Praise for *LAKE LIFE*

A *New York Times* "Editors' Choice" selection • One of the *Atlanta Journal-Constitution*'s "10 Best Southern Books of 2020" • A *Publishers Weekly* "2020 Summer Read" • A *Lit Hub* Book Marks "Rave" title • A *Millions* "Most Anticipated" book of 2020 • A *Southern Review of Books* "Best Southern Book" of July 2020

"If your . . . summer vacation was canceled this year, console and distract yourself with *Lake Life*, the tale of a family getaway gone very wrong. . . . There's a lot of bad behavior here, perhaps because Poissant is so good at writing it. His prose throughout is sure-footed and intelligent. . . . [He] also leaves room for absorbing discussions of art, the socioeconomics of vacation property development, and religion."

—Jean Thompson,
The New York Times Book Review

"Masterfully crafted . . . simultaneously heartbreaking and hilarious . . . A totally engrossing story of the long shadows cast by troubled relationships and the glimmer of hope that dawns after painful confrontation."

—*Booklist* (starred review)

"Impressive . . . A well-wrought family tale from a talented writer."

—*Kirkus Reviews*

"Most stunning in this debut novel is Poissant's remarkable facility and fluency with point of view. . . . Each character's trajectory is masterfully rendered. . . . For a perfect summer read, look no further. You're not likely to find more beautiful, more distinctive prose anywhere."

—Melanie Bishop,
New York Journal of Books

"Poissant is one of our most talented local writers and we've been waiting for this, his first novel, for what feels like *a very long time*. If 2020 did nothing else good, at least it brought us this book."

—*Orlando Weekly* (Staff Pick and Best Book of 2020)

"When you find yourself thinking about a novel's characters well after you've finished reading it, wondering about them and how they're doing as though they were friends of yours, family, it means that you've found something truly special: one of those books that's not just about life but somehow contains it. Poissant's characters linger just that hauntingly, and his novel breathes with just that kind of life."

—Kevin Brockmeier, author of
The Illumination

"A humane and wise book about a family getting into all sorts of trouble. I am obsessed with the Starlings."

—CJ Hauser, author of
The From-Aways and *Family of Origin*

"*Lake Life* is a terrific story, one that delves into a family's messy history, and finds there not only pain, but—thrillingly—stubborn survival, hope, and love. I'm grateful for this book."

—Christopher Coake, author of
You Would Have Told Me Not To

"Told in stirring language, *Lake Life* is the complex story of contemporary Americans, each dealing with a brand of loss: of children, of youth, of self-control, and of destiny. Here is a book that is heartbreaking and true, lilting and swooping, dark and light, wry and touching."

—Michael Carroll, author of
Little Reef and *Stella Maris*

"*Lake Life* drew me into the kind of narrative dream that I'm unable and unwilling to leave. I read past daylight, and when I closed the book I had no memory of having turned on the lamp by my chair. The conflicts and themes of the novel are timeless and universal, and the prose sings."

—Allen Wier, author of
Tehano and *Late Night, Early Morning*

"A gorgeous, nuanced portrait of a deeply funny, somewhat dysfunctional, strangely lovable bunch."

—Hannah Orenstein, author of
Head Over Heels

"*Lake Life* captures the complex truths of familial and romantic relationships better than any novel I've read in years. This book is a triumph!"

—Joe Oestreich, author of
Hitless Wonder

"*Lake Life* is a tour de force. Heartbreaking and filled with characters that will haunt you long after you read the book, this is one of the year's finest novels."

—*Largehearted Boy*

"With . . . *Lake Life*, Poissant rises so far above expectations that it seems like he's been writing novels his entire existence. The form and execution of the work here are masterful, and the characters and settings are brilliantly painted."

—Barrett Bowlin, *Fiction Writers Review*

"Poissant has cooked up a deliciously satisfying novel, sharpened with suspense and psychological acuity."

—*The National Book Review* ("5 Hot Books")

"David James Poissant's prose, often rare and structurally both fierce and elegant, is a joy to read."

—Shann Ray, *Northwest Book Lovers*

"A fantastic book . . . outstanding . . . remarkable."

—Eliot Parker, *Now, Appalachia*

"Poissant's absorbing first novel . . . is fueled by moonshine and melancholia. . . . Death ripples through a family as riven by secrets as it is united in love."

—Matt Seidel, *The Millions*

LAKE LIFE

DAVID JAMES POISSANT

SIMON & SCHUSTER PAPERBACKS

NEW YORK   LONDON   TORONTO   SYDNEY   NEW DELHI

Simon & Schuster Paperbacks
An Imprint of Simon & Schuster, Inc.
1230 Avenue of the Americas
New York, NY 10020

First Simon & Schuster trade paperback edition July 2021

SIMON & SCHUSTER PAPERBACKS and colophon are
registered trademarks of Simon & Schuster, Inc.

For information about special discounts for bulk purchases, please contact Simon & Schuster Special Sales at 1-866-506-1949 or business@simonandschuster.com.

The Simon & Schuster Speakers Bureau can bring authors to your live event. For more information or to book an event, contact the Simon & Schuster Speakers Bureau at 1-866-248-3049 or visit our website at www.simonspeakers.com.

Interior design by Carly Loman

Manufactured in the United States of America

10 9 8 7 6 5 4 3 2 1

Library of Congress Cataloging-in-Publication Data
Names: Poissant, David James, author.
Title: Lake life / David James Poissant.
Description: New York : Simon & Schuster, [2020]
Identifiers: LCCN 2019043350 (print) | LCCN 2019043351 (ebook) | ISBN 9781476729992 (hardcover) | ISBN 9781476730011 (ebook)
Classification: LCC PS3616.O5467 L35 2020 (print) | LCC PS3616.O5467 (ebook) | DDC 813/.6—dc23
LC record available at https://lccn.loc.gov/2019043350
LC ebook record available at https://lccn.loc.gov/2019043351

ISBN 978-1-4767-2999-2
ISBN 978-1-4767-3000-4 (pbk)
ISBN 978-1-4767-3001-1 (ebook)

for my parents, who gave me water
and for Marla, who taught me to swim

PART ONE
FRIDAY

1.

The boy on the back of the boat, laughing.

The sky, pewter-stamped and threatening rain.

Michael Starling, age thirty-three, warm on his father's boat, watches the other boat, the boy, the bay—the water that will never be his because Michael's parents are selling the house.

Yesterday, they arrived—Michael and Diane, Jake and Thad—and were given the news: Richard and Lisa Starling will not be retiring to the lake. In a week, the Starling family summer home will be sold so that Michael and Thad's parents may retire, instead, to a pocket of Florida shore that screams margaritas and sand and all things distinctly un-Starling.

This decision, it's not like Michael's parents. They are not Florida people. They are ex-hippies, academics. They are lovers of cold mountain lakes and clear, cool streams, of trees that change color in the fall. Their summers are North Carolina summers, starry skies and the converted double-wide the family affectionately calls its *cabin in the woods*.

What has become of Michael's parents? Who are these brave fools who splash before him, bobbing in swimsuits and inner tubes in the calm waters of a Lake Christopher summer day?

Onshore, a heron picks through reeds for fish. Above, clouds cover and uncover the sun.

A morning on the lake—sandwiches, swimming—this was the Starlings' plan before the rogue vessel arrived, unzipping the water behind it, never mind swimmers or the bay's enforced no-wake speed. The boat dropped anchor too close, and the man at the wheel uncovered his head and waved with a hat—a captain's hat!—from the deck. He whooped, spat a wad of tobacco overboard, then turned up his music very, very loud.

This is not good lake etiquette. This is not done.

Lake Christopher is not a party lake, and this is not a noisy bay. Longtime residents work hard to keep it that way, having survived decades of development and two challenges—one public, one corporate—of eminent domain.

The interloper boat blasts Jimmy Buffett, *The Party Barge* stenciled pink along its side. Its pontoons gleam gray under a gray sky.

Michael's father doesn't seem to mind. "Join us!" he calls to the man with the captain's hat. Then everyone from *The Party Barge* is in the water, all but the boy (*swimmer's ear*, his mother says, *a shame*) and his older sister, left aboard to watch the boy. Soon, though, the sister is under the canopy on her back on the deck of the boat, eyes closed, earbuds in.

Michael watches the boy and wants a drink.

The boy is four, maybe five. Where the boy's biceps should be are pumpkin-colored water wings. He moves to the outboard motor, then straddles the cover, a jockey in silver swim trunks. His horse is tattooed *Evinrude*, his racetrack the sun-dappled water in his wake. "Giddy-up!" he screams.

Some might find this cute. Michael doesn't.

The inflatables bulge like blood pressure cuffs around the boy's arms. One hand releases an invisible rein, and the boy mines a bag of Cheetos in his lap. He turns his head to observe his sister in the boat, his parents swimming fifty yards away. Michael follows the boy's line of sight. When he looks back, he finds a finger. It is a middle finger, the signature neon of Cheetos, and it is raised in Michael's direction.

Michael shuts his eyes. Why is he watching over this kid? He doesn't even *like* kids. He opens his eyes. The boy sticks out his tongue.

Hey, Michael wants to call to the negligent parents, *your shitty kid's giving me the finger, and your other shitty kid's asleep.*

Michael should be swimming, but his head has bats in it. Sobriety is wings in the skull. It's echolocation behind the eyes. He needs vodka, stat, but this morning he woke to an empty orange juice jug and no way to sneak liquor undetected onto the boat. His family will put up with a lot, but not vodka before noon.

The boy raises the chip bag to his mouth, and his chin and chest are dusted orange. Then he drops the bag into the lake. He stares at Michael, daring him to speak.

It's a new sensation, being bullied by a child, and Michael can't say he cares for it.

He cradles his head. He misses his liquor cabinet. He doesn't miss his house. He'd rather be here than back in Texas. He's spent every summer on this lake since he was two, and if there's a place he feels at peace, it's here.

The boy draws himself to his knees and peers over the motor cover's edge.

The boy's family, they aren't from here. Michael had them pegged for out-of-towners. But out-of-towners pilot marina-rentals, and this is no marina-rental. This pontoon is an Avalon Ambassador, 90K on a good day, a watercraft that makes the Starlings' six-seat fishing boat the seafaring equivalent of Tom Hanks's *Cast Away* raft. (Michael's father christened theirs *The Sea Cow*, hand-painting the name on the gunwale in blue house paint that, thirty years later, has faded to a wavery *a Cow*.) No, these people—the mother with her Dolce & Gabbana sunglasses, the father with his faux naval captain's cap—they aren't locals or vacationers. They're newly minted lake house owners breaking in the captain's midlife-crisis present to himself. Even as the Ambassador entered the bay, the mother was probably cutting price tags from the stack of towels at her side.

These are loud people who loudly flash their wealth around. To Michael, these people are everything that is wrong with America in 2018.

Speakers thump. Guitars strum. And for the love of all that is holy, would someone get Jimmy Buffett a goddamn cheeseburger already?

At the shoreline, the heron lunges and comes up with mud.

On the other boat, the girl who's supposed to be watching her brother is definitely asleep. She's young, late teens, bikinied, body toned and honey-tan. She's roughly the age and shape Diane was when she and Michael met here, in this bay, fifteen summers ago.

The boy leaves his knees. He's squatting on the motor now. His sister shifts in sleep, and it occurs to Michael that these siblings are far enough apart in age that the boy might be a mistake. Perhaps the accident waiting to happen has been an accident all his life.

The first one you smother. The others, he's heard, raise themselves.

Michael doesn't want a first one, never did. That was their agreement. That was *always* the agreement.

Diane floats on a raft in blue water, belly-up. She won't show for a few weeks, though sometimes Michael swears he sees the hint of something, a contour, a fattening. His wife isn't fat, but she's no longer the girl on the boat. He wishes she was, and, wishing, knows this makes him *hashtag something or other*. He doesn't want to be whatever wanting a fit, young wife makes him. But wanting not to be won't ease the want. He misses youth, his and his wife's.

Does this make him sexist? His mother would say yes. His father would say no. Thad, his brother, wouldn't care, and Jake wouldn't know what Michael was talking about. Jake, Thad's rich, attractive, slender boyfriend, is young. He's naive. He lives in New York and makes paintings for other rich, attractive, slender people who live in New York. As far as Michael can tell, Jake's interest in other people extends only as far as the dollar signs attached to his canvases.

In the water, Jake and Thad toss a football. Michael's father and the captain laugh, water noodles rising from their crotches, red, obscene. The mothers tread water, talking, Diane between them on her raft.

The girl on the pontoon boat sits up. She says something to her brother that Michael can't make out over the Jimmy Buffett din. She pokes at her phone a minute, then lowers the phone, lies down, and shuts her eyes.

From her raft, Diane won't look at Michael.

For fifteen years, they were so happy. Happy enough. Content, at least, before Diane upended everything. *People change*, she said. Michael's not so sure. Did Diane change, or did she trick him? Is this what she wanted all along?

Michael moves to his father's chair at the helm and flips on the fish finder. The depth here measures sixty feet. At the fifty-foot mark, something big drifts gray across the screen, a catfish, maybe, or a tree branch settling into underwater rot.

His mother adjusts her broad-brimmed sun hat—*the cancer hat*, she calls it, an attempt at levity that, every time, makes Michael cringe. Probably, she's telling the other mother about the skin cancer she beat. Again, Michael thinks, *Florida? Seriously?*

The bats cavort. Soon his hands will shake. He really, really, really needs a drink.

The boy perched on the motor flips him off again. The sister's earbuds have popped out, and her mouth is slack with sleep.

The heron in the reeds gives up and lifts off, fishless. The boy watches, and Michael follows the boy's eyes following the bird.

The boy smiles. He stands. Then he's overboard.

His body tugs him under, and the water wings rocket from his arms like champagne corks. A hand breaks the surface, slaps, but the floats slither, amphibious, from his grasp. The hand does not break the surface a second time.

And only Michael's seen—seen the boy stand, then fall, the seat of his swim trunks hitting the shell of the outboard motor, hard; seen him slip over the side; seen, in the eyes of the child, water below and sun above, a transmission, one word telegraphed from boy to man, and that word was: *Please*.

Michael rises, kicks off his shoes and sheds his shirt. He calls to the others, a cry he can't be sure is heard over the music blasting from the boat. He dives. He swims. He turns his face to take a breath and calls for help again, but he cannot stop. He cannot break his stride.

No splashing ahead, no hands.

Three more strokes, and Michael's close enough. He takes a breath and dives. He's seeking silver swim trunks, teeth, anything that might catch light in the belly of a lake. But ten feet down the light is scarce, the water turned to murk.

He pinches his nose, pushes air from his ears to equalize the pressure.

Fifteen feet. Twenty. Blind, but grasping. Water in fistfuls, but no boy.

Come on.

He tunnels, pulls. How deep is he? How fast does a body sink?

The light is gone, and the water grows colder the deeper he goes. Whatever happens, he must not lose track of up and down.

In high school, he could hold his breath for a minute at a time, but high school was a long time ago. His ears throb. His lungs are lit coals. Wait too long, and he'll take a breath reflexively. He can't be underwater when that happens.

He has to surface. Surface or drown. Except. *Except.*

A whisper. The dance of something just out of reach. Swim trunks, fluttering. The pink of fingernails. Either the boy's below or Michael's dead and dreaming this.

Then he has the hand.

He can't see it, can't make out the boy's hand in his own, but he has it. The hand is there, and it is good. It's a hand he can swim with. He'll rise and hold the hand and not let go.

Later, in the hospital, Michael will wonder. Say he'd had a drink that morning, just to calm him down. Say the shock of his parents' revelation, the house for sale, hadn't led him to drink so much the night before. He might have held on tighter, risen true.

But that isn't what happens.

What happens is that Michael kicks the boy.

He doesn't mean to, but a body underwater isn't weightless, and swimming with one arm is hard to do. The boy's body drags. It is kicked. And just like that, the hand is gone.

He exhales, but there's no air left to leave his lungs.

He's swimming the wrong way. The boy is below. Why, then, does

Michael rise? He cannot rise without the child. He must turn back, but his body will not let him. Something in him has taken over, and the something in him wants to live.

He kicks, he claws, but there's no light. Impossible to gauge direction without the compass of the sun.

Then, a vague illumination. An object passing overhead.

He's heard stories. Catfish the size of zeppelins. Sturgeon armored like gators, ten feet long. Unless the thing he sees is his soul rising, leaving him behind.

No.

He is alive. He lives, and he is swimming. The fish or soul, it grows, and he swims toward it.

He's lost all sense of distance, space, and time. All dimensions are *water*. Fireworks go off behind his eyes, and a siren screams for him to breathe.

Breathe, then, he thinks. *Join the boy. Be done with this.*

Except that Michael's life is not his own. He is a *father*. His life is marked by that which is in bloom. This truth hits him with a force so great he hardly notices his head striking the bottom of the boat.

All is water. Then light. Then air.

He coughs, gasps, and throws up. He breathes.

Above him, the girl is screaming. Her brother is at the bottom of the lake. Surely, by now, he rests. Surely, he's stopped fighting, stopped water-calling, now, his sister's name.

Michael tastes salt. The salt is blood and the blood is his.

He cannot dive. He dives again, he'll die.

He is a father.

His life is not his own.

Beyond the boat, others fling themselves from rafts and swim to him. And in the distance, wings, severed from their body, spin, orange and current-caught. They orbit each other, knowing. They tumble, ocular with water's awful wink.

2.

Boats cross the bay, trolling for the boy. Through binoculars, Lisa Starling watches. She could have changed clothes. After swimming to shore, after dialing 911 and helping Michael into the ambulance, before grabbing her binoculars and returning to the water's edge, she could have put on something dry. But it's only just occurred to her that she's in her swimsuit still. Anyway, she's dry enough. The warm air has sipped the water from her skin.

This morning, when she woke, the sky was blue. Now the sky is gray, cloud-clotted. The color of carrion, she thinks, though she isn't sure this thinking makes much sense. But a boy is at the bottom of a lake, therefore the world does not make sense.

Lisa believes in God, though God is no one she'd like to meet today.

All over the bay, neighbors stand on decks and sit on docks. They huddle on shorelines and along the point. Across the bay, a man emerges from his house with scuba gear, then enters the water, tank on back, fins on feet, a regulator bulb in his mouth.

A pair of police boats keep other vessels from entering the bay. The boats are white and blue, and from the top of each, lights flash beneath the leaden sky. Above, a helicopter breaks up clouds.

Lisa lowers her binoculars. They are Swarovski Swarovisions. They're eights because she likes her birds bright. They're small because she likes her bins lightweight. They're among the best binoculars in the world. She knows. She helped rank them for last year's *Cornell Lab Review*.

She raises the binoculars again. The Starlings' boat is still out there, anchored alongside the other family's pontoon. A third police boat bobs between. This is the boat from which, minutes ago, two divers leapt with flashlights big as megaphones.

Her husband, Richard, has joined the other family on their boat. He looks tired, face yellow, resin-stiff. He stands, a hand on the shoulder of the man they met just hours ago. The man's removed his sunglasses, his captain's cap. He holds his wife's hand. Their daughter's face is hidden in her mother's lap. The daughter and the mother cry. For an hour they've cried while the men watch the water, saying nothing.

Lisa lowers the binoculars. Their strap is cool on her neck.

She should have gone to the hospital with Michael and Diane, but she feels needed here. There are stories of children gone under, recovered twenty, thirty minutes later, then revived. Not miracles, biology. If the conditions are right. If the water is cold. If one stands onshore and watches long enough.

But, if she's being honest, they're only looking for a body now.

She starts up the hill to the house.

The house is small and old. *Distinguished*, Richard would say. *Not old, and neither am I*. Oh, but they're getting up there. Lisa is sixty. Soon her husband will be seventy. The lake house is older than Lisa's children, a '70s-model double-wide converted in the '80s to a house. She and Richard bought the place on impulse not long after Michael's birth. Their marriage was rocky. Twice they'd separated, then come to an arrangement: *No more maybes*. They would stay married, for better or worse. The summer home was the handshake on the deal.

And what a home it had been, years ago. Long and low to the ground, the house lolled at the top of the hill like an errant fire truck, white-shuttered, cedar siding painted red. A porch, low-banistered in the style of those old Sears Roebuck build-'em-yourself bungalows, wrapped the house, the back screened. A quilted hammock hung in the yard between two trees. A sprinkler system set to a timer kept the lawn green while they were away, and a detached two-car garage became a place to store research when their offices in Ithaca filled up.

Then came the storms of '86 and '90, the blizzard of '93, the tornado—a near miss—of 2011. And don't even get her started on the great ant invasion of 2017. They tried to keep up, but maintaining a summer home was work, and they had work already, Richard teaching at Cornell, Lisa conducting research in the labs, both of them publishing. Summers were for resting, not repairs. So they'd let the house go a little. Okay, a lot.

These days, the porch sags. The siding is gray and mildew-stained. The roof is missing shingles, and what shingles remain hang furred with moss. And is it Lisa's imagination, or does the whole house kind of *lean* a little? The hammock in the yard has long since rotted away, and the lawn is a patchwork of grass and dead places, of anthills and weeds.

Last month, during negotiations, Lisa and Richard made so many concessions to the inspector's damage report that they stood to lose tens of thousands. "Hold off," their Realtor cautioned. "Fix up the place. The market's only getting better. In a year, you might make twenty thousand more."

But what's the point? The concessions are a way to tank the asking price, nothing more. Even pristine, the house, sold, would greet a wrecking ball. The lake is changing, investors coming in. In the end, it's not the house that she and Richard are selling. It's the land.

Unless Lisa calls off the sale. Closing is a week away. Barring a lawsuit, it's not too late. Keep or sell, stay or go, Richard won't fight her. Because they had a deal. And Richard broke the deal, forgot what marriage meant. The handshake—the house—it has to go. This isn't punishment. It's more that the equation must be balanced. To stay together, they must start over. To start over, they must sell the house. That much, to Lisa, seems clear. And just because Richard doesn't know she knows, that's no reason to go on as though nothing's happened. Is it?

She isn't sure.

She's sure of this: The choice is hers. Richard already made his choice. Richard gave up his right to have a say.

Up the hill. Up the porch steps. The staircase gasps underfoot.

Beneath it, where her children used to play, ivy's taken over, a hiding place for snakes. She skips the fifth step, run through with rot. The railing shakes. The wood is soft as cork, the kind left too long in the bottle that crumbles at the corkscrew's kiss.

On the top step, she turns and once more brings the binoculars to her face. She focuses, and the mother is there. Lisa should be with her on the boat. But, being on the boat, she would become the mother, and she has already been the mother. She will not touch the hem of that particular misery again.

And why is this happening now, their last week at the lake? Why rob her of the beauty of this time with her family?

But these thoughts are evil. For a moment, she can't stand herself.

The other mother is Wendy. In the water, she gave her name, and Lisa thought of *Peter Pan*, not the play or Disney movie, but the book, a favorite of Lisa's mother, whom Lisa lost three summers ago. Cancer, parents—the indignities of growing *distinguished*.

God, Wendy's face when those inflatables bobbed into view.

Who was watching the boy? Who was *supposed* to be watching him? Not Michael, who saw and dove and rose beneath a boat.

Poor Michael. Poor Wendy. Wendy is ruined. Wendy will never forgive herself.

And where do they go? Lisa wonders not for the first time, not for anything like the first time in her life. Where have they gone, Wendy's son and Lisa's firstborn, all the souls of children gone too soon?

If heaven exists, it has received them. They're children, after all. If not innocent, then innocent enough. Lisa imagines a Neverland for them, a place the ghosts of children go to wait, to fly, until their parents come for them.

She hopes for this. She prays.

Some days, all that keeps her going is this thought: If God is love, she'll see her girl again.

3.

Jake showers, and Thad leans against the sink. Thad still can't be sure how it happened—the boy, the boat, his brother's head. He searches the bathroom mirror for answers, but all he finds is his pale, unshaven face. The mirror fogs, and he wipes the condensation away. His eyebrows need trimming.

From the bay, they swam ashore and ran uphill. His mother made the call while Thad tried to convince his brother he needed an ambulance, Michael insisting he was fine, that he could drive, while Diane cried and pressed a blood-soaked washcloth to her husband's head. When the ambulance arrived, Michael reluctantly got in, Diane with him, and Thad's mother stationed herself at the edge of the lake. When at last Thad thought to check on his boyfriend, he found him in the bathroom.

"Are you still there?" Jake says, steam from the shower filling the room.

"I'm here," Thad says.

And who is this boy he's been with the past two years? Jake is twenty-six, four years younger than Thad, though there are times the gap feels wider, days Jake acts sixteen. They've reached the point they should get serious, commit or go their separate ways. That Jake might not recognize this makes Thad sad.

"Can I have some privacy?" Jake asks.

Thad wants to believe he's misheard. He pulls the shower curtain aside. Jake stands beneath the water. He's small and lithe, with acne on his chest. There's lather in his hands, and he's erect.

"You've got to be kidding me."

Jake pulls the curtain back. "Leave me alone."

"A kid's at the bottom of the lake," Thad says. "   the hospital."

"I'm stressed," Jake says. "This happens when I'   .

Thad leaves the bathroom, slams the door.

Stressed. There's an explanation for Jake's behavior, but *stressed* isn't it. Jake's horny. Jake's *always* horny.

Thad used to be. Before weed. Before the regimen of Xanax, Paxil, and Seroquel. His dick works, it's just the want that's waned. He should want Jake. Jake's gorgeous. He's successful. He's good to Thad, or good enough. And *good enough*, given Thad's track record with men, ought to be enough. But it isn't.

If only Jake listened, asked about his day, showed him affection unattached to sex. That, to Thad, would look like love.

He moves to the kitchen table.

In a double-wide, even a converted one, rooms run together: kitchen, dining area, family room. Two table legs rise from carpet, two from linoleum the color of uncooked pasta. The floor's old, the kind that sticks to your feet with every step. Thad's feeling hungry, then ashamed for feeling hungry. How long, in the aftermath of tragedy, does one wait to eat?

Outside, his mother's coming up the hill. The grass is high. If she's not careful, she'll take a horseshoe stake to the shin.

From the bathroom comes Jake's whistling. This one's a hymn, "Come Thou Fount of Every Blessing" in a minor key. A recovering Baptist, Jake knows every hymn, each word of every verse. For him, growing up meant church on Wednesday, Saturday, and twice on Sunday. For Thad, church was Sunday mornings once or twice a month, and only if his mother insisted. (She never managed to get his father through the door of any house of worship.) Thad gave his mother's church a chance, but he knew early on who he was, and while her church wasn't the kind to condemn him, neither was it a place where Thad might raise his head from prayer to find others like

.n seated in the pews. Couples, there, were straight. Singles were straight. The minister was a woman married to a man. None of this felt particularly welcoming. None of it felt *his*.

He hasn't been to church since he was twelve. And, while he judges Jake's occasional childishness, there are days Thad, too, feels like a child. It's as though, having dropped out of college, he missed some class everyone else got to take. *Here's how to pay taxes. Here's how to balance a checkbook. Here's how to keep a job.*

How have his parents done it, stayed employed for thirty years, stayed married thirty-seven? Their love is real. Their work is important. Google either name, a thousand hits come up.

How, then, did they raise such dumbfuck sons?

Thad's mother reaches the porch, but she does not come in. She stands on the top step and watches the water through binoculars.

Thad will miss this house, house of summers, of card games and horseshoes, of fish fries and music and ice cream and love. But this isn't the home Thad remembers. The walls are marked by holes and hooks where paintings used to hang. Boxes crowd the corners, stacked or open, half-packed. Bookshelves stand empty. His mother's knickknacks and flea market ceramics have all been newspapered away. Framed family portraits, wrapped in brown paper, lean against the walls.

The room's one concession to ornamentation is Jake's painting—a gift last year upon his first visit to the lake. In the painting, a girl palms a pomegranate half. A cherub hovers over one shoulder. A compass at her feet points north. One of the girl's breasts is out. All of these add up to something symbolic, though, gun to his head, Thad couldn't say what. Part of him wonders whether Jake could say. Jake might be a genius, or he might be making shit up as he goes. Could be anyone who tries to analyze his work, the joke's on them. Thad merely remembers being relieved his mother hadn't protested the wayward boob.

His mother, as a rule, is thoughtful, unfailingly polite. He imagines her packing, fretting over whether to take the painting down or leave it for Jake's benefit. Thad can't say such worry is undue. Jake's got an ego and the sensitivity to go with it. Then again, it's possible he hasn't even noticed that his painting is the only one still up. Jake sometimes has trouble getting past himself. By twenty-four, he'd had two solo exhibitions. At twenty-five, he was the subject of pieces in *Artforum*, *New American Paintings*, and the *Times*. Just last week, the *New Yorker* gave his third solo show three pages, dubbing him Brooklyn's next big thing and praising his work's "mordant irony" and "refreshing excess." Jake pretended not to care, but Thad's caught him reading the article half a dozen times. He's had only one bad review. An *Art in America* piece celebrated a group show before singling out Jake's work as "clumsy, desperate, and eager to please," a line that sent Thad's boyfriend to bed for three full days.

The whistling tapers off, replaced by a bassline. Jake has switched on the Sharper Image plastic-capped bath radio he gave Thad's parents for Christmas and which nobody but Jake has likely ever used.

Thad moves to the hallway. He presses an ear to the bathroom door, and that's when he hears it. Over the rush of water, the buzz of the bathroom fan, the hum of Bell Biv DeVoe singing "Poison," Thad can just make out the gentle slap of his boyfriend jerking off.

Thad's mother crosses the porch. Thad steps into the bathroom and shuts the door. Immediately he's underwater, the room more steam than air.

How did his brother do it? Push himself past so much silt and dark?

"You have to stop," Thad says. "Or be quiet about it."

The slapping grows frenzied.

"Jake," he says. He doesn't want to pull the curtain aside.

The sound slackens. Jake's done. The radio cuts off. The water stops. The curtain draws back, and Jake's head appears, eyes blue, teeth so white you'd think he modeled for some product four out of five dentists recommend.

Those eyes, though. He loves this boy. Jake's sledgehammered Thad's heart a hundred times, but it's Thad who's let him. You can only blame the hammer so long before you have to blame yourself for not stepping aside.

Jake wipes the water from his face.

The plans for tomorrow are set, and Thad should call them off. Say he did, would Jake go to Asheville without him, or would he stay? Either way, a boy is at the bottom of the lake. There are more pressing concerns than tomorrow's lunch with Jake's art school ex.

"I can't believe you did that," Thad says.

"Don't shame me," Jake says.

"I'm not shaming you. I just think it's disrespectful."

"*Disrespectful?* What I do with my dick—"

"Do you even care?"

Standing in this room is like being in a mouth. Everything is wet—the mirror, faucet, knobs all slick and glistening. Jake stands dripping, and Thad offers him a towel, which he takes.

"Do I care that a boy is dead?" Jake says. "Of course. I'm not a monster."

Thad lowers the toilet lid and sits. In the shower, Jake towels off his hair, which is short and dark. There's little in the world that Thad likes more than running his hands through that hair—clean and soft—before Jake slathers product into it. He likes Jake's hair the way it is. Jake prefers the electrocuted hedgehog look.

"All I'm saying is there's a time and there's a place," Thad says.

Jake laughs. "You don't believe that. You think you believe that because that's what you've been taught to believe. No sex for you. Not at a time like this. You're *respectful.*"

"My mom is—"

"Your mom?"

Thad's arm itches. He runs a finger along the raised scar, swollen in the steam. "I could hear you halfway across the house. You want her hearing that?"

"Ah," Jake says. "That's different. That's manners. Manners I can get behind."

Jake's big on manners. In the city, he's as well-known for his charm as he is for his art. Frank DiFazio—respected, feared, beloved owner of Chelsea's Gallery East, the man who made Jake and named Jake (before Frank, Jake was *Jacob*)—has Jake trained. "I took the boy out of Memphis *and* the Memphis out of the boy," Thad once overheard Frank tell a friend.

"I'm sorry I was impolite," Jake says. He's drying off. He's lean but not boyish, muscled but not buff. Thad had a body like that once, but he's put on weight the past few years. Too much pot. Too many late-night snacks.

Jake smiles. It's tough staying mad at him.

Thad stands, and Jake drops the towel. He reaches past the shower curtain and places one hand on Thad's cheek.

"I can make you feel better," Jake says. His hand drops to Thad's waistband. "Come on. I'll keep it real respectful." Then Jake's hand is down his shorts.

Thad pushes him, and Jake hits the wall, hard.

"Jesus," Jake says.

Thad moves to the door. He needs to leave the room before he cries. He doesn't want to meet Jake's ex. He doesn't want to lose Jake. He doesn't want a child to be dead.

"You think they'll find him?" Thad asks, but Jake won't look at him.

When Jake turns, his back is latticework, squares where the shower tiles have left their mark.

"I'm sorry," Thad says.

But he no longer has Jake's attention. Jake's stepped out of the shower, and his attention is on the small, black jar he's just fished from his toiletry kit. He uncaps the jar, dips two fingers in, then gently works the product into his hair.

4.

Diane Maddox exhales. Diane Maddox who traded Tennessee for Texas. Diane Maddox whose parents are divorced. Diane Maddox who married Michael ten years ago and wouldn't take her husband's name. Diane Maddox who carries a child inside her. Diane Maddox who had an abortion in high school and who does not regret that choice, but who is not in favor of making that choice a second time. Diane Maddox who went to school to be a painter before settling for being a those-who-can't-do art teacher. Diane Maddox who wonders whether thirty-three is too early for a midlife crisis, were women said to have those and if those meant more than a red motorcycle and the affair to go with it. Diane Maddox who has been reassessing her infinitesimal place in the cruel and sideways-pressing world. Diane Maddox who likes dangly earrings. Diane Maddox who has always longed to visit Reykjavík. Diane Maddox who grew up watching *Mad About You* and wanted to *be* Helen Hunt. Diane Maddox who, in eighth grade, cried—*cried*— through the *Mad About You* finale, cried over the fact that Paul and Jamie weren't together anymore. They would give it another try, the way Diane's parents gave it another try too many times to count, *giving it another try* code for the pain a daughter feels when some mornings Dad's there, eating Cheerios, and some mornings Mom says, "I hope that fucker drives that thing off a fucking bridge." Diane Maddox who is unhappy but for whom divorce does not feel like an option (whether to prove something to her parents or to *Mad About You*, she isn't sure). Diane Maddox who wonders whether things would have gone better had she taken her husband's name, though of course a name can't save you. A name can't save a marriage, can't save a house from sale or a boy from the bottom of a lake.

Diane in the ambulance. Diane not crying, keeping calm. Diane following the paramedic's instructions as the ambulance navigates country roads and the paramedic measures Michael's blood pressure. Diane Maddox-not-Starling—and it's never too late to change a thing, except sometimes it is—pressing the damp cloth to the head of the man she loves. Or loved. Some days, let's face it, she's not sure. Blood pooling beneath the cloth, the forehead *an awfully vascular area*, the paramedic says, *worse than it looks*, which Diane takes to mean *looks worse than it is*, though she can't be sure. There will be stitches, though she hopes against concussion, against brain injury, against anything permanent because, in all fairness, can the girl who said *in sickness and in health* still speak for Diane at thirty-three? Say Michael slips into a coma or spends his life in diapers, drinking through a straw? Does the Diane who said *I do* love this man enough to wipe his ass another fifty years? And how to love a man who's made it clear, if not in words, then in scowls and sighs, in the way he picks strings from the frayed cuffs of his jeans, that he'd rather her not have their kid? Does she love Michael enough to stay? Does she love herself enough to leave? Diane doesn't know, knows only that Michael's blood is real and warm and won't stop rising from his head.

The ambulance brakes, the doors open, and Diane breathes.

The hospital is not what she was expecting. Small and beige and boxy, the building looks less like a hospital than a bank someone dropped onto an acre in the woods. Gently, Diane is pushed aside by a nurse at the curb, Michael lowered into a wheelchair and asked to hold the cloth to his own head. Of all the fears Diane has ever known—fear of flying, of snakes, of seeing the stick's minus sign become a plus—never has she known a fear like watching her husband's face paint the water red. The paramedic pushes the wheelchair forward, the nurse holds the door open for Michael to be pushed through, and Diane follows, feeling useless.

Inside, the waiting room is empty, the floor a checkerboard. The woman at the front desk is rude. The hallways are hot. The X-ray room is cold.

Then Michael's on a table, and she's at his side. The Betadine goes on, and Michael winces, his forehead orange. The needles go in, and she has to look away. She holds his hand. The next time she looks, eight Frankensteinian stitches hold his head together. They fill the gap between eyebrow and hairline, as though Michael's left eyebrow has an eyebrow of its own.

Then the X-rays are in and all is well—*Good enough for this country doctor, anyway*—though Michael gives Diane a look that says, *When we get home, I'm getting a second opinion.* Not that they can afford a second opinion, what with a mortgage they can hardly handle on a house that's worth half what they paid in 2007, four maxed-out credit cards, plus Diane's student loans, which, no matter how hard she ignores them, aren't exactly going anywhere. Still, she's glad to see Michael talking, smiling. Mostly, though, she's happy she won't have to change his diapers till death do them part.

That said, there *is* a diaper she wouldn't mind changing in fewer than seven months.

This love for a thing unborn, a thing that isn't even yet a thing—how to explain this love to her husband? She promised him she'd never want a child, and she'd meant it at the time. The mistake wasn't getting pregnant. The mistake was making a promise that was never hers to keep.

The doctor scrubs his hands. A nurse will be with them shortly to discuss care and cleaning, he says, then dries his hands and leaves.

Michael's still on the table, lying down. His eyes are on her middle, as though he can see beyond her waist into her womb.

We're keeping it, she wants to say, but doesn't, not yet.

She's not religious, but she is superstitious. It seems bad luck to fight about the pregnancy today, as though doing so might invite the spirit of the dead boy into her, might curse her with a baby born blue-lipped, without breath.

If fates are steered by thoughts, by words, the least Diane can do, on this day, is keep quiet. So she lets her husband hold her hand. She smiles. And there are many, many, many, many, many, many things she does not say.

5.

Three times Richard Starling has given the officer his statement. Three times he's explained he didn't know what happened until what happened was over, Michael in the water, head cracked open, the girl on the boat wailing in a way Richard hopes never to hear again.

The officer's face is downy, lips pursed in a spittle-glistening pout. He turns to the others. They are the Mallory family. The father is Glenn, the mother Wendy, the daughter Trish. Richard misses the boy's name and can't bring himself to ask.

Glenn gives his version of the story, then Wendy. Trish won't stop crying. Again, the officer asks for the daughter's statement. Glenn stands. Richard stands.

Richard's not a violent man. He was a hippie. He was at Woodstock. He turned twenty-one in 1969. A December birthday doomed him, but flat feet saved his life. Instead of Vietnam, he got to finish school. He's never thrown a punch, but, before Cornell, he taught high school in Atlanta for fifteen years, so he's broken up his share of fights. He knows when a fist and a face are a parabola away.

The officer's young, the kind who drinks hard on days off and makes his wife iron his uniform each night. He has yet to know loss, can't register the grief beside him on this boat.

Richard's hand finds Glenn's shoulder.

"Why don't you let me take them home?" Richard says.

The officer frowns. They're on Glenn's boat, bobbing. Richard holds a seatback to stay upright. He looks to shore, but Lisa's left.

Police boats circle. Divers dive.

The day Richard discovered his daughter dead in her bassinet, he believed she might yet be revived. Even in the face of facts, he assumed, for hours, some new cure would be found. That was years ago, and not a day goes by he doesn't miss his daughter.

These parents, though, Glenn and Wendy. Has it hit? Or do they hold out hope their son will surface still, will wave and swim ashore?

"Sir," the officer says, "I'm going to need you to sit down. Both of you." He won't look Glenn in the eye. That's a start, a sign—if this young man isn't ashamed of the tone of his voice, at the very least he knows he ought to be. Glenn doesn't sit, and neither does Richard.

"Sir!" the officer says, but another police boat has pulled up.

The man at the wheel is older, and the eyes beneath his visored cap are pinched in kindness. "Brockmeier," he says, "a word."

"Corporal—" the young officer says, but the expression on his superior's face cuts him off. He climbs from gunwale to gunwale and hands the visored officer the clipboard onto which he's recorded the day's statements. From behind the wheel, the older officer touches the brim of his cap. He looks each family member in the eye, saying, "Ma'am. Ma'am. Sir." When he gets to Richard, he says, "Sir, I think we've got it from here. If you'd kindly remove your boat from the premises, I'll see the family makes it home."

"We're not leaving," Glenn says. But his wife's hands are on him, face pressed to his shirtfront. "Okay. Get us out of here."

The young officer extends a hand that no one takes, and into the police boat they go, first Trish, then Wendy. Glenn turns to Richard, and it's only then he sees his hand is still on the man's shoulder. He lets go, and the other father leaves his side.

Richard watches the police boat depart, then climbs aboard *The Sea Cow*. He crosses the bay and navigates into the boathouse. He cranks the lift, and the boat rises from the water. The boathouse, like the house above, is crumbling. Wasp nests paper the eaves, insects funneling in and out like copper drones. Richard's fishing poles lean in one corner. They're in rough shape. They need new line, new reels. He's not sure they're worth bringing to Florida. He's never fished the ocean. He might need all new gear.

An ache in his stomach, thinking this.

Florida's all right. He likes Florida fine. There will be birds for Lisa and libraries for him. He likes those Florida potboilers—Miami mysteries, murders on the beach—likes solving the crime in the first fifty pages, flipping to the end, and being right. Plus there are colleges down there, plenty of them. If he gets bored, he can always teach again.

But Florida's not Lake Christopher. Florida was never in the cards. The plan was *here*, always. He doesn't want to leave the lake, but given what he's done, who is he to say no?

Why *did* he do it? Why, last summer, did he join Katrina at MCA in Montreal, not expecting anything to happen, but not putting up a single boundary to keep said anything from happening, save the thin wall between their adjoining hotel rooms? Hadn't he gone so far as to leave the door on his side open, just to see?

What are you doing? he asked himself all week, as though watching, from a distance, another man do things he'd never do.

He never should have joined her at the club. He offered her a drink, but Katrina only wanted to dance. She danced. Richard watched. When she returned to the bar, she was sweaty, smiling. "These Canadians are nice boys," she said. "Too nice." It was forty years since he'd been with anyone but Lisa, but Richard knew, right then, what would happen next. Katrina didn't have to wink. She didn't have to run her hand down his arm.

Katrina was brilliant, a fellow full professor—Stanford, physics. Her interest in Richard was in Lie theory and exceptional groups, and in their application to mathematical physics. She needed more math, and he was the reason, she said, she'd picked Cornell for her sabbatical. Early in the new century, Richard had joined another mathematician and a physicist in debunking Lisi's E8 theory. This made him briefly famous (by mathematician standards) and won him some grant money, job offers leveraged into course releases, and the contract for a book he wrote and which sold well (again, by mathematician standards). Though in the end, who knows? History might be on Lisi's side. A grand unified theory could prove true. Perhaps there will even be a convincing theory of everything, though Richard doubts he'll live to see the day.

In his time at Cornell, he had many genius colleagues, but never one so young as Katrina. She was in her thirties and already a full professor. She'd skipped grades in elementary school, she told him, finished college in three years, and defended her doctoral dissertation at twenty-four. This was more or less unheard of, and Richard found himself worshipping her for it.

"Relax," she said. "It's sex. It's not a trap."

They traded the club for Katrina's hotel bed. Richard had trouble getting it up, then he didn't. He lay back, she rode him, and all he could think was how, once, he'd been young too.

He didn't love Katrina, and she made it clear that she did not love him. He loved Lisa—*loves* his wife. But one life will never be enough. If he could, he'd do it all again a hundred different ways. He's sure he could live a hundred lifetimes and never grow bored.

In the boathouse, a wasp dive-bombs, and he returns the lifejackets to their hooks. He pulls the cooler with the day's uneaten sandwiches from the boat. The cooler's heavy. It will hurt his back to drag it up the hill.

At the door to the boathouse, he looks back, and it occurs to him this might have been his last day on the water. Given what's happened, his family may not want to fish or swim. They may not want to stay the week.

He starts up the hill. The grass needs mowing. Above, the sky is dark, rain on the way. He sets the cooler down and stops to catch his breath. He used to race his boys up this hill. He's always been an older father, forty by the time Thad was born, but he used to be in better shape.

In the grass, there's a horseshoe. He bends to pick it up, then straightens, thinking of his back.

His affair with Katrina lasted three months. They were careful.

They always used condoms, a new sensation that took some getting used to, and not once did Katrina call him at his home. In the end, it was Richard who called it off, more from guilt than fear of being caught. Katrina hugged him, straightened his bow tie, and said she understood. She accepted no blame for his infidelity, nor did he blame her. If a marriage was worth protecting, it was the duty of the married one to keep the vows.

That fall, then spring, they worked side by side as though nothing happened. On Friday afternoons, Katrina's new boyfriend picked her up at the lab. He seemed nice, was handsome and much closer to her age. They were happy together, and Richard wished them well. He should have been relieved. Why, then, did he feel hurt?

What does he *want*?

He wants his body back, for one. He wants the stamina and muscle tone of someone half his age. He wants to be adored, not as a mathematician, but as a man.

He wants Lisa not to leave him. He fears she suspects, though how could she know?

On his cell phone, Katrina used to come up as *K*. What he wouldn't give, some days, to see that letter blink green on the black screen of his phone. But they haven't talked since spring semester's end. She was not at his retirement party in May, a modest reception in Malott Hall. Chances are, they won't speak again unless Katrina needs a reference for a grant or residency, a letter Richard will gladly write.

A screen door bangs, and Lisa meets him in the yard. She helps him lug the cooler up the hill, and they rest on the bottom porch step.

"Did they find him?" she asks, and Richard shakes his head. She's been crying, face puffy, red. "Diane called. Michael got stitches, but he'll be fine. They just need a ride home."

"I'll go," he says.

The helicopter, departing, passes overhead. In the bay, divers climb onto their boats.

"Are they giving up already?" Lisa asks.

He doesn't know. He guesses it's the weather, takes her hand.

"Those poor people," she says. "That poor boy."

"Are you going to be okay?" he asks.

"No," she says. "Absolutely not."

They stand, and together they carry the cooler up the steps and across the porch, then Richard follows Lisa into the house.

6.

In dreams, Jake is running. His father has him in his sights.

In dreams, the Remington never wavers, and the buckshot, when it comes, arrives like lightning down his back.

In dreams, he's in Phoenix at the Road to Manhood camp. He prays and prays and prays, and still he's gay. Men scream at him. A counselor presses his erection to Jake's back.

In dreams, his father calls him *faggot*, *pussy*, *queer*.

In dreams, his father says, *You're not my son*.

From dreams, Jake wakes, and Thad is watching him from across the room.

"How long was I out?"

"Not long," Thad says. "My dad went to get Michael and Diane. Mom's making dinner. You can sleep more if you want."

Jake sits up. The towel slips from his waist, and he's naked on the bed. Thad's seated at the desk his parents purchased for this room when Thad insisted he was a poet and needed a place at the lake to work. It's the kind with hinges that opens to make a surface for your work.

"What's that kind of desk called?"

"Secretary," Thad says. He turns back to his work, writing in one of the little notebooks he carries with him everywhere he goes, a choice Jake finds insufferable. Jake doesn't keep a sketchpad on him, never has. Maybe Thad's poems are competent. Jake can't be sure. With paintings, he can eye a piece and tell you in two seconds if it's any good, what the artist was after, and how long it took—or should have taken—to paint. Whether he *likes* the painting is beside the point. What matters is conviction, is evidence of care and craft.

Thad has conviction. Jake's not so sure about the rest. The world of Thad's poems is mostly a blur, like a moon glimpsed through a backward-facing telescope. Then again, Jake's never really gotten poetry.

He stands. He moves to the desk and takes Thad's shoulders in his hands. He kneads, and Thad closes the notebook and puts down his pen.

"Please don't," Thad says. "I want to get this down."

"Get it down," Jake says. "No one's stopping you."

He massages. Thad's shirt is blue and scratchy, the collared kind, Lacoste alligator openmouthed at nipple-height. Thad needs new shirts. The past year, his clothes have gotten tight, which Thad blamed on the dry cleaner before admitting he was the proud owner of what their friend Wes called a *muffin top*. "Welcome to thirty," Wes said, and Thad gave Jake a look that said no way were they going to bed with Wes again.

Jake runs his palms down Thad's back, lifts the hem, then slides his hands inside Thad's shirt.

Thad stiffens. "I said *don't*. I said *please*."

Jake withdraws his hands. "I was being nice."

"You weren't." Thad flicks his pen, which rolls off the desk onto the floor.

Jake leaves Thad's side. He retrieves his laptop from his backpack and opens it on the bed. He gets comfortable, pillow under his head, then navigates to Chat-N-Bate, clicks *Male on Male*, then, changing his mind, clicks *Male Solo*.

Onscreen, a man sits on a bed. The bed is long and narrow, and there are posters on the wall: Metallica, Korn, Tool. A lava lamp shares a table with a stack of books. It's a thirty-year-old's idea of what a dorm room looks like, and this man is thirty if he's a day. But Jake gets it. The college look is in, and being *in* is what gets you tips. Jake's never tipped, but he likes to watch.

The man onscreen wears no shirt. His jeans are around his ankles. He's shaven, long, uncut. He's tugging at himself, looking into the camera like he can see Jake through the lens. He can't, of course, but that's the illusion: to make the other person feel seen.

The guy's screen name is DannyK. Beside the livestream, a message board scrolls viewer comments. There's a beep when someone posts and a ding when someone tips. Supposedly, hot twinks get rich off this, though Jake's never seen anyone clear more than fifty an hour. A hell of a way to grind out a living. He can't fathom jerking off that much. Three, four times a day he'll do, but every hour, eight hours a day? You'd get sore. Or bored. Maybe not bored. Jake can't imagine getting bored of sex.

The kid tugs and tugs until Jake finds himself hard. He looks up. Thad's watching.

"Seriously?" Thad says. He stands. He slips his notebook into his pocket and leaves the room.

Jake shuts his eyes. The laptop's warm on his stomach, cool where the machine's fan blows air across his skin.

He was sixteen when his father caught him masturbating. Masturbation alone, given their faith—Southern Baptist—and their church—the Church of the Glorious Redeemer, West Memphis campus—was bad enough. But Jake wasn't just caught masturbating, he was caught masturbating to *porn*. And he wasn't just caught masturbating to porn, he was caught masturbating to *gay* porn, a sin-packed trifecta that pretty much guaranteed him an eternity of pitchforks and fire.

His father didn't beat him, not that time. Instead, he opened Jake's Bible. The Bible had been a birthday present, Jake's name embossed in gold leaf on one leather cover corner. Bible between them on the bed, his father led him through a dozen passages. He skipped Song of Songs, opting for passages condemning sexual sin. His father was versed in apologetics, and they got into the Greek, the multiple interpretations of *arsenokoites*. They talked David and Bathsheba. The Onan story got a lot of play.

His father admitted that boys Jake's age had urges. Still, he must never act on them. No alternative was offered, merely the acknowledgment that, from time to time, Jake might mess up, at which point his only hope was to beg forgiveness and pray that God would make his boners go away. His father also assured him that he wasn't gay, merely confused.

Jake wasn't *confused*. In middle school, a friend had shared his stepfather's videos. The women in the movies did nothing for him. Instead, he found himself watching the men, then watching his friend. "Don't watch me," the friend said. "Watch them."

By high school, he'd had many crushes, though none he'd acted on until a youth group camping trip and the tent he shared with Sam McIntosh. All they'd done was kiss, but the next day, Sam went to their youth leader, Mr. Doug. The boys were the same age, same standing in the church, but no matter. Sam repented first. Jake had "made him do it." Sam was forgiven, rebaptized, cleansed. Jake was all but excommunicated. No more youth group. No Wednesday nights or mission trips. He could accompany his parents to church on Sundays, nothing more. His mother cried. His father beat him, then didn't speak to him for weeks.

Months later, when Jake turned eighteen, he was sent to the three-day Arizona camp staffed by old queens pretending that they weren't. He heard testimony after testimony: God could intercede. God could make you straight. The scales could fall from your eyes, and just like that, you'd be really into boobs.

Jake tried. He took part in every ceremony, answered every question, sang every sparkly, halo-making song. He wanted to be a good Christian. He wanted to make his father proud. He wanted to love and to be loved by God.

Jake opens his eyes. Onscreen, DannyK's still going at it. The chat thread scrolls by, stuffed with images and GIFs. Beeps and dings like crazy. Someone types: *Go, dawg, go!*

Jake's lost his erection. He slaps the laptop closed. From the kitchen, he hears Thad's mother on the phone.

The bedroom door opens, and Thad pokes his head in. "They're on their way home," he says. "Michael's fine. Just stitches."

"Good," Jake says. He's never cared much for Thad's brother because Thad's brother's never cared much for him, but he wouldn't want to see the guy hurt.

"You might want to dress for dinner," Thad says.

Their eyes lock. Jake won't apologize for his sex drive. Still, he feels bad. Thad's good at guilt. Jake's good at feeling guilty.

Thad's stomach brushes the doorknob. That shirt. The hemline used to reach his crotch. Now it rides his waist. With Thad, everything's skinny but his gut. *Muffin top.* It's noticeable enough that, more than once, walking through Brooklyn, Jake's caught eyes on them, expressions that seem to ask why he's with Thad.

Thad backs out of the room and shuts the door.

A thunderclap. Jake doesn't look outside. He doesn't want to see the police boats, the lake. He checks his phone. A text. *Marco.*

Tomorrow's a mistake. He shouldn't go, and knowing he shouldn't go, he will.

Blame curiosity. Blame fate. Blame Facebook. When Marco IMed him and said he lived in Asheville, and when, a week later, Thad's mom called, insisting they visit the lake before month's end, the timing seemed too providential to ignore. Asheville awaits, an hour away. Only a matter of getting Thad on board.

Every open relationship has boundaries, and theirs are these: Always together. Only if both are comfortable. Never if it's an ex.

A kind of mantra: *Always. Only. If.*

For two years the rules have served them well. Thad wasn't crazy about the *open* part at first, but Jake won't have it any other way. He won't have strictures imposed on him, not by church or any man. Better to be a fuckboy than an altar boy. Better to suffer one bad night than regret the torment of *what if.*

Marco's different, though. Not only is he an ex, he's Jake's first time, first love. With Marco, *just lunch* can't possibly mean *just lunch,* can it?

Tomorrow? Marco's texted. *We still on?*

We're on, Jake texts. He hasn't mentioned Thad. He texts a string of x's and o's, goofy enough for built-in deniability should Thad raid his phone, but bold enough to mean something to Marco if there's something there to mean.

Jake stands and slides the laptop into his bag. He slips on boxer briefs and pants.

Outside, the wind makes maracas of the trees. Beyond the trees, the lake is wavy, and the boats have left the bay.

He drops to the floor and searches for Thad's pen, which he finds under the desk. The pen isn't a nice one. It's a Bic—white-barreled, black-tipped, the kind that comes cellophaned in packs of ten. Thad will write with anything, a quality Jake finds endearing. And annoying. He caps the pen and returns it to the desk.

A little time until dinner. Really, he should do something productive. He went to the trouble of getting his oils through security, brought the material safety data sheets, though in the end he hadn't needed them. The woman at security hardly noticed the tubes. "Paints," he said, and she let him continue to his plane. Turps and mineral spirits wouldn't have made it through, but he can siphon gas from the lawn mower if he needs a thinner. He has a pair of canvases and pushpins for the pushpin/trash bag trick to get the canvases home wet. He has brushes and a palette. He has his collapsible travel easel. Minus palette knives, he has everything he needs.

He also has a secret.

Jake Russell, the toast of Bushwick, Frank DiFazio's youngest client, the man *Artforum* called a *New Symbolist for the Twenty-First Century* and an *American Munch*, hasn't finished a painting in six months.

7.

Dusk, or not quite dusk. That cadaverous hour approaching dinner—doom.

Lisa sits at the kitchen table. She is hungry, and the smell of chicken and rosemary and onions makes her hungrier. Before her, a cantaloupe half rests on a plate in a pool of its own brine, its middle molten, like a geode neatly cracked. She has only to dig the seed tangle from the melon's center, but the spoon in her hand feels small, the task too much.

Richard should be back by now.

The windows are dirty, and she rises to wipe them. She unlatches a window, opens it. The lake's gone gray. The boats are gone.

Wind hits the window screen and dislodges a beetle—emerald husk, legs like twigs. The screen is red with rust. She can't remember the last time the windows were cleaned. She can't remember the last time she or Richard dusted or mopped the kitchen floor. Neglect might mean they don't deserve the house. No matter. Soon, they'll have no house to come to and not clean.

On the sill, the insect reclines abdomen-up, an accusation. Thunder rattles the window in its frame, and at least this gives her something useful to do.

She gathers the household rain buckets and sets them in place, handles tipped like smiles on their sides. One bucket catches drips from the roof's peak, the other from a large, tarantula-shaped water stain.

All rot, the inspector said, descending the ladder from the roof. Lisa worried the sale might not go through, but the buyers didn't flinch. Which is when she knew they weren't here for the house. In a week, her life's best decades will be bulldozed into dust.

Never again will Lisa see Thad's little butt cheeks gallop haphazard through the house (there'd been a toddler streaker phase). Or watch Michael heft a catfish, tail flapping, up the hill. Or study a kingfisher, its punk-rock crest and heavy bill, from her back porch.

Nor will they navigate the mountains, years from now, and find the driveway, ring the bell. "We used to live here," they won't say, hoping for a tour of the updated kitchen or rescreened porch. Because there will be no kitchen, no porch. Or, there will be, just not theirs. Their house will be gone, something preposterous and glamorous in its place.

Why, then, these buckets? Why not let the water stain the floor?

Because the house is hers. It's hers a few days more, and Lisa cares for what is hers.

She has only to cancel the closing, has only to say *no*. But that is the one thing she cannot do. A sacrifice is required. Except, a sacrifice to whom? For whom? In the name of . . . what?

But these are the wrong questions. One might as well ask who owns our grief, who strips the incandescence from the matchbook of our days?

The first time Lisa made love was to a boy named Nick. The year was 1978. She was a college junior, twenty years old, and they did it in her '71 Chevy Vega. Two years later, she met Richard. Soon after, she married him, at which point she insisted they sell the car. Richard pushed back. The car was fine. If she hated the Vega, she could drive his Dart. But she wouldn't have it. She refused to watch Richard drive the car or ride in it. Sex meant too much to her. Sex branded everything it touched. So the car was sold. And if this house wasn't where Richard had trespassed, it's where she'd waited, last summer, while he did. It's the house to which he returned from his convention, bow tie askew, and she knew another woman's hands had touched his neck. His laundry, when Lisa did it, smelled like her.

No, the house must go, the crooked page made straight, spine of their days reset.

There will be a winnowing, followed by a relocation: new state, new house, new birds, new friends, new lives. It isn't the only way forward, except, having made up her mind, it is.

She adjusts the rain buckets. It's a job she's done a hundred times, but there's a comfort in rituals like these, security in the knowledge that, if nothing else, what rain comes will be caught.

8.

Thad drags a croquet mallet across the yard, over anthills, unmown grass. A red ball lounges tumorous beside a wicket, and he bends to excavate it from a dandelion patch.

The day before, his father pulled the set from the garage, unboxed the mallets and affixed wickets to the lawn, though no one got around to playing. Not that they've ever played properly. Their family version of croquet involves balls whacked at random and however many points per wicket they've agreed to for that game. Official rules grace the back of the box, but Thad's never read them. Arguing the finer points of croquet sounds to him like some fucked-up Tom and Daisy shit. His parents may own a lake house, but that house is still a trailer, a double-wide in disguise, purchased before word on Christopher, North Carolina, got out and the Home Depot guy bought up half the lake.

That Thad's father would break out croquet, of all things, is confirmation of a growing fear: his parents intend to resurrect the whole world in a week, everything they love about this place. Every boat ride and fishing trip. Every picnic. Every entertainment—horseshoes, lawn darts, cards. A forced march down memory lane.

Jake loves the lake house games, loves competition. Whatever spring winds the clockwork of Thad's father winds Thad's boyfriend, as well. For Jake, life is art and sex and games. That, or art and sex *are* games. The way Jake does them, all three feel competitive.

A rumble drifts polyphonic over the lawn. The croquet balls glow in the gloaming. Thad pulls his Moleskine from his pocket, but he has no pen. He could go inside, but he doesn't want to deal with Jake.

Glow in the gloaming. And he calls himself a poet. Bullshit.

He unfastens the wickets and returns them to their bag. He's found one mallet, and one's in the box. Two to go. He wanders the yard, praying against snakes, until he finds the third mallet in the grass. It's beat-up, the knocker gouged.

When Dad wasn't looking, Thad's brother used to hammer slugs. The Slug Hunter 3000, Michael called his favorite croquet mallet. He'd raise the mallet, give a *Mortal Kombat* cry of "Finish him!" and bring the hammer down. What remained was magic, a glistening, mercury-leavened pool. Once, Michael malleted a snail, which, he reasoned, was just a slug with a hat. But the accompanying crunch was too much. Michael threw up. Thad cried. They never killed a slug or snail again.

The storm is close, Thad's shadow lengthening across the lawn. Cloud bottoms brighten overhead. He finds the last mallet and returns it to the garage just as the rain arrives.

The garage, detached, was never a place for cars. Now it bulges with everything that once filled the house. Boxes tower and jostle, the uniform tan of U-Haul cardboard. Not one is labeled, which is just like his parents. The absentminded professors. But it's not moving boxes Thad's after. The boxes he wants are long and white.

In middle and high school, he collected comic books. College, too, before he dropped out. The collection was X-Men, mostly, though he abandoned his beloved mutants once Matt Fraction's run ended and the X-Men stopped making any sense. He still picks up an issue here and there. In the latest, Gambit and Rogue, the will-they-or-won't-they Ross and Rachel of the superhero team, finally tied the knot, a development that would have thrilled him twenty years ago. These days, he'd trade the couple for a few gay X-Men in any story central to the plot.

Most of his comics made it from Ithaca to Jake's place, but, because Thad spent summers at the lake, the rest are here. He's no completionist, but with every series interrupted by gaps in any given year, it would be nice to reunite the books. He could take some time, reread the best runs. Maybe eBay them. He isn't sure what they're worth. A few thousand dollars, probably. Enough to get him through a couple of months in the event that—

But Thad doesn't want to dwell on *in the event that*.

He moves piles and reassembles stacks, but the long, white boxes are not here. Unless they've been boxed inside other boxes, they're gone. Which can't be. Surely his parents haven't thrown out their son's comic books. Surely he's not that dated cautionary tale.

He does find the old family telescope, secure in its dusty, patent leather case. He lifts it and the handle comes off. The case clatters to the floor. He drops the handle, leans the case like a rifle on one shoulder, lowers the garage door, and runs through the rain into the house.

His mother is in the kitchen. A large roast chicken has been pulled from the oven, and the air is fragrant, the house warm.

"I found the telescope," he says. He's back in boy mode. Despite himself, he wants her to be proud of him.

"Okay, but don't rearrange the garage. The movers charge more if the boxes aren't consolidated."

He sets the telescope on the table, then moves to the kitchen counter where his mother whisks melted butter in a bowl. The counter's horseshoe-shaped, and he stands across from her.

"Did you put the croquet set away?" she asks.

"I did."

Two more days and they'll all adopt their family roles: his father withdrawn, his mother smothering, Michael moody, Thad jockeying for everybody's love.

"Mallets in the box," she asks, "hoops in the bag?"

"*Wickets.*"

"In England, where the sport began, they're *hoops*."

Thad smiles. "Pretty liberal interpretation of the word *sport*."

His mother butters the chicken with a basting brush. The skin is gold, not yet her trademark golden-brown.

"I haven't seen Jake all afternoon," she says.

"He's painting," Thad lies. "Hard at work on the next show."

"That's wonderful," his mother says, but she's not really listening.

She slips her hands into yellow oven mitts, opens the oven door, and slides the chicken in.

The house is quiet. The thunder's given up. Now it's just rain on the roof and buckets catching drips.

"Mom," he says, but the timing's wrong. His mother's eyes are shut, arms folded over her chest. This day's too big, and he'd sound monstrous raising the question of missing comic books.

Let them eat first. Let them play a game. Maybe this week can still work out all right.

Thad thinks this, then thinks of the other family, the boy. Immediately he feels selfish, then weak for feeling selfish, then self-conscious for feeling weak. "Analysis paralysis," Steve would say, a term Thad's pretty sure his therapist shoplifted from AA.

Tomorrow, Thad will wake and go to the window. If the boats are back, they haven't found the boy.

His mother weeps. He shuts his eyes.

There's only one thing to do in the face of all this grief. Thad is going to get stoned out of his fucking mind.

9.

Richard shuffles, and Diane cuts the deck.

The Spades they play is modified for six. They work in teams of three, rotating who plays. Richard keeps track of rotation and score.

They're at the kitchen table. Lisa's made tea, which only she drinks, and filled a bowl with pretzels, which no one eats. No one ever eats the pretzels, but they're nice to look at, a little hillock of clipped trefoil knots. Outside, the rain is steady.

Richard deals. He, Michael, and Jake make up one team, Lisa, Diane, and Thad the other. This is how it's been since Jake entered the picture. Richard plays best with Jake. Jake gets the game. He follows Richard's lead. And, most important, he plays to win. Ambition matters. Sure, it's only family fun, but it's no fun if it's *all* in fun. Richard would rather play and lose than no one ever win.

Jake's a good kid, charming, successful. A little full of himself, but who wouldn't be with money and prestige like that at twenty-six? Richard watches him across the table and wishes, forgive him, that his boys were more like Jake. Wishes *he'd* been more like Jake, everything he wanted at so young an age. Richard was late to marry, late to have kids, late to his career. Perhaps it's not too late for his sons. Michael's smart. He's sensible enough. And Thad's okay when he's not off his meds. There was that nasty business in the winter of '05 and a second attempt a decade ago. But Thad says that's over now, and Richard wants to believe it's true.

Lisa stirs her tea.

When it comes to cards, he and his wife make terrible partners. Thirty-seven years of marriage should translate to mind reading and knowing winks, but Richard has no patience for Lisa's underbidding or her forgetting, each hand, what's been played. *There are only fifty-two cards*, he wants to say. *Keep up!* He loves his wife. He'd step in front of a bus for her. But he hates how she plays Spades.

She pulls the tea bag from her mug, lets it hang over the tea, dripping, then drops the pouch onto the tabletop. Where she sits, a constellation marks the place tea bags have steamed the finish from the wood. Richard can see her heart's not in the game. His either. He's just better at pretending. Fake contentedness until you feel it, that kind of thing.

Dinner was a quiet affair, the chicken tough, the veggies rubbery, which is not the norm. Still, everyone ate. Everyone said how good the chicken was, everyone lying, everyone knowing everyone was lying and saying nothing, because that's what families do. Lisa said little, Jake and Thad appeared to ignore each other, and Michael, high on painkillers, raised a hand every few minutes to probe the sizable bandage on his head, Diane scolding, pushing the fingers away.

Dinner last night was uncomfortable for other reasons. "Your father and I," Lisa began, and Richard watched his children's faces fall as the family home was taken from them.

Richard deals the last card. Let them play a hand. Maybe if they just start playing—

"Should we leave?" Diane has addressed the table as a whole, and Richard knows better than to respond.

"What do you mean, dear?" Lisa asks.

Always, Lisa's called Diane *dear*, though never Jake. Jake will get a term of endearment if he and Thad marry, Richard guesses, not before. With Lisa, everything is earned.

"Given what's happened," Diane says. "Do we want to stay?"

To witness a drowning and keep going, keep playing cards. Is it unreasonable? Are they in shock, Diane the only one who's thinking straight?

Lisa smiles the smile of someone trying not to cry and working her way toward angry all at once.

"Where would we go?" she asks.

Let them leave, Richard wants to say. *Release them if that's what they want.*

He doesn't want to hurt his wife. He only means to stick up for Diane. He loves Diane. She's good to Michael, kind to all of them, and still Lisa's tough on her, which Richard finds hard to watch.

"You kids can go," he says. "We'd love for you to stay, but—"

Lisa frowns. Her knuckles whiten around the handle of her mug.

"We won't blame you if you want to call the week off," he says.

His wife watches him. She wants him to meet her eyes, and he won't. He keeps her in his periphery, and his eyes settle on Michael's bandage, the cotton square stained orange by Betadine. When the stitches come out, his son will have a scar.

"At least give it a good night's sleep," Lisa says. "In the morning, if you still want to leave, you can leave." She's watching Richard, talking to Diane. Richard watches Michael. Michael watches his lap.

Jake reaches for a pretzel, seems to change his mind, and gives the ceramic pretzel bowl a spin. The bowl's one of Diane's. She's good with pots, less good with paints. She's no Jake, of course, another thing everyone knows and no one says.

Sword in head, the king of hearts watches Richard from his hand. The hand is weak. Too few face cards to take tricks, too many trumps to go nil. Unless Jake's cradling some monster spades, they'll be off to a slow start.

"I could use a drink," Richard says, leaving his seat.

"Me too," Michael says.

His son can drink. More than he should. More than the others seem to notice. Richard only sees his son a week at Christmas and a week each summer, so maybe it's a vacation thing. He hopes Diane would tell them if Michael had a problem. Unless Diane knows something and is afraid to say, the way Richard suspects and is afraid to ask.

He pulls the last of the summer mason jars from the freezer and two tumblers from the cabinet above the sink. He pours two fingers into each. The moonshine is called Apple Pie, and he's never met the locals who distill it. Instead, he calls a number, leaves a message, drives his car to the county dump, then takes a twenty-minute walk. When he returns, the money under his front seat is gone, the moonshine in the trunk. His Cornell friends would find this procedure troubling, dangerous, but it's been done this way for decades. It's a North Carolina thing, and Richard gets it. These are his people. He was born a Southerner, and he'll die a Southerner. No PhD or professorship can change this fact.

He sets a tumbler before his son and sits.

"Go slow with that," he says, and Michael nods, then gulps. Moonshine, plus wine with dinner, plus painkillers can't be safe, but Richard bites his tongue.

The rain is slowing.

"It's a brave thing you tried," he said, driving Michael and Diane home from the hospital. *Did*, he should have said. *Did*, not *tried*. He wanted to say more, though anyone who's watched someone die knows just how cold cold comfort in the face of death can be.

At the table, he examines his cards, though he memorized them the second he saw them. This round, it's him and Jake against Thad and Diane. Diane's good. She carries Thad and Lisa. Every third turn, when Thad and Lisa are paired, that's when Richard makes his move.

Diane bids. Richard sips his drink, and he's pummeled in the face by bright, unfiltered joy. The moonshine, which he's been drinking all summer, doesn't mess around. His tongue fills his mouth. His spine is light.

Jake bids low, which means his hand is garbage. Thad bids high, so he has all the cards. Richard bids, throws down his club, and Michael leaves his seat. At the kitchen counter, Michael takes a shot, then returns to the table, tumbler refilled. In all his life, Richard's never had three moonshines in one night.

He looks from one son to the other. "Michael got the skinny genes, and Thad got the skinny jeans," Jake once joked. Both boys look like Richard—high cheekbones, sunken eyes, hawk's nose—but Michael's height and slenderness make him more his father's son.

When the boys were growing up, Lisa sometimes invoked a

thought experiment she called *Smart, Happy, Good*. Lisa believes people can be all three. Richard feels the best most can hope for is two. He's smart. (Modesty's dishonest—worse, a waste of time.) He's happy off and on. But rarely is he good. Not that he's *bad. Good*, the way Lisa puts it, means giving, serving others with a sacrificial love. That's the game: Is your life a quest for knowledge, happiness, or good works? They need not be mutually exclusive, except that they so often are. He's known colleagues who were giddy in their meanness, had friends who were kindhearted idiots. Seven combinations, then. Seven kinds of people in the world, eight counting those with no virtue at all. Far more permutations taking rank into account, though Richard's never taken it that far.

Thad is smart. He's good. It's happiness that eludes him. Michael is smart, though he has a knack for making poor choices, saying stupid things. Lisa, well, Lisa might just be all three.

Thad plays the ace of hearts, which Jake takes with a trump. Richard will have to watch Jake's discards for hearts. Occasionally Jake cheats, which destroys the integrity of the game, which Richard can't abide. No fun winning if the winning isn't real.

"What I want to know," Michael says, "what I want to know is what the *fuck* those parents were thinking." His voice is liquor and painkillers. He downs his third glass and sets the tumbler on the tabletop too hard.

"Michael," Lisa says. Her voice is firm, but there's fear there too. *Don't*, she seems to say. *Don't mess this up*. As if the week isn't already wrecked.

"Those people," Michael says.

"Glenn and Wendy," Richard says. He lays his cards on the table, facedown.

"Who?" Michael asks.

"The people you're about to slander," Richard says. "They have names, and their names are Wendy and Glenn."

"Wendy and Glenn," Michael says. "I've got a few choice fucking words for Wendy and Glenn."

"Language!" Lisa says.

His wife is not a stickler. She *is* a person of faith, but she's the crunchy, progressive, God-is-love kind, not the turn-or-burn, no-bad-words kind. The lake house, though, is sacred. She's ecclesiastical in this, if nothing else. A time to curse, a time to refrain. A place for anger, a place for peace. For her, this house has always been a place for peace.

For Richard, peace is illusory. There's beauty in the world, sure, but look closer. The world wants you dead and will not rest until it gets its way.

Jake plays the queen of diamonds, a wasted play. Thad plays the two of diamonds. Richard discards a club, and Diane takes the trick.

"I mean, who brings a kid who can't swim on a boat?" Michael says.

"Darling," Diane says, but Michael slaps the table. The pretzels tremble. The rain has stopped.

"Those people are everything that's wrong with America," Michael says, voice loose with moonshine. "Rude and white and upper middle class."

"Michael," Lisa says, "*we're* white and upper middle class."

"*You're* upper middle class." Michael shakes his head. "Those people should be in jail."

Lisa stands. She sits. She so rarely grows angry, Richard had forgotten what it looks like when she does. But Lisa's angry now.

"Some things are no one's fault," she says. "They just happen. They happen, and they're no one's fault."

She watches the ceiling. She is a mother. She had three children. Now she has two.

"Please," she says. "Leave those poor people alone."

All eyes on Michael. What happens next depends on him. Around this table, they've had some mighty blowouts, thanks mostly to things Michael has said. Just two years ago, he made his mother cry. "No son of mine is voting for Donald Trump," Lisa said, storming from the room. This evening, though, she's going for diplomacy.

Michael lifts his empty glass, and Richard can't say whether it's a surrender or a toast. It's no apology. Then Michael burps. The burp is loud and long, with more than one octave in it. It's meant to break the tension, but tonight no one's laughing.

Michael shuts his eyes. When he opens them, he's focused. An old trick, Richard's noticed, how his boy blinks to sober himself up.

"What say we drop all this and get some 'scream?" Michael says.

Lisa moves to her son and stands behind his chair.

"That sounds lovely," she says.

She rubs his shoulders and kisses the top of his head. She doesn't mention his thinning hair. She doesn't give his shoulders an *I'm still your mother, and you will respect me* shake. Already she's forgiven him, unasked.

And can Richard be blamed for wondering if there's grace enough for him? But Richard's not the son. The son you love no matter what.

He rises, and his family follows. Tumblers are rinsed, pretzels bagged, cards put away.

They will go to Highlands, and they'll get ice cream.

It's not too late. The ice cream will save them. All will be well.

He thinks this, and it's such a simple idea that, for a minute, he almost believes it's true.

10.

In Thad's memory, Nico's stands a turreted wonder on a hill, a citadel rising from the roadside, gabled, rococoed, daffodilled. In memory, Nico's towers proudly, a beacon in the dark announcing ice cream, waffles curled to cones before your very eyes. Nico's and the river below Nico's crowded with trout—rainbows, browns, brook trout—fish thick as bodybuilders' arms. On the porch of Nico's, domes perch on the deck rails, waiting for your quarter, waiting to drop food into your small hand, fish waiting for the pellets to be flung. Then into the river the sand-tan pellets go, and *this* is what you've come for, this more than ice cream, this cacophony of food inhaled in pops and smacks, of gills like bellows, echolalia of fin and scale, and *you* have done this, with your quarter, with the cast of your hand, you've brought the river, writhing, into life. In memory—

But Nico's, like the lake house, is merely what Nico's has become. Paint-faded, chestnut-pocked, the building on the hill appears to be deflating. The domes on the deck rails are gone, the railing replaced by mismatched two-by-fours. A mistake, Nico leaving his empire to Teddy. Teddy is the dead man's perpetually stoned only son who, since inheriting Nico's two years ago, has used the storefront to push merchandise that probably hasn't hurt his ice cream sales.

Yes, if you're looking to get high in Highlands, Nico's is the place to go. Ask for the tubby guy, the one who can work up a sweat just tugging the lid off a canister of rocky road, the one with the twin cobra tattoos (one for each forearm). That's Teddy. And Teddy doesn't just sell weed. He sells *weed*. Indica, sativa, hybrids, crossbreeds, loose leaf, pre-rolls, edibles. Anything Thad can get in Brooklyn, he can get cheaper and better from Teddy's mahogany chest.

Evenings, Nico's is usually packed. But it's late. The after-dinner crowd has come and gone. Probably the rain's kept customers away. Everything is wet: the staircase, the mildew-slicked front stoop, the pink-stenciled *Nico's* logo peeling from the windowpane beside the pink front door. Thad holds the door for everyone but Michael, who won't have doors held for him, who always nods and waves the holder in.

Inside, the ice cream parlor's empty. The man behind the counter is not behind the counter, which has Thad quietly freaking out. What if Teddy was arrested? What if he's dead? Thad's not sure he'll sleep tonight without a hit.

Then, there descends over the parlor, a smell. It's a smell Thad's smelled before, a body odor composed of perspiration, weed, and chicken soup. The smell is trailed by a clatter, beyond the counter, of white, saloon-style doors. A stomach passes through the doors, and the rest of Teddy follows it.

"Thaddeus!" he booms. Teddy's been peddling to Thad since they were teenagers, when he sold dime bags from the heavily bumper-stickered trunk of his beat-up Corolla. They're friends, as much as you can be friends with the dealer you see twice a year.

Teddy approaches the counter, but he's stopped short by the prodigiousness of his own gut. Thad sympathizes. What Thad can't relate to, though, is Teddy's general dishevelment. Gone are Nico's pink-and-white-striped shirt and paper hat. Instead, Teddy wears a turned-back Boston Bruins cap and tea-colored Mossimo tee that Thad remembers being white once upon a time. The shirt is snug as a singlet, Teddy's nipples like jacket fasteners showing through the front. From his collar, a tuft of hair uncurls, pubic and obscene. Saddam just after capture, is the look Teddy seems to be going for. Saddam in a hockey hat.

Teddy extends a beefy hand, which Thad shakes. Only Michael and Jake know this man is Thad's dealer. The rest, let them assume whatever they'd like.

Teddy moves to the sink behind the counter, washes his hands, and pulls on plastic gloves.

Jake's first, and he starts in, a complicated order not on the menu. To hear Jake order food, you'd never know he grew up on milk and cornbread, on hens whose heads and feathers he removed himself. At least, that's how Thad imagines Jake's childhood from what he's been given, which isn't much. "Tell me a story," Thad will say, and Jake will say, "Once, there was a boy whose parents loved God more than they loved him."

If only he'd known Jacob the boy, but, when Thad met Jake, Frank had already traded Jacob the boy for a New York story the rich pay five figures a canvas to hear. Assuming Jake's popularity keeps up, it's only a matter of time before some enterprising journalist makes a Memphis pilgrimage, knocking on doors and taking quotes from neighbors, family, friends. Even then, Frank will find a way to spin it: *Country Mouse Makes Good in Big City!*

Jake's order goes on longer than the longest order Thad's heard in a Starbucks line. Teddy pulls on the brim of his cap. He appears to have stopped listening some time ago.

"Hold up," Teddy says, cutting Jake off. "Cup or cone?"

Thad doesn't have to look to see the expression of anger and dismay that now crowds his boyfriend's face.

Jake isn't a bad guy. Thad's seen him offer his seat on crowded subway cars, seen him break his stride to drop a twenty into a homeless person's cup. Turn on a Sarah McLachlan animal adoption ad, and watch Jake sob. Jake's never met a stranger or an animal he didn't like. But people he gets to know get on his nerves. Take Thad's family. He's pretty sure Jake dislikes all but Thad's dad. If this is true, poor Teddy doesn't stand a chance.

"Cup," Jake says, then repeats his order, word for word. There's a *please* at the end, though the *please* feels more like an *I dare you to get this wrong*.

Teddy frowns, wipes his forehead with the back of his hand, then makes Jake's order so quickly and precisely, Thad's sure he was fucking with him all along. Teddy serves the rest of them, then rings up Thad's father, who never lets anyone else pay.

Once everyone's outside, seated in yellow patio chairs or peering past the railing, riverward, for fish, Thad skirts the counter and follows Teddy through the saloon doors. In back sit two upturned buckets, the white, five-gallon tubs ice cream comes in. Between the buckets, a sheet of particle board serves as a makeshift table, cinderblocks for legs. Teddy's mahogany box rests on top, and Thad sets his dish of ice cream next to it.

"Your boyfriend's kind of an asshole," Teddy says, the way only an old friend who's also your drug dealer can say.

"I'm sorry," Thad says. "It's been a rough day. We saw something." But he doesn't want to talk about it, or wants to talk but doesn't have the words. Better to get what he came here for and go.

"Saw?" Teddy says.

"A deer," Thad says. "We saw someone hit a deer."

The lie comes easy as exhalation. Teddy removes his cap. Beneath, white scalp, brown hair, a perfect Friar Tuck.

"Dude," Teddy says. "That sucks."

"Yeah."

"That's some heavy shit."

"Yeah."

"Bambi, '*your mother can't be with you anymore.*'" Teddy opens the box, and Thad relaxes into the familiarity of the transaction.

Thad needs a job, and he could do this. He could totally sell weed. More than once, his therapist's suggested he find work. Not so much for the money—Jake has plenty—but because this is America. Because here, work equals self-esteem and self-respect. And, if Thad's honest with himself, being a lightly published poet doesn't exactly fill the hours of his days. The best reason, though, is this: He can't count on Jake forever, and what becomes of him when that day comes?

At the very least, Thad needs *routine*. Something repetitious, like an assembly line. The satisfaction of fitting lids to miles and miles of shampoo bottles, or the calm familiarity of checking cuffs for stitching, then slipping your tag into a pocket: *Inspector #5*. Thad could be Inspector #5. No one to hassle Inspector #5. No one to check *Needs*

Improvement under *Work Habits*, as Thad's grade school teachers used to do.

Except, a pocket can't converse with you. A shampoo bottle can't trade its thoughts on the latest Spike Jonze flick. And Thad needs people. When he's not with Jake, he's high or he's asleep. He's never been good at being alone.

He *could* get serious about his writing. How does Jake do it, stand for hours, painting the same canvas day after day? Locked in a room alone, Thad would lose his mind. Plus, ten lines into a poem, he loses focus. Jake blames Thad's habit, and maybe he's right. Jake never smokes.

Thad should flush his system, go a week un-stoned. Except, without weed, he isn't sure how best to wrestle with the world. He isn't like the rest of them. He doesn't have his father's brilliance, Jake's talent, Diane's grace. He doesn't have Michael's cynicism to keep him warm at night, or his mother's faith to fold into when things get rough. He wants to be happy. But how to get there without a joint in his hand? How to live without the love of someone else? How to be happy sober and alone?

The bucket under Thad has grown uncomfortable, the back room hot, but what's in Teddy's box is beautiful. Each compartment holds a canister, each canister a bud, each bud a promise: *The world would miss you if you went.* Thad needs to believe this.

His ice cream is softening fast, but he's not really here for ice cream, so he lets it melt in the bowl.

"This Blueberry's new," Teddy says. He holds a canister at eye level, gives it a gentle shake. Through the glass lid, Thad glimpses the blue-green-purple plant matter inside. "It's an indica, so we're talking relaxi-taxi. There's Northern Lights—classic—but you've had that before. On the sativa side, I've got a K2 and some pretty decent Kiwi Green. Then there are the blends: I've got Kushes, OG and Kandy. Some other hybrids over here."

Teddy touches each canister as he talks. His fingers are long. His hands are huge.

"Now, this," Teddy says, "this is Blue Cross. Enough sativa to keep you sharp, but not so much you're checking your back for ghosts."

"That one," Thad says.

"Good choice. You want, I'll roll you one right here."

"Thanks, but, you know." Thad hooks a thumb in the direction of the doors. By now, his family's wondering where he is. Then again, maybe a big fat joint is just what his family needs. He can picture it, his mother laughing, Dad doing a box step with Diane across the deck. Michael snuck hits with Thad in high school, so who knows? He might be down.

Thad produces two hundred-dollar bills from the wallet he holds for Jake, and Teddy drops two baggies in his palm, plus rolling papers and a lighter.

"You run out, you know where to find me." Teddy smiles, and his teeth are yellow. He shuts the mahogany chest, then fixes the front with a combination lock.

Thad studies the bags. There's more weed here than he can burn up before heading through airport security. Which means he won't be back for more. Which means he may never see Teddy again. He should say something, but he's bad at goodbyes. Easier to let Teddy believe, next summer, he'll be back. Easier, but not kinder.

Shaking Teddy's hand, he knows this week will be long and filled with lasts: Last swim in the lake. Last game of horseshoes on the lawn. Last night on the dock, watching the moon climb, star by star, into the sky.

He pockets the lighter, the papers and the bags. He picks up his ice cream dish. Then he's through the saloon doors, past the counter, and out the door onto the deck.

Michael and his father stand at the rail, ice cream cones in hand, river below. Diane sits in a high-backed patio chair, knees pulled to her chin. His mother stands beside her. Jake is nowhere to be seen.

"I just want to know what's happening," Michael says. "I have a right to know. *We* have a right to know." He casts a glance that says,

Back me up here, bro, but whatever Thad's walked into, he wants no part of this.

Plus, in any disagreement, Thad's rarely on Michael's side. For years, his brother's been a stranger to him. He couldn't say why Michael threw away his free ride at Cornell to follow Diane to Georgia, why he turned Republican, why he and Diane relocated to Texas, of all places.

"How long have you two been planning this?" Michael asks.

Their father chuckles. "There's no conspiracy, Son. Your mother and I never promised we'd retire to the lake."

So that's what this is about. Michael, who can barely afford his home in Dallas, wants the house. That, or he's pissed he wasn't consulted first. Thad gets it. He shares Michael's disappointment. Still, how can they ask their parents to maintain a place their sons visit, at most, two weeks a year? Their father's turning seventy. Why shouldn't they keep upkeep to a minimum, start over somewhere things are cared for, property managed, home warrantied?

"It may not be a conspiracy," Michael says, "but it sure feels like an awfully big *fuck you*." His face bulges, forehead swollen, bandage huge.

Thad wishes he were home, safe under Jake's Egyptian cotton sheets. Popcorn, a bong, a bad movie on TV. Someone get him back to Bushwick. Someone deliver him from the South.

"Just promise me no one's dying," Diane says. Feet in her chair, chin soldered to her knees, she looks as though she might cry.

"Dying?" Thad's mother says. "Oh, honey, no." She kneels beside the chair, takes Diane's hand. "No one's dying. No one's going anywhere."

"It seemed sudden, that's all," Diane says. "I worried someone might be sick."

Thad's mother stands. She turns to them. Her forehead's lined, and there are age spots on her face Thad hasn't seen before. How strange to look upon a parent and recognize that, in the short time since you saw her last, she's grown old.

"Clearly, your father and I went about this the wrong way," she says. "This decision has been in the works for years. We could have given you more notice. We should have, and I apologize. You're sweet to worry, but there's no secret. We're just ready for a change." She frowns, as though she hasn't gotten what she means to say quite right, but she goes on. "The lake house sells next week, I'll put in my last year at the lab, then we'll find a place to settle down."

"What about the Ithaca house?" Michael asks.

"There are any number of newly tenured professors who will gladly take that off our hands."

Michael looks away.

Thad's father takes the last bite of his ice cream cone and crosses his arms. "If it's your inheritance you're worried about—"

"Dad," Thad says, "please, we don't care about that."

"I care about that," Michael says.

A breeze whips the limbs of trees along the riverbank. Somewhere in all of this, the nighttime crickets have turned on.

Michael leans against the rail. Thad waits for more, some accusation from Michael of mismanaged funds or a request for proof he's still executor of their will, but Michael's quiet. Whatever's on his mind is intercepted only by the river. Maybe none of this is about money. Maybe Michael's just sad. That thought opens Thad's heart a little, but not enough to go to the railing, to be at his brother's side.

Diane rises from her chair and hugs Thad's parents. Thad moves to a nearby trash barrel and drops his ice cream in.

Where is *Jake*? He descends the staircase to the deck below, but Jake's not there. A trail of fieldstones leads to the river, and he follows it.

He's ready to get high, ready for the hand that readjusts the rabbit ears, clears the reception in his head and knocks the laugh track down a dozen decibels. He does some of his best thinking high, unless he only thinks that because he's high so much. Already he can taste the paper on his tongue, feel the sweet, hot inhalation in his chest.

The river rushes by. He follows the path downstream to where the river widens and the trout congregate too deep to see. Ahead, a light glows between trees. He follows the light into a clearing, and there's Jake on the riverbank, hair moussed, pants tight, teeth electric in his cell phone's glow.

"I can't get a signal," he says.

Who's Jake wanting to call, Marco? Thad dislikes Marco. He's never met the man, but he dislikes the idea of him. Your first lingers, love-wet and memory-heavy, and Thad is sure that Marco lingers just that way for Jake.

Just lunch, Jake's said, but what lunch of Jake's is ever only lunch?

"About tomorrow," Thad says.

"You don't have to come," Jake says, but his eyes are on his phone.

"And if I don't come?"

"If you don't, you don't. I'm fine with that."

"And what if I'm not fine with it?"

Jake lowers the phone.

"I don't like it," Thad says. "I don't want this lunch."

He pulls the weed and papers from his pocket, rolls a joint, lights it, and takes a drag. His brain un-fogs. The static clears. The sound gets crisp.

Jake crosses the clearing, and Thad offers the joint, knowing he won't take it. Jake was raised religious, and religion left a mark on him. For an artist in an open relationship with another man, it's surprising the number of things that, to Jake, still feel like sin.

Jake pulls him close. "I love you. Do you believe that?"

Thad nods. He'd like to believe it.

"Marco's a friend. He used to be more. Now he's not. It's lunch. That's all."

Jake's hand finds Thad's face, but Thad steps back. He takes another drag, exhales.

"Michael doesn't want my parents to sell the house."

Jake checks his phone. "That's dumb. Your parents can do better than that house. They have pensions, right?"

"You don't get it."

"Oh, I get it," Jake says. "I understand the feeling of attachment. You think I want to sell everything I paint? But your parents, they need to think long-term. Sometimes you have to let go of what you love to love what you have."

Thad swears he's heard Frank utter these same words. That, or they're from a movie, some scene where the music swells and the lead utters the kind of truth that only sounds profound when accompanied by violins.

"I get that the house has sentimental value," Jake says. "But *value*? If I found some sucker to take that trailer off my hands, I'd take the money and run. Your dad gets it. I don't know why Michael's arguing with him. Who argues with a genius?"

Thad shakes his head. "Dad's not a genius."

"He won that grant."

"A MacArthur," Thad says. "*Genius Grant*'s a nickname. That doesn't mean he's actually—"

"You sound threatened."

"I'm not."

Thad takes a hit. Teddy's stuff is stronger than it used to be, and for a second the world goes wobbly. He wants to sit, but he doesn't trust himself to stand back up. Plus, nature makes him anxious. Leaf litter and worms, ants and grass. Plants are for smoking, not sitting on.

Overhead, ten thousand stars turn on. Fuck it. He sits.

"Anyway," he says, "this isn't Dad's decision. The way they're talking, I'd guess this is all Mom."

He takes a last drag and grinds the joint into the ground.

"Whoever's choice it is," Jake says, "it's the smart choice. They're better off someplace nicer, someplace warm, someplace with no state income tax. Florida's cheesy, sure, but there's a reason people flock to it. It's, like, old-person paradise."

Thad wants to cry. Maybe it's the weed. Maybe it's the boy, maybe the long day. Maybe it's his fear of Marco and what tomorrow brings. But, more than he wants to cry, he wants Jake to understand. He wants him to have seen the house thirty years ago. How bright it was. How clean. How you pulled off your shoes, and the carpet rose to meet your feet. How the kitchen filled with the smell of fish and potatoes fried in the same cast-iron pan. How, after a year away, your throat would tighten walking through the door.

He wants Jake to see that you can't hang an asking price on memories like that, that time is a fickle thing, and any way to slow its passing, to hold on to the past, is worth a hundred Florida beachfront condos.

But mostly he wants to remind Jake that none of this has anything to do with him.

"Just lunch?" he says. Beneath him, the earth turns. Beside him, the river cuts a corridor to the sea.

Jake sighs. He pockets his phone. He says nothing, and Thad says nothing in return. Instead, Jake turns and walks upriver, and Thad is left alone.

On the riverbank is a rock, a big one, and he crawls to it. The rock is wet and weathered, lichen-rough. He sits. He takes a breath. And finally, he cries.

11.

Lisa's story is sad, but her story's not unique. Over three thousand families a year lose babies just by putting them to bed. Sudden infant death syndrome: a death mis-monikered. There's nothing *sudden* about smothering. Suffocation can take up to seven minutes. Nowadays, there are distinctions: SIDS, suffocation, death by unknown cause. Back then, everything was SIDS, a catchall when you couldn't bring yourself to tell the parents, *Hey, we said no bumpers, no blankets, no stuffed duck in the crib. We told you, lay the baby on her back.* Today, people know better, the deaths a third what they were the year June died. This reduction should bring Lisa comfort. She had something to do with it. Fund-raisers and research, awareness, telethons. She's walked so many miles. She has so many shirts to show for it. But, losing a child, there's no real comfort to be found.

What the other family's going through, there's not a word for it, no word to accommodate that degree of sorrow laced with rage, no word for what Lisa felt the morning her daughter stopped breathing and no one would say why.

Lisa brushes her teeth. She combs her hair. She smooths on a cream that's meant to melt the wrinkles from the skin around her eyes. The cream's never worked, and it's expensive, but she applies it anyway, just as her mother did, half out of habit, half out of vanity.

When she met Richard, she was twenty-two. Great age, great skin. This was 1980. Great year. Gas was a dollar a gallon. Her rent was three hundred dollars a month. A Democrat was in the White House, Bowie was on the radio, and, right out of college, she was employed.

Her first day, a man nine years her senior showed her how to use the photocopier. He was handsome, and he did not have a mustache.

In those days, high school teachers were mostly women. What men there were wore mustaches. Maybe it's still that way. She isn't sure. She was a terrible teacher, she's sure of that. The man with no mustache was not a terrible teacher. She'd noticed him that morning, as he was pulling into the parking spot reserved for Teacher of the Year.

"Like this," he said beside the copier. He poked at a panoply of buttons, and the copier whirred and churned. Soon, paper was spilling from its side.

"I'm Richard," the man said, and to her dismay, Lisa felt herself blush.

She'd been with men in college, but always they'd been men her age. This man, though. She could imagine standing on tiptoe to kiss him at the altar, imagine their eyeglasses clicking as their lips touched.

Richard waited a week to ask her out, six months to ask her to marry him. They married quietly that summer, and returned to school in August as Mr. and Mrs. Starling. She was twenty-three years old.

"Why the rush?" they sometimes ask each other. "What were we in such a hurry for?" They can't remember. Someone shot Ronald Reagan. Someone shot the pope. Life in the dark, early days of 1981 seemed suddenly short and fraught. A sniper's bullet might take you out at any time, so why not love the one you're with? Why not marry the one you love?

Lisa caps the skin cream and returns it to the bathroom drawer. She washes her hands. She trims her nails.

By October of '82, she was pregnant. By July of '83, their daughter, one month old, was dead. Over the next two years, she and Richard separated, came together, left high school teaching to pursue PhDs, and separated once more. But seeing as the chief occupational hazard of separating is reuniting for sad, nostalgic sex, Lisa found herself, in time, pregnant again.

But it wasn't the new baby that rebooted their lives together. Once Michael was born, she considered leaving Richard for good. Too much shared anguish. Too much of June in her husband's lips, his eyes, the delicate Ss of his ears. No, what started the marriage over was the house.

Listen: Do you know what it's like to fall in love, not with a person, but a *place*? Hill slope and dock creak. Sunlight and breeze. A V of geese reflected on the surface of a lake.

Lisa does.

Summer of '86, Michael a year old, they rented a lake house. They'd hoped to summer near the Finger Lakes or on the Cape, but money was tight, and they could stay a week in the Carolinas for the cost of a weekend in New England or New York. Which was how they found themselves on Lake Christopher, a mostly undeveloped lake in the Blue Ridge Mountains an hour west of Asheville, a lake Richard had visited as a boy.

They found they were other people at the lake. Happier people. *Better* people. At the lake, they were no longer the harried parents of a screaming toddler but the loving caregivers of a sometimes-fussy son. No longer were they the bored couple that bickers over sex, they were attentive lovers, generous and kind. With the last of their money, they rented the house a second week. The third week, they offered to buy the property outright.

The purchase proved nearly impossible, the house a terrible investment that required they borrow money from both sets of parents (neither of whom had much to lend) at a time when interest rates were 10.5 percent. Not to mention that the house wasn't for sale. The owner was an investor who maintained several rental properties and saw no reason to part with one. In the end, and against their Realtor's advice, Lisa and Richard paid more than the house was worth. They might have picked another house on this same lake. But no. It had to be this house. This house, this bay—this was where they'd rediscovered love.

It was a bad idea, and it was the best decision they ever made.

The lake didn't just save their marriage. That summer set their lives on track. Over the next two years they completed their degrees, defended dissertations, Richard landed the Cornell job, and Lisa found work at the Cornell Lab of Ornithology, a dream spousal hire coup that would never happen in 2018. Thad was born, and the Starling family settled quietly into what they would come to think of as *their lives* for the next thirty years.

"Are you coming to bed?" Richard calls from the bedroom.

Lisa leaves the bathroom. She should put peroxide drops in her ears. They swam in lake water today. But she's so tired. She wants to burrow into bed and never leave.

Dinner was bad, ice cream worse. Is she forcing the week? Should she let them go? But how to sell the house before giving everyone the chance to say goodbye?

"I'm going to make some tea," she says in the doorway. "Would you like some?"

In bed, Richard reads. The book is one of those Florida noir things, garish cover and dead girls. He puts the book down. His smile is thin, forced. Lines radiate from his lips the way she's seen with smokers, though Richard's never smoked.

"Sleepytime?" he asks. She nods, and he nods in return.

In the kitchen, she fills the kettle. Her crockery and pans are packed. She's kept just enough unboxed to get them through the week: six plates, six glasses, six tumblers, six mugs, six sets of silverware. A roasting pan. A teakettle. A pot. A carving knife. She likes cloth napkins, but she's conceded paper and plastic for the week—recyclable, of course. "Just do Styrofoam," Richard said, and she'd given him a look like *Don't you know me at all?*

She touches the kettle to the burner, listens for the sizzle, and flips on the stovetop fan. In the kitchen light, wallpaper ivy climbs the walls, leaves like trowels. This happens to her: Once she sees things one way, she can only see them that way forever after. For years, the leaves have been trowels.

She locks the front door. She rinses a wayward dinner plate. She walks a wet hand towel to the laundry room and pulls a dry one from its drawer. In the morning, one son will slice a grapefruit, leaving the counter slick with juice. The other will leave his bowl on the table, Rice Krispies clinging to the lip. These she'll clean without complaint. She's a proper hostess, but it's more than that. She misses feeling like a mom. Her sons no longer need her the way they did in their youth. This is good. They shouldn't need her. They're in their thirties. But it hurts, not being needed. So she'll scrub their bowls. She'll pick up after them. It's how she says *I love you*, whether the boys notice or not.

She misses her boys at eight and eleven, eating sandwiches cut out by cookie cutter, surprise Oreos tucked underneath. She misses Michael on the dock, pole in hand, always a fish at the end of his line. She misses Thad, her beamish boy, forestalling bedtime, reciting "Jabberwocky" from memory before he lets her tuck him in.

But those boys are gone. In their place are men, furious men, bewildered and afraid. Her whole life she's been surrounded by men—men and the voices of men, urgent, demanding, and oh-so self-assured. The house is for sale. Who cares if it's too much to ask of them? Haven't the men been asking all their lives?

In the kettle, the water churns.

She anticipated resistance from Michael, but not a scene. He even pulled a *sorry* from her, and for what? For selling *her* house without *his* permission? He has no right. Although, the house is a family home, Lake Christopher the place he met his wife. If Michael must be mad, she hopes it's this, not money, that he's mad about.

No more apologies. If Richard suspects the reason for the move, fine. One day he'll confess to his affair, or he won't. So be it. Confession isn't the thing she needs. The thing she needs is change.

When June died, a grief counselor encouraged them to slow down. "Don't make any huge life changes," he said. "Escaping grief isn't as simple as crossing state lines."

Isn't it, though? Hadn't it been? And wouldn't it work again? Plenty of people live just that way, forever crisscrossing a vast geography of despair and keeping hope alive.

A whistle, and Lisa lifts the pot and tips it, steaming, over one mug, then the other. The tea bags spin. The water swirls. She turns a knob, and the burner's coil shrinks to black. She returns the kettle to the stove and stirs her tea.

To trust scripture, God never gives you more than you can bear. Ha. Tell that to any parent who's lost a child. It's been a long time since Lisa's looked to the Bible for advice, a long time since, eyes closed, in bed or back against a pew, she's felt the hand or heard the voice of God. Still, morning and evening, she prays. She prays for comfort. She prays that she might be a comfort to others. She prays that she'll be heard.

With a spoon, she presses a tea bag to the inside of the mug. *Don't*, Richard always tells her. *Let it steep.* But she can't help herself. She likes the way the water tans when spoon meets mesh. She moves the spoon to Richard's mug and presses, hard.

In the bedroom, Richard is asleep. She removes the book from his chest and pulls the chain on his bedside lamp. In the kitchen, she pours his tea into the sink.

Down on the dock, her boys are talking. The rest are in their rooms, asleep or pretending to be.

She moves to her favorite chair and sits. How many birds has she watched from this seat? How many books has she read? What will the rest of her life with Richard be?

Be still, the Psalms say. *Be still and know that I am God.*

Stillness she has covered. It's the *knowing* part that gives her trouble every time.

Lisa tucks her feet beneath her and sips her tea against the house's air-conditioned chill. She watches the water, waiting for a child to rise. She waits, she watches, and soon, the tea has done its job. She must move to bed or risk falling asleep in the chair and waking sore.

She will not be here when her boys come up from the dock, will not be here to kiss their foreheads and send them to bed. But she can imagine it, how, her sons asleep, she might crack their doors and look at them, ignoring the arms in which their lives are wrapped, ignoring the bodies of the men they have become. How she might stand in their doorways, watching their chests rise and fall, and remember nights not so long ago when she would watch her children sleep—how she could hardly bear it, all that love.

12.

Nights used to be better. Before the resort and golf course, before builders bought up land on other bays, used to be you saw more stars. The stars are there, but faint, sky pinholed where, once, the night hung gouged and leaking light.

Michael sits on the dock beside his brother. Their feet are in the water, and Thad casts a fishing pole, a joint smoldering at his side. Michael drinks, the tumbler sweaty in his fist, the fuzzy love-buzz of moonshine quietly decapitating the bats inside his head. He drinks too much, a fact he's hidden so well from others that there are days he hides it from himself.

Once, as a boy, Michael had the flu and his fever hit 103 degrees. The worst part of being sick wasn't the chills or aches, or all the weight he lost. The worst part was being unable to think clearly. His brain, at 103 degrees, was fat in a skillet, sizzling, his thoughts sautéed. Grown Michael, sober, feels the same. He has to drink, or he's that boy again, his brain a pan, his thinking fried.

The worst is in the morning, waking up. He has yet to drink before 10:00 a.m., and if he's proud of nothing else, he's proud of that. Of course, he used to wait until noon. Then eleven. But something in him says that a drink before 10:00 a.m. means problems. Which isn't to say he doesn't have the drink poured and ready by nine thirty.

In the evensong of frogs and night bugs, Michael sips. Thad smokes.

"I don't want to talk about the house," Thad says.

"I don't want to talk about the boy," Michael says.

The bay before them is three football fields wide, a spit of land reaching a rocky point halfway across. A flagpole rises from the point.

Someone's forgotten to lower the flag for the night, and it flaps in the wind. As boys, on a night like tonight, they would swim to the point, climb the rocks, touch the pole, and race back. Michael always won.

"What's your bait?"

Thad reels. A lead sinker hangs steel gray at the end of his line— no hook, no lure, only weight.

"Just trying to get it out there," Thad says. Then he pulls his Southern accent out. "Practicin' my castin'. Been a year since I wet a line."

Michael smiles. All their lives they've played the fake-twang game, though less lately than when they were boys. "Don't make fun," their mother would say. "How a person speaks is no indication of their intellect." Michael knows this. He was never making fun.

As a Northerner turned part-time Southerner turned Texan, he's always been fascinated by ways of speaking, how a day's drive earns everyday objects new names: *Shopping carts* become *buggies*, *wolves* become *woofs*, and what goes out isn't your *power*, it's the *'lectric*. And don't even get him started on Texas. Texas has a language all its own.

His parents are Southerners who came by their accents honestly, though those accents were stronger when Michael was a boy, the Starlings fresh transplants from Atlanta. Michael never picked up their accent. Neither did Thad. But summers at the lake were enough to learn the cadences. By nine, ten years old, Michael could do a spot-on imitation of the neighbors, of Clyde at the marina or the butcher at the meat market. He's always slipped other's voices on with ease.

"Wanna cast?" Thad asks.

"I reckon," Michael says, and Thad hands him the pole.

The rod's a cheap one. It's fitted with a Zebco spincaster, the closed-face kind with plastic push button and metal cone. When he was a kid, this was the only kind of reel Michael could cast. Others tangled the second his thumb left the line.

Michael sets his drink on the dock. He weighs the rod in both hands.

Thad's not practicing casting. They both know what's at the bottom of the lake, what Thad's hoping not to hook.

Michael whips the rod like a willow switch, and the weight sails over the bay before smacking the water and sinking, enough moonlight tonight to make a show of where the sinker's hit, far out, rings multiplying then widening toward the dock.

It's been a year, but he'll be damned if it isn't a perfect cast.

"Damn," Thad says. "That was a perfect cast." Brothers.

Michael reels the sinker in, drops the rod, and lifts his glass. He takes a long swallow. The moonshine, on top of the painkillers, is doing its thing. He can't feel the stitches anymore. He can't feel his face. He extends the glass, and Thad takes it, sips, and passes the glass back.

"You still get high?" Thad asks.

"Can't. Pot shows up on drug tests."

"You get drug tested?"

"I could any time. It's in my contract."

There's a joke to be made about the price one pays for holding down a job, but Michael doesn't make it. Thad's proven sensitive to the suggestion that he's sponging off Jake, though not so sensitive that he's looked for work the past two years.

"Better hold your breath," Thad says. He lights the joint, which has gone out, and takes a drag. He exhales away from Michael, but the wind blows smoke in Michael's face.

Fuck it. All the years he's been there, not once has his company followed through on the threat of random screenings. Too expensive. Too much work. The threat *is* the deterrent.

He extends his hand.

"You sure?" Thad says, then passes the joint.

Michael inhales. His throat burns, but the bats are gone. Better yet, the bats, the cave, all of it has been detonated, his skull cracked open, cupping night. He feels *good*.

He returns the joint and lies back on the dock. His feet leave the water. His limbs loosen, and it's as though he's in a hammock, as though the dry, warped boards beneath him are rocking him to sleep.

"This is *not* the shit we smoked in high school," Michael says.

"No shit it's not that shit. This shit is light-years beyond the weed we smoked as kids. We're talking hydroponics, grow lights, engineers."

"They found a way to science the shit out of pot?"

"They found a way to science the shit out of pot."

Michael wants another hit. It's as if all his life he's eaten TV dinners. Then along comes steak. Steak with, like, a side of shrimp. And scallops. With butter.

"This weed is butter," Michael says.

The stars shimmer. The breeze is fingers up and down his arms. Thad is laughing, and the sounds around them, frog song and cricket call, keep time with the laughs. Not just time, the creatures seem to be in tune. For a second, Michael can make out the opening bars of "Sweet Caroline."

"Dude," Michael says. "The crickets are doing Neil Diamond tonight."

But Thad can't reply. He's laughing too hard. Is he laughing at Michael? It would appear that he is.

"I'm gonna be a papa," Michael says. He laughs, but Thad's not laughing anymore.

"What did you say?"

"'*Hands*,'" Michael says. "'*Touching hands. Reaching out. Touching me, touching you.*'"

The dock is silk. The stars won't stay in place.

"'*Sweet Caroline!*'" he sings. "'*Good times never seemed so good!*'"

Thad's hands shake him. "Too loud, buddy. Way too loud."

But Michael can't help it. His body wants to sing.

"'*I'd be inclined,*'" his voice echoes across the bay, "'*to believe they never would!*'"

Thad's hand is suddenly on his mouth—sweaty, meaty—and Michael licks it, at which point Thad yelps and lets go.

Stars cartwheel. The moon melts. Michael stands, strips off his clothes, and the water, when he hits it, is cold and wakes him up. The bandage slips over his eye, and he pulls it off, dropping the patchwork of tape and cotton, sopping, onto the dock.

"Michael," Thad says. "I don't think you're supposed to get those stitches wet."

He tries to remember what the surgeon said. Either way, lake water's gross. It's got amoebas in it. He wants another drink. He doesn't want a kid. Although, a boy might be cool. But expensive. Kids are expensive. Everyone says so.

He treads water, and the water is cold. The animal sounds have returned to burps and chirps. No more Neil Diamond, no more "Sweet Caroline."

He misses the music. He misses his *brother* and the way things used to be, that got-your-back blessedness of boyhood and the certainty that one would walk through fire for the other, through shit and sharks and chainsaw-wielding clowns. At what age is that love lost for good?

Michael swims to the ladder and pulls himself onto the dock.

"Don't move," Thad says, and he's up the hill. A minute later, he returns with a towel, fresh bandages, and rubbing alcohol.

Michael dries himself and slips his clothes back on. He's not embarrassed by his nakedness. He's not embarrassed to be drunk and high in front of his brother. Mostly he's concerned that he may have just confessed the pregnancy, though perhaps Thad missed that amid the singing and the jumping in the lake.

What Michael needs now is a distraction. What he needs is a different secret. He seats himself on the edge of the dock, feet in the water, and Thad sits beside him.

"Diane and I are broke," he says. He towels his hair. He smells like the lake, which, for all its silt and goose shit, is a smell he loves. "We both work our asses off, and we still can't pay the bills."

"That's awful," Thad says. "But how is that possible?"

Michael drops the towel. He finds his glass empty and eats the ice.

"Too much house," he says. "We were approved for the loan, but we shouldn't have been. Not for that much, and not at an adjustable rate. We should have done the math. Our salaries, her loans, two cars, credit card debt. We bought in '07, just in time for the collapse, then Diane's school district took pay cuts. Our house will never be worth what we paid for it. The developers didn't even finish the neighborhood."

Thad pours rubbing alcohol onto a cotton ball, which makes Michael thirsty. These days, even at the scent of Windex, his throat aches.

"Your turn," Michael says.

"My turn what?"

"Your turn to tell a secret."

Thad presses the cotton ball to the stitches, and Michael winces. Even through the giddy radiance of marijuana, of moonshine and pills, pain envelops his head at his brother's touch.

"I didn't know we were playing that game," Thad says. "*Fuck.*"

"What?"

"The cotton ball," Thad says. "It's stuck in the stitches." He tugs at the cotton, and it Silly Putties, wet and cirrus-stretched. "The stitches, they're like Velcro."

"Just stick a bandage over it."

"I don't know if —"

"It's fine," Michael says. "Pop a Band-Aid on and tell me a fucking secret."

Somewhere, a dog barks, and a second dog barks to answer it.

"You're a mean drunk," Thad says.

A third dog joins the fray, and for a minute, the world is blotted out with barks. Across the bay, lights come on and the dogs are brought inside.

"I think Mom and Dad threw away my comics," Thad says.

"That's a shitty secret. Give me something good."

Across the bay, the lights go out — one, two, three.

"We fuck guys," Thad says, "me and Jake."

Michael laughs. "How is that a secret?"

"No," Thad says. "Guy-*zuh*. As in ménage à trois. As in couples seeking couples. As in open relationship."

Michael isn't sure *what* to say to that. Without a drink, he never knows what to do with his hands. He takes up the fishing pole, but his arms feel too heavy to cast. Instead, he holds the rod tip over the water. He lets some line out, and the sinker taps the surface of the lake. More concentric circles. The quiet's killing him.

"Is that common?" Michael asks.

Thad caps the rubbing alcohol, pulls a bandage from the box, and peels the backing off.

"Well," Thad says, "I can't speak—"

"For the entire gay community. I get it. But what are the statistics?"

"*Statistics?*"

"Are most gay guys open, or what? I mean, in my world, that's considered pretty far out."

"Less far out than you'd think. Plenty of straight swingers too, I'd imagine. Now, hold still."

The bandage approaching Michael's face is huge. If Thad gets it right, it will fill a rectangle of skin between his eyebrow and his hairline without touching any hair. If he gets it wrong, the next change of dressing is going to suck.

"So, Jake goes to town on some other guy," Michael says. "You're cool with that?"

"I know Jake loves me."

Something about this bothers Michael, not because he cares what Thad does, but because this doesn't sound like Thad. It sounds like something Jake's trained Thad to say.

The bandage goes on, and Michael feels his eyebrow catch.

"Shit," Thad says.

"It's fine. You're telling me you don't get jealous?"

"Of Jake? Of course not. I'm involved. At the very least, I'm in the room."

Michael pulls in the fishing line and sets down the rod. He reaches for the glass, remembers it's empty, then feels the bandage. It's definitely affixed to his eyebrow.

"I don't know," he says. "I couldn't do it."

He imagines Diane, some dude above her, thrusting. Instantly he's angry—real fury toward some guy he just made up.

"You never worry he'll fall in love with someone else?" Michael asks.

"Do you worry Diane will fall in love with someone else?"

"No, but we're not fucking other people."

Thad shakes his head. "Trust me, our little rendezvous, love's got nothing to do with it."

Except that Thad can't hide things from his brother, and the look on his face betrays him. There's something there. Not fear, necessarily, but concern. Bewilderment, at least. It's as though, with his line of questioning, Michael's rearranged Thad's mental furniture. Or else Jake rearranged the furniture long ago, and Thad's just now noticing that something's out of place.

Thad lights his joint. He takes a drag. He flicks what's left into the water.

"Say, one day, Diane comes to you," Thad says, "and she says, 'Michael, I love you. I'm happy. But you know what would make me *really* happy? If sometimes we had sex with other people.' What would you say?"

" '*Fuck* no.' "

"Not even for her happiness?"

Michael stands. He's cold. He wants his bed. "She might think she'd be happier, but who's to say? Who says sex with other people wouldn't raise all sorts of questions for her?"

"Say it did? Don't questions deserve to be raised?"

"Sure," Michael says. "Before the wedding day. Before you make a commitment."

Thad gathers the towels, the bandages, the rubbing alcohol. "That's fair. You two took vows. But people change. You're no longer the people you were at twenty-three."

"I don't want to watch my wife with another dude."

"Another woman, then. Isn't that every straight man's fantasy? What are the statistics on that?"

Michael watches the water. He can feel himself swaying.

He and Diane were eighteen when they met. She's the only woman he's been with. Some days, he's proud of this. Other days, the thought embarrasses him. Either way, it's rare he worries that he's missing out. Diane is good in bed. *Was* good. They haven't been together since before the fight, the morning, weeks ago, when Diane opened the bathroom door and Michael saw the white stick in her hand.

"You think happiness is getting what you want," Michael says. "Whatever you want, as much as you want, whenever you want it." His voice is trembling. "But what if that's not happiness? What if true happiness is about saying *fuck you* to what you want, then sticking together, even when things get hard, even when you're not the people you once were?"

He burps. Something's churning in his gut. Drunk as he is, it's not lost on him that he's just articulated his wife's argument for the baby that he doesn't want.

How fiercely we defend those we love, even to the annihilation of ourselves.

Michael laughs. He laughs, and, laughing, throws up on Thad. Just drenches him. He's like a fire hydrant, uncapped, his stomach emptied in a colorful and urgent gush. He drops to the dock, and his knees rattle the boards.

"I'm sorry," he says, but when he turns, the world's stopped spinning, and his brother's halfway up the hill.

PART TWO
SATURDAY

13.

"It's been a while since I've seen the falls," Diane's father-in-law calls from the backseat. "Years."

Polite to a fault, Richard insisted Diane ride up front, though the car that he and Lisa share is a hybrid and tiny. His knees grind Diane's seatback. No one's comfortable.

Michael pulls away from the gas station, and they follow the country road west. His thumbs drum the steering wheel. A silver coffee tumbler rests between his legs.

This morning, when she offered to drive, Michael only frowned and gave her the look. Diane hates *the look*—the way Michael narrows his eyes to make her feel dumb. "You're so lucky to have a husband who doesn't raise his voice," her friends say. How to explain, though, that a few fights would be better than all this *not* fighting, this slow dance toward separate lives lived side by side.

Michael turns the radio up, and Buddy Holly is between them, crooning about a roller coaster and undying love. Anyone would think her husband is relaxed, but Diane recognizes the telltale grind of his jaw. At night, he wears a mouth guard just to keep from chewing through his tongue in his sleep.

"It can't be five more miles," Richard says.

"I'm just saying what the guy at the gas station said," Michael says.

They pass a farmhouse, an apple orchard, a wandering cow.

After sleeping badly, Diane woke to more boats in the bay. She scrambled eggs, made toast, but couldn't eat. Lisa stayed in bed. Thad and Jake were off to see a friend. "We have to get out of here," she said, and Michael suggested the falls. So they changed into swimsuits,

Richard joined them, and at Diane's insistence they stopped at CVS for waterproof bandages, at which point Michael and his father began arguing about their destination and how long it took to reach.

"Set the odometer," Richard says. He's watching trees go by.

What is he thinking about? Diane wonders. Her father-in-law meditates at wavelengths well beyond them all. *The absentminded professor,* Lisa calls him, but there's something gorgeous in the way he's always lost in thought. Diane doesn't regret art school, only the quality of instruction she got in everything that wasn't art. More math and, who knows, maybe she could balance a budget. More geography and maybe she could find Iceland on a map.

"The odometer, Son," Richard says. "I want to know if it's five miles or not."

Michael does as he's asked. Of course, it's been a mile since the gas station. This will launch an argument when they arrive, so they'll have to clock the mileage going back. But this is the way of families — the inconsequential elevated to the imperative. Bring three couples together for a week under one roof, and everything is code for something else.

Michael drinks from his mug and wipes his mouth with the back of his hand. His eyes say, *Can you believe my dad?* Richard leans across the backseat. In the rearview, his eyes say, *Don't worry, I know you're on my side.*

She shuts her eyes. For the next one to four miles, she'll pretend to be asleep.

These men with their loud emotions, their quiet power grabs. Some days, she imagines a life without men, just her and her daughter on a blanket in a field of poppies and cardinals and bright blue sky. Even the flowers, in this dream, have had their stamens plucked. Diane and her daughter. Then again, who says the child won't be a boy?

The car slows, and she opens her eyes. Vehicles clog the roadside. No sign or gravel lot, just grass trammeled by a half century of tire tread on sunny days. Michael steers the car onto the shoulder, parks, then pulls the key from the ignition.

Outside the car, the day is hot, air heavy with last night's rain, and she moves through soupy, sun-bleached sky. Beyond the tree line, a gentle echo, water cascading into other water.

Two shaggy-haired boys emerge from the woods. One boy raises a hand for the other to high-five. "Bust yo' ass *falls*!" he says. The other slaps his hand so hard, the first boy staggers. Meanwhile, Michael and Richard lean against the car, arguing over mileage and who said what. From a distance, Michael's forehead looks coraled — bulbous and purpled in some otherworldly, underwater way.

"Gentlemen," she calls. She will not be their referee.

Michael steps away from the car, and his father follows. They wear towels around their necks, ceremonial as stoles. They fall into step — same height, same stride — Michael and the man he will be forty years from now.

Beyond the high-fiving boys and past the trees, a trail leads them through the woods. She remembers the way. After all, Michael's not the only one who grew up here. While her parents may not have had the money for a summer home, they had friends who let them visit every year.

She was eighteen the summer she and Michael met, back when she wore a two-piece and Michael's abs still showed. He was funny and smart, and she liked the way one front tooth overlapped the other just a bit. He was tall and gangly, big-eared, like a friendly rabbit, and his eyes were kind. Plus he was surprisingly big below the belt, which shouldn't have been a big deal, though she couldn't help feeling shyly proud of this.

The trail bends, and pine trees beckon, needles silvered by sunlight, trunks ambered with sap. The falls grow louder, the tumble of water over rocks and the splash of bodies, airborne, touching down. Voices rise, river to woods and woods to sky. Then they're around the bend, the river a ribbon, the water wide. The footpath forks, a choice: Follow the river downstream, or take the trail to the top of the falls.

All is as she left it. She's not sure why she worried things would change. A river needs no tending. A river need only not be polluted, dammed, or cut off at the source. This river has been here millennia and will be here millennia more.

Yips, a yodel, and a boy is riding down the falls. The falls don't *fall*, exactly. They don't crest a ledge and drop in a postcard-perfect way. Instead, the water rushes down an incline, ski slope–steep, three stories, maybe four. Children slalom the falls on stomachs and backs, laughing, screaming, singing songs. Along the riverbank, the path is gentle. The middle, though, is like a luge. More than once, Diane's watched a girl slide down and rise without her top.

The falls are tricky too. The water zips and wishbones so that, no matter where you push off, there's no guarantee you won't be pinballed to the middle, which is why Diane's never braved the falls herself.

The boy sliding now is tall, long hair. He slaloms, all ass and holler, down the incline and rodeos into the current below. He surfaces, shakes his mane, then leaves the river, charging up the trail, a whir of pink swim trunks and skinny, hairy legs.

He's not from here. Men from here wear cutoffs or jean shorts, or drop their pants and swim in underwear. The bills of their caps are frayed, ornamented by a single fishing hook. Their tans are real, their Oakleys fake, and they drink beer from cans that aren't in paper bags. Plus, around here, men don't wear pink.

Vacationers are just as easy to spot. They aren't rich, but they have money, enough to rent summer homes or stay at Blackstone Inn. Their board shorts are plaid or paisley or have *Corona* emblazoned on the front. They're clean-cut, shaved faces, shaven chests. Their tans are fake. Their Oakleys are real.

Then again, distinctions are becoming hazier. Hipsters and trustafarians. All that denim. All those PBRs.

Meeting Michael, she took him for a local before learning his parents taught at Cornell. Michael didn't talk like he had money, which is to say he didn't speak the way Diane, at eighteen, assumed people with money spoke. He spoke like her. He loved her, and, in time, she loved him back.

In the water, a woman swims with a baby. She blows on the baby's face, dips her underwater, then, quick, brings her back up. Each time, the baby comes up laughing. The woman brings the baby to her chest, and she clings there, water beading on her cheeks.

Diane turns, but Michael's already up the trail. "Michael," she calls.

I love you, she should say. *I forgive you the grief you've caused me these six weeks. Now, come back, take my hand, and together let's wade downstream.* She should say this, and she won't. She won't because what she needs most is to hear these words from him.

Instead, she says, "Watch your head."

At the top of the trail, Michael pulls off his shirt. He's still in shape, minus the abs, chest defined, nipples pert as baby peas. She likes the parts of him that stick out, the oversized ears, the bob of Adam's apple and curl of collarbone. Richard follows Michael up the trail, and Diane removes her shoes and steps into the pool below the falls.

The mother cups water onto her daughter's head. She sings. The song's not one Diane knows. There is a verse about a creek, red clay, a sun at the bottom of the sea. The baby coos, and the mother pulls her swimsuit top aside. Then the baby is nursing, and the mother shuts her eyes. *Bliss.*

Diane knows better than to touch a baby without asking, but the child summons her, seems to send out lassoes of beckoning light from the top of her suckling head. And suddenly Diane's beside them, suddenly reaching, suddenly touching two fingers to the child's tender scalp. Fingers to head and head to breast, a current runs up her arm and through her womb, the four of them briefly, magnificently, one.

"How far along are you?" the mother asks, opening her eyes.

Diane's face must give her away, because the mother puts a hand on her arm and gives a gentle squeeze. "I'm sorry. You're not telling people yet."

"No," Diane says. "That's all right. I just . . . how?"

Above, boys whoop and taunt the falls.

"You're not showing," the woman says. "A mother can just tell. *Sometimes.* I was wrong last week. *That* was an uncomfortable Piggly Wiggly checkout line."

Diane laughs. She wants to hug this stranger. She wants to hold the nursing child. Together, she and this mother could raise their children, free from needy men and the trappings of romantic love. Some members of the animal kingdom must do this, dispense with the males once the deed is done.

Oh, but she'd miss Michael. She would. That charming overlap of teeth. His ability to home in on every ring of keys that she's misplaced. How, when she cries, he holds her for as long as she needs without ever asking why.

The child has fallen asleep at the mother's breast, milk running down one cheek. The mother wades to the far shore and lowers herself onto a quilt, the child in her arms. In time, she notices that her breast is exposed and pulls her swimsuit up. She gives Diane a wave, but the wave is not an invitation to join them, and Diane returns to the foot of the waterfall.

Others hike the trail, emerge from the trees, and stand onshore. Overhead, swimmers wait their turn at the top of the falls, Michael and Richard among them.

Earlier, Diane wondered whether they'd have the river to themselves, whether news of the drowning would make visitors wary or keep locals indoors. Except, that's the thing about death—it reminds you you're alive. The world spins, and those with lives continue risking them. Had the Starlings not been there, the drowning would feel no more substantial than the front page on which its story, this morning, was printed. What happened only hurts because they saw. But such things happen every day.

Had she spoken to the boy? She hadn't. Though she can picture his face, his buzz cut and blue eyes.

Diane lets herself slip beneath the surface where the falls give way to underwater roar. She examines her hand. How easily a ring in water might slip off. She spins her wedding band, but she does not tug. She rises, and her husband calls to her, something in his expression that reminds her of a child's *Look at me*.

The week they met, she swam here. She watched Michael above, light caught in his hair, light burnishing his legs, light racing with him down the falls. How her stomach hurt that day, her heart gone papery with want. How young they'd been, backs pimpled, skin soft. She knew, watching him ride the falls, she'd sleep with him that night.

But that was fifteen years ago. At thirty-three, Michael has far less hair on his head for light to tangle in, and his legs' golden hair has turned a wiry black. He crouches, apprehensive at the water's edge, his godhood all used up.

Sit, she thinks. *Sit before you slip and crack your head open again.*

A pair of teenagers goes down the falls holding hands, a bikinied girl and bowl cut–headed boy. Halfway down they're ripped apart, then rejoined at the bottom. In froth and foam, they rise laughing, holding hands again.

Above, Richard joins Michael. He sits, the current parting at his back.

Michael stands. And slips. The seat of his swim trunks hit, and the current carries him. It's like a stickup, how his hands reach for the sky. Then he's down the falls and under, Richard close behind. Michael comes up. Richard rises too, and Diane hurries to their sides.

"My ass hurts," Michael says, rubbing the back of his trunks, his waist. "Like, really hurts."

"You might have bruised your coccyx," Richard says.

"You're not that kind of doctor," Michael says.

Diane slips a hand down Michael's shorts, but all she feels is butt.

"Did you hit your head?" she asks.

"No."

"Do you want to go back to the hospital?"

"Never."

The bandage she applied to his forehead in the CVS parking lot is still in place. Through the little plastic viewfinder, the stitches advertise themselves as dry.

"It's looking better," she says.

The wound does not look better. It looks like torn flesh shoelaced shut. The scar will be ugly.

"I'm sorry about your coccyx," she says, but her husband doesn't laugh. He's talking to his father.

"I can't believe you actually went down," Michael says.

He doesn't know. How, when he fell, his father was behind him, reaching for his son. How his father chased him, reaching, the whole way.

They walk the river's shallows and swim its depths. They let the current carry them a mile to where the water yawns into another pool. Fewer people know this spot than know the falls, making this a sanctuary for locals. More beer coolers, fewer clothes. A dozen people splash and swim. On the riverbank, a boy of one or two makes naked circles chasing a lizard with a stick.

From the water, a carved stairway of rock ascends to a fist of stone a story high. Men and women dive from the boulder. They belly flop, can opener, and all the other tricks. In every way, the jump is safer than the falls. The water's deep, and there's room enough for just one jumper at a time. It isn't far to fall, though from the top, the edge feels awfully high. Her first trip here, Diane leapt. She hasn't found the courage to leap again.

"Michael," she says, but already he's at the stairs, in line behind a boy in yellow boxers, a smiley face plastered on the back.

Onshore, a man in cutoff jeans, Michelob in hand, squats on a slab of river rock. Crushed cans litter the ground at his feet. He's the father of the naked lizard chaser, Diane is guessing, as well as the yellow-boxered boy.

Richard moves to her side. He's so tall, the water hits his waist while she's chest-deep. Her father-in-law is pale, but fit, well-groomed, no earholes clogged with hair. She'd be pleased if Michael looked like Richard at his age, assuming she and Michael are together forty years from now, which, given the circumstances, might be assuming too much.

"Is he okay?" Richard asks.

A girl jumps, followed by her father. Michael's almost reached the top of the stone staircase.

He's not, Diane wants to say. *He hasn't been himself for years.* But all she says is, "I'm not sure."

On the bank, the lizard's gotten away, and the boy's on hands and knees, turning over stones.

"You two don't have to stay," Richard says. "I know Lisa wants you here, but that's not as important as you kids taking care of yourselves."

"No," Diane says. "I want to stay."

She didn't last night. Today she does. She wants to see Christopher, North Carolina, one last time—the river, the falls, the lake, the land, the town. She wants to paint a sunset on the dock. She's no Jake. Still, she loves making art. And she'd like to make peace with Michael. If that's meant to happen anywhere, it's here.

A cry. The lizard lost, the child screams and runs to his father. The man takes a long pull from his Michelob, lays a hand on the child's head, and at his touch, the screaming stops. The boy drops, cross-legged, onto the rock beside his father, then pulls at himself, inspecting his foreskin with a level of intensity typically reserved for police procedurals on TV.

"You think one day you two might want one of those?" Richard asks.

It's a question women her age are used to being asked. *Why no kids? Will you have kids? When will you have kids?* Friends and colleagues, strangers, Diane's mom. Diane's never understood it, this need to know who's breeding, and, if not, *why*? Coming from Richard, though, the question's a surprise. Of all the people in her life, Richard is the most private. His standards of decorum belong to another generation, and if they seem at times old-fashioned, at times fussy, Diane finds them admirable too. He's not a man who asks a woman whether she wants kids, and momentarily she wonders whether Michael's told.

Her hand, underwater, finds her waist. At ten weeks, what's inside her is an inch long. She looked it up. There are toes and fingers, fingernails and hair.

"We'll see," she says.

The boy in yellow boxers jumps, splashes down, and comes up spitting water. The man on the riverbank whistles, and the toddler halts his self-examination to watch his brother swim to shore.

"Terrible about yesterday," Richard says.

He looks away, and a revelation settles on Diane's shoulders like snow. This quiet, private man needs someone to talk to. Well, who says she can't be that person? She can talk to him. But she doesn't want to talk about the boy.

"I know Michael's mad about the house, but I understand your position," she says, unsure what makes her say it. She feels like a traitor, not taking her husband's side. Plus, she *doesn't* understand the reason for the sale. She has a habit of saying what she thinks others want to hear. She knows this about herself, and it worries her. Is she desperate to be loved, or just like everybody else?

"Thank you," Richard says, "but I'm not sure Michael will forgive me."

"It was a surprise, that's all. Michael will adjust."

Michael won't adjust. Her husband can hold a grudge better than anyone she knows.

Onshore, the father stands. He finishes his beer in one gulp and pulls something from his pocket. The something turns out to be a plastic shopping bag that he shakes open and fills with the beer cans at his feet.

Diane's not used to long conversations with her father-in-law. What do mathematical physicists talk about?

"That multiverse stuff you study," she says. "You once said every combination of things that *could* happen *is* happening all at once."

"That's just a theory," Richard says. "I'm skeptical."

True or not, it's an idea Diane likes and thinks about a lot. On bad days she consoles herself that, somewhere, she is happy. Somewhere, there's no debt and Michael's always kind. Somewhere, they have a baby, and she never doubts her husband's love.

Overhead, Michael has summited the rock. He stands on one foot, crane kick–style, arms up. He's looking for a laugh, and she gives it to him.

"Are you all right, dear?" Richard says. "You're shaking."

"I'm all right," she says. "I just got cold."

She's more than cold. She's sad. Also hopeful, excited, enraptured, scared. She's going to be a mother. With or without Michael, she'll bring new life into the world.

"Cannonball!" her husband cries.

A windmill of limbs, and Michael's in the air.

Diane cradles the promise of her abdomen.

Chin to knees and knees to chest, Michael grasps his ankles. For a second he seems to levitate. Then, like the iron projectile for which the dive is named, her husband falls.

14.

Antoine's is one of a dozen buildings squeezed onto a busy, parking-metered Asheville block. The storefronts rise from the sidewalk, competitive in their pastels. A cigar store. A delicatessen. Restaurants with sidewalk chalkboards advertising lunch specials and signature drinks. Of all the restaurants, Antoine's is the scrappiest. Its peach topcoat flakes, teal swatches peeking out from underneath.

Thad pictures a younger crowd, arms graffitied, earlobes gauged, but, inside, the clientele is suit and tie. This is not a place for tattoos. This is a place for working lunches and company credit cards.

Jake wears the black crushed velvet blazer he wears to gallery openings and dinners with buyers. The coat is loud. It's garish, the kind of coat a gay boy dreams of, the dream outgrown following his first trip to John Varvatos, or slipping on his first Brooks Brothers suit. Somehow, Jake never outgrew the dream.

Thad brought no clothes for the occasion, and, an hour earlier, outside Asheville, Jake steered their rental into a JCPenney parking lot. "We need to look nice," Jake said—*we* is the word he uses when he means Thad.

Inside the department store, Jake pulled khaki pants and a gray blazer off the rack. Thad tried them on. The blazer was wooly and thick. The pants had pleats.

"I look like a pallbearer," Thad said.

"You look fine," Jake said, then went back to studying his phone. All morning there'd been dings and beeps, texts about when and where to meet.

At the register, the clerk presented scissors, and Jake cut the tags off Thad. Thad's sneakers didn't match, but there was no time. Jake cared about appearances, but he cared more about punctuality.

Now Jake strides through the restaurant, shoes polished, cuff links flashing, hair gelled, and Thad can't say whether Jake meant to dress him up or make him look so lackluster, so drab by comparison, that Marco's eyes would never stray from Jake.

A hostess leads them to a door that opens to a courtyard. Outside, the day is hot, and there are no umbrellas, only an ivy-laced trellis overhead. A couple sits at one table, the girl tall and pale and thin, the man Latino, red shirt, dark hair. The man stands. "Jacob!" he says. The girl does not stand, but she's so tall, her posture so fine, that it's as if she stands already.

Like Thad, Jake seems surprised to see the girl. There's a hitch in his step, then Jake's in Marco's arms. With Jake, long hugs mean nothing, but this is not a long hug, which means everything: restraint in the brevity, premeditation in the pulling away. Marco's hand finds Jake's lapel, and his thumb runs its length.

"This old thing," Marco says.

"Frank makes me wear it," Jake says.

In reality, Frank's tried to talk Jake out of the velvet coat for years. But the lie is clever, a dodge and name-drop in one. Jake has confirmed his place in the art world along with his obligatory contempt for it. Near as Thad can tell, this is the goal of all of Jake's painter friends, to make it big enough to be able to disparage everything they used to want.

"How *is* old Frank?" Marco asks.

"Frank's fine," Jake says. "This is Thad."

Marco takes his hand, and Thad understands the appeal of this man. His touch is soft. His jaw is strong. His hair's slicked back, shirt open at the collar, chest waxed. His sleeves strain to hold the muscles in. He's a specimen every bit as impressive as Thad had been prepared to expect, except in one crucial way. The man who stands before him is a J.Crew model—clean-cut, corporate, *safe*. Whatever element of danger, of excitement, made Marco an art school idol, that element's long gone. Though for Jake, perhaps he'll always be young Marco the way that Jake will always be the shy boy in the black blazer for Thad.

Thad met Jake on an April evening two years ago. The night was cold, rain imminent. Thad trudged through Chelsea. He was low on money, exhausted, out of weed. His destination was a poetry open mic where he might find a joint or someone to spend the night with, preferably both. He had a month left on his lease, then it was back to Ithaca. Better to admit defeat and return home than starve. Then, through a wide gallery window, Thad saw him, a boy of twenty-four afloat in a sea of suits. The boy wore a velvet coat, a rose pinned to the lapel. His hair was wild. His eyes were wide. Where the boy moved, the crowd parted, and Thad realized that these people, all of them, were here for him. Who was this boy, and why was he beloved? Then it was raining, and Thad stepped inside to find out.

Marco shakes Thad's hand for too long.

"It's nice to meet you," Marco says, and Thad nods. He doesn't like this guy.

The girl at the table does not get up. Her dress is short and black. Her legs are crossed.

"My girlfriend," Marco says, "Amelia," and suddenly Thad likes Marco very much.

Jake looks to Amelia, then Marco. Thad sees he's shocked, but Jake remains composed.

They sit. The table holds four place settings and a pitcher of what must be margaritas. The pitcher glistens, a lemon halved and floating in the drink, and Amelia pours them each a glass. Thad's drink reaches the rim, and a rivulet escapes and streaks the side.

"Sorry," Amelia says, and there's something flirtatious in the way she reaches over him to dab his glass with her napkin, in the way her eyes settle on him.

In high school, Thad was with two girls. He left one girl crying, one bemused. "I think I love you," the first girl said. The second said, "I think you might be gay."

Amelia looks young enough to be one of those girls, too young to be dating Marco. She lifts her glass to her mouth and sips.

Across from him, Jake talks and talks. Thad sits between Marco and Amelia so that Jake shouldn't be able to turn his head without Thad interrupting his field of vision, but Jake finds a way, the table lengthening to a galaxy's inky gulf. In the car, they agreed that if Thad grew uncomfortable, they'd leave, but how to communicate this when he can't even enter his boyfriend's line of sight?

Finally, it's Marco who cuts Jake off. "Thad, what do you do?"

There's honeysuckle in the air, and Thad feels a sneeze coming. North Carolina always makes him sneeze.

"Oh, Thad doesn't paint," Jake says.

"It's okay," Amelia says, a hand on Thad's shoulder. "I don't paint either."

A parade of bracelets encircles her arm. A character marks her wrist, another language's word for love or peace, or feces, because tattoo artists have a sense of humor, too. Thad's glad that, at her age, there was nothing he believed in badly enough to have it engraved on his skin. Perhaps in time he'll find something, someone, he loves enough to earn his flesh. Some days, he thinks that someone might be Jake. But not today.

He sneezes.

"Bless you," Amelia says.

"Thank you," he says. He drinks, and the margarita is potent, a lime squeezed between his teeth. Amelia's hand leaves his shoulder.

"C'mon, mystery man," Marco says. "What do you do?"

Marco turns from Jake. His torso swivels, legs apart, the kind of body language that assures you of a person's full attention. Having that attention entirely, nothing feigned, Thad feels the ache of just how long it's been since he felt seen.

"Thad's writing a book," Jake says, and Thad has Jake's eyes now. The eyes are big. They beg Thad not to let him down.

"A book," Marco says. "Fantastic! What about?"

"Oh," Jake says, "he won't talk about it. It's a process thing. A little pretentious, I know, but—"

"Birds," Thad says, thinking of his mother's book. He tried to read it once, but the book's no introduction to birding. It's a text for ornithologists, one concerning the subtleties of bird taxonomy— class, order, family—that kind of thing, including an entire chapter on a bird called a wallcreeper and the degree to which it does or does not belong in the nuthatch family. Thad made it three pages before giving up, though as a boy, he often turned to the middle, a color insert on pages glossier than the rest. He liked the bird illustrations, their bright beaks and twiggy legs. He liked the diagrams, how a tail feather or wing was marked with a Roman numeral tied to a sidebar by a dotted line. Some nights, he lay in bed and imagined himself small, a cowboy, lasso in hand. He saddled birds and rode them, dotted lines for reins: Thaddeus, King of the Birds.

"It's a book of poems about birds," he says. It isn't such a bad idea, really.

"No way," Amelia says. "Marco totally paints birds."

Everyone turns to Marco for confirmation. Marco shrugs. He brings two fingers to his face and scratches his chin. "It's true," he says.

"Oh my God," Amelia says. "Marco, you should do the cover!"

"You should!" Thad says. He's watching Jake. "I would *love* for you to do the cover."

Jake doesn't glare, but his tongue bobs in the pocket of his cheek. He smiles weakly.

"I appreciate that," Marco says, "but I'm sure your publisher would want to consider my work first."

"No, no, no," Thad says. "It's *yours*. Jake says you're great, and I trust Jake. In fact, the publisher's a friend of Jake's. He'll put you two in touch."

If Jake were a cartoon, his face would be freshly frying-panned.

"Well," Marco says, "I guess lunch is on me." He leans forward, elbows on the table. His eyes are bright, teeth big as Chiclets. Where

Marco's muscled, Thad is mostly fat. Where Thad's chest dimples at the center, Marco's pecs bulge.

"This book of yours," Marco says. "Does it have a name?"

"*Birds of a Feather*," Thad says. It's the worst title he can think of. Still, Marco and Amelia smile. Then Amelia's hand is on his shoulder, accompanied by a flourish of bracelet clicks. He doesn't mind the touch, but he's uncomfortable not knowing what it means.

A server arrives, and at Marco's insistence, everyone but Amelia orders swordfish.

"I have a thing," she says, ordering chicken.

"She won't eat anything that swims," Marco says.

A pair of men in suits take a table nearby. They hang their coats on their chairs and loosen their ties. They sit and light cigarettes.

Soon, the server reappears with four Caesar salads.

Amelia pushes a forkful of lettuce into her mouth, and Thad wonders whether she knows about Caesars—the dressing, all those anchovies. He wants to warn her but doesn't want to make a scene. He eats his salad. He drinks his drink. The closer he gets to the bottom of the glass, the stronger the margarita gets. When he sets his glass down, Amelia is quick to refill it.

"So, what do *you* do?" he asks.

Amelia holds up a finger. She chews. She wears no makeup, no lipstick in danger of smearing when she touches her napkin to her mouth. She folds the napkin and returns it to her lap. Her table manners are impeccable.

"I'm in school," she says. "Western Carolina, but I might transfer to NC State, depending on what major I pick."

"Thad studied English," Jake says. "At Cornell." He doesn't mention that Thad dropped out after sophomore year.

"Cornell," Amelia says. "Fancy."

Writing a book, going to Cornell. Thad wants to protest. He's not the trust fund kid Jake's making him out to be. Without Jake, Thad's homeless. Michael's broke. Neither brother has been shown a will, and for all Thad knows, his mother's money will go to birds, his father's to Cornell or NASA or that supercollider thing in Switzerland that's always messing up. His parents assembled their wealth from nothing, which is nice for them, though less nice for the sons who seem to be expected to do the same.

"How did you like Cornell?" Marco asks, body still turned toward Thad.

Thad talks, and Jake's expression is pained. He's not used to being anything other than the center of attention at meals. This is not the lunch he was looking for.

"How did you two meet?" Thad asks.

Amelia wipes her mouth. Again, she folds her napkin, puts it in her lap.

"Marco had a show downtown," she says, "and my Art in Society professor got a bunch of us to go. It was extra credit." She reaches across the table and takes Marco's hand. "That's what I call him, sometimes. My little *extra credit*."

Their hands release, and Amelia's bracelets rake the table with her wrist's retreat.

"You're showing work?" Jake says.

Thad almost feels sorry for Jake. The desperation to control the conversation. The need to make sure Marco's here for him. If it's not sex Jake's after, it's the assurance that Marco is Jake's for the taking. But Marco *isn't* his for the taking, despite any impressions Jake had sitting down to lunch. Thad's not the type to read his boyfriend's texts, so he can't say whether Marco led Jake on or Jake led himself on all along.

"Oh, Marco's showing work," Amelia says. "Marco's a pretty big deal around here. His stuff is at Zuzu's, in the River Arts District, which is *the* place to be."

"It's no Gallery East," Marco says, "but it's good for Asheville."

"Good?" Amelia says. She lifts her glass and finds it empty. She shakes the margarita pitcher and finds it empty too. "Marco's being modest. He's huge. Wait until you see our place."

Marco's quiet. *Our place* hangs over the table, an exclamation point.

"I wouldn't mind seeing your place," Jake says.

Amelia turns to Thad, and the day feels dangerous again. He'd decided he liked her. He isn't sure he likes her anymore.

Again Amelia lifts her drink. Again she finds it empty.

Jake watches Marco. Marco watches Thad. Thad watches Amelia, and Amelia watches her empty glass, everyone waiting for whatever Thad says next. But there is no next, for, mercifully, at that moment the food arrives.

Plates hit the table. Waters are refilled. Salad bowls are cleared, and Marco orders another pitcher of margaritas. A phone shrieks the opening bars of James Taylor's "Carolina in My Mind," and one of the men at the nearby table stands to answer it. There's an open gate, and the man on the phone walks through it. He's saying something about *residuals*, and he keeps saying it, emphatically. The other man lights another cigarette. Already their table's ashtray is a ziggurat of butts.

A thirty-dollar piece of fish stares up at Thad from his plate. The fish wears grill marks and a crust that's dusted gold. Salsa hugs one side. A salad of purple leaves nuzzles the other. Something elevates the fish an inch or two, and, over everything, a sauce the color of molasses has been drizzled. This fish, Marco says, is special, a darling of the Asheville foodie scene. But this kind of thing is everywhere in New York. Thad's been to more lunches than he can count, more benefits and gallery openings as Jake's plus-one, where something very much like this was served. These days, the foods Thad craves are simple: peanut butter, box cakes, soup straight from the can. The very thought of lifting this fish to see what hominy or chutney's underneath makes Thad tired.

He could send the swordfish back, order something he actually wants to eat, but he won't. He'll eat cold food before he'll flag down a server or complain. Jake, on the other hand, sends meals back all the time.

Thad takes a bite and tastes saffron, then honey, then balsamic vinegar, then brine. He takes another bite. Maybe Asheville's not so bad.

"Marvelous," Jake says. His fish is halved, the hominy beneath—
it *is* hominy—spilled across the plate.

Marco waves a hand in front of his face. "Is that smoke bothering
anyone else?"

Thad isn't bothered. He smoked cigarettes for years. He only quit
for Jake, who's sensitive to smells, cigarette smoke most of all. Thad
sees, then, that Jake's eyes are bloodshot. Oh, God. Did Marco notice
first? *Was* Marco a better, more attentive boyfriend than Thad?

Marco stands and pushes in his chair.

"Honey," Amelia says, "it's fine."

"I'm just going to talk to him," Marco says.

Marco stands, and here's the passion Thad's been waiting for, the
magma roiling under rock. But Marco isn't showing off for Amelia.
If Thad had to guess, he'd guess that Marco's showing off for Jake.
If this is true, this isn't lunch. This is a war, a tournament of self-
important men, each gesture, every word, a way of saying: *I don't
need you. Look how far I've come.*

How long, Thad wonders, has Marco planned this? The girlfriend,
the expensive restaurant, *Lunch is on me*? The smoker, however, is
not part of the plan. Marco wants Jake jealous, not eyes watering,
wanting to leave.

At the other table, the man with the cigarette says something, and
Marco leans in close. When he returns to the table, the man's cigarette
is out. Marco sits. Amelia rolls her eyes. Jake looks impressed, which
was, of course, the point.

The other man, no longer on the phone, rejoins his friend, and the
two whisper, casting glances Marco's way. Marco smirks. Jake fawns.

Thad wants to go home.

He excuses himself to the men's room and calls Jake's phone, but
Jake doesn't pick up.

Bathroom, Thad texts, *now, or find your own ride home.*

A minute later, Jake is through the door.

Thad wants to shout. He wants to cry. He wants to give Jake hell.
But first he'll give him one more chance. He opens his arms and pulls

Jake into them. He kisses Jake's cheek, his ear. He holds him tight. All can still be forgiven.

"Let's not do this," Thad says. Jake tries to pull away. "Please."

The only way out of Thad's grasp is down, but, slipping through his arms, Jake falls and hits the bathroom floor. His coat rides up, the collar at his ears. On the floor, he looks small, a boy swallowed by his father's clothes.

"Admit that this is more than lunch," Thad says.

"Grow up," Jake says. He stands. He moves to the mirror and smooths his lapels.

A pair of sinks perch beneath the bathroom mirror, and Thad moves to one of them. He opens the tap and water rushes out. He cups his hands. The water's cold.

Jake examines himself in the mirror. He pulls the thin, plastic arrows from his shirt collar, then reinserts them. Sure enough, the collar hangs straighter, sharper at each end.

"Look at me," Thad says. He's tried kindness, sympathy, mutual respect. Time to pull the pin from the grenade.

Jake fusses with his hair. He picks something from between his teeth.

"Look at me," Thad says again, and when Jake turns, Thad opens his cupped hands onto Jake's front. It couldn't look more like Jake wet his pants.

Thad dries his hands and walks out of the bathroom.

"You're a child," Jake calls after him. There's more, but Thad can't hear it. The door has already swung shut.

15.

Iron rings the day bright. The horseshoe hits the stake and spins, and Richard smiles.

Down the sloping yard, midway between the water and the house, is a plateau, land leveled and rock-walled against erosion. The wall is low, knee-high, an echo of the seawall that follows the curve of shore below. Each summer Richard walks the wall, finds the horseshoe pits hidden in grass, then kneels and pulls up the earth around each stake. The stakes are regulation: fifteen inches tall, twelve degrees from vertical, forty feet apart.

The horseshoes are rusted. Richard found one embroidered, a vine grown through the eyelet meant for nail and hoof. The vine twined the horseshoe, a creeping helix, and Richard gently untangled the iron from the plant, then tapped the horseshoe to the wall, rust flaking and falling away.

A truck rumbles in the distance. A lawn mower starts up. Birds carol.

Back from the waterfall, Richard didn't expect Michael to join him on the hill, but here they are, horseshoes in hand.

"Three to you, old man," Michael says. The bruise has escaped its bandage, painting Michael's forehead indigo. He cradles the mug he's had all morning, the travel kind with spill-proof lid, but Richard never saw any coffee go in.

Below, the morning boats are gone. They've found the body, or they've given up, following the current's drift to another leg of the lake.

He wants to tell his son that he is brave, that he did his best. For all the good this will do. Michael will never forgive himself for not moving faster, diving deeper, just as the boy's parents will never forgive themselves for the water wings, just as the daughter will never forgive herself for falling asleep. Just as Richard will never, ever forgive himself for putting his daughter to sleep with a stuffed duck. June's little fist. In memory, she forever grips the foot of that green duck.

They thought one day they'd tell the boys, then thought better of it. Michael and Thad had no reason to know they had a sister. Why upset them? Why conjure a girl to life only to smother her before their eyes?

Even now, June is a balloon bound to Richard's wrist. She hovers behind him, just out of view. He turns, and she turns with him. But she's there, always, afloat at the periphery.

Richard removes his glasses. He polishes the lenses with his shirt. A second horseshoe waits to be flung, and he flings it.

The clang quiets the birds. Another ringer.

Michael shakes his head. "You join a league, or what?"

Richard blinks, surprised by luck.

"Seriously," Michael says. "Are those your first two throws this year?"

They are, and Richard wonders at the odds. His pitcher/ringer average at his peak was one in eight, but he hasn't been at his peak in twenty years. The past few years, Richard's lost to Michael badly.

Michael sips from his mug. Two horseshoes wait on the wall, but he seems in no hurry to pitch them.

The house above is quiet. Thad and Jake have gone to Asheville, and Lisa hasn't left the bedroom all day. He could go to her, but his impulse is to be with his son. Does this make him a good father or a bad husband?

He doesn't know. He knows enough to know he doesn't know himself that well. When June died, Lisa's attempts to put him "in touch with his feelings" were lost on him. Grief groups, couples counseling, psychotherapy. In therapy, he sat in a chair across the room from a man in another chair, each session a game of Battleship. When the other man got close, Richard simply moved his ships.

There would be no going back into that bedroom, no looking in the bassinet.

He should go to Lisa. He should climb the hill and comfort his wife. But the sun is up, and the stake has two horseshoes around it. Michael is laughing at the improbable six points, and that laugh fills Richard's heart.

"All right, old man," Michael says. "You're going down."

Michael grabs the horseshoes and approaches the pinecones they've arranged to mark the throwing line. Then Michael's eyes are searching. Two boats have entered the bay.

"He's still out there," Michael says.

"Let's go inside," Richard says. Hand to shoulder, he tries to spin the compass of his son, but the water is magnetic north, and Michael's tuned to it. He hops the rock wall, jogs downhill to the dock, and Richard follows, slow.

The first boat is one from yesterday, an officer in uniform at the wheel. The second boat is brown and red, three times the other's size, a man at the helm and two men at the stern. These men are not in uniform. One wears a T-shirt with the Warner Brothers Tasmanian Devil on the front. The other wears a ball cap and a sweatshirt, forest green. They both wear work gloves. The first man turns a crank, and an enormous hook and chain are lowered into the bay. The chain unspools from the boat's middle, threaded through what looks like the neck of a yellow bulldozer.

Hook submerged, the boat makes a lap around the bay before anchoring. The men turn the crank, and the chain coils with a ratcheting cackle, links big as tractor tires.

"Oh my God," Michael says. "They're *fishing* for him."

The surface breaks. The chain catches. What's hooked spins, dripping.

It is not a body. It is a refrigerator door, algaed and mud-slick. It hangs a moment before the handle snaps and the door drops back into the lake.

Richard expected a net, some kind of scoop. He hadn't prepared himself for the sight of a three-pronged grappling hook. The logic, of course, is sound. The lake bed must be a mess of litter and logs. One pass, and any net would be in shreds. But a *hook*.

"Come on," he says. He can't watch this.

He turns, and his son is smiling. Why is Michael smiling?

"I was just thinking of this joke you told us when we were kids. This awful, awful joke."

"Son," Richard says.

"No, stay with me. So the joke goes: 'Did you hear the one about the dredge operator who couldn't keep up with the duck?'" Michael pauses, whether for emphasis or searching for the punch line, it's hard to tell.

"They say he was lagging a drake," Richard says.

"Lagging a drake," Michael says.

"Why don't we go inside?" Richard says. Michael is pale. The day is hot.

"Spoken like someone who's afraid to lose at horseshoes," Michael says, and they climb the hill, the chain unraveling into water at their backs.

Above, Diane waits for them. She wears a summer dress, white with whorls of gray and green. She sits on the rock wall, ankles crossed. Her legs are long, and her sandals touch the grass. She offers Richard a hand, and he takes it, clambering over the wall.

She and Michael won't look at each other. *I'm imagining this*, Richard thinks, but the longer he watches, the clearer it becomes. Something's going on between these two.

"I brought water," Diane says.

On the wall sit Solo cups sweating in the sun, and Richard takes one and drinks.

"Lisa's up," Diane says.

"I should check on her," he says.

"She's in the tub," Diane says. "At least, I heard the water running for a while."

"Mom's fine," Michael says. "Can't we finish one goddamn game?"

Richard can't account for Michael's change of mood. On the dock, he told a joke. With Diane, there's a look of fury on his face.

"Are you in pain?" she asks.

She reaches for the bandage, and Michael pulls away. He holds a horseshoe, but he seems determined not to throw until Diane has left.

"Are those boats doing what I think they're doing?" she asks.

Richard nods. He hopes she hasn't seen the hook. He wishes he had some words of wisdom, something to say to comfort these two, but he comes up short.

Across the bay, dogs fill the air with their cries.

"I'm going up," Diane says. "If Lisa needs you, I'll let you know."

She's several steps away before she returns and hugs Michael. He doesn't put the horseshoe down, and he doesn't hug her back. Her cheek finds his chest. She stays that way awhile, then kisses his shoulder and departs.

She's up the hill before Michael will look at him.

"What the hell was that?" Richard says.

"The hell was what?" Michael's got the travel mug to his mouth again. He sips, sets down the mug, then drinks from the Solo cup.

"I know you're upset about the boy. I know you're sad. But don't take it out on your wife."

It's briefly back, the look of rage that Michael flashed Diane, but Michael says nothing. Instead, he takes his place at the pinecone line, steps back, steps forward, then launches the horseshoe from his hand. For a second it seems the *U* will sail over the stake, but only for a second. At its apex, the horseshoe drops, collars the rebar, and wrings its neck.

Richard howls. Two dead and three, three ringers in a row.

"Back to three for you," Michael says. "Want to see if I can make it zilch?" He watches the stake. He won't look Richard's way.

"Talk to me, Son." He wants to touch his boy, but something warns his hand away. "Have a seat."

Michael frowns.

"I'm your father," Richard says. "Sit down."

Michael does as he's told. Cross-legged on the wall, he looks ready for meditation, were meditation practiced with a scowl.

Richard sits beside him. The wall is chalky, stones gummed together with quick-dry concrete. He built the wall himself, years ago. As a younger man, he never let another hand repair his home, rotate his tires or change the oil in his car. Then came tenure, research, fellowships, and time grew more valuable than saving money on odd jobs. In the hour it took him to mow the lawn, he could draft the abstract for a grant that might net his department half a million dollars. But that part of his life is over. No more stipends. No more travel funds or research requests. No more technology fee proposals. Richard is retired. From here on out, life is one big unfunded sabbatical.

"You know," he says, "your mother and I have had our troubles too."

"I'm sorry?"

A dragonfly lands on Richard's leg, lifts off.

"You and Diane. You seem unhappy."

Michael sighs. "We're just going through something at the moment. Something happened that I can't discuss."

Richard suspects, no, *knows*. Right then, he's sure he knows the thing his son has done.

"Michael," he says, "you're not alone in this."

"We promised each other we wouldn't . . . we didn't want—" Michael waves a hand, and his travel mug tumbles to the ground. He uncrosses his legs and retrieves the mug. He sips. He's slouching now, feet in the grass.

Richard sits up straighter. "I know it feels like the end, but it doesn't have to be."

"I love Diane, but— I really shouldn't talk about this."

"It's okay," Richard says. He is ashamed, but he can say it. They are men of the same mistake. Michael will understand. "I had an affair too."

Michael's head turns in his direction, but slow. It's as though the head has been severed and centered on a lazy Susan, the tray turned a quarter-revolution at a speed designed to maximize the agony of the father coming face-to-face with the disapproving son.

Richard has miscalculated, grossly.

"*Too?*" Michael says. "You cheated on Mom?"

"There was a woman—"

"Oh my God."

"—another professor."

"Oh my *God.*"

"I made a mistake."

"And *you* thought *I*—"

"Michael," Richard says, "please lower your voice."

Michael puts down the mug and grips his knees. His head drops. "I don't want to know. I don't want to hear it, and I definitely don't want to know."

"I'm sorry," Richard says. "I thought—"

"You thought I'd fuck around on my wife? I wouldn't do that, Dad. I'm not that man." Michael's head lifts to search his father's face. "How are *you* that man?"

His boy thinks he's better than him. His boy with a mug full of moonshine and a mountain of debt thinks he's better than the father who made one mistake.

Michael runs a hand over the stone wall. A rock is loose, and he pushes on it.

"Does Mom know?"

"Some days, I think she knows, though I'm not sure how she could."

Richard searches the windows of the house above, but no sign of Lisa. He should have gone to her. He should be up there with his wife.

"I wish you hadn't told me," Michael says. He has the stone in both hands now. He pushes on it, hard, and Richard remembers the weeks he spent assembling this wall. But what does it matter, really? The wall may well be razed next week.

"First Thad," Michael says. "Now you."

"Thad?" Richard says.

"Thad and Jake are open."

"Open?"

"*Open*. As in fucking other dudes."

"Oh," Richard says. "Thad told you that?"

He's not naive. Over a generation separates him from his sons, and younger people do things differently. He'd just always pegged Thad as the old-fashioned type.

Michael lets go of the stone. The mortar has chipped and crumbled, and he brushes dust and pebbles to the ground.

"Did Thad tell you this in confidence?"

Michael nods, and Richard shakes his head.

"You shouldn't have told me," Richard says.

"You shouldn't have told me you had an affair."

"That's different," Richard says, careful not to raise his voice. "That was my secret to tell. You owe it to your brother to respect his privacy."

"And you owe it to Mom not to fuck other women."

Woman, Richard wants to say, but what's the use? Michael is determined to attack anything he says.

A rattle turns both of their heads. In the bay, the men on the boat work the giant chain. The hook breaks the surface and comes up clean.

"Be a better brother," Richard says. "Also, Diane loves you. My advice? Whatever's gotten into you, don't mess that up. You don't have much, but you have her."

Richard dismounts the wall. He presents the last horseshoe to Michael. No more words, just this. The horseshoe waits in his hand. One more word, then: "Throw."

Then the horseshoe's out of his hand, and Michael's moving fast. He doesn't take his time, doesn't line up the shot at the pinecones. But the throw, when it happens, is even better than the first. The first was the basketball equivalent of a granny shot, up and down and around the stake by the dumbest of luck. This pitch, though, is vigorous, a fiery *fuck you*.

The horseshoe, that age-old symbol—*U* up for luck—cups sunlight in its rusty hoof. It spins. It sails like it will detonate the stake.

Three points on the line, and both men wait. They wait without breath or blink of eye, wait to see whether what remains will be negated or upheld.

16.

In Bushwick, Marco's apartment would rent for three thousand a month. But this is Asheville. Jake's guessing Marco pays fifteen hundred, tops. The apartment is white in a way that feels sterile: white carpet, white ceiling, white walls. Not cream. Not eggshell. *White*. Jake hasn't seen an apartment with this much carpet in a while and tries to imagine Marco vacuuming. Marco mentions three bedrooms, but, down the hallway, the first two doors are shut, and he doesn't offer to open them. The third door opens to a tidy bedroom. The room is huge—walk-in closet, king-sized bed.

"Can I get anyone anything?" Marco says. He's undone another button, waxed chest aglow. He's in even better shape than when they were together.

"I'd drink coffee," Jake says. He checks his pants. No water stain, but he's feeling self-conscious. In the bathroom at Antoine's, he stood beneath the hand dryer until it burned.

They return to the main room and a pair of couches, plump and white, a glass-top coffee table squeezed between. Jake removes his coat and drapes it on the back of one couch, then sits. Thad joins him, Amelia sits opposite, and Marco moves to the kitchen. Jake can't help looking at Thad beside him, then Marco in the kitchen. Thad's not chiseled like Marco, but he's cute, still boyish, baby-faced. Jake cares about him. He does.

Thad smiles, making small talk with Amelia. Whatever had him so worked up at lunch seems to have left his system. Jake takes his hand, and Thad lets him take it.

In the kitchen, Marco makes a show of making coffee, opening and closing numerous silver-handled cabinet doors and filling the counter with coffee bags, a grinder, a French press.

From her couch, Amelia smiles, long legs buckled beneath her. Jake doesn't know what to make of her. No way is Marco straight. He'd be surprised were Marco bi. Not *his* Marco. Not the Marco he knew in art school.

Amelia asks what brings them to town, and Thad tells her about Lake Christopher, his parents' place, the visit before the closing on the house. She runs a hand through her hair and tilts her head, eyes so suggestive Jake nearly laughs out loud. *Good luck with that.*

"The house is a trailer," Jake says. Thad releases his hand, and Jake can't say why he said it. What compels him to act this way? What makes him mean?

"My parents live in a trailer," Amelia says. "Lots of people do."

Thad sinks into the couch cushions and studies the ceiling. Jake looks up, but there's nothing there, just the crumbly popcorn finish used by contractors too lazy to hang drywall without leaving seams.

"That must be tough," Amelia says to Thad. "Losing the family home."

There's a lull in the conversation before Amelia unfolds her legs and stands.

"Honey," she calls to the kitchen, "can we do some coke?"

"I don't know," Marco says. "How do our guests feel about that?"

"Your guests are quite taken by the idea," Thad says.

Jake's pretty sure Thad's never done coke, and right then he knows he's in trouble. Thad hasn't calmed down. He's been waiting to strike. He doesn't want cocaine. He just wants to fuck with Jake.

"Jake?" Marco says. "You cool with that?"

"Absolutely," he says. He's thinking of PSAs, high school assemblies, videos of eggs sizzling in a pan. *Just say no!* How much harder to say *no* in real life, though.

In the kitchen, a kettle whistles.

Amelia leaves the room, then returns with a Boggle box. She lifts the lid and dumps the contents onto the coffee table. There's a plastic segmented tray, an hourglass, a couple dozen dice with letters where the numbers ought to be. If they played, Thad would destroy them all. Words are kind of his thing. But they aren't here to play.

Amelia pries the plastic cap from one end of the hourglass and pours half of what's inside onto the table. With the box top, she shuffles the pile into anthills, the anthills into lines, then runs a finger along the lid and licks her finger clean.

Jake's been to parties in every corner of every borough, watched artists snort or smoke or gobble or shoot up just about every drug there is, and never, never, has he seen someone go to all this trouble for some coke. Seriously, who takes the time to fill a Boggle hourglass? Why not keep their drugs in baggies the way respectable recreational users do?

"Closest to *A* goes first," Amelia says.

Thad plucks a die from the tabletop and rolls a *Q*.

And, at last, here's Marco. He carries a silver serving dish with four teacups, a creamer, and a sugar bowl. The teacups are dainty, brittle-looking. At the tray's center sits the French press. The plunger is gold, and, where a bulb should be, a skull bares its teeth at them, gemstones for eyes.

Amelia clears a place on the table, and Marco lowers the tray.

"Thad rolled a *Q*," she says.

Marco laughs. He sits. He rolls.

Jake hates this. The only time he did cocaine, his heart beat so fast he thought he'd die, and he's in no mood to try again. He looks to Thad to bail him out, but Thad's studying the ceiling once more.

Jake excuses himself to the bathroom, ducks around the corner, and hurries down the hall. But it's not a bathroom he's after. He needs a place to hide, just for a minute, just to calm down before he hits the point that he can't breathe. Also, he's feeling nosy.

Given a thousand guesses, Jake couldn't have predicted what's behind door number one. Painters don't hang their own paintings, let alone set up mini-galleries for themselves, but that's what the door opens to: a Marco shrine. Filling the walls are all the paintings Marco did in art school that never sold. Jake knows these paintings. The bullfight series. The acrylics of gutted goats. The self-portrait in iodine and blood. The work is brutal, better than Jake remembered, but none of it is new.

Jake's favorite is the hardest to look at, the way his favorites often are. It's from a series Marco began after touring a slaughterhouse. The painting is a collage of dripping snouts, pig ears tattooed or tagged, hooves bound by wire, streaked with blood. Authenticity is hard to fake, and Marco's old work makes Jake want to see the new. Perhaps there *is* life after Asheville. Maybe someone in New York would still take Marco on.

Jake backs out of the room and shuts the door. With no one coming down the hall, he opens the next door and slips inside. This room has a window, good natural light, and he sees that it's a studio. Canvases crowd the floor, each draped by a pillowcase or else turned toward a wall. Two easels face away from him. He wants to see a canvas, get a look at these birds Marco's been working on, but he hears a voice and leaves the room.

He follows the hallway to the bedroom, then steps into the master bath and locks the door. The bathroom is luxurious: double sinks, ten-foot ceiling, a glassed-in shower *and* a whirlpool tub.

He sits on the edge of the tub, and it's back, the feeling that he can't catch his breath.

What if Marco's a better painter than him?

What if Marco moves back to New York and people like him more, and Jake's sales slip?

What if Thad leaves him? Already, on one of those white couches, he's planning his escape. Soon, Jake will be alone. Then broke. Then homeless. The rats will gnaw his fingers in the night.

He's going to throw up. No, he's going to die. He's going to die on the floor of his ex-boyfriend's bathroom while his boyfriend and ex-boyfriend do cocaine. Should make for a nice write-up in the *Times*.

At one sink, he splashes water on his face. On the counter, a blue mug features an outline in the shape of North Carolina. A pair of toothbrushes occupy the mug. One toothbrush is new, bristles compact and uniform. The other's bristles are like the hair of someone waking up. Jake can't even guess which toothbrush is Marco's. He's not sure he knows this man anymore.

The water helps. He breathes. There's a hand towel, and he dries his face. There's a medicine cabinet, and he opens it. He looks for lube, prescription meds—anything Marco might consider private— but he finds only toothpaste, combs and creams, the usual. He finds floss and threads a sliver of swordfish from his teeth.

He returns to the main room, where the French press has been plunged. Marco and Amelia sip from their teacups. Jake sits and reaches for a cup. On a normal day, he'd take cream and sugar with his coffee, but this is not a normal day. He's not sure his shaky hands would survive the delicate ballet of sugar and spoon, so he brings the teacup to his lips with two hands and sips the coffee black.

"Last line is yours," Marco says.

Cocaine adorns the tabletop, white and caterpillar-thick. Polite as he can, Jake shakes his head.

"Oh, c'mon," Thad says. He moves close, and their thighs touch. On the couch across from them, Amelia is practically in Marco's lap. Her nose is dusted white.

A green Starbucks straw lies beside the Boggle box, and the hourglass has tipped over. Jake takes the straw between two fingers, bows his head, and brings the straw to his nose, but something's changed—a current in the air—and Thad's face is at his ear.

"I forgive you," Thad whispers. "All we have to do is leave right now."

Half of Jake wants to turn and embrace the man he loves, to leave this place and go about their lives. The other half, the half that hates ultimatums, hates shame—the half whispering in his other ear that pride is superior to love—steadies his hand, pinches one nostril to the straw, and inhales.

At first he feels nothing. Then the nothing's followed by a buzz, electricity coming on inside his head. Sparks, lightning. His brain's a Tesla coil, current racing down his throat, electrifying his spine. His eyes are bulbs, his lips fluorescent lights.

He looks for Thad, but Thad is gone. On the other couch, Amelia and Marco kiss, which is hard to watch. The sight of Marco with a woman is unsettling.

Then Thad's back. The JCPenney pants Jake bought him this morning are off. His boxers are bright red. He unbuttons his shirt and lets it fall to the floor.

"This is good?" Marco says. "We're all good with this?"

"I'm good," Thad says.

"I'm great," Amelia says.

This isn't right. This isn't what Jake wants.

Words—someone's saying his name. Then Marco's on the couch with him.

"Let's do a bump, all right?" Marco says.

Marco shakes the hourglass, and more cocaine comes out. He doesn't bother with dice or straws or careful lines. A spoon protrudes from the tea tray's silver sugar bowl, and Marco removes it. He untucks his shirt from the waistband of his pants, polishes the spoon with one shirttail, does a bump, and passes the spoon to Jake.

Across the table, Amelia and Thad now share a couch. Amelia's dress has dropped to her waist, and her bra, if she was wearing one, is nowhere to be seen.

Her breasts aren't large so much as long, and Thad lifts them and lets go. They smack her ribs, which looks like it hurts, but Amelia only laughs.

Unlike Jake, Thad was with girls in high school, so this isn't a first, but this isn't like Thad. This is an act designed to torture Jake.

He doesn't want more coke—already his heart is hammering away—and he scoops just enough to powder the surface of the spoon. He sniffs. He coughs.

"It's the postnasal drip," Marco says. "Bothers some people more than others."

Then Marco's hands are on him, kneading his shoulders, running the length of his spine. The hands feel good. They feel . . . *familiar*. And when did Jake's shirt come off? He doesn't want to watch Thad and Amelia, but he doesn't want to leave the couch, doesn't want these hands to stop.

"Like this," Amelia is saying. Her breasts are in her hands, then, startlingly, one is in her mouth, a thing Jake didn't know women could do. Amelia sucks at her nipple for a minute, then lowers the breast, glistening, to her chest. She holds the other breast, and Thad guides his mouth to it. He catches Jake's eyes. There's a moment's hesitation, then the nipple's in Thad's mouth.

Fuck it. Jake taps the hourglass onto the spoon, a mighty bump, and snorts the coke up. And it is good. The cocaine is good. He *feels* good. His heart is a metronome on high.

"Slow down there," Marco says. "That shit's the shit." His hands move to Jake's stomach, his belt.

Jake considers his boyfriend, but Thad's mouth is full, his eyes closed on the couch.

Jake's belt comes undone, and he lets his eyes shut too. He's readied himself for weeks, imagining the many ways this day might go. Not one scenario included Amelia or cocaine, but that's okay. That's fine. He won't let those stop him. His pants are down. He's ready.

Except, his body won't respond. Marco's hands are on him, and he's limp, which is not a thing that happens, not to Jake.

"It can be this way with cocaine," Marco says. "Easy to get horny, hard to get hard. I've got Viagra if you need some."

Fuck that. Jake's twenty-six years old. He's good in bed. He doesn't need a pill to get him hard.

A rhythm tap-dances itself into his head, and he traces the tempo to a white clock on the wall. On the other couch, Amelia tugs at Thad's boxers. Jake unholsters himself from Marco's grip and zips his pants back up.

"What's wrong?" Marco says, voice buttery with a concern Jake wants to believe is real.

So many things to say, they tangle, Pentecostal, on his tongue.

How to explain the need to be admired, praised, and the wanting not to need such things so much? How to explain the desire to be seen not as he is but as he wants to be seen?

How to explain the desperation, paranoia, shame? Such shame! The horniness and the shame for the horniness he feels. The jerk-off sessions several times a day. The three-ways. The *four*-ways. The times with Thad, and the times Thad doesn't know about. Men come to him, beautiful men with designer jeans and rock star hair, painters and men who want to be painters and men who will never be painters but just don't know that yet.

And how to explain his feelings for Thad? Jake never asked to love one man, but he does. He does, and what now? What can he do?

Like me. Fuck me. Love me.

Maybe Marco's the same way. Maybe Thad. Everyone on planet Earth, bursting, desperate to be adored. Maybe Jake's *not* special, and maybe it's *this* that scares him most of all.

There are no good words, no way to transmit this, but that's no matter, because Marco is standing, pulling him from the couch and toward the bedroom down the hall.

They sit at the end of Marco's bed. Pillows cover the headboard, more pillows than any two people could ever need. The bed is covered by a quilt, and Jake knows this quilt. Once, drunk, he and Marco argued over whether the quilt's color was seafoam or green, the kind of argument art school students have when all they have to show for all the work they've done, so far in life, are their opinions and inflexibility.

Jake runs a hand over the quilt. The stitching swirls and loops, rising through the cloth like Morse code.

"My grandmother made it," Marco says.

"From Puerto Rico," Jake says. "I remember." *I still love you*, he might as well have said.

A wet, slapping sound works its way into the room from down the hall, and Marco stands and shuts the door. He moves to the bathroom, and when he returns, his shirt is off. His stomach ripples, abdominal muscles pronounced as tire tracks in mud. In one hand, he holds the blue North Carolina mug. The other hand, palm up, holds a blue pill.

Jake takes the mug, the pill. He swallows, drinks.

He grips the quilt and watches his crotch.

Marco laughs and joins him on the bed. "This isn't 'The Incredible Hulk.' It takes some time."

"Is this even safe? Mixing Viagra with cocaine?" Jake listens for sex sounds, but the closed door does its job.

"My last boyfriend did it all the time," Marco says.

Boyfriend. Jake doesn't know how to ask tactfully, so he just asks. "Amelia. What's the story there?"

Marco shrugs. "She gives good head."

Jake must look bewildered, because suddenly Marco's gripping his shoulder, shaking him too hard.

"I'm kidding," Marco says. "Jesus. I don't know. We clicked. You're telling me you've never clicked with someone who isn't your type?"

"Sure," Jake says, "but they were guys."

"I still like guys, but I like her too. She's sexy, and she loves talking art."

Jake wants to say that the only people *talking art* in New York aren't people you want to talk art with. Talkers are buyers, blowhards, students, wannabes. When Jake sees his painter friends, the last thing they *talk* is *art*.

"Amelia reminds me of you, actually," Marco says. "Not you, but *you*. You before success went to your head." He runs two fingers down Jake's arm. "I loved you, you know."

Jake wants to feel something, but the words sound calculated, rehearsed, and he can't say whether they're meant as a kindness or a cruelty.

"So, you and Amelia, you're what?"

"It is what it is," Marco says. "We don't like putting labels on it."

Which makes Jake laugh. How many times has he heard this line from married men trying to get him into bed?

"We have fun," Marco says. "That's all."

And is that all Jake is to Marco, *fun*?

"Did you really love me?" Jake asks. It's easier than asking: *Do you love me now?*

Marco lets go of a sigh he may well have been holding in for years.

"Who knows, Jacob?" he says, and that extra syllable is a hatchet in Jake's heart.

The quilt bunches in his hands. More than sex, right now Jake wants to be alone. The cocaine, while it's quickened his heartrate, has slowed his thinking. Or else it's the blue pill rerouting blood from his brain. He needs to think, but his mind isn't working right.

"I wasn't jealous," Marco says.

"I'm sorry?"

Marco rises. He wanders the room. "When Frank took you on, when all those paintings sold, you said I was jealous. But I wasn't jealous. I was happy for you. That isn't why I left."

Jake wants to know. He doesn't want to know. "Why did you leave?"

"Because, Jacob, you were fucking *everyone*. Every time was the last time. Every time you said you wouldn't do it again."

"There weren't that many," Jake says.

"Spencer," Marco says. "Roger."

"I *never* had sex with Roger," Jake says. He's sure he didn't. He's almost sure.

"Clifton. Alan. Ned. Demetrius."

"Okay."

"That guy at Heather's opening," Marco says. "He had a septum ring. A *septum ring*."

"I *loved* you," Jake says.

Marco returns to the foot of the bed. He kneels.

"I believe you believe that," Marco says. "But here's the thing. You don't know what love is. There's something wrong with you. Something's broken. You don't love anyone. Because you can't."

Marco pulls off Jake's pants, pulls down his underwear, and Jake, in spite of himself, sees that the blue pill's worked.

There's so much he wants to say, but Marco shushes him.

"No more talking," Marco says. "Let me do the thing you came here for me to do."

17.

In the kitchen, carrots, chopped for soup, clutter a cutting board. On the stove, a pot of water sits, unboiled. On the counter, a pyramid of bouillon cubes, a wooden spoon, an onion snug in its golden skin. Diane unstacks the cubes, stacks them again.

She knows better than to knock. What's happening in the bathroom is not her business. But even from the kitchen she can hear her mother-in-law crying. Diane goes to the door. She knocks.

Either Lisa can't hear over the running water, or Diane is being ignored. She knocks again.

She gets it. She's a private person too. But even a private person shouldn't be left alone, crying, for an hour in the tub. Lisa needs to know she's not alone, and if Richard won't be a husband today, Diane will do her best to be a daughter.

She tries the door, and it's unlocked.

"Lisa," she calls, "I'm coming in."

Inside, the bathroom is condensation and fog. The sink's brass knobs are dewed. Even the toilet tank is slick with sweat. Four bulbs are meant to light the mirror above the sink, but two are burnt out, giving the room the feel of dusk, the calm after a day's rain. Somewhere behind a perspiring shower curtain, Lisa bathes.

Diane's skin pinks. Her sleeves, in the humidity, grip her arms. The water shuts off.

"Hello?" Lisa says.

"It's me," Diane says. "Are you all right?"

"I'm fine. Just having a day at the spa. Steam's good for the pores."

Diane nods, but the shower curtain isn't giving her much to work with. She pulls a towel from the bar, drapes it over the damp toilet lid, and sits. Beside her, a gap between the curtain and the wall reveals Lisa's feet and, above them, the polished silver of the bathtub faucet. The silver is at odds with the sink's brass, something Diane loves about this place, the house a mishmash, each broken part swapped out, over time, so that nothing matches because nothing needs to match. This is not a place for suppering with colleagues or entertaining guests. This is a summer home, a place for family. The bathroom fixtures clash, but there's a harmony in the discord.

Lisa's toes retreat into the water. The faucet drips.

Diane wants very much to say something, anything, but she has the strong impression that it's not her turn to talk.

"That boy," Lisa says. "That family."

Her foot leaves the water, and the toes, prehensile, grip the knob marked *H*. The foot retreats as the water rushes, steam spilling past the curtain into the room. There must be something in the tub, salts or bubble bath, because there is an aroma of fresh-cut flowers, eucalyptus, mint. The toes return, and the water is cut off.

They're quiet after that, the only sounds the faucet's drip and Lisa's ragged, tear-filled breathing.

"Can I get you anything?" Diane asks. "Is there—"

"I lost one too," Lisa says. The curtain ripples, its far end pushed aside so that Diane can take in Lisa's face, the puffy eyes and tear-tracked cheeks. "We had a daughter. Her name was June. She lived a month. This summer, she'd be thirty-five."

Diane wants to go to her, to hug her, but the nakedness, the tub, makes it impossible.

"I'm so sorry," she says. "Michael never told me."

"Michael doesn't know."

Surely Diane's heard wrong. This secret, it's not the kind you keep thirty-five years, then tell your daughter-in-law from the tub.

"We never told the boys," Lisa says. Her hands cup water, which she splashes on her face. "You're wondering why we didn't tell them. You're wondering why I'm telling you."

Diane is dizzy. She's sweating, the room too hot, the air too thick to breathe.

"Richard wanted to tell the boys," Lisa says, "but we couldn't agree on an age. You can't tell a toddler he had a sister that he'll never see. You can't tell a child that children die. You can, of course, but it's a risk, developmentally, emotionally. The age of seven, then. That was our agreement, based on what we read. Except, when Michael turned seven, Thad was four, and we didn't trust Michael not to tell. When Thad was seven, Michael was ten, and we worried we'd waited too long. The more we worried, the longer we waited, until telling the boys felt like something we'd be doing for ourselves more than for them. If there were any risk they'd find out some other way, we'd have said something. But June was born in Georgia, and Georgia's where she died. In New York, no one knew. Which is how we wanted it when we left those lives behind."

Diane's nose runs in the steam, but she's afraid to lift a finger, afraid to break the spell. She's never doubted Lisa loves her, in the obligatory way that mothers love the wives and husbands of their sons, but she and Lisa have never been particularly close. This disclosure, though, it feels like love.

"There's no name for it, you know," Lisa says. "We have words for all the rest: orphan, widow, widower. But no name for the parent of a child who goes first."

Diane pulls toilet paper from the roll. She dries her eyes, her nose. She's always been a person you can't cry in front of without her joining in.

"Should we have told the boys?" Lisa says. "I don't know. Should we tell them now? Who can say? Which is more selfish, telling them when it will only make them sad, or holding back the truth because you can't bear reliving it again?"

"There's no good choice," Diane says.

"Precisely. No good choice. No right way. People say, *Work the steps, grieve in this order for this much time*, but no one gets to say. No one gets to tell you how to grieve."

Lisa ladles more water onto her face. The steam has thinned.

"I don't want my sons feeling sorry for me. I don't want them to look and see *Mom who lost a child*. I want them to look and see *Mom*. In Georgia, for a year, everywhere I went, people asked what happened, asked if I was okay. The grieving mother, that was me. Do you know what that's like, being defined by one thing?"

"No," Diane says, though she does.

At restaurants or walking the neighborhood, Diane sees students, students and the parents of students, or those who were her students once upon a time. To them, she is not Diane. She is Mrs. Maddox, elementary school art teacher. To them, she is pinch pots and papier-mâché and finger paints. She is bathroom passes and tardy slips. Even among her colleagues, she is *the art teacher*, which makes her lunch monitor, bus duty coordinator, the one whose room unruly children are sent to for time-out. Each person, every aspect of her job, is a reminder that she lives in Texas, not New York, that she is defined by the dream she gave up long ago.

"Sympathy is exhausting," Lisa says. "I know that sounds terrible, but there are days you'd rather pretend you're fine, rather everyone pretend around you too. It's not fair to ask that of others, I know. And who knows if it's healthy? Who knows what *healthy* even is. I watch these shows, in waiting rooms, in airports—daytime TV—and these people, they feel compelled to say what they feel, *everything* they feel. To strangers. On national television. You can't convince me *that's* healthy."

A curl of hair, steam-spun, falls over Lisa's eyes, and she pushes the hair from her face.

"Sometimes I imagine June isn't my daughter, more an old friend I haven't seen in a while. Last I heard, she was in Madagascar studying lemurs. She likes mangoes and dry-roasted cashews, and her favorite color's something odd—chartreuse. *I should call her*, I'll think. Then my heart breaks because, for a minute there, I let myself forget. And that forgetting is a failure. To lose a child is to spend the rest of your life failing the child you've already lost."

More toilet paper. More tears. Through the hand towel, Diane feels the seat of her pants wet from the toilet's damp. She watches Lisa. Lisa watches her. And it's as though a tether, noosed at either end, binds both their hearts. From the tether, the ghosts of children dangle alongside children not yet born, bodies hauling themselves hand over hand.

"That boy's mother," Lisa says. "She'll never forgive herself. She'll never understand it's not her fault."

Diane's feet leave the floor. Her knees find her chin, then she's balled up tight on the toilet lid.

The list of things she'll do for Michael is long. But there's something she can't do. Yes, they had an understanding when they married. Yes, she promised. But she's a human being, and human beings are allowed to change their minds.

No one is taking this child from her. No one.

And though this room, and the hurt in it, belongs to Lisa, Diane can't keep quiet anymore. She has to speak.

"I'm pregnant," she says, and Lisa beams.

A new kind of crying fills the room.

"There's more," Diane says.

The rest will be hard for Lisa to hear. Her son's feelings. Michael's suggestion that they call the baby off. Still, Diane confesses everything.

And watches Lisa's face fall.

18.

Fuck Jake.

They're done. As far as Thad's concerned, they're *finished*.

"Sweetie," Jake says.

Thad didn't speak on the car ride back from Asheville, and he doesn't speak now.

"If anyone should be mad, it's me," Jake says. "You're the one who fucked them both."

Thad regrets his revenge, petty and mean. To be inside a woman. Consensual, yes, but he used Amelia, used her body to get back at Jake.

He regrets the look on Jake's face entering the room. Regrets how they locked eyes, Thad behind Amelia on the couch, then pulling out, tearing off the condom, and grabbing himself, four quick bursts from his fist, and Jake the first to look away. Regrets how Marco joined him on the couch, how Thad let himself be fondled, kissed. How Thad kissed back.

Which, for Jake, must have been worse than watching him with Amelia. The feelings Jake no doubt still has for Marco. Surely, this was the worst thing Thad could do. And he did it. And, all the while, no one beckoned Jake to join.

We're through, Thad wants to say, but dinner is soon and everyone is home. He'd rather sulk than start a shouting match.

"Just talk to me," Jake says. "Please." He's begging, which is not a thing Jake does.

The bedroom walls press in, claustrophobic in their 1970's faux wood paneling.

"I can't believe you made me wear this," Thad says, pulling off the JCPenney shirt. He heads to the bathroom to change pants. He doesn't want Jake seeing him right now.

Changed, he finds Jake in bed pretending to sleep. Jake's laptop lies beside him on Thad's pillow. The laptop is shut. Thad sits on the bed and rests the computer, still warm, on his lap. He pulls Jake's pillow from beneath his head and throws it to the floor.

"I was sleeping," Jake says.

"If I open this laptop, am I going to find porn?"

Jake has no reply, and Thad opens the laptop. Jake sits up, and the bedsheet falls to his waist. He's shirtless.

"What's your password?" Thad says.

Jake smooths the sheet across his lap.

"I will smash this laptop to pieces, I swear to God."

"Your birthday," Jake says, which gives Thad pause. If he weren't so mad, the moment would be sweet.

He types the date. The screen goes black, then bright, then there is a naked man. The picture is blurry, a selfie snapped on someone's phone. Thad drags the cursor to Search History, and it's what he expected. Hundreds of sites. Thousands. Nothing illegal or underage, from what he can tell in the minutes he spends scrolling. Still: So. Much. Porn.

"You have a problem," Thad says.

Jake stands. He fishes his shirt from beneath the covers and pulls it on. "I'm a healthy American male."

"This isn't healthy."

"I'm twenty-six years old," Jake says. "It's normal."

"*This* isn't normal. It's too much. You know these are time-stamped, right? That you can see how long you spent on every site?"

Jake cracks the blinds with two fingers and watches the yard.

"Jake, this is *hours* every day. This doesn't even look like fun. This looks like a compulsion."

Thad scrolls, tabulating time stamps. These aren't just furtive searches when Thad's left the building or gone to bed. They're off and on all day, most days, especially midday when Jake's in his studio. Which is when Thad realizes the reason he hasn't seen a canvas leave that room in months.

"Jake, what do you do all day?"

Jake's back tenses, but he doesn't leave the window. The blinds snap shut with a spray of dust. "It's research."

Bullshit. "That's a lot of research."

"A new series," Jake says, not even trying, really, to sound convincing.

But when he turns, Thad's unprepared for the sight before him. Jake's face is ashen. His chest heaves. His knuckles are white, hands balled around the hem of his shirt.

"You don't get to do this," Jake says, his voice faraway-sounding. "I support you. You don't even have a job. What I do in my studio is my business, and what I do with my dick is my business."

"Jake."

"You fucked *Marco*," Jake says, face twisted by whatever sobs he's holding back.

Thad shakes his head. "Don't turn this around on me. You fucked him first."

"We didn't fuck," Jake says. "He just—no, *fuck you.*"

For all they have in common, it's the four years' difference in their age that, some days, matters most. *What's four years?* Thad thought meeting Jake, kissing him, climbing into bed. But the bridge from twenty-six to thirty is wide, and Jake is a young twenty-six.

"You need help," Thad says. "Either you're an addict, or you're depressed and medicating with sex."

Jake laughs. "You think everyone's depressed."

He's not wrong. Thad tends to project. But he isn't projecting now. Happy, well-adjusted adults masturbate. Plenty look at porn. But they don't do so for hours every day.

"I'll call Steve," Thad says. "Maybe he can fit you in next week."

But Jake's not listening. He appears to be in a trance, jaw slack, eyes wide. Then the trance is over, and Jake's on his knees on the floor. He grips his chest. He wheezes. There's fright in his eyes, and, right then, Thad doesn't care about pornography or Marco or the things Jake's said. Right then, all Thad wants is to help the man he loves.

He doesn't hesitate. He joins Jake on the floor.

Time passes. He holds Jake's hand. Gradually, Jake's breathing slows. His tears subside.

"They're called panic attacks," Thad says.

"I know what they're called."

They move to the bed, Thad's back to the headboard, Jake's head in his lap. Thad runs his fingers through Jake's hair.

"This has happened before?"

"Yes."

"How often?" he asks, but Jake shuts his eyes, and Thad knows better than to press. He doesn't want to trigger another episode. The first was hard enough to watch. For all Thad's history with depression, with anxiety and suicidal ideation, he's never suffered panic attacks.

"No shrinks," Jake says.

"No shrinks," Thad says, though Steve will hear about this, if not from Jake, then from Thad next week.

Jake's hair is damp, as though from a fever freshly broken.

"So," Jake says, opening his eyes, "are you disappointed or relieved to learn your boyfriend's more fucked-up than you?"

It's not a contest, Thad wants to say. Instead, he says, "Everyone's fucked-up."

The room's so bare, it's hard to be in, the walls adorned with hooks and nails where family photos used to hang. The house may still belong to his parents, but Thad can't say the house still feels like home.

"I think that kid's death messed me up more than I've been letting on," Jake says.

In Bushwick, they aren't the kind of people who keep blinds closed. Here, they've grown afraid to lift a shade or leave the room for fear of what they'll see outside. Boats and divers. Hooks and chains.

"Yesterday, I didn't feel a thing," Jake says.

"Yesterday you were in shock."

Jake takes deep breaths. His hands unclench.

"I've never been afraid of death before," Jake says. A *very* young twenty-six. "When I believed in heaven, death wasn't scary. You die, you go to Disney in the clouds, then it's cotton candy and Space Mountain forever."

"You don't believe in heaven?" Thad asks.

"*'Ooh, heaven is a place on earth.'*"

Jake's hair has so much product in it, Thad's hands feel oil-slicked, and he wipes them on the sheets.

"What is it with you and eighties songs?"

"I'm a child of the nineties," Jake says. "We all want what we can't have."

Of the many things Thad wants but doesn't have, he wants most to be well.

He was seventeen the first time he tried to kill himself. He stood on a chair and used a belt cinched to a basement pipe. A quick kick should have ushered in oblivion, but the belt was old. It snapped and sent him to the floor. Embarrassing to end it all only to have to end it all again. In school, they'd read Jack London's "To Build a Fire," and the teacher had talked about how freezing was like falling asleep. That sounded peaceful, so Thad left the belt, the chair, climbed the basement steps, shed his clothes, and stumbled, in his underwear, outdoors into the snow.

What came next was not peaceful. He remembers shivering, then shaking, the shaking so violent he feared his teeth would pierce his tongue. A motorist found him facedown on the side of Stone Quarry Road, delirious, frostbite setting in. He still has a four-toed foot to show for it.

He tried playing the incident off as a drunken accident, which might have worked, had he been a drinker, had he thought to pull the belt down from the pipe. But there it hung, an accusation in leather and brass, the first thing his father saw coming down the stairs.

Thad spent two days in a hospital bed, foot bandaged, IV X-ed in the crook of his arm. A man was there, a man in a sweater vest who smelled like peppermint and called himself a *mental health professional*. The mental health professional asked him about his motives, his fears, his hopes for what came next.

But how to put a thing like that into words when so many things made him anxious — crowds, loud noises, parties, loneliness — when so many things inspired fear — failure, disease, rejection, suffering, death? This last one tripped the mental health professional up. If Thad feared death, maybe he didn't really want to die? Which was when Thad knew this wasn't the mental health professional for him.

In the future, better doctors would help him see. Depression doesn't need a *why*. Depression is a maze you can't logic your way out of. In Thad's case, depression means medicine, and on good days, the medicine helps.

Thad's mother, after, was the hardest to face. Her mouth said, *I love you*, but her eyes said, *How could you?* Hadn't they been good parents? Hadn't they loved him, supported him, taken him to his first pride parade when he came out?

She hadn't meant to make his suicide attempt about herself. Thad has to believe that or hate his mother for making him feel so bad.

These days, he takes his pills. He sees Steve. He does his best to keep bad thoughts at bay.

"If Jake left you," Steve asked once, "what would you do?"

"I'd be fine," Thad said, lying, knowing Steve knew he was lying. Steve didn't have to ask what happened if Thad left Jake. Deep down, both knew who'd be the first to leave.

But that was before today. Thad's stronger now. He knows what he wants.

Jake's head in his lap is heavy, but he doesn't ask Jake to move.

"Why no therapists?" Thad asks.

"I don't do drugs."

"I'm not talking pharmacology," Thad says. "Just conversation. Professional help."

He rubs Jake's temples, massages his ears.

"When I turned eighteen," Jake says, "my parents sent me to Arizona, one of those turn-you-straight camps. No exit, no phones."

Oh, Jake.

"Every night we had to cuddle with a counselor. They didn't call it *cuddling*. They said our fathers didn't love us right, that we needed 'the right kind' of masculine affection."

Thad's read about these places, though Jake's the first person he knows who's been to one. A reminder that Thad is fortunate. Fortunate to have the parents he has. Fortunate to grow up in a college town.

"Ten minutes a night," Jake says, "we got on the floor. Each of us was paired with a counselor, and my counselor was Charles."

"Jake, if you're not ready, you don't have to tell me this."

"There were three positions. Side by side was easy, like posing for a picture. The counselor put his arm around you, no big deal. The second position, you had to sit between his legs, but there was breathing room. The third they called the 'motorcycle.' Between the legs, and back to chest. Butt to crotch. The patient was supposed to choose. I always chose side by side. But the last night, Charles said, 'Tonight, God's telling me you need the motorcycle.'"

Jake brings a hand to his face, bites a thumbnail, and spits.

"And what could I do?" Jake says. "This guy's forty. I'm eighteen. Plus, he's a *man of God*. And I wanted to get better. I wanted to be cured."

He offers Thad his hand, and Thad takes it.

"So I get between his legs, Charles pulls me to him, and that's when I feel it. He doesn't thrust. He doesn't move. But it's there, pressing against the small of my back. For ten minutes. And *that* was the last time I sought 'professional help.' Honestly, I'd kill myself before I'd see another shrink."

The second time Thad attempted, he was twenty.

This time, he meant it, razor up the arm and not across. Seeing the blood, he passed out before he could do arm number two, then woke on his dorm room floor wanting to live.

Fifty-eight stitches and a quart of blood later, he was alive.

"Lucky duck," the doctor said, a kind woman, Indian, sari on under her white coat. She wore a visor over her face, the plastic kind cops wear to break up fights—surgical riot gear.

"I'm supposed to be on a date right now," she said. "I was almost out the door when you came in. Lucky for you, because I'm the best."

Thad watched the needle burrow in, wink out, watched his arm close up like a turkey, stuffing trussed. At some point, he realized he couldn't move. He was shackled to the table.

"Sorry," the doctor said. "It's the rule."

"Never again," Thad said, "I promise," and the doctor nodded like she'd heard those words before.

"I hope not," she said. "When I'm finished with it, this arm will be a masterpiece."

The next week, he sent the doctor flowers. The week after, he stopped in to say hi, but the man at the check-in desk only eyed him before asking him to leave. They were not in the habit of bringing former patients back to say hello.

Thad never got the doctor's name, or else he got her name and lost it in the frenzy of post-surgery Percocets. But he thinks about her often. He hopes that she made that dinner, that her date stayed at the restaurant table, waiting. He hopes that the doctor is happy and in love and saving lives.

Nine toes and a ribbon of scar tissue up his arm. And never again. Never, unless—

No. *Unless* is the end. *Unless* is how the thoughts start every time.

Jake's quiet so long, Thad thinks he's fallen asleep. But when he releases Jake's hand, Jake's eyes open.

"I'm sorry that happened to you," Thad says.

"I'm over it," Jake says, though of course he isn't. No one ever is.

In the next bedroom, murmuring, sighs. Michael and Diane are fighting, or else they're fucking. The wall is thick enough, it's hard to tell.

The smell of dinner creeps under the door, last night's chicken recycled into soup.

Jake's head leaves Thad's lap, and Jake sits up. They face each other on the bed.

"What do we do, then?" Jake says. "About us?"

But Thad is staying quiet. It's Jake's turn to talk. They've moved into one of those rare spaces, a planet inhabited by them and them alone—this moment, these bodies, this bed. There's less gravity here, more goodwill. Here, you have to tell the truth, and Thad welcomes it. Time to say the things that need saying.

"It's my fault," Jake says.

Of all the things Thad thought Jake might say, he hadn't expected this. But confession is a coin flipped, spinning, and Thad waits to glimpse the other side.

"I pushed you into something you didn't want," Jake says.

"We said no exes."

"I'm not talking about Marco," Jake says. "I knew the first month we were together. I told you I only did open, and I saw the worry written on your face. I thought you'd come around. You thought I'd change. But here's the thing." Jake takes a breath, exhales. "It's never going to be just us. I don't want that. But I want *you*. I can't imagine life without you. But I can't imagine life with you alone. I need more experiences than that."

Gravity, goodwill. Thad floats, and for the first time, sees himself through Jake's eyes.

Before Jake, he'd been with one man at a time. He's tried to change, for Jake, but he's never loved the love they make with other men. Still, he's gone along with it, refused to speak up, afraid to be alone. And Thad can't say who's selfish here, can't say which is worse, to coerce openness or compel monogamy. Which is when he knows this isn't just Jake's fault.

Or, *fuck* fault. Fuck blame. They are men who want different things. To be together, one must bend, and Thad's been bending for two years.

"Jake, if you want to be with other people, you should be with other people. But I can't join you. I need to be with one man, and, for that man, I need to be enough."

The atmosphere evaporates, and gravity returns. Thad's stomach hurts, and there's an ache behind his eyes.

"Maybe there's a way," Jake says. "I could let you pick the guys. I—"

"Jake."

"Seriously? You're going to make me do the hard part? You're going to make me choose?"

"I can't make the choice for you," Thad says.

Jake stands. He puts on pants. Then he's out the door, and Thad returns the laptop to his lap. He opens Jake's browser history. With a click, he erases it all. Then it's on to files, folders, cookies, cache.

If only he could find his way back to that bubble of no judgment, no gravity. But there are so many men.

He deletes. He empties the recycle bin. He purges the other bodies from Jake's life.

19.

Always, there is more to pack.

Soup on the stove and a while until it's warmed, Lisa builds a box. *Fold, fold, tape. Fold, fold, tape.* Her fingers are pruned, skin still pink from the bath. She could use a tall glass of cold water, but she doesn't want to leave the bedroom to get it. Beyond the bedroom, family members lurk. They want to make her feel better. They want to help. But Lisa doesn't need help. She needs to be left alone. Too much has happened the past twenty-four hours. A family has lost a son. Her son doesn't want a family.

What's wrong with her boy? She'll talk sense into him. Michael will be a father. Lisa will be a grandmother. Everyone will be happy. End of discussion.

Diane asked her to keep the pregnancy a secret, just as Lisa asked Diane not to speak of June. Neither, of course, is a promise either's bound to keep. It will be hard keeping track of who knows what, who doesn't, who's pretending not to know, but this is what it means to be a mother. Open secrets. Broken promises.

She fills the box with lake house clothes she won't need for the week: spare underwear, a bra, old bathing suits, some of which haven't fit since Bill Clinton was in office. She's never been big on clothes, but she likes swimsuits. One piece, two piece, solids, florals. There must be ten of them. In Florida, she'll buy new ones. These should go to Goodwill, but they won't. Always, she's had trouble getting rid of things.

The door opens, and Richard's in the room.

There's still space, but she tapes the box shut. In Sharpie, she writes *Swimwear, Undies, Bras.*

"How was your bath?" Richard asks. He sits on the bed. He doesn't ask her to join him, and she doesn't.

"You know what next week is?" she says, then apologizes for asking. He knows. Of course he knows. A mistake thinking fathers love their children less, though it took her some time, figuring that out.

They only forgot June's birthday once, years ago. It was Richard who remembered. He was quiet, too quiet, the next day, and she knew. She'll never forgive herself for forgetting. And though the forgetting doesn't mean she loves her daughter less, still she hopes never to forget again.

June's birthday is always a question of what to feel or say, of how to be in the world. Summers the boys are with them, Thad will notice— *Mom, you seem sad today.* Summers when the boys have yet to visit, when it's she and Richard, they eat dinner in silence and go to bed as early as they can. Those nights, all of it is there in her husband's eyes: the ambulance ride, the wake, the funeral; the casseroles she threw out by the trash can full because people believe that, grieving, you can't cook; the tranquilizers, grief groups, couples counseling; then church, then work, the big move to New York; then the making of Michael— tentative, accidental— and the lake house, before life began anew.

This time next week, the house will not be theirs to eat their dinner in. Already they will have vacated the premises, the moving van ferrying their possessions to New York. The morning of June's birthday, they will sign on the dotted line. By midmorning, the closing will be done, and they will spend the day making the twelve-hour drive from Christopher to Ithaca. Dinner, if they bother to stop, will be McDonald's or IHOP, something unappetizing and fast.

On the bed, Richard is quiet, perfectly composed. Some days she wishes he weren't so even-tempered. Just once, she'd love to see him scream, to throw a lamp or punch a wall, to see him helpless in a bathtub, sobbing. But that's not her Richard.

After June died, they attended an interfaith support group. One night, a Catholic mother prayed for the souls of unbaptized babies in limbo. That was the first time Richard walked out. He left quietly, but the next week, after enduring a laying on of hands, he left loudly, and he left for good. Lisa continued to attend without him. She didn't need to agree with everyone's ideas of God to go. Being with other grieving parents was enough. Richard seemed happier saying nothing, staying home. *Seemed,* for in reality, Richard's silence disguised a kaleidoscope of hurt. Lisa couldn't see it then. She's spent her marriage learning how to look.

"Not the weekend we were hoping for," Richard says, and she moves to him.

She takes his head in her hands and kisses the top of it. She holds his face to her chest. She can be mad at him and love him at the same time. No one stays married thirty-seven years without learning that trick. And she's no saint. She can be unkind.

One night, years ago, they reached a disagreement. She wanted a fight, Richard wouldn't engage, and she locked him out of the house. They'd been budgeting toward retirement, and the numbers weren't adding up. Turned out, Richard had been sending checks to Michael and Diane. Not small checks, hefty sums. What Lisa called enabling, Richard called love, and they disagreed until she pushed him out the door. He spent half an hour in the rain before she let him in, and he caught pneumonia the next week. Maybe the rain and illness were unrelated. Maybe the pneumonia was her fault. Either way, at his age, he could have died. And if he can forgive her that—

Richard raises a hand to her waist, and she steps away.

"Thad's looking for his comic books," she says.

Richard doesn't say, *I told you so.* "Don't," he'd warned her. "Thad will come looking for those." Still, cleaning the house, she'd dragged the comic boxes to the curb.

"I feel like I threw out his childhood," she says.

"We can replace them," Richard says. "There's a comic shop in Highlands."

"I think they were X-Men," she says. "Didn't Thad like X-Men?"

"I don't know," Richard says, "I never asked," which more or less sums up the riches and limits of his parenting. On the one hand, he was not the father attempting to live vicariously through his sons. He never asked too much or raised a bar they couldn't clear. On the other hand, he didn't know his sons. He never missed a graduation, and rarely missed a performance or baseball game. But ask him, the next day, which team won, and he could tell you only the equation running through his head while, just beyond the chain-link, his boy hit a home run.

Lisa joins him on the bed and lets him take her hand. If asked, she'd have trouble explaining the tenderness she feels in this moment for this man. His hair's gone white and wiry. His eyes are blue. He's no longer the man she married, but he's still the man she loves.

My dear, how much regret do you carry with you in your heart?

"Something's going on with Michael and Diane," Richard says.

She must make a choice. Her husband is warm beside her. His hand is soft. But she'll keep her word. She promised Diane.

"I think they're just upset about the house," she says. She doesn't like to lie to him.

"Well, that's not their call. It's simply not their call."

Richard stands, moves to the dresser, and builds a cardboard box. He pulls shoes from the closet floor: a pair for fishing, a pair for town, a pair to mow the lawn. He is a fussy man, exacting and precise. Every day, to work, he wore a bow tie. When Richard saw that Lisa tied it better, straighter, he asked her, each morning, to tie his tie. And she did, for nearly thirty years.

The tie was the first clue, the tie and the smell.

Richard lowers the shoes into the box, then spends a minute arranging them, pulling a pair out, squeezing them back in.

"They want us to keep a house and maintain a property, just for them, when they're here two weeks a year, at most," Richard says. "They have no appreciation for what we pay in property taxes, insurance, utilities, maintenance. They have no idea how money works."

Then stop giving it to them, she wants to say. *Maybe they'll learn.* But that's an argument for another day.

He grumbles, filling up the box: slippers, hangers, a bathrobe he hasn't worn in years.

The lake house isn't a logical place to retire, he reminds her. It requires too much repair. Even with the house repaired, he's not sure he can picture wintering here. Lake Christopher, in the off-season, is lonely, desolate, and the mountain roads can quickly turn to ice.

Still, Lisa finds it vexing, measuring *logic* beside *longing*, memory beside saying goodbye.

Richard paces and packs, speaking authoritatively, but also like he's trying to convince himself of this decision that she's made for them.

"Do you want to keep the house?" she says.

Richard need only say a few words, and she'd take it all back. Skip the closing, cancel the sale, risk a lawsuit, pay what it takes. The words, though. She needs them to be right.

"I want what you want," Richard says.

What she wants? What she wants is for Richard to go back in time. What she wants is for him not to do the thing he's done. *I want what you want* are not the right words.

Richard wears the face he wears for Spades, inscrutable to the point of infuriating.

And she wonders if she's being petty. What if selling the house isn't about starting over? What if she *is* punishing him?

When Lisa tied Richard's bow ties, she practiced the twisted knot method, that last bend in the fastening that rendered the knot fuller, puffier. It suited Richard's *warbler*, her pet name for his Adam's apple, one more pronounced than most men's. His voice wasn't deeper for it, it was just the shape of him, but Richard was self-conscious. He believed bow ties distracted from the feature, and she let him believe it.

One evening last year, Richard, home from work, walked through the door, and she knew that the knot at his neck was not the knot she'd made. This knot was untwisted, the product of a less-skilled hand.

"Darling," she asked, "did your tie come undone?"

"No," he said. "You tied it perfectly." But he didn't smell right. He didn't smell like himself. Then he kissed her on the nose and retreated to the shower, though he seldom showered at night, and Lisa knew.

She said nothing, but watched as Richard returned home, several days a week, his bow tie retied by another hand. There were no emails, voice mail messages, or texts, no wayward love note left in the pocket of a shirt. His cell phone showed no history, which meant he was deleting all records of his calls. But his list of contacts showed a new addition: *K.* Lisa had only to call the number to hear the voice of the woman welcoming her husband into bed, but she couldn't bring herself to call. After a few months of this, Richard's bow ties came home, each night, the way they'd left the house, and when Lisa checked his contacts, *K* was gone.

"What do *you* want?" Richard says. He leans over the open box. Meticulous as he is, he seems not to notice he's built it upside down, *UP* arrows pointing to the floor.

"I want to sell the house," Lisa says, and stands to help her husband pack his things.

20.

Michael finds Diane in the bedroom they've shared in this house for as long as they've been together. The room is dark. The shades are drawn. But Diane isn't napping. The bed is made, and she sits at the end of it.

"I've made a decision," she says, and Michael shuts the door and joins her on the bed.

He doesn't have to ask to know what the decision is. He wants to face her, but she's rarely seen him drink before dinner, and he needs her not to smell the moonshine on his breath.

Back home, it's easier. Fifteen ounces a day of vodka will keep his hands from shaking. Pop a few Altoids coming home from work, and she won't smell the alcohol on his breath. Of course, the worse their finances have gotten, the cheaper the vodka. The cheaper the vodka, the worse his headaches the next day. He's heard charcoal filtration helps, but it's hard enough hiding liquor bottles around the house without having to hide a Brita, too.

"Before you say anything," he says, but her hand grips his knee.

"I'm having this baby," she says. "It's not up for discussion."

Michael rises and moves to the window. Their window doesn't face the lake. Their view is pine trees and sunlight. His parents' mailbox is a plastic bass whose mouth opens for the mail, and the road beside the mailbox is empty. This far back on the bay, the only traffic would be neighbors or the friends of neighbors come for weekend getaways.

Michael could live here. He thought one day he would.

"We don't have to make a decision today," he says.

"You've said that for weeks," she says. "I'm tired of waiting. The decision's made. I love you, but it's made."

His forehead throbs. His bandage needs changing. He needs another drink. "Don't I have some say in this?"

"Some say in my body?"

"Some say in our baby."

The room is dangerous with happy memories.

As teenagers, they spent a lot of time on this bed. She wore his shirts. They were kids, practically. But that was a long time ago, when money was no concern and pregnancy was unthinkable. On a rainy day, they'd sneak back here and make love, and no one knew, or, knowing, no one cared. They'd shower after, and sometimes, in the shower, they'd make love again. It's been so long since they've been together that way, any way at all. Since before news of the pregnancy, certainly. The last time may well have been the conception itself.

God, how he misses young Michael, young Diane. Time, take him back. Make him young. Let him be eighteen again.

"We can't afford a kid," he says.

"We can. If you make assistant manager, that's another two dollars an hour. That's an extra eighty bucks a week."

"I don't want to talk about work."

"You brought it up."

"I brought up money."

"Work *is* money, Michael."

Diane pulls her feet from the floor and crosses her legs on the bed. The fan creaks overhead.

"I'm not asking for a divorce," she says. "I don't want one, but I'm ready if it comes to that."

Beyond the window, the world goes gray. He wants air. He wants to be out of this room.

"Also," Diane says, "I told your mom."

Then he's on the bed. He's at her side. Let her say that to his face. Let her smell the moonshine on his breath.

"We had a deal!" he says. He's whispering, but, to his ears, the whisper is a shout.

"I don't remember a notary. I don't remember any dotted line."

"I don't want my mom involved in our decision."

"My decision."

He can't stand it. Who is this woman before him? What happened to the girl in the shirts too big for her, caressing him, promising to love him for all time?

"I didn't plan to tell her," Diane says. "I meant to comfort her, and it slipped out."

"How is that a comfort? How is that anyone's business but our own? Yesterday a child died. I get it. I was there. More than anybody, I was *there*. We're all grieving. But—"

"She lost a child too," Diane says, a look on her face that says she's said too much.

The room pulses. For a moment Michael can't hear, sound suspended, then muffled, then roaring back, the bedroom big, then small, then big again.

"I'm sorry," she says. "That wasn't mine to say."

He never knows he's been grinding his teeth until they hurt. He unclenches, rubs his jaw.

"I would have had a . . ."

"Sister." Diane takes his hand, but he doesn't want her touch, and he lets go.

"Why would you tell me that?" he asks. "Why would *she* tell *you*?" Thirty-three years he's lived without this loss. Why now?

"I'm sorry," Diane says.

"Please don't tell Thad."

"I wouldn't do that."

"I don't know. You had no trouble telling me."

"Don't be mean," Diane says.

Kitchen sounds. The dinner hour has arrived.

"Was there a name picked out?" he asks.

"Her name was June."

"How far along was she?" he asks. "When she lost the baby, how far along was my mom?"

"Oh," Diane says. "Oh, Michael, I'm sorry. I wasn't clear. The baby was born. She was a month old."

The bedroom is a heart, beating. He feels Diane's hands on him, but her touch, it drains him. Her very nearness leaves him cold. He needs a drink, needs to be out the door. He can't get away from her fast enough.

21.

The table is set, air thick with the delicious stink of chicken soup.

Jake tried vegetarianism once, but found he ate healthier as a carnivore. Short of meat, he stuffed his face with chips and fries. Sure, there are alternatives, proteins minus slaughter and blood. But slaughter and blood taste best. Screw tofu. Screw nuts and beans. Give him chicken any day. Deliver unto him a xylophone of beef with smoke-kissed ribs.

Lisa stirs the soup. "It's a throw-together," she says. "I hope that's okay." She unclips a cellophane bag and removes a stack of thin red bowls. "It kills me, using this stuff. But don't worry. I'll rinse these and bring them back to Ithaca. They have a plastics plant that takes number six recyclables."

Jake wasn't worried. Recycling isn't the kind of thing he gives much thought. The planet has, what, thirty good years left? How big the landfills get, in the meantime, seems beside the point.

"I'm sorry the week's turned out this way," Lisa says, and Jake joins her at the stove. In a wide, cast-iron pot, last night's chicken bobs in stock. Lisa salts and stirs. There are carrots in the soup, celery and noodles, little leaves.

He and Thad don't cook. For dinner, there's the good Thai place and the bad Thai place. There's the Korean barbecue taco truck. There's pizza and ramen. So much pizza and ramen.

Eight years since he sat in his mother's kitchen. Eight years since he drank her tea or sipped *her* chicken soup. Eight years since Arizona. He left the facility early—he was eighteen, no one could make him stay—and he did not go home. He couldn't be near the people who had sent him there. Never mind that his mother thought she was helping. Never mind that she lived under the crush of her husband's thumb. She was his *mother*. She should have protected him from Arizona, from his father, from all bad things. She should have loved him, no exceptions, no matter what.

Eight years since he's spoken to his parents. If they know he's a painter in New York, they have not reached out. He will not reach out to them, will not give them the chance to prove their love conditional again.

Jake holds the bowls, and Lisa ladles. Richard moves to the table, then Michael. They sit, men ready to be fed, men used to being served. Thad wouldn't sit. Thad, were he here, would help his mother, but Thad is in the bedroom, sulking.

"Dinner," Lisa calls, but still no sign of Thad or, come to think of it, Diane.

The table is set with waters, and Michael makes a trip to the freezer. When he returns, a tumbler sweats beside his bowl. He's an alcoholic. Jake's 90 percent sure. He doesn't know whether to be sad or amused that no one in the family seems to have picked up on this. How Michael downs moonshine at every meal. How, away from the table, his hand is a fist around a travel mug. Could be everyone knows and says nothing, the way Jake suspects his parents knew who he was long before they let on. But whether the Starlings suspect Michael, whether they don't know, whether they know and hope for the best, they have certainly been good to Jake. They can be intense—Michael's outbursts, Richard's stoicism, Lisa's earnestness—all that unrestrained, unasked-for love. But as found families go, he could do worse.

Jake and Lisa sit. Jake sips his soup.

"It's wonderful," he says.

Michael and Richard sip, saying nothing, the son looking so much like the father, it gives Jake pause. He could paint them. These men, side by side. Still life with soup. A little *American Gothic*. A little Munch. But it's been done. Everything good has been done before.

A door opens, and Diane joins them. She's been crying, anyone can see. But then, maybe they all have, given what they witnessed yesterday.

For Jake, what lingers is the sister on the boat, screaming, pointing at the empty water wings, at the lake that swallowed her brother whole. The screaming never stopped. Not after Michael surfaced, blind with blood. Not once the police arrived. Not even when Jake stood, hours later, in the shower, ears filling up with water that would not wash away the sound of that girl's voice. Not until he turned the shower radio on and let the music in. Not until he took himself in his hand and made himself relax. He's not a monster. He's had a sad life. And he knows what to do when the sadness gets to be too much.

Diane sits between Michael and Lisa, and Lisa places a hand on her shoulder. It stays there, which seems to comfort Diane, though no one's talking. Michael drinks. He won't look at his mother. He won't look at his wife. Something's up.

Finally, Thad emerges from the bedroom. His hair is combed. His shirt is changed. He really is sweet-looking, the kind of eyes that grab you, a face that, seeing it, you want to kiss. He's no Marco. He's the boy next door, the sensible choice. Which is boring, or else lovely, depending on your mood.

"Sorry," Thad says. "I was reading the news."

Lisa's hand leaves Diane's shoulder.

"I don't want to know," Lisa says. "I don't want to know what that maniac is up to." Thad tries to speak, but his mother cuts him off. "This house is a place of peace. This food is a dinner that I made. That man gets enough of our attention. He's not welcome here. Not this week. Not at my table. Not in my home."

"It's not your home," Michael says.

"For one more week it is."

If Michael wanted everyone's attention, he has it now. He stands, grips the table, and gently pushes off. He's drunk. He hardly lets it show, but Jake doesn't miss much. Michael pours himself another drink and sits.

"So, what's the scoop?" Michael asks. "What's the latest Oval Office gossip?"

"Please respect your mother's wishes," Richard says. He's hardly touched his soup.

Michael drains his glass. "This is ridiculous. A boy is dead. The house is sold. And you're afraid politics will wreck the week?"

Michael's face is sweaty, lips twisted in an unrelenting sneer. His bandage comes loose, flashing the family with the puffy, ointment-smeared stitches, before Michael fumbles with the cotton and, wincing, thumbs the bandage into place.

"You want to talk politics?" Diane says. "Fine. Richard, Lisa, it's your son's fault we're in this mess."

Michael laughs. He pushes his soup bowl away from him. His chair scoots back, as if to make room for his rage.

"Say it," Michael says.

Diane looks stricken. This isn't her. In the two summers and two Christmases Jake's spent with her, he's never heard her utter an unkind word. Never heard her raise her voice. Never seen her contradict a thing her husband says, and Michael says some pretty stupid shit.

"Say it!"

Diane's head drops. "Michael voted for . . ." But she can't make herself finish the sentence.

"Oh, Son," Lisa says.

"Oh, Christ," Thad says.

"I'm sorry," Diane says, but the destination of her *sorry* is unclear. The apology bounces off the ceiling, the light fixtures, Jake's painting on the wall. It sails around the room until it falls, dissolving, at their feet.

"Why the fuck?" Thad says. "You're not that dumb."

"Don't call me dumb," Michael says.

"Don't call your brother dumb," Richard says.

"Son," Lisa says. "What were you thinking?"

"*Thinking*," Michael says. "That's the problem." He waves a hand, indicting all of them. "All this thinking, all the time. And where did all that thinking get us? Did it get the country out of debt? Out of Afghanistan? Out of Iraq? Did all that thinking save Detroit? Or save our jobs from going overseas? Did that thinking find new work for coal miners? Or raise salaries for teachers nationwide? Did that thinking bail out homeowners trying to keep their homes?"

The bandage slips and, once more, Michael pushes it into place.

"Did everyone get to keep their health care?"

Michael looks at Thad. Thad looks into his soup.

"'If you like your health plan, you can keep it.' Did that turn out to be true?"

"No," Thad says, "except—"

"No, it did not turn out to be true," Michael says.

"It's more complicated than that," Lisa says. "The law set standards. For co-pays. For deductibles. Prescription benefits. People who lost their plans, those plans weren't health care. They were rip-offs, shams. Those aren't the plans he meant."

"But that's not what Obama said." Michael's eyes are huge. His teeth gleam.

"*President* Obama," Lisa says.

Michael smiles. "*President* Obama. I've never once heard you say *President* Trump."

"I'll call him *president* the day he acts like one," Lisa says.

Michael lifts the spoon from his soup bowl and licks it clean. He taps the spoon on the table once, twice, half a dozen times.

"Let's talk drones," he says.

"Enough," Richard says.

"Your president," Michael says. "Your Nobel Peace Prize–winning president. Do you know how many people he killed?"

"Besides bin Laden?" Thad says.

"Almost four thousand," Michael says. "*Four thousand*, over three hundred of whom were civilians. Wedding guests. Doctors. Mothers walking children home from school. And that's just the *drones*."

Lisa shakes her head. "I'm sure that's not—"

"It's true," Diane says. "I didn't want to believe it either, so I looked it up. I'm afraid it's true."

Michael leans back, and his chair's front legs leave the floor. He rights himself. He drops the spoon. "See, Mom, while you were busy saving all those birds, your favorite president ordered machines to kill people, then sat in a war room and watched those machines murder people on TV. Let me ask you this. Which is more valuable, a person or a bird?"

"Jesus, Michael," Thad says, "leave Mom alone."

"Why?" Michael says. "Who'd you vote for?"

"Hillary," Thad says. "Obviously."

"Dad?" Michael says.

"Not that it's anybody's business," Richard says, "but Hillary."

"Mom?"

Lisa, however, refuses to play Michael's game. She sits, quiet, dignified. Jake finds this commendable. Also anticlimactic. Had he spoken to his mother this way, she'd have slapped him across the face, assuming Jake's father hadn't already thrown his face across the room. But Lisa remains composed. And is this love, or something less?

"This is my fault," Diane says. "I shouldn't have said anything."

"No," Lisa says. "This is *not* your fault. But we're finished discussing that monster."

"That monster lowered your taxes," Michael says.

"Spoken like a true deplorable," Thad says.

"Deplorable?" Michael says. "*I'm* the deplorable? You don't even have a job!"

"I don't collect social services," Thad says.

"You don't have to," Michael says. He looks at Jake, but stops short of what he wants to say. Jake knows what Michael thinks of him, and Jake doesn't give a fuck. He has half a million in the bank and owns his loft. He gives more to The Trevor Project annually than Michael makes in any given year. When it comes to Michael, Jake has nothing to prove.

Thad, on the other hand, has let his brother get the best of him.

"I'm looking for work," Thad says.

"You've been 'looking' for two years," Michael says.

"Just because I'm not willing to dress up like a fucking referee—"

"Fuck you," Michael says, and here, Thad's gone too far. Michael's fiercest ache, his greatest shame. The family calls him a businessman. They say he's in sales. No one mentions the fact that, for years, Michael's worked the floor at a dingy Foot Locker at one of America's dying indoor malls. Honest work, though Michael insists it's beneath him, insists without saying what he'd rather do.

Michael stands, a finger in Thad's face. The bandage slips, and Michael rips it off.

"*You* have the nerve to call *me* a deplorable. You contribute *nothing* to society. And the second Jake leaves you, you won't hesitate to let taxpayers pay for you. And *you*." He turns to Lisa. "Two houses. Two ivory-tower pensions. And you talk about how a child had the nerve to drown and ruin your family's special week. And *you*." He turns to Diane. "You didn't even vote for Hillary! You voted for *Stein*. You say Trump's my fault. At least I didn't throw away my vote! All this while we sit here in a double-wide trailer in a red state. Don't you get it? *We're* the deplorables! Hillary doesn't care about you, or you, or you. You think Hillary Clinton ever spent the night in a trailer? You think she cares about the states she didn't win? And, hell, whichever liberals aren't judging Mom and Dad for being from the South are judging them for the people they've displaced. You think this lake was always called Lake Christopher? That's a *developer's* name. This lake had a Native American name, but that name had too many syllables, too hard for white people to say, so some company buys the land and, presto, it's *Lake Christopher*. Pretty, pronounceable, *marketable*. From there, development is easy. Buy out the locals. Those you can't buy out, condemn with eminent domain. Sell the land to the owners of Home Depot and RaceTrac and Coke. Stock the lake with largemouth bass. Then lie back and cash the checks as they come in. That's Lake Christopher, a town built on the backs of the working class on land stolen from Native Americans, now owned by business moguls. But it's okay. You worked *hard* nine months a year. You've earned your peace and quiet, haven't you?"

Michael takes a breath.

"I may be a deplorable, but so are you. All of you. Because guess what? This is America. Everybody's somebody's deplorable."

Then they're yelling at each other, Thad calling Michael an asshole, Diane demanding Thad not call her husband names, Lisa scolding Diane for voting third party with so much on the line, Richard asking Michael not to yell, and Michael asking why his father never takes his side. Everyone arguing, no one listening.

Except Jake. Jake takes it all in.

This family. These miserable, well-meaning people. They've never liked a thing Jake's given them. The forsaken shower radio, the painting on the wall. But there's another offering, something no one else can give.

"You guys," Jake says. They're the first words he's spoken since the start of dinner when he complimented Lisa's soup. No one hears him over the lather of their attacks, so he stands. He tries again. "I have something to say."

And Jake gives the Starlings a gift that also has the convenience of being true.

"You guys," he says, "I didn't vote."

Eyes turn. Temples throb. And Jake can't help but smile. He has, if only for one night, become, for this family, the thing he's always been for his own. He is the common enemy, the scourge upon whom all might heap their scorn. Tonight he is the voice that saves them from themselves.

22.

Water, moonlight, wind. A tumbler, sides condensing, drink so strong Michael imagines the moonshine eating through the glass, the dock, sees the poison hit the lake and, in seconds, the surface is bubbles and fish bellies.

He sits, shoes off, feet in the water. He's seen snakes here, big ones, watched them move through the water, between reeds, black heads like periscopes.

Above, the stars are bright, the moon a crescent. Below, the lake is a bowl that holds the sky.

On the point, the flag flies half-staff. Michael wonders who died, then recognizes the tribute for what it is. A kindness to the locals, the bay, the boy. There is not enough kindness in this world. Michael should know. He's more than contributed his share to this insufficiency. The world won't miss him when he's gone. Diane might. A child would. But giving yourself someone new to miss you—that's not a reason to bring life into the world.

Frogs bleat and insects pulse. A clump of cattails clack atonal in the breeze. An owl calls, and Michael calls back, but he's not his mother. His mother can make herself into any bird.

He wonders what it's like, having a kid. He's not afraid he'll shake the baby, or whatever parents do that lands them in grisly reenactments on daytime TV. Neither is he worried, seeing the child for the first time, that he'll feel nothing. He'll love the child. He knows he will. That's what scares him. He'll love the child, and all that love will push his resentment down the road, what, ten, twenty years? Still, one day he'll wonder who he might have been, given a few more years, given the time to figure out his dreams. When that day comes, he'll look back on his life and blame the child. He will. And he doesn't want to be that father.

Of course, this argument would be easier to make with himself if he had dreams. What does he want?

More moonshine, for starters. He knocks back his glass. Another owl calls, and he responds.

The dock creaks, and Michael knows who's behind him before the first word leaves her mouth. His mother sits and, sitting, sits too close. She's wearing shorts, her thighs a topography of age spots and spider veins.

"You make a lousy great horned owl," she says.

"Was I answering you?"

"No. That was a tiger, all right. I was about to vocalize, but you beat me to it."

Michael rattles the ice in his glass. He has yet to find the warm, pillowy center of tonight's drunk. He's too on guard, too tense, back stiff and forehead still ablaze.

"That was quite the show you put on at dinner," his mother says.

He grips the glass. The glass will keep him safe. Even empty, it's a wall between himself and whatever his mother will say next.

"How come we don't talk anymore?"

He can't do this, not tonight. He hasn't had enough to drink.

"We talk," he says. "We're talking right now."

"I mean *talk*-talk. There was a time you *wanted* to talk to me. Now it's like we hardly know each other."

"I don't know what you're talking about." He knows exactly what she's talking about.

If his mother died, if he had to speak at her memorial, Michael has no idea what he'd say. She loves birds. She loves her boys. He knows how much she loves him and how much he's let her down. But he doesn't know *her*.

"I don't mind that you don't call to ask about my day," she says. "It's not a son's job to be invested in his parents' lives. But it hurts thinking you don't want me to know *you*."

Which *you*, though, Michael wonders. It's a rare day even he knows his own mind.

"I want to talk to you about something," his mother says, "but I don't want you getting mad at me."

"Not a great way to start."

"I mean it."

"I mean it too. That's maybe the worst way to start. I'm on the defensive, and I don't even know what you're going to say."

His mother's eyes are no longer tender. Resolve has smacked the kindness from her face. "I'm just going to come out and say it."

"I wish you would."

"I think you two should keep the baby."

The glass has gone warm in his hand, and he puts it down. He watches the surface of the lake. If he watches long enough, maybe his mother will rise and walk away.

"Honestly," she says, "I can't believe it's up for discussion. I can't believe it's a question of *if*."

"This has nothing to do with you."

"I'm the grandmother. I'd like to think I play some part in the decision-making process."

"You don't." He isn't trying to be mean about it, then he is. "You don't even enter into the equation."

She looks away, and he feels shitty. But only briefly. Because this *isn't* her business. This isn't her marriage. He may be her son, but his life is still his own.

His mother's knee grazes his. "You shouldn't say things you don't mean."

"I mean it," he says. "But I shouldn't have put it that way. I'm sorry."

Across the bay, the dogs let out a reverie of barks and howls. Then, just as they did last night, the lights come on, the dogs are brought inside, and the evening settles into chirps and croaks. A fin breaks the water a few yards past the dock. Carp or gar, Michael can't make the fish out.

"If this is about June," Michael says, and hears the intake of his mother's breath.

He's trespassed. He feels it. He's sullied the memory of his sister, and all he's done is speak her name.

His mother straightens. "That was a secret."

"Diane sucks at secrets. But you knew that. She told you ours."

"I suppose . . ." she says, but her thought goes unfinished. She was about to say that when it comes to family, there should be no secrets. Michael's almost sure of this. But something stopped her. Perhaps another secret changed her mind.

"I get not wanting to scare us when we were younger," he says. "But once we were older, grown-up, why not tell us then?"

But the look his mother gives him says he'll never be grown-up enough for this.

"What age?" she says. "When would you have had me tell?"

"I don't know. Once we were old enough to understand."

His mother laughs, but the laugh is a flower bloomed and dead and withered all at once.

"*Understand*? Son, there is no understanding. When a child dies, there's no bigger picture, no reconciling death with destiny or God. When a child dies, the only thing to understand is that there's nothing to be understood. Nothing. I wanted to protect you boys from that."

Michael wants to say that, as June's brother, he deserved to know, but the fight they've just had over babies, over whose business is whose, makes that a tough argument to win.

"Your father wanted to tell you both," his mother says. "Then Thad had his thing."

He hates that she calls Thad's suicide attempts his *things*, as though transforming the word transforms the truth.

"After that, we worried it might upset Thad too much, that he might . . . self-harm."

"Then why not just tell me?"

His mother nods. "We considered it, but we weren't sure that was fair."

"Except, you told Diane. You must have wanted me to know."

"Maybe you're right. Maybe, deep down, I did."

Her nose shines, the scar pink where they carved the cancer out, one nostril a little deflated, slowly closing in on itself.

"The timing's bad, Mom. We just don't have the means."

"No one ever thinks they have the means. You just have to go for it."

"Everyone who says that has *money*."

But he isn't sure she's hearing him. She can't fathom his salary or what Diane's school district pays—how, incomes combined, he and Diane make less than his mother will take home in retirement each year. She's forgotten what it's like, starting out. Or else she always lived within her means, never splurged.

"What about what Diane wants?" his mother says.

"Diane doesn't know what she wants," he says. This isn't true. Her mind's made up. The baby will be born. But Michael's not ready to give his mother the satisfaction of this answer, not yet.

Plus, what about what *he* wants?

So he picked out their house, their cars, the state in which they live? So the decisions that left them broke were mostly his? If sacrificing for the one you love is better than getting your own way, Michael's merely given his wife numerous opportunities to feel good about herself. If this is true, isn't an abortion the perfect way for Diane to prove her love to him?

Even buzzed, Michael's not buying his own bullshit.

"You know," his mother says. "You get a tax credit with every kid."

Hard not to laugh out loud. Where reason and shame have failed, she's appealing to his avarice.

"Hey," she says, which is when he feels her hand on his cheek, her palm turning his face to hers. Then her face is so close he thinks she means to kiss his lips like when he was a boy. But she only touches her forehead to his, her scarred nose to his own.

"I *love* you," she says. "I'm your mother, and I love you. That's all I mean to say. That most of all."

Moments like these, a corner of Michael's brain lights up. It's the corner that distrusts sentiment, that tells him not to fall for shit like this, that keeps him safe from emotional manipulation at all costs.

But not tonight. Tonight, that corner of his brain stays dark, and he has only to look into his mother's eyes to know that he is loved.

And any part of him that wants to dismiss this truth as childish is dwarfed not by the love that he returns—slender in comparison to hers—nor by the guilt he feels not sharing equal love, but by the certainty that to bring a child into the world is to surrender your happiness to someone else, to trust your heart to cavalier, unsteady hands.

To have a child is to ruin yourself, forever, in the name of love.

PART THREE

SUNDAY

23.

Lisa's seen the church but never been before today.

Lake Christopher First Baptist stands beyond the north side of the lake. The north side is the less developed side. No marina, no inn, older houses with fewer floors. The water on the northern end is shallow, the shoreline jagged, erosion beyond the reach of cost-effective land development. Poor to the north, rich to the south. This is how prestige lakes work. The rich want deep water, manicured shores, good lots. The locals are left with land the rich don't want, land they share with the water treatment plant, the power station, the county dump.

Beyond the lake, north on I-64 and down a dirt road, is the church, its gravel lot piled deep with cars.

All of these people, have they come as mourners or as spectators? Lisa would like to believe that *her* intentions are noble, but then, who doesn't believe the best of themselves?

This morning, she woke no longer sad but angry, furious with no good destination for her fury, a sure sign she could use some church. Let her meditate awhile in the house of God. Let her comfort a family whose hurt is far greater than her own.

She leaves her car and smooths her dress. Tan with a floral pattern, the outfit is among her least favorite. It blouses at the top and squeezes her waist, but it's modest, drab, appropriate for the tenor of the day. To wear black seemed bad luck, as the body has yet to be found.

She's late, and she squeezes between cars to cross the parking lot.

The church is white, two stories, with a peaked roof and a tin cross at the top. The siding is vinyl. Lisa doesn't know how to feel about a vinyl-sided church. Then again, vinyl is practical, long-lasting, cheap.

If God exists, if Jesus is God's son and if he said all he's meant to have said, then wouldn't God prefer vinyl to the Vatican? Save your gold leaf. Feed the poor. Amen.

Beyond the church, stones rise from the lawn like teeth erupting crooked from the mouths of children. The headstones are different heights and mineral shades, some tall, some small and crumbling. Toward the tree line, newer stones stand uniform in color and design.

If asked, Lisa couldn't say where she and Richard will be buried. She would have said the lake. Now she supposes they'll be laid to rest in Florida. Does Florida even inter their dead? That close to sea level, won't the buried rise and go out with the tide? There are mausoleums, of course, though Lisa hates the thought of bodies cupboarded aboveground, those card catalogs of corpses, each rotting in a box.

Maybe she won't be buried. Better, perhaps, to be burned. Let her ashes be scattered or kept on a mantel, she doesn't care. Let the living sort it out. What becomes of her remains is for their benefit, not hers. The rest is in writing, the DNR indisputable, the will signed, the money set: a third to Michael, a third to Thad, a third to the National Audubon Society. Let the boys decide the rest, which heirlooms to keep or sell or give away. Let them respect her wishes, or let them lament their failure to inherit every cent.

With June, she kept a onesie in a Ziploc bag. When she missed her daughter—which was often, many times a day—she opened the bag and breathed her daughter in. She has the outfit still, though the smell went out of it long ago. Even now, she can close her eyes and summon June's scent with a thought—the damp sweetness, like maple syrup strained through moss, or muffins lightly burnt.

June's body was donated to the Medical College of Georgia through the state anatomical board, so that future doctors might better understand SIDS. The right choice, though there are days Lisa wonders what became of June's remains, days she wishes there were a gravestone to visit or an urn to hold in her hand.

Lisa stands on the church steps. She checks her watch. She's very late.

She only means to crack the door, but it swings wide to let her in. A man in a gray suit shuts the door behind her. He wears thick glasses, and his head is mostly scalp, a few strands combed from one ear to the other. He smiles and offers her a bulletin from a stack beside the door. The front of the sheet is hymns, the back Bible verses, plus an outline for the service: *music, prayers, offering, a sermon by Pastor Lance, prayers, communion, music, closing prayers.* The order of worship is asterisked in places, and Lisa follows the asterisks to the bottom of the page where a note of explanation reads: *PLEASE RISE.* In Ithaca, the minister of the small interfaith church Lisa attends a couple of times a month will say, "Please stand as you'd like or as you're able," language Lisa always found pedantic, though now she understands. In faith, as in life, there are commands and there are invitations. She's left the land of invitations. She's entered a Southern Baptist church.

The church is not ornate, no choir loft or baptismal font, no mosaics or stained glass, just a red rug and wooden pews. The pews are full, every folding chair along the back wall taken too, so Lisa makes her way past the chairs to stand beside a woman leaning on a far wall. The woman smiles. She's young, early twenties. She wears a yellow dress, pearls around her neck.

The man at the front has been speaking since Lisa stepped inside. He stands at an amber-colored pulpit, a table to his left, a piano to his right. The wall behind the man is windowless. Where, in a different church, a window might be, a plaster crucifix depicts Christ at the apex of his agony, head back, eyes heavenward. Below the cross, and a little to the left, hangs an American flag.

Pastor Lance, at the pulpit, is tall and Ichabod-thin. He wears no robe or collar, no vestment or stole. He has on a black sport coat and, under this, a button-up, no tie. His shirt is white. His hair is short. He's handsome, young, too young to preach the word of God, Lisa thinks, but she's trying not to judge. Different region of the country, different brand of faith.

The woman who stands beside Lisa is in love with the man behind the pulpit. There's no mistaking it, the way she watches him, absent-mindedly running a hand over her pearls.

"Brothers and sisters," Pastor Lance says, and his voice croons more than booms. "Death is not the end. Death is the *door*."

He smiles, and Lisa's fingers tingle. The man's charisma is not due to his youth, but despite it.

"'*Behold, I stand at the door and knock.*' Then, what does Jesus say? '*If anyone hears my voice and opens the door, I will come in and eat with him, and he with me.*'"

Regardless of whether, beyond these walls, Pastor Lance is confident, the confidence he projects feels authentic. Regardless of whether he is wise, the wisdom feels unfeigned. He speaks, and Lisa understands how one so young has his own church.

"Let's think about that," Pastor Lance says. "Let's think about what it will be like to eat with Jesus. Good table manners will be important, I imagine."

He smiles again, and the congregation laughs. It is not a morning meant for laughter, but he's given them permission to feel joy. Gently, he's disarmed them with his words. He beams, and his eyes turn to the first pew. They rest there so long, Lisa has to look.

And there they are—Wendy, Glenn, and Trish. The father sits between his wife and daughter, an arm around each.

"Maybe you've met the Mallory family. They're new to Lake Christopher, but they've been here every week since April. Generous givers. Faithful Sunday school attendees. You always know Glenn's in a room by his laugh. And Wendy brought the tastiest peach pie I've ever had to our spring picnic on the lawn. Trish starts college at Duke this fall. Bright girl, very sharp."

Pastor Lance looks away. His eyes land on the woman at Lisa's side, and the woman nods, as if to say, *Go on*.

"And you might remember their son, Robbie," he says.

Robbie. How Wendy screamed the name, calling for her boy. It's a name Lisa will never again hear any other way.

"Always a ball of energy, that child," Pastor Lance says. "A bright spot on a dark day. Robbie was a *pistol*, as my father would put it. But the best kind of pistol there is. Not the kind that fires bullets. No. The kind that fires God's love."

Lisa fears the direction the sermon is taking, but Pastor Lance seems in no hurry to get where he's going.

"Brothers. Sisters. I'm going to share a hard truth with you today, and let me be clear that it gives me no pleasure doing so. What gives me pleasure is imagining the choice I hope *you'll* make. *Today.* A choice that, if you make it, will change the rest of your life."

He waits, as though the effort required to say what comes next is too great. He takes a breath, and Lisa has to look away. She hopes he will not say the thing she knows he'll say, and then he says it.

"The truth is this," he says. "Brothers. Sisters. Hell is real."

Lisa leans, and the wall holds her up. She looks to the woman at her side, but the woman seems unflustered. The usher at the door seems unflustered. The congregation doesn't stir or protest or speak, and, for all the bodies in the room, Lisa suddenly feels very much alone.

"'*I am the way, the truth, and the life, and no man comes to the Father but by me.*' Do you hear that, brothers and sisters? *No* man. Not you. Not me. Think of the best person you know. The kindest. The gentlest. Gives all his money to feed the poor. Not him either. Not unless he's repented of his sins and given his life to Jesus Christ."

Pastor Lance's hands leave the pulpit, and he steps out from behind it. His shirt, it turns out, is tucked into jeans, the jeans cinched to his waist by a brown weave belt, the kind Thad and Michael wore long, tails swinging from their fronts, when that was the elementary school trend. The pastor's belt does not hang. Nor does it match his shoes. He would stick out at Cornell. But she's being a snob. She's a Southern girl, born and raised. Here, this is how men dress.

"Is the way narrow?" Pastor Lance continues. "It is. But is the reward great? It is *indeed*. Which is why it is so important that we accept Jesus Christ as our personal Lord and Savior and give our lives to him. Because Jesus didn't say, 'No man comes to the Father except through

Buddha.' He didn't say, 'No man comes to the Father except through Vishnu.' He didn't say, 'No man comes to the Father except through *Zeus*.'"

The congregation chuckles, and Pastor Lance clasps his hands.

"No, we know better. We know what Jesus said. We have the book. We've been given the good news. We know how the story ends, and we know there's just one way."

Lisa leans and wonders, has this man read the Bible? Front to back? She has, and she has a few questions for him. She wants to ask which *Genesis* creation story he believes. She wants to ask about the sheep in other pens. She wants to ask what this man ate for breakfast and whether he washed his hands and whether the shirt he's wearing is a cotton-polyester blend.

Pastor Lance moves to the aisle, unclasps his hands, and grips the arm of the first pew. The Mallory family turns and, in profile, Lisa sees each face, the mother's tear-lined, the father's pained from holding back his tears, the daughter catatonic, as though she's been drugged.

"I don't know about our brother, Robbie," Pastor Lance says. "I don't know whether he's in heaven. I don't know because I don't know whether he had that personal relationship with Jesus Christ. That sounds like an awful thing to say, I know, and I was hesitant to say it. But this morning, Marcy—" He gestures, and there's no mistaking that the woman at Lisa's side is this man's wife. "Marcy and I were talking, and I said, 'Marcy, a terrible thing has happened, but *darn it* if we can't use this to bring people to Jesus. If we keep even one soul out of hell, just one, then that boy's death will not have been in vain.' Isn't that right, honey?"

Marcy nods, and her smile is sympathetic, genuine.

Lisa's trembling. The church is warm with bodies, with air-conditioning that can't keep up with the summer day, but Lisa's never felt so cold.

"I'd like to think that Robbie's not in hell," Pastor Lance says, "but that's between Robbie and God. That choice is made. All I know, all any of us know, is that *we* still have a choice. Each of us, the living. We have the choice to side with the Prince of Darkness or the Prince of Peace. The chance to open the door or slam the door in Christ's loving face."

The pastor surveys the congregation, letting his gaze drift, so that his eyes seem to land on every face, then lift.

"This life is an election, and your soul's your vote. Now tell me, brothers and sisters, would you rather vote for heaven or for hell?"

Robbie's father's face contorts. His head drops, and Pastor Lance reaches past Wendy to put a hand on the man's shoulder. The shoulder shakes. Glenn's arms untwine from his wife and daughter, and he slides, knees-first, to the floor, head bowed in prayer.

Lisa can't take any more. She follows the wall the way she came, past folding chairs and the people who fill them. The man who let her in blocks the door. He doesn't mean to block it. He's rapt. Like the rest of them, he stares, hypnotized, ahead, whether from fear of hell or hope for heaven, Lisa can't say.

"Excuse me," she whispers.

"Now, some of you may be wondering what hell is like," Pastor Lance says. "Whether there's actually a lake of fire. Whether the darkness is eternal or just until the sin is burned away."

Lisa taps the man's shoulder.

" 'How,' you might ask, 'can hell be on fire and still be dark? And just what *is* a *gnashing* of teeth?' "

Pastor Lance bares his teeth—pristine, orthodontist-straight— and grinds them side to side, his face a mask of puzzled wonderment.

Another chuckle from the congregants.

"You laugh," he says. "But hell is no joke. Hell is real, and it is forever."

"Please," Lisa says.

"Picture the thing you're most afraid of," Pastor Lance says. He leaves the family's side, leaves Glenn praying on the floor, and returns to his place behind the pulpit. "Maybe it's needles or spiders. Maybe it's snakes. Maybe what you're most afraid of is waking up one day to find that everyone you love is gone. I want you to think about that for a second. Let that fear sink in. Now imagine that fear multiplied by—"

"Excuse me!" She screams it. There's a hush, and the pastor's words fall off a cliff. Then everyone is watching her: the congregation, Pastor Lance, the man at the door, the family of the boy.

Wendy, I'm so sorry.

"I'm sorry for your loss," Lisa says, then she's out the door and down the stairs. Her flats touch the gravel lot, and she sits on the bottom step to catch her breath. Then stands. Let her catch her breath in the car. Let her get away from here as quickly as she can.

But there is a voice at her back. "Wait," the voice calls, "please," and Lisa turns.

It's the wife of Pastor Lance. She's shorter than Lisa, but she stands on the bottom step so that they are eye-to-eye. The hem of her dress sways at her ankles, and her face is pinched in unashamed concern.

"I'm Marcy," she says. "I'm Pastor Lance's wife."

It's not too late to turn and walk away, but Lisa feels compelled to give her name.

"Lisa."

Marcy smiles. "It's nice to meet you, Lisa. I haven't seen you here before. You heard about the drowning?"

Lisa nods. She won't say she was there. She won't give Marcy a reason to give her a hug. Let Marcy's sympathy extend to those who need it, those heaped on the front pew hearing how hell is fire and spiders, how their only son might be there even now.

"I know it's hard to hear," Marcy says. "Which part upset you?"

"All of it. All of it upsets me. Watching a church exploit a tragedy. Watching a family in need of compassion get threats of hell."

Marcy looks past Lisa to the graveyard. She looks so long, Lisa's tempted to walk away.

"You don't believe in hell, do you?" Marcy says.

"I don't. I never have."

For Lisa, hell is an appendix. Perhaps, long ago, it was essential to the evolution of some religions. But hell has long outlived its usefulness. When it comes to faith, hell is a rotting organ waiting to be excised.

"I'm sorry," Marcy says, "but hell is in the Bible."

"As are rape, incest, genocide ordained by God."

Marcy nods. "It's a difficult book. But without the Bible, what's your source of authority? How do you know good from evil? How do you communicate with God?"

"Reason," Lisa says. "Faith and prayer too, but let's not forget God gave humans brains. Why have logic at our disposal if not to figure things out on our own? As for good and evil, you don't need a book to tell you which is which."

"You don't put your faith in scripture, then?"

"I put my faith in intuition," Lisa says. "I put my faith in the fact that a book written millennia ago, then assembled by hundreds of men over hundreds of years, is bound to suffer from some flaws. Some cruelties. Some inconsistencies. Men have agendas. Churches retract things all the time. We change our minds. So does God."

"God can't change His mind," Marcy says.

"Can't or won't?"

"Doesn't," Marcy says, but her face says she isn't sure.

"If God doesn't change God's mind, what's the point of prayer? Why did Jacob wrestle the angel? Why petition a deity whose decisions are already made?"

Marcy leaves the church step with a gravel crunch. She looks up to meet Lisa's eyes.

"We pray," Marcy says, "because God likes us thinking about Him. It brings Him pleasure to hear from us."

"Maybe," Lisa says. "Or maybe God's not that needy."

Marcy's quiet after that. This girl a third her age, what does she know about loss? About the strength it takes to love God when the person you love most in this world is taken from you?

"Do you have children?" Lisa asks.

Marcy's head tips to one side like a dog angling its ears to hear, and there's a smile on her face that she can't hide. "Second trimester. The doctor said I should start showing any week."

"Congratulations," Lisa says.

"You were going to say that having a child will change my mind about God. About hell."

"I was," Lisa says. "You're about to learn what real love is. That sounds condescending, but I don't mean it to be. It's just, you're young. You think you know what love is, and you don't. But you will."

A bird alights on the stair railing at Marcy's back, a flycatcher, judging by the bill, but Lisa doesn't have time to ID the species before it takes off.

"I know what love is," Marcy says. So far her tone has been measured, calm, but now it's turned defensive, hurt.

"In six months, chambers are going to open in your heart, rooms you never knew were there. When they do, you'll know there's no hell. There can't be. Because God would never send a child there."

Marcy's voice, when she speaks, has regained its footing. "For God to love us with a perfect love, He has to let us choose. Humans want everyone to go to heaven, but that's because we're fallen. God knows better. His love is just. Our love is imperfect."

"Imperfect love?" Lisa says. "There's no such thing."

Politely, Marcy shakes her head. "Our job is not to question God. God made us. God can do with us as He sees fit."

It's no use. Lisa's too late. This girl, her mind's made up, chiseled by a thousand Sunday mornings, a thousand rounds of Sunday school. Marcy has her Bible, her church, her verses quivered, ready for the bow. All Lisa has is life.

The bird is back. It lands on the top step. It's an Acadian flycatcher, common, olive and yellow and white, with a song like it's screaming for pizza. The Acadian can hover, fly backward, even. Great bird. It hops once, twice beside the church door, then it's gone.

Next week, June would have been thirty-five. Lisa can almost feel June with her, watching her.

What are you doing? June asks. Her hair is long. Her eyes are alabaster. She gestures at Marcy, then moves to stand at Marcy's side. *All this unpleasantness. Is this for me?*

She's right.

"Boy or girl?" Lisa says.

Marcy hesitates.

It's okay, Lisa wants to say. *It's not a trap.*

"We're waiting to find out," Marcy says. "But if I'm being honest, I hope it's a girl. I know that's terrible to say, and I'll be happy with whatever God gives us. I just can't help wanting a girl."

A song escapes the church, the sound of the piano being played.

"I'd like you to do something for me," Lisa says. "When the service is over, I want you to find Wendy, and I want you to tell her that her son is not in hell."

The piano plays. The sun beats down. A truck rattles down the main road between towns.

"I can't do that," Marcy says. "I don't know if it's true."

"It's true. That's a mother in there. Two days ago, she lost her son. Imagine, God forbid, but imagine what you'd need to hear if that were you."

"Me?" Marcy says. She pulls at her pearls as though the strand has tightened around her neck.

"If your child died," Lisa says, but sees too late she's gone too far. This isn't helping Wendy. It won't bring back June. She's taunting a pregnant woman in front of a church, trying to change a mind that won't be changed.

"I think you should leave," Marcy says. Lisa wants to believe that she's heard wrong, but she has not. "You contradict the teachings of the Bible, you challenge my husband's message, you haven't been particularly nice to me, and now you talk about my child dying?"

When June died, Lisa received visits from friends and neighbors, mothers who wanted to share their same, sad stories. They used up Lisa's Kleenex, crushed her hand, then left, more at peace with their own losses, happy for the difference they were sure they'd made in Lisa's life.

Today, Lisa meant to tell Robbie's mother about June, to promise her that she is not alone. If nothing else, Marcy has saved Wendy from this, for when is shared loss ever a comfort? When, in one's darkest, soul-fucked moments, is it helpful knowing others suffer too? Better to leave Wendy to her family, her grief.

Lisa watches Marcy, but she's done arguing. She turns to go, but there's one last thing she wants to say, and she turns back.

"I hope you get your wish," Lisa says.

"What wish?" Marcy says.

"I hope that it's a girl."

24.

Jake's never seen a gallery outside of New York.

There must have been galleries in Tennessee, though his father never would have taken him to one. As a child, Jake rarely saw art outside of books, and he didn't set foot in a museum until the school trip to the Memphis Brooks Museum of Art. The other sixth graders jostled and postured, bored with what hung on the walls. Jake tried to ignore the walls, but every room lit him up until he could no longer pretend and stood, instead, searching painting after painting, for what made each so beautiful. He wanted to weep. He was twelve years old, and he was home.

"Which painting flipped the switch?" *Artforum* would ask, years later.

That was easy: Margaret Keane, *Waiting*, 1962, a gorgeous painting full of indigos and blues. A woman, framed by violet shutters and white curtains, leans out an open window. Behind her, the house is dark, but beyond the house is day. Her hair is brown, up in a bun but loose at the sides, framing her face. So many frames: the hair, the curtains, the shutters, the window frame. She's trapped. She's tired. Why, though, does she stand at the window looking sad? What is it that this woman's waiting for?

The painting made Jake think of his mother. She was often sad, often tired, beautiful in a way that perhaps Jake's father couldn't see.

Jake learned that day that every painting tells two stories: the story the painter gives you, and the story you bring to what the painter paints. And both are valid. In their brushstrokes, composition, balance, both are true.

Of course, that's only true of *art*. What hangs before Jake in the sprawling Asheville gallery is not art. The gallery is not even a proper gallery, and, in his velvet coat, he feels silly, overdressed.

What gets him first is the floor. It is not marble or tile or refinished wood. It is wall-to-wall Berber, the dark-flecked, soulless kind that carpets elementary school classrooms. This is a floor installed for Wine Night Wednesdays, a color picked for hiding spills. The second thing that gets him is the glare. Too much track lighting. Too much glass. Shadows take odd shapes and interrupt the paintings on the walls. Then there are the walls themselves, paintings saturating every inch of real estate, walls so crowded Jake doesn't know where to look first.

The first room is a floral tantrum, tulips in planters and roses in jugs. The flowers aren't even interesting. No Dalis or O'Keeffe close-ups here, merely arrangements, still lifes from America's most ordinary homes. The paintings have the look of bad photographs transferred to canvas with pastels, which perhaps they are.

The second room is landscapes. One catches his eye, a log vaulting a river at an angle that almost lowers Jake into the painting. He likes the composition, except for the chipmunk the painter's dropped into the foreground, cheeks stuffed for winter, cartoonish with its buckteeth and tucked arms. The rest is dreck: meadows, rivers, a forest glen, light filtered through the trees. Why must light always fight its way, in paintings, through tree branches and clouds? Boring, boring, boring. He surveys the room once more, but nothing here is lovely. Nothing is sincere. They are paintings of paintings, the Kinkades and Bob Rosses of the amateur painter set.

He checks the prices. The largest—a seascape, 36 by 48—is two thousand. A painting that size, in Frank's gallery, might fetch fifty times as much. But a painting that size would take Jake weeks. This seascape was painted in a day.

Jake went to some trouble to be here: rented a car when Thad said he'd need their rental for the day, drove the hour back to Asheville, then tracked down what he thought would be a gallery but turns out to be the art equivalent of an antiques mall, painters renting rooms and stocking them with their wares. At the entrance, he ran into a woman changing out *her own show*, another thing he's never seen before. He asked where he might find Marco, and she pointed to the back, past the flower madness, through the landscapes, and beyond a series of interconnected rooms.

The next room turns out to be photography. The prints are sepia, mostly, and the person behind the camera feels *very* strongly about the rule of thirds. There are the obligatory beaches at sunset. There are children with balloons. There is a mouse perched on the forehead of a cat. Motivational posters, most of them, minus the accompanying captions underneath.

Jake walks on. The gallery is long, a nineteenth-century shotgun house reinvented for commerce, and the final showroom, when Jake reaches the very back, is Marco's. The paintings, here, are coming down, others going up. But it isn't Marco he finds at the center of the room. It's Amelia surrounded by brown boxes and packing materials. She holds a small framed painting, a falcon with its talons around a snake. Seeing Jake, she sets the painting on the floor with the exaggerated care of someone who's been scolded for being careless in the past. From the wall at her back, a grumpy-looking seagull watches Jake, its bill crimson-spotted, wings spread for flight.

"I never got my chance with you," she says.

Jake takes a step back. "I'm gay, Amelia."

"Marco said the same thing when we met."

She's so young. Sexually, Marco will teach her everything he knows, then, once she's good and in love with him, he'll leave. Jake knows because he's been there. She's the new Jake.

Around the room, birds eye him: cardinals, jays, a pair of ducks navigating a stretch of pond. They're Audubons, all of them. They're Audubons without quite being Audubons.

A box of paper rests on the floor, and Amelia sits and wraps the falcon painting in it. A corner pokes through, and she gives the frame a second wrap. The paper is thin, newsprint-gray, and looks nothing like the paper Frank's assistants use.

"Is that paper acid-free?" Jake asks.

Amelia eyes him from the floor. "Is Marco expecting you?"

"No."

She slides the wrapped painting into a cardboard box. The box overflows with balled up paper, and she pushes the paper down. Then, with packing tape, she seals the box shut. Wrong. All wrong. Bad for the canvas. Bad for the frame.

"He's out back," Amelia says. "He's stressed. Mel wants everything up by noon, even though it's Sunday and no one comes in on Sundays until two at the earliest."

"Mel?"

"Mel Gleason. The owner. You have to meet him. He's the best."

Jake doesn't have the patience to explain the gulf between this world and his own. What's more, explaining it would make him an asshole. Let Amelia believe her boyfriend's a star. Let her think Marco and Mel are names people should know.

"How long has Marco done the birds?" he asks.

"As long as I've known him." She's removed a robin from the wall. She's on the floor, more paper, more cardboard flaps and tape. "They sell better than anything he's ever done, so that's what all of his shows are these days: birds."

Jake imagines Thad's imaginary book of poetry and wonders which bird would be right for the cover.

"Tourists love the birds," Amelia says. "Locals, too. One guy, he's got seventeen. He keeps inviting us to dinner to see how he's displayed them, but Marco never wants to go. He says there's a bridge between a painter and a customer that must never be crossed."

Today is a mistake. Jake came to see Marco's art, to see if it's evolved, and now he's seen it hasn't. He should go.

"You're not impressed," Amelia says. "You're thinking Audubon, right? You're thinking Marco ripped him off."

Jake surveys the walls.

Amelia stands. "See, Audubon didn't work from live birds either. He worked from taxidermies. Audubon's paintings were paintings of *sculptures* of birds. Marco's birds are *paintings of paintings* of sculptures of birds. Three removes from the animal itself. What does Marco call it? A *meta-commentary*. By mimicking Audubon, he comments on Audubon's style."

Jake has to look away from Amelia to keep from laughing. He can't decide whether this line of reasoning sounds more like a bad undergrad art theory paper or something Frank might say to move some paint. Then, of course, there's the fact that the meta element isn't what's making these things sell. People buy them for the pretty birds.

"You should see his latest," Amelia says. "Marco's branched out. The new ones are all pairs. Some have chicks. My favorite is the blue jays. They're here somewhere. They've got this worm. I think they'd be perfect for Thad's book."

"There's no book."

Amelia crosses her arms. She looks confused. The floor, where she stands, is a minefield of mats and frames, paper bunched into balls.

"Thad and I were fighting," he says.

"I gathered."

"And you and Marco got caught in the cross fire. The made-up book was part of that. I mean, Thad writes poems, but he's only published a few. Plus, birds are his mother's thing. If he had a book, I don't think it would be about birds."

"If he had a book, what would it be about?"

"I don't even know." It hurts, saying this, because it's true.

"Well, what are the poems about?"

He should be able to say. But he can't seem to remember the subject of a single poem. He can't conjure an image or a title, a catchy line.

"They must be bad," Amelia says.

"What makes you say that?"

"Good poems aren't easy to forget."

That can't be true. Thad's poems are good. Jake's been told they're good. They've been in magazines. Not magazine-magazines, but journals, quarterlies. Something out of Montana. The *Something Something Review*. Thad was proud of that one. But if the poems are so good, why can't Jake remember even one?

Oh, God. Is Jake *Amelia*, oblivious, his boyfriend a hack? Or is Jake's head so far up his own ass he can't see Thad's poetry for what it is? Is Thad a shitty poet, or is Jake a shitty boyfriend?

He can't decide, and now is not the time, because now Marco's in the room.

"Jacob," Marco says. His eyes shine, but his hair is uncombed. His clothes are clothes for tearing down and setting up a space, paint-stained shorts and an old T-shirt, collar stretched to Marco's chest. He asks Amelia to give them a minute, and, on tiptoes, she kisses Marco's cheek. Then she hugs Jake.

"It was fun meeting someone famous," she says.

Jake wants to protest, but before he can get a word out, Amelia's raised a hand to his coat. She rubs the crushed velvet, elbow to cuff, then cuff to elbow, the material darkening, then brightening, under the harsh gallery lights.

"You think we don't know the difference between what we have here and what you have in New York," she says. "But we do. You made your point. You rubbed his face in it."

"Amelia," Marco says.

Jake has no words. He underestimated her. He's underestimated them both.

"I just have to ask," Amelia says. "Your boyfriend, does he come to your openings?"

He does. Dresses nicely, and always knows the perfect thing to say to Frank, or to a buyer, or to a painter Jake's enamored with. Thad's always there, always gently teasing him about his coat.

"All of them," Jake says.

"I thought so," Amelia says. "He seems really, really nice."

Then she's gone.

"Sorry about that," Marco says. "She's not herself today."

He moves around the room. With far less care than Amelia, he pulls five paintings from the wall. The clatter of frames makes Jake wince. Marco piles the paintings on the floor, and, kneeling, opens an unlabeled cardboard box. He wraps the paintings quickly, without fanfare.

"You could have called," Marco says.

"I thought if I called, you'd tell me not to come."

The bird in Marco's hands, Jake thinks it's called a spoonbill, feathers pink, beak ladle-shaped. Five minutes ago, he wanted nothing more than to be rid of these people, be gone from this place. But seeing Marco on his knees, boxing birds, he feels a rush of sympathy, urgent and intense.

"I can help you," Jake says. "I saw your old work, the slaughter-house, the pigs. You have talent, but that talent's wasted here. If you moved back—"

"Fuck you."

Marco sets the spoonbill down. He stands and moves to the far side of the room. There are three paintings left hanging, and all three come down. "I have *talent*? You arrogant prick. You think I don't know that? You think I've been waiting half a decade for Jacob Percival Russell to tell me that?"

"I only—"

"Here's how this ends, Jake. You're going to have a bad show. Maybe not the next show. Or the next. But somewhere down the line, some critic will decide they've had enough of you. *Your work's become derivative*, they'll say, *a parody of itself*. A second critic will echo that critic, then another, until there's a consensus and you're done."

Marco grabs the spoonbill, wraps it, and stuffs it in the box. He tapes the box shut.

"Best-case scenario? When you're seventy, someone floats a 'forgotten masters' puff piece in the *Times*. Your name gets dropped, but so do twenty others. One of those names ends up in lights, and, if it's yours, people buy your work again. But let's not kid ourselves. We both know your name won't be the one that's called. Because it's not about the art.

It's about the artist. And what are you? You're white, you're cis, you're upper-class, you're male. You're not what the art world needs right now. Fifty years from now, they'll need you even less."

Marco wraps the last three paintings. He's out of boxes, and he leans the frames against the wall. He won't look at Jake. He's said too much, or else he hasn't said enough.

"Ask Frank to show you a list of his clients sometime," Marco says. "Ask to see the past thirty years. See how few names you recognize, and you'll see just how ruthless this business is. Maybe then you'll wonder what's so wrong with picking a city you love, settling down, and making work that sells. Because, trust me, in twenty years, when you're broke, when you don't know where to go, when people are cracking jokes that *Jake Russell* sounds like a fucking dog breed, I'll still be here, happy, painting birds."

Marco straightens. He stares at Jake.

"*I have talent*. Fuck you."

Jake loved this man. He loves him still. He wants to hug him, wants to hit him.

"Paint your birds," Jake says. "But make real art too."

"*Real art.*"

"I didn't mean—"

"It's fine. You can't help it. It's who you are. But here's the truth. I've *tried*. I've tried, and I can't paint that way anymore. Whatever dreamland I was in at twenty, I can't find my way back to that place. I don't expect you to understand."

Jake wants to say he understands, that he hasn't worked a paintbrush in months, but that shame is private. If too intimate to share with Thad, it's certainly too intimate for Marco.

Marco stacks sealed boxes against one wall and begins unpacking boxes of new work. He unwraps a painting and hands it to Jake. A pair of robins watch Jake from a nest.

Marco unwraps more and hangs them on the wall. The paintings are uniform, same frames, same size, which makes it easy, putting up a show. Marco gestures, and Jake hangs the robins on a hook.

"Is it that hard to believe I'm happy?" Marco asks.

It is. Because Jake would not be happy. He'd rather take Michael's route. He'd rather sell men's shoes than make bad art. At least that would be honest work. But this, this gallery, these paintings on the wall, nothing about this strikes Jake as honest.

"I thought you'd be different," Marco says. "When I reached out, I thought we'd have both grown up, calmed down. But you're still the little boy in the black jacket who thinks he's better than everybody else. It must kill you, knowing I don't envy what you have."

Jake moves to touch him, and Marco pushes his hand away.

All around them, the birds seem to flutter, come to life, warble and hum, wingbeat and song.

"Look at you," Marco says. "How Thad puts up with you, I'll never know."

Jake rests his hands on Marco's shoulders, and Marco lets himself be touched. Then Marco does the same, Jake's shoulders in his hands.

They don't hug. They'll never hug again. They're wrestlers, swaying, weary from the fight. Their foreheads touch, and there's no love in it. Still, they stand that way a long, long time.

25

Tackle fills the kitchen table. Hooks and spinners, floats and lures, swivels and sinkers and weights. This morning, when Richard set out to tidy and consolidate his tackle, he hadn't realized just how much he had. Even once he's inserted the extra table leaf, there isn't enough surface to spread out all of his gear.

Wastebasket beside him, Richard tosses what he can into the trash. A pink jig with half a hook. A cracked rattletrap. A spinnerbait minus skirt and blades.

Amazing, the merchandise a person can amass in thirty years. Richard's father would be disgusted. Growing up with little, Richard was raised to look down on the type of person he's become: elitist, academic, upper middle class—someone who has more than he needs, who, most days, fails to appreciate all he has. There are more lures here than he'll use in this lifetime, more Florida potboilers in the garage than he can read before he's dead.

His sons are the same.

Every Christmas Michael shows up with the latest, most expensive phone. Meanwhile he can't pay his bills and asks Richard to write another check.

Thad, at least, is frugal, his accumulation contained to the books and comics he can afford. There's a passion attached to these purchases, and Richard hopes that lasts, hopes books make Thad happy the rest of his life. As a boy, Thad had trouble sticking to one thing. First he liked to draw. Then it was sports, football and baseball. By high school it was theater, then music. He had a band—what was the name of it? Thad played the keyboard, the most dispensable of high school garage band instruments, and sure enough, within a year the band had dispensed with him.

Richard throws out more rusty lures, a hook without a barb.

Diane joins him from the kitchen, and Richard clears a place for her to set her plate, the sandwich she's made herself for lunch.

"They're beautiful," Diane says, running a finger over the exaggerated eyes of a Hula Popper. In all the years she's joined them on the lake, she's never accompanied Richard fishing.

"Where'd everyone run off to?" Richard asks. Sleeping late, he was surprised to wake to a half-empty house.

"Michael went to Highlands. Lisa's at church. Jake left early, not sure where, but Thad wouldn't let him take their car, so he got a rental. Not sure what that's about. I didn't even know we *had* Enterprise out here. If you're heading into town, there's Thad's car. I can't tell if he's not sharing or just not sharing with Jake."

"That's all right," Richard says. "A day at the lake will be nice."

Beyond the window, the boats are gone, sun up, the water like glass. This is the bay he remembers. This is the lake he loves.

Then Thad is with them. The coffeepot's gone cold, but he pours what's left into a mug and microwaves the mug. He asks where everybody's gone, Diane gives him the same spiel she gave Richard, and he joins them at the table. He sips his coffee and pokes at a silver spoon lure, its surface scored like the handles of a walnut cracker.

"Careful, Son," Richard says, then feels bad. All this time, he's let Diane browse the tackle, undisturbed. He tries not to do this, to treat his sons' partners with more respect than he treats his sons, but it's hard not to, the way his sons behave at times, the questionable choices they make. He loves them, fully, unconditionally. But respect comes harder than love.

"I think Mom threw my comics out," Thad says.

"I'm sure they'll turn up," Richard says. "Hand me that float."

Thad slides a red bobber across the table. "The boxes were white cardboard. Long ones, a few hundred comics in each. Some were pretty valuable."

"Hey," Richard says, "how about a joke?"

His son's not stupid. It won't be lost on him that his old man's changing the subject. Still, Richard draws from his dusty arsenal of well-worn jokes.

"What's the difference between a hippo and a Zippo?"

"I don't know," Diane says. "What's the difference?"

"One's heavy, and one's a little lighter."

Diane laughs appreciatively. Thad's heard the joke before. He's heard all of Richard's jokes before.

"That band you were in," Richard says, "what was it called?"

"You were in a band?" Diane asks.

"Dad's using the word *band* pretty liberally," Thad says. "More like five high school guys and a garage. We did some Weezer, some Blink-182, a lot of Green Day. This was 2004, so we knew *American Idiot* inside and out."

"But the band name," Richard says.

"Inadequate Grass," Thad says.

"That's it. That's the name."

"You remember the computer game?" Thad asks Diane. "*Oregon Trail*?"

"Sure," Diane says. "'*Little Timmy has died of typhoid.*'"

"Exactly. You'd be on the trail, there'd be a drought, and your oxen would die from '*Inadequate Grass.*'"

Richard isn't following any of this. He's trying to remember if he's ever even played a video game.

"We had T-shirts, too," Thad says. "Name on the front, a pot leaf on the back. We thought we were so edgy. *We* couldn't wear them, since you aren't supposed to wear the shirt of the band you're in, so we tried to sell them. We did a few gigs, battles of the bands. We dragged that box of shirts to every show and never sold a single one." He turns to Richard. "Maybe that box of shirts is around here too. In the garage. With my comic books."

The table cleared of damaged gear, Richard files bobbers and lures into the trays of his tackle box.

"I believe I'll go fishing this afternoon," he announces.

"I'm off to Nico's," Thad says.

Diane says nothing, and Richard hates picturing her left alone with her sandwich. He wishes he knew why she and Michael are at odds. He wishes he knew how to help.

"If you'd like to come with me . . . ?" he says.

The invitation isn't insincere, but Diane waves it away, and he wonders if she thinks it was. Or perhaps she'd rather have some time to herself. He's not the best conversationalist.

Diane eats her sandwich. Thad goes to his room. Richard stands.

The wastebasket beside him is filled with broken things, gouged Styrofoam floats, bent hooks, lures too rusty to attract fish. The tackle box, when he picks it up, is lighter, packed only with what might still be of use.

26.

Highlands doesn't have a good bar, let alone a good dive bar, and nothing like the loud, dark-cornered bars back home. Days off, or after work, Michael's butt has warmed the stools of every Dallas–Fort Worth bar there is. He pays cash so Diane can't track his movements on the credit cards, though she has been known to ask him why so many ATM withdrawals.

There was one place in Highlands last year. Decent. Cheap. Henry's, maybe? Harry's? Something with an *H*. Or else a *W*. Willy's? He's not sure. He had moonshine this morning, before he left the house, and he's having trouble combing through his thoughts.

He passes Nico's and pulls onto Main Street, a three-block strip of boutique shops and cafés. He turns onto a side street and parallel parks his Hyundai between a new model Mercedes and a stately Lincoln Town Car. The people who live here have money. He checks his wallet—he has enough cash for three drinks, maybe four—then he's out of the car and looking for Henry's. Or Willy's. Any bar will do.

Church bells sing out eleven o'clock. Fuck him, it's Sunday. State blue laws mean he has an hour to kill, assuming he can even find a place that serves on Sundays. Blood floods his hands, his face, adrenaline at the thought he might not get his liquor. Which is pathetic. It's not like he doesn't know how pathetic that is.

He'll stop drinking soon.

He can't stop. Half a day, and his hands shake. Next come the headaches, cold sweats, stomachaches and cramps.

He hurries down the sidewalk, checking every awning, every window for signs of alcohol. The day is overcast, like the sky wants to rain again but can't. The street isn't yet bustling, most people are at church or waiting for places to open up. Ahead, an older woman guides her Chihuahua into a purveyor of gluten-free dog treats.

Michael stops in at two brunch places, thinking of mimosas, but both give him the same answer—no alcohol before noon—and he walks on.

He passes the bakery, the coffeehouse that has a different name each year, the old theater that's been a storefront for at least five businesses since Michael was a kid. Still, the frontage is the same, the Galaxy logo where the single-screen movie theater used to be, the missing *G*, letters rusted red. Spines erupt from each letter's peak—pigeon repellant—and Michael can't help wondering whether a bird's ever been skewered, and whose job it was to clean up the mess.

He passes the Highlands Fine Art Gallery, then doubles back. The window is wide. It drips, recently squeegeed. Inside, brightly colored canvases interrupt the walls. He can't tell if they're any good. He doesn't understand abstract art. He likes Jake's stuff all right. Jake doesn't just splash a canvas and call it art. His paintings may not make sense, but at least the objects in them look like objects from real life. At least there's skill involved.

Once, Michael asked Jake what the painting he made for the lake house meant, but Jake only laughed at him. "What does it *mean?*" he asked. "What do your shoes mean? What's the meaning of the sun?" Michael wanted to argue that such meanings were self-evident. Shoes protect your feet. The sun's essential to life on earth. But Michael had already learned his lesson. No matter how nice Jake seems, no matter the gifts or cash he throws around, no matter his upbringing or how much he's overcome, Thad's boyfriend is still a dick.

Plus, Jake's never given Diane his time or professional counsel as an artist, never asked to see her work, and Diane, all this time, has been too shy to ask. Jake knows she sculpts, she paints, and he couldn't act less interested.

Fuck Jake. Michael will do something nice for Diane. A present. Something that says, *Please don't divorce me. I'm sorry. I'm scared.*

The gallery is open, and he goes in. He may not know what's

good, but he knows what his wife likes. Given a dozen paintings, he could pick the one that best matches the work hanging on their walls, none of which is Diane's, a fact Michael finds bewildering. *Artists don't display their own work, they sell it*, his wife says. Never mind that no one's buying, that their spare bedroom's packed with Diane's paintings, vases, pots.

The gallery is wide, Pac-Manned with low, freestanding walls like office cubicles, a labyrinth of art. Michael hears voices and follows them to the middle of the maze where a man and woman stand, talking. The man is older, gray hair, gray suit. The woman's middle-aged, enormous glasses balanced on her nose. Her hair is bobbed, her forehead bangs. What is it about turning forty that makes every woman cut her hair so short?

The man holds a framed painting, and the woman examines it. The painting depicts the northern lights over a mountain range, and it's beautiful. Michael's shocked, actually, to find such beauty in this place. The woman moves toward the painting until her face is inches from the canvas, then backs away. She pushes her glasses up the bridge of her nose.

"Original," she asks, "or—" then she says something that sounds to Michael like *g-clay*.

"It's a g-clay," the man says.

Michael half expects the guy to call her *madam*. He must be the owner or curator, or whatever you call the person who runs a gallery. He wears glasses of his own, lenses nickel-rimmed and round. He gives Michael's presence no acknowledgment. Neither of them do.

The woman stares at the painting awhile longer. Everything about the man's posture, the expression on his face, says he's not a man who's used to holding paintings, but that for this customer he makes an exception.

"I was hoping for an original, not a g-clay," she says.

Michael really needs these people to stop saying *g-clay*.

"It's a fine print," the man says.

So *g-clay* means *print*? Why not say *print*? Is there something special about a g-clay, or does it just make buyers feel special saying it?

"I assure you," the man says. "This g-clay is number four of fifty. Very limited."

Say the word again, and Michael will g-*clay* the nearest canvas with his fist.

"The only *original* in this series," the man says, "is the Reykjavík."

Michael's turned to leave, but *Reykjavík* turns him around. *Reykjavík* is a word he knows. It is the capital of Iceland. He knows this because Diane has always said she'd like to go.

Michael turns back, and the man holds up a painting of Iceland's capital at night. The image is mostly grays and greens, a little dull, a little rushed-looking compared to the print.

The woman brings a hand to her cheek. Her thumb worries her ear. "I prefer the g-clay. But I'd love to have an original. I'd take both, except we're running out of room. I never should have had that kitchen wall knocked down."

Michael doesn't mean to laugh. They turn.

"I'll be with you shortly," the man says.

The woman looks away. "I'll have to think about this. Can you hold them for me?"

"Absolutely," the man says. "Just remember, twenty-four hours."

"Of course. I won't make that mistake again."

It's only once the man has returned the painting to the wall and escorted the woman slowly, talkatively, out, that Michael sees the painting he wants. It's neither of the paintings the woman's put on reserve. It's a landscape. Nothing grand, which is good. Diane doesn't do grand. She prefers understated, would have, for example, preferred a smaller house. She'd love the landscape on the wall. A black road runs between green hills, blue sky above, not one cloud creeping in.

He has to have it. A painting can't rewrite the past two months, but it's something. This painting says *I know you deserve better, and I'll try harder to deserve your love.* And, if this painting doesn't say that, at least it says *I care. I pay attention. I know what you like.*

"I noticed you admiring this one."

The man is back. His jacket pocket, Michael's just noticed, sports a yellow pocket square. Michael wears sneakers, jeans, and a T-shirt, and feels, suddenly, very underdressed.

"Your head," the man says, looking for all the world like someone who speaks with an English accent, someone whose name should be *Gerald*.

"My horse," Michael says, trying on his best English accent. Fuck it. He'll never see this guy again.

"Your . . . horse?"

"He has a mighty kick," Michael says, his voice as British as he can get it.

"Oh dear."

"It's all right," Michael says. "You should see what I did to the horse."

The man's eyes widen, and Michael moves closer to the landscape that Diane would like.

"This is Iceland too?" Michael asks.

The man nods.

"I thought so. The wife and I were driving through the Icelandic countryside this spring, and I'm quite certain we passed these very hills."

He clears his throat. The man brightens. Perhaps he disbelieves the accent, the story of the horse, but he believes in Michael's money, and that's enough.

"It's a lovely print," the man says. "My favorite in the series."

Michael is confused. He looks closer. The landscape looks like a painting to him. "This isn't a painting?"

"It's a g-clay."

"I'm sorry," Michael says. "I don't believe we have those in London."

"My apologies," the man says, spelling out the word. "The *giclée* process is the best high-resolution inkjet reproduction method there is. Better than screen printing. Better than lasers."

How badly he wants to run a finger over the canvas, just to feel. "This isn't paint?"

"It's ink, but pigment-based. No dyes. And light-fast, a fifty-year guarantee against fading. Better than paint, really. It won't chip, won't crack, won't craze. Why, would you believe that some insects have been known to eat paint?"

"Except the artist didn't *paint* this," Michael says.

"The artist painted this landscape, yes."

"But the artist didn't paint *this one*."

The gallery owner appears put out. How many times a week does he have this talk? How often must he defend the work he sells?

"The artist didn't paint *this one*," the man says, "but he signed and numbered it. The signature—his signature is paint."

"The kind of paint that insects eat?"

The owner studies his wingtips, and already Michael can see it: Michael is the story this man will tell his spouse tonight. They'll shake their heads. They'll laugh at his expense. For dinner, they'll eat the fancy food that Highlands people eat. They'll listen to music on their phonograph, or whatever Highlands people play their music on. The man with the fake English accent and the bandaged head will be a dinner party anecdote for years.

"You mentioned an original?" Michael says.

"Just one in the series," the man says. "The portrait of Reykjavík."

Michael moves to the second of the two pieces the woman put on hold. He looks close. To his surprise, Reykjavík looks about as much like a capital city as Ithaca, where he grew up. The buildings are boxy, small. A single concrete church rises above the rest.

Michael likes the bright landscape better. Diane would like the landscape better. But he can't get over the fact that it's a canvas some fancy machine spit ink onto. No, this gift, to mean something, it needs to be paint. It needs to be real.

Michael looks closer, and the man asks him to take a step back. The paint on this one is real, all right, textured, layered thick. A bristle nestles the edge of a building. He steps away. The gallery owner removes a handkerchief from his back pocket and blows his nose.

"How much?" Michael asks.

"I'm sorry?" the man says, returning the handkerchief to his pocket, and Michael wonders whether he's doing this wrong. He's never bought real art before.

"The painting. What's the price?"

"Well, it *is* an original."

"Not just the signature?"

"Sir, I assure you, this painting was painted by the artist. It's priced at six thousand dollars."

Michael takes another step back from the wall. He was not prepared for that. The painting is no bigger than a shoebox lid. "*Six grand? For this?*"

"Yes, sir, though as you may have overheard, this one is on reserve for one of our best customers. I can't let it go until this time tomorrow."

He gives Michael a look that says *You clearly have no money, go away*, a look Michael finds infuriating. Sure, he's mishandled his finances. Sure, he's facing potential foreclosure and crippling credit card debt. But those aren't things this pompous ass can tell just by looking at him. Michael *could* have money. If he'd been a little wiser. If he hadn't made them house-poor. If he'd known better how interest rates work, how credit cards work, how adjustable rate mortgages tend to play out. If they'd known that, by 2018, their house wouldn't be worth what they paid in 2007. If he'd known then what he knows now, hell, he might be a wealthy man.

"I'll pay you seven," Michael says.

The gallery owner's eyebrows lift. "I'm sorry, sir, but Mrs. Lynn is one of our dearest—"

"Eight. Eight grand."

The owner chuckles. "Extremely flattering, but I'm afraid—"

"Nine," Michael says. "I won't go higher. That painting's overvalued as it is."

Overvalued. It's not a word he's used before, but it's a word he's heard Jake toss around.

The owner reaches for the painting before his hand falls to his side.

"You drive a hard bargain," Michael says.

He's dropped the phony accent entirely. He doesn't care. He's wiped the smug look off this fucker's face.

"Twelve thousand," Michael says. "Twice what it's worth. I'll even write two checks. Six grand to the gallery. Six grand to you."

The owner will not look at him.

"Or to a charitable organization of your choosing," Michael says. He likes that. It sounds like the kind of thing a rich person might say.

"I wish I could," the owner says.

"Come on."

"We could use the revenue."

"Take the money."

The owner shuts his eyes. It's once he's opened them that Michael knows he's won. The man pulls the painting from the wall, and Michael follows him to a desk near the front door.

"One last thing," Michael says. "I need you to call her."

"Call . . . whom?"

"The buyer with the painting on reserve. Call Mrs. Lynn."

"I don't think that will be necessary." The man is agitated, sweating. He pulls his hankie from his pocket and pats his brow. "The way these things go, she may not want the painting after all. No need to upset her unless—"

"It's necessary," Michael says. "I can't in good conscience make this deal until I'm sure the previous agreement has been terminated. I will not be in business with someone who isn't honest."

The owner offers another nervous chuckle, but Michael isn't laughing.

Church bells ring beyond the gallery walls. It's noon.

The man stands behind the desk. A landline telephone sits beside a glass dish stuffed with mints. Michael unwraps a mint and pops it in his mouth. He lets the wrapper fall to the floor.

"I really don't see why this is necessary," the man says.

"I've given you my terms." His throat burns. He's overdue for a drink.

From a desk drawer, the man retrieves a small, leather-bound notebook. He flips several pages, then lifts the phone's receiver. But he doesn't dial. He stares at Michael, and Michael can't tell, by his expression, whether the man pities him or fears him, whether he suspects him eccentric or insane. But the man wants the money. That much he can tell.

"Your call," Michael says.

The man hesitates, then dials.

What happens next is hard to listen to. Over the phone, the gallery owner tells his customer that the painting is no longer hers. This development does not go over well, and the man is on the phone a while, begging the woman not to cry, promising her she's still his favorite customer. By the time the call is over, he's pale. He wipes his eyes. There's spittle at the corners of his mouth. He won't look at Michael.

"The painting's yours," he says.

On the desk, beside the bowl of mints, Reykjavík glitters silver green in the night sky.

"Sorry," Michael says. "I changed my mind."

27.

Highlands Comics and Collectibles is not what Lisa expected.

She expected a darkened cave, cobwebbed and wet. She expected the stench of a used bookstore—mildew and dust, book pages yellowed by time. She expected teenage boys in glasses, braces stapled to their teeth. What she gets, instead, is a woman, late twenties, in a blue and red Supergirl tee.

The woman's hair is brown, waist-length, the way Lisa's was in college, but hers is bathed in purple-pink highlights. She reads a Spider-Man comic behind a register. Beneath the register, a glass case displays row upon row of comic books and action figures.

The rest of the store is clean and orderly. Colors assault the senses. Merchandise fills every corner and hangs on every wall, sculptures and posters, capes and hoods. Tables capped with narrow boxes make an island at the center of the store. The boxes are bloated with comic books, the comics sealed in Mylar bags with cardboard backs to keep the paper stiff.

She doesn't know whether Thad still collects comics or concentrates solely on his poetry, whether he wants his old books back to read again or merely for the memories they hold. She doesn't know Thad the way she once did, and that's a loss. Parents don't have favorites, though, if they did, her favorite would be Thad.

For years she couldn't get him to read. She tried sci-fi, westerns, Richard's mysteries, biographies, supermarket magazines. She loved reading, and, as a mother, it disturbed her that her son did not. She thought she might trick him into reading through comic books slipped into his backpack and under his bedroom door. Batman. Fantastic Four. The Hulk. But nothing stuck. Until X-Men.

Looking back, the comic was a perfect fit. A team of mutants whose powers manifested, unbidden, at puberty? Unlike other heroes, the X-Men were misunderstood, feared and hated for who they were, how they were born. The metaphor wasn't exactly subtle, but the books got Thad through middle school, then high school, where he felt comfortable coming out.

It was a great-aunt who gave Thad a book of verse as a high school graduation present. In all of Lisa's years of pushing books, she'd never thought to offer poetry. But who would have guessed that the kid who grew up hating books would grow up to be a poet? Home from college, Thad left his books in piles around the house, slim volumes with Pulitzer Prize stickers on the covers and authors' names she didn't recognize. She tried reading them, to have something to talk about with her son, but she found the books impenetrable, most of them, the poems bewildering and dark and sad. She hoped they weren't making his depression worse. She hopes this still.

He has a big brain, her boy. He only needs the drive to match. She knows he writes. She sees him scribble in a notebook now and then. But he's never shared his work with her, and she's afraid to ask to see. It would hurt too much if he said *no.*

The woman at the register slides Spider-Man into a Mylar bag.

Thad did this too, reading each comic with care, bagging it, slipping the cardboard in, and taping the bag shut. What was Lisa thinking, even in her hurry to clean out the house? How, how, how could she have thrown his X-Men out?

The woman steps back from the register. "How may I help you?"

"I'm looking for some comics. Except, I'm not sure what I'm looking for."

"That's okay. I'm Maya. I'm here to help."

In the display case, three monsters recline side by side. All are the slug from Star Wars, the one Leia strangles with her chain. For no reason Lisa is able to ascertain, each is tagged with a different price.

"I'm here for my son," Lisa says.

"What age is your son?" Maya's nails are red and blue to match her shirt, colors alternating with every finger. They click the display case above the slugs.

"He's thirty. He likes the X-Men. Or, he used to. He might still. I don't know."

"I'm sure he does," Maya says. "X-Men fans are pretty ride or die."

At Cornell, Lisa dreaded each visit to the IT guy. Say she had a file she couldn't unzip. She'd ask her question, and the man would do three things. First, he'd laugh to let her know just how pedestrian her question was. Next, he'd ask a question he knew she couldn't answer. (*Are the files encrypted? Have you extracted the folder yet?*) Finally, he'd sigh and perform the task himself without teaching her how it was done.

Lisa feared similar treatment visiting a comic shop, but Maya is not the IT guy. That is, until Lisa says what she must say next.

"What happened," she says, "is that I kind of threw his comics out."

Maya laughs. She looks at Lisa. She stops laughing. "Wait, you're serious?"

Outside, a car honks. Across the street, people line up at a popular pizza spot.

"I'm sorry," Maya says. "Stay put for one second."

She hurries across the store, disappears behind a curtain at the back, and returns with another employee. This man wears a Superman shirt, but he's not pulling it off in quite the way that Maya is, the shirt a size or two too small. But he's handsome, clear skin, dark eyes. He's in his twenties, black, hair in an Afro.

"This is Ken," Maya says. "Will you tell Ken what you just told me?"

Lisa doesn't feel good about this. "I threw away my son's comic books."

Ken covers his mouth, and this is not mock horror. The man is horrified.

"Oh, shit," he says. "How many?"

Lisa gestures toward the tables at the center of the store. The boxes come in two sizes, and she knows which size she dragged to the curb. "The shorter ones. How many comic books would fit in two of those?"

"Three hundred," Ken says. "Maybe four."

"Three or four hundred, then," Lisa says.

"Fuck," Ken says.

Maya shakes her head.

"Hang on," Ken says.

He heads to the back, then returns with a *third* employee. Which begs the question, how many people can one tiny comic shop employ?

This man is older than the others—fifty, maybe. He has a thick gray beard, and instead of Superman, he wears a button-up Hawaiian shirt. An inflatable red rubber fish hangs from his belt, like one of those Swedish candies in the blue and yellow box. The fish hangs waist to knee.

"Sorry," Ken says, "just one more time."

But Lisa doesn't want to play this game anymore. If they make her say it again, she'll cry. And the man in the Hawaiian shirt must sense this because, soon, he's leading her to the back of the store, past the curtain, to a folding chair, and offering her a cup of tea.

"I'm really sorry," he says.

A card table faces the folding chair, and he sets the mug down. Tea leaves float in a wire basket in the shape of the Batman logo, the bat's wing clipped to the lip of the mug. Steam rises from the water. The tea steeps.

"I'm sorry too," Maya says. "It's just, we've been waiting for this day for years. The mom who throws her kid's comic books out. The cautionary tale. You're a *legend*."

"You're the '98 Pikachu Illustrator card of moms," Ken says.

The older man, the storeowner whose name turns out to be Matthew, clears his throat. "What they mean to say is that we're pleased to meet you. We've never had the chance to reassemble a lost collection. It's kind of the Holy Grail of this job."

They join her, pulling chairs up to the table. The tabletop is lit-
tered with playing cards. Except the cards aren't kings and queens,
they're creatures. Beneath each creature are numbers, like baseball
stats, but the statistics are indecipherable.

"You picked a good day to come in," Maya says. "We only sort
inventory a few times a year, which is why you've got all three of us."

The back room is how Lisa imagined the front would be: poorly
lit, linoleum floor weirdly sticky on her shoes. Comics lean in
plastic-bagged piles everywhere, and everywhere loiter those white
boxes—some full, some half-full, some with lids and some without.

Lisa sips her tea, which is too hot and still too watery. The Batman
infuser clicks against her teeth.

"So," Ken says, "what titles are we talking?"

"X-Men," Lisa says. "All of them."

"Easy," Ken says. "What years?"

"Around 2000 to 2010. But just the summers. The rest he has. The
summer issues he kept here."

Matthew studies the ceiling. "That would be Whedon, Casey,
Austen, Claremont, Brubaker, and . . . Fraction."

"Don't forget Grant Morrison," Ken says.

Maya picks up a card, studies the stats, and returns it to the table.
"Grant Morrison fucked everything up."

"What are you talking about?" Ken says. "Grant Morrison's awe-
some."

"He had Magneto pretend to be Chinese for two years! Imagine
you're a Chinese reader. You're like, cool, a Chinese X-Man! Then
it's like, *nope*, that was Magneto the whole time."

"That was—"

"Racist," Maya says. "The word you're looking for is *racist*."

Ken shakes his head. "Are you seriously lecturing me on race?"

"Are you seriously mansplaining identity politics to a lesbian?"

"We get it," Matthew says. "Enough." He turns to Lisa, apology
in his eyes.

"Oh, this is nothing," she says. "I work at Cornell."

Lisa tries to keep up. She's liberal. She's progressive. She's a feminist. But, the ever-changing language, good Lord. Disorienting to be called *intolerant* by one grad student for learning the term *non-binary* too late. She likes this generation. She does. She admires their compassion, their drive for inclusion, social justice, civil rights. Still, they could learn a little patience, show a little more respect to those who came before. She was marching before these kids were born. Lisa will miss her students, but not the self-righteous ones, the ones so sure they have it all figured out at twenty-two.

But Ken and Maya aren't those people. They're passionate. They care about the art they love and how groups are depicted in that art. That's different than berating someone for not knowing the right words. By the look on his face, Lisa's not sure Matthew appreciates Ken's and Maya's arguments, and that's okay. He's trying. He hired them, after all. Better to let him evolve at his own pace than shame him into fighting for the other side.

Matthew pulls the fish from his belt into his lap. It resembles a balloon animal, the fish expressionless, mouth closed, eyes shut. It's a fashion choice Lisa can't comprehend. But then, she's lived through bell-bottoms and Jams, shoulder pads and stiletto heels. Feathers in the hair were big for a while. Why not fish for belts?

"Belt fish," Matthew says. "A friend makes them. I keep thinking they'll catch on."

Ken and Maya lock eyes, clearly trying hard not to laugh at their employer's expense, already friends again.

Matthew stands, and they follow him past the curtain to the boxes at the center of the store.

"It will take some time," he says, "but I think we can re-create your son's collection. Where it gets tricky is the months. Marvel cover dates and release dates didn't always match. A June book might be stamped August."

"I'll buy June through September, then," Lisa says. "Just to be safe."

Matthew stares at her. "That could be four hundred books. And some may be valuable. I'll give you a discount for buying in bulk, but you're still looking at over a thousand dollars out the door. And that's if we have the issues. Probably, there will be some gaps."

"Whatever you have, I'll take it. And I'll need them rebagged. No stickers. No prices on the front. I want him to think these were his."

"You're a good mom," Maya says.

Lisa would like to believe that. But were she a better mother, would Thad be so maladjusted, so damn sad? She's not stupid. She knows how depression works, the stranglehold that nature has over nurture. But she's a mother, and as a mother, it's hard to believe that a child's unhappiness is not your fault.

Comic books won't cure Thad's depression, of course, but they might make him happy for a day, maybe for a few, and for Thad, any number of happy days is a lot.

"Okay then," Matthew says. He turns to the others with the seriousness of a coach rallying players for a big game. "Maya, you're on X-Force, X-Factor, Excalibur, and Generation X. Ken, you're on Wolverine, Cable, X-Man, and Deadpool." He turns to Lisa. "Did your son collect Deadpool?"

For all the ivory-bills that ever lived, Lisa couldn't say. "Is Deadpool X-Men?"

"It's tangential," Ken says, "but it's canon."

"I don't know what that means," Lisa says.

"Better grab Deadpool," Matthew says. "I'll take care of X-Men, Uncanny, and Astonishing. Ken, grab a couple of old Wizards for reference. I don't want to miss an issue."

Lisa half expects the man to say *On three* and make the others huddle up.

"I'm so excited," Maya says.

"I'm gonna bag the fuck out of those comics," Ken says.

They're giddy, all of them.

"You're welcome to sit in back, enjoy your tea," Matthew says. "This may take a while."

"Thank you," Lisa says. "I appreciate your time."

Matthew smiles, and it's refreshing seeing someone who loves his job, who's good at it. She wants that for her boys. She doesn't care that they're not professors or scientists. She doesn't care whether they make much money doing what they do, though enough to live on would be nice. She'd just like them to come home satisfied at the end of each day, knowing that they've done good work. She wants that for them, that sense of purpose, purpose and the belief their time has been well spent.

"You really are a good mom," Matthew says.

Lisa nods. She'll take the compliment.

"One last thing," he says. He hesitates, steadies the fish swinging from his belt. "Just to be clear."

"What's that?" Lisa asks.

"All sales are final."

28.

Hand at the tiller, Richard follows the shoreline, careful to keep the trolling motor's prop away from rocks. Ahead, a fallen tree breaks the plane of the bay, and Richard pilots past it. The day is breezy, which will make fishing the shallows a challenge, wind and low-hanging branches the fiercest enemies of fishing line.

Richard slows, cuts the motor, and anchors. Here, this cove, is where his father taught him to fish.

This lake, it wasn't picked at random for the vacation during which he and Lisa found their home. As a boy, Richard's family traveled to Lake Christopher for a week one summer. The drive was three hours, Georgia to North Carolina, an easy trip. His father was a high school teacher, a man of modest means, and the family camped—father, mother, and son in matching sleeping bags. That's when there was land enough around Lake Christopher to pitch a tent. Probably the land was someone's lot or hunting property, but back then no one noticed, or, noticing, no one cared. These days people care, the land bought up, developed, lots bulldozed, new houses going up each year.

Richard checks the anchor line. The sun is high, light traveling eight minutes and twenty seconds to bounce off the ball cap he wears to protect his head. The lake bed is six feet below the boat, the water three feet deep where he will cast. All things are, at this moment, as Richard wants them. Where he can't impose order on his family, let him at least impose a pattern on the lake. Let him anchor where he's anchored a thousand times before. Let him bait his hook with the day's first fat, glorious worm. Let him cast as he was trained to cast by his father sixty years ago.

What has he done with the worms? He is . . . he is stepping on them.

The blue, plastic tub leaves his boot heel with a suctioned exhalation, and Richard pries free the pinpricked lid. The worms writhe, unhurt, and he hooks one, casts it, and watches his bobber drop.

The bobber does not bob. No fish bite. Impatient, Richard reels in his line. He casts again. He likes the shape the line makes letting out, the saddle horn silhouette of filament followed by the bobber's thunk. He likes how the float dips before righting itself. So satisfying, like mowing a lawn, which Richard's always done himself. An economy of lines, one way to do it right. Not like physics. Physics is messy, mathematical physics the work of prying a design from inside the mess. Or trying to. Trying and failing, then trying again.

Richard casts once more. He'd have made a good fly fisherman had he taken time to learn the Carolina rivers or the ways of trout. Instead, he is what he is: a bass and panfish fisherman. No fancy flies or waders for him, just a fishing boat and a push-button Zebco reel, both inelegant but good enough.

A tension in the line, and the bobber is under. Richard tightens his drag. He reels. The rod bows. The fish pulls hard, and Richard loosens the drag. He's fishing on last summer's line. Each year he restrings the reels, but this summer he's been lazy. Hard to make himself go to the trouble when he won't get a full summer out of it. He hopes the line will hold. It's eight-pound test, but bluegill are wily. He's watched small ones snap new lines with their pulls.

He kneels at the bow and pulls the trolling motor from the water. The fish pulls more line, headed toward the fallen tree. If the fish reaches the branches, it's over. He'll tangle in the limbs, and no amount of tugging will untangle him. Nothing to do but tighten the drag and hope the line doesn't snap.

Richard reels. Nothing breaks. He dips the net, and the fish is caught.

It's a bluegill all right, but not any old bluegill. Richard has just landed the biggest bream he's ever seen. The world record, if he remembers right, stands at a little over five pounds. This fish isn't that big, but it's big enough to look transfigured out of all proportion, demon-possessed. Its forehead is humped, and its stomach bulges, scales like thumbnails. It's as though someone stuck a bicycle pump in the mouth and inflated the fish. Tie a string to its tail, and you'd have a balloon.

Bluegill are his favorite fish to catch because they're always a surprise. They might break the surface green or blue, or leave the water with scales the color of pumpkin skin. The gill plates can be solid or striped, earflaps black or red.

Richard Starling doesn't get emotional about much, but he can get misty about fish.

No one he knows would throw this fish back.

He throws it back.

He doesn't need to eat it. Doesn't need a picture or a wall mount to remember its size. He stows his rod and pulls the anchor up.

The gas gauge is approaching E, and the marina isn't far.

For as long as Richard's owned the house on Lake Christopher, Clyde has worked the marina gas pumps, filling boats, and Clyde is there today. He's tall, back bent with age, and wears plaid long-sleeved button-downs, which he rolls to his elbows, arms speckled by the sun.

The marina is small, a few dozen docks, a half-dozen boats tied up. The gas pumps are the old bubble-headed kind, their displays spooled like the faces of slot machines. A silver freezer advertises ice. On the west side of the lake, a mighty new marina's being built. No doubt, it will put Clyde out of business in a matter of years.

"How's things, Rich?" Clyde's the only one who calls him *Rich*. Just started doing it one day, and Richard never felt compelled to correct him.

"Things are fine," he says. "Thanks for asking."

Clyde ties him off and moves to the nearest pump. He doesn't have to ask which octane. He's been gassing up *The Sea Cow* for decades, through the lives of three engines, two props, and a reconstructed hull.

"How's your family?" Richard asks.

He's never met them, but he knows that Clyde has a wife, Nadine, and a daughter, Cece. Cece is Thad's age. She's the rebel, the girl run off to Asheville. For a while, Clyde wouldn't speak of her. Then Cece had a son, and all was forgiven, the way it is when grandkids are involved, or so he's heard. Richard doesn't expect to be a grandfather. Neither of his sons have expressed an interest in having kids. And maybe that's for the best. He can't quite picture them as fathers, as much as he'd love having grandchildren of his own.

"Family's good," Clyde says. He fits the nozzle into the side of the boat and opens the valve, then seats himself in a battered lawn chair, vinyl straps, once red, now sun-washed pink. "Survived a tornado last year. Took the house, right down to the root cellar."

"Good Lord."

"Everyone's okay. Insurance paid up, and the new house is nicer than the first. We lost the F-150. Never had insurance on that. Nadine got the cat and photo albums to the cellar in time. My father's flag, too. I lost my Purple Heart, though. That one hurts."

Richard is of an age where most of his friends served. That he didn't serve sometimes embarrasses him. Though of all the stories Clyde's shared over the years, he's never shared a war story, not once.

"How's your girl?" Richard asks.

"Still in Asheville."

Clyde's never mentioned a husband or boyfriend, or who the child's father might be, and Richard knows better than to ask.

"Cece makes clothes now," Clyde says. "They sell in shops all over town. You wouldn't believe what a dress sells for these days."

"Everything's getting expensive."

Clyde shakes his head. "I'm ashamed. I helped vote that yahoo into office thinking things would change. I feel like a fuckin'—" Clyde winces. "Pardon me. I feel like a chump."

Richard says nothing. He's never picked his friends by how they vote, and he's in no mood, after last night, to talk politics again.

"How's Lisa?" Clyde says. "Cancer stay away?"

"It did. She's good, healthy. One year until retirement. I retired last month."

Clyde stands, extends his hand, and they shake. The valve clicks, and he pulls the nozzle from the tank. "Retirement. They give you a watch, or what?"

Besides emeritus status and the standard compensation package, there were no gifts and little fanfare. There was a small reception, cake, a few words from the dean, and pats on the back, a bit of a letdown after so many years of service. Not that he'd expected much. He'd hoped Katrina would be there. He'd hoped to see her one last time.

"No watch," he says. "How about you? Nervous about the new marina?"

"We'll survive," Clyde says, but, saying it, he won't meet Richard's eye, and Clyde is not a man to speak and look away. He returns the gas hose to the pump. "How are your boys?"

It's hard being a genius, harder still being the father of sons who aren't, another thing Richard knows better than to say aloud. Instead, he says, "The boys are good."

They aren't good. His sons have let him down. He loves them, and it pains him thinking so, but they have. He only wishes he knew where, as a father, he went wrong.

Clyde gives Richard the price, and Richard pays in cash, telling Clyde to keep the change, just as he has for over thirty years.

"Hug that grandbaby for me," Richard says.

Clyde unhitches the line from the cleat, and the boat rocks, untethered from the dock. "Shame about that boy."

"I heard," Richard says, and leaves it at that.

"How on earth does a thing like that happen?"

How? Because drownings happen, thousands a year just in the United States, according to data Richard found last night on his phone. Drownings are more common than even SIDS. No consolation in this, of course, but neither is Lake Christopher somehow cursed. A lake this size, it was bound to happen. It's a statistical inevitability.

Clyde places a foot on the side of the boat, ready to push off.

"Wait," Richard says.

Clyde returns his foot to the dock. He pulls the line taut.

"Tie me off," Richard says. "Before I go, I want to tell you the story of my daughter. I want to tell you about my little girl."

29.

There's no bar where the bar is supposed to be. What used to be the bar is now an antiques shop. Outside the shop, a man reads the paper on a bench.

"Henry moved to Asheville," the man says, not looking up, and Michael hurries on.

Two more blocks, two turns, and Michael finds himself beneath a green marquee that reads *Winter Wine Bar* in red letters. He's not in the mood for wine, but it will have to do. He'll have two glasses, maybe three. No more than a bottle. Enough to keep his hands from shaking, but not so much he can't drive home.

Inside, chairs huddle empty around tables that Michael passes on his way to the bar.

"Welcome to Winter," the bartender says, any conviction his greeting ever had long since sapped by the tedium of the work he does. He smells like cigarettes and a generous dousing of cologne intended, and failing, to cover up the cigarettes. The man's handlebar mustache hangs limp, unwaxed, and a white apron covers his shirt, so that he looks more like a 1920s barber than a man tending bar.

The bartender pulls down a glass. The glass catches the light, and he turns it, inspecting it from every angle. The glass is spotless. Still, the man tugs a white rag from a hook on the wall and runs the rag over the lip of the glass. The rag leaves fibers on the rim, and the bartender lowers the wineglass, a little hairy now, onto the bar.

Michael doesn't need to see a wine menu to know the only thing in here that he'll be able to afford is the house red. He orders a bottle, then asks for nuts.

"Nuts?" the bartender says.

"Peanuts?" Michael says. "Cashews?"

The bartender holds a wine bottle in one hand, a corkscrew in the other. He threads the cork expertly, without looking, which feels show-offy, gratuitous.

"Something to munch on?" Michael says. "Pretzels? Chips?" Something for the gut. A barrier against the acidity to come.

"We have a very pleasant baked brie," the bartender says. "We also have a cheese plate and a fruit plate. Or there's the combo plate. That's both."

The cork leaves the bottle with a wet pop. The bartender pours a sip of wine into the rag-furred glass, but Michael waves him on until the wine has nearly reached the rim.

Michael lifts the glass and brings it to his nose. The smell is pungent, over-oaked, too sweet. Fine, then: Don't think of it as wine. Think of it as an alcohol-delivery system.

He wants to sip, but something slows him for a moment, then a moment more. It's a feeling like when you really have to pee. You've unzipped your fly. The toilet's there. The breeze is on your balls, and sweet relief will soon be yours. Still, you savor the moment, the pressure leading up to the release, the exquisite torture of *almost*. Michael relishes the suspense, then tips the glass and guzzles it.

His eyes shut. He's warm all over. He is loved.

The bartender looks concerned.

"Don't be concerned," Michael says.

He sets his glass, empty, on the bar, and the bartender refills it. The bartender glances at his forehead, and Michael taps the bandage. He considers breaking out the English accent again, but it's too late. The man's already heard his voice.

"Snakebite," Michael says.

The look on the bartender's face betrays his disbelief.

"Cobra. Big motherfucker. People think there aren't serpents in Iceland, but let me tell you."

It's fun watching the bartender decide how to proceed, watching him weigh how much work a tip is worth.

Michael starts in on the second glass, but the wine has begun to burn. The burn isn't the warehouse fire of moonshine or the blowtorch of scotch on the rocks. No, this fire's sneakier, a bouquet of flowers lightly gasolined. Lean in to get a whiff, and the red wine strikes a match. He needs something to eat, something to settle the tannin-acid churn, so he orders the cheese plate, hoping it comes with crackers.

The cheese plate, when it comes, does not come with crackers, just cheese, a big ol' helping of gourmet mold, thin slices arranged in geometric patterns on the plate. Very well, then. He'll eat cheese.

The bartender asks where in Iceland Michael's from.

"Reykjavík," Michael says.

"You're serious?" the bartender says. "I've never met someone from there."

"You probably have. We're all over. We blend in. We're like those insects shaped like sticks."

Michael feels himself smiling. He feels strangely good, like maybe everything will be all right. Maybe they'll drag the lake and find the boy alive. Maybe Diane will miscarry and things will go back to how they were. He thinks this and does not feel bad. A minute later, he feels bad for how bad he didn't feel.

He drains his glass, and the bartender upends the wine bottle, filling the glass again. People say five glasses to a bottle, but when you pour them right, it's three.

"It must be cold there," the bartender says.

"A common misconception," Michael says. "Greenland's ice, and Iceland's green. In summer, we wear shorts. That's when the snakes come out."

The bartender wipes the bar down with his rag.

"And we have special horses, little fellas. They're trained to keep the snakes away."

"Jesus," the bartender says. "I had no idea."

"Sharks too. We harpoon them, let them rot for half a year, then eat them. In Iceland, rotten shark's a delicacy."

This part, the most farfetched, is true. And with this truth, he's lost his audience. The bartender looks away. He brings two fingers to his mustache, pulls on it, and lets go. Michael wants the mustache to coil into place, like that of a villain perched over a woman tied to the train tracks, but the mustache only droops.

He eats more cheese. He watches the wine, determined to make this glass last.

The wine's definitely kicking in, and he's adrift. A friendly buzz electrifies his frontal lobe. He should be getting home. There's moonshine at the house to drink, fish in the lake to help his father catch.

"Just one more bottle," Michael says.

The bartender hesitates, then pulls a second bottle from the wall, but he's interrupted by a dark-haired woman coming through the door.

"Shit, Lou," she says, "don't pour him that."

The woman slips onto a stool beside Michael. She wears a silver necklace and a shimmery black dress. Michael doesn't know anything about fabrics, but this one undulates under the bar lights like the lake under the moon. She's too dressed up for church, too elegant for a funeral, and well overdressed for a bar in the middle of the day.

"You don't want that red," she says. "If you're on a budget, at least go for the La Crema, the pinot. The house wine here is swill."

Michael nods, and the bartender swaps bottles. If he's offended by *swill*, he doesn't show it, and Michael senses these two are friends.

The woman's lipstick is too red, her cheeks too rouged. She's overly made-up, like an older woman trying to pass for young, except she's young already, younger than Michael, thirty at the most.

"I didn't catch your name," she says.

"I didn't give it," Michael says. He's not flirting. He's flustered. He was happy drinking with the miserable mustached man, but this woman's arrival has thrown off the afternoon.

"This is Miss Gwendolyn DeMarco," Lou says. "Gwen, this man's from Iceland."

"I'm Michael," he tells them.

Lou smiles at Gwen, but Gwen's eyes stay on Michael.

"My dad's from Iceland," Gwen says.

Lou grins and hits Michael on the arm. "Hey," he says, "you're right. Stick bugs!"

Lou pours Michael a glass, then opens a second bottle and pours glasses for Gwen and himself. This wine smells better than the first, raspberries and lavender, and goes down smooth, no cheese required.

"What part of Iceland are you from?" Gwen asks.

"Reykjavík," he says. It's the only Icelandic city he knows.

"Which district?"

"District?"

"East or west of the city center?"

Michael shuts his eyes. The buzz is getting to be too much. He can't do this anymore.

"I'm not from Iceland," he says.

"Neither is my father," she says. "I'm just fucking with you. I wanted to see how long you'd keep it going."

She smiles, and there's so much makeup, but the smile seems genuine. Lou doesn't smile. He turns to the sink behind the bar and runs his dishrag under water.

"He's sensitive," Gwen whispers.

They drink, and Michael offers Gwen his cheese, from which she picks a piece. She opens her mouth wide enough to keep her lipstick in place. Already, her wineglass rim is red.

Lou shuts off the sink. He stands in steam. By now, his rag must be glistening. He turns and tops off all three glasses.

"What are we drinking to?" Gwen asks.

Michael would like to drink to the memory of the boy, but trying to remember his name, all he comes up with are those orange floats spinning, bumping the side of the boat.

"To Iceland," Michael says.

Gwen laughs. Lou doesn't. "To Iceland." They drink. They set their glasses down.

Lou pulls a pack of Marlboros from his apron pocket and a cigarette from the pack.

"Back in a minute," he says, and leaves through a door behind the bar.

Michael drinks more wine. It's soothing, being away from his family, but he misses Diane. He's sure she loves him still. Like, a couple of nights ago, he forgot his mouth guard before bed, and she woke him in his grinding, then brought the mouth guard to him, freshly scrubbed. To hand-wash another person's spitty dental appliance, now *that* is love, the kind that never leaves you, the kind that stays beside you when you're old. His father's right. He needs to fix this. He'd be a fool to lose Diane.

Yet, given the chance to prove, if not love, his affection at least, what does he do? He fucks it up. He trades the inexpensive print Diane would have treasured for the chance to fuck over some guy he'll never see again. All because he thought the man thought he was better than Michael.

And who knows if even *that* is true? What if everyone with money isn't always looking down on him? What if thinking so is easier than admitting the things he thinks about himself?

Behind the bar, the wall is mirrored where a row of bottles ought to be, and Michael watches Gwen in the mirror. Her stool creaks, and she turns to face him. Her dress cut low, the silver necklace disappears between her breasts. She wears no wedding ring. She splays her hands on the bar, as though to emphasize this point.

"Where are you from, really?" Gwen says. Her lips are very red.

He tells her Texas. He lifts his glass, finds it empty, and fills his glass halfway. Already his second bottle is getting awfully low.

"Here," Gwen says, tipping her bottle and topping off his glass. Her hand finds his arm, two fingers at his wrist, as though checking for a pulse. He lets the hand linger there a second, which is a second too long, before he pulls his arm away.

He should leave. He's never cheated, and he ought to pay and leave right now.

Alternatively, he could keep drinking and see where this goes. He doesn't want Gwen. The attention, it's just so flattering, like he's stumbled into someone else's life. Michael's life isn't like this. In all the afternoons and evenings he's spent in bars, for all the desperate men he's seen trying to pick women up, he can't think of a time a woman's hit on him.

And is this how it happened to his father, attention turned to flattery turned to indiscretion before he knew what he was doing? He can't picture it, can't fathom who would want to fuck his dad.

The bar's air-conditioning kicks on, and cool air shoots from a dust-encrusted vent overhead.

"What do you do in Texas, Michael?" Gwen asks. "Wait, let me guess. You're an architect."

Michael shakes his head. If the bruising and the bandage hasn't scared her off, maybe learning what he does will do the trick.

"Lawyer."

"Nope."

"You're a doctor. No. CFO! You're head of finance for a Fortune 500 company."

"Stop," he says. "Please. Every guess makes it worse when you find out."

Gwen frowns. "Come on. How bad could it be?"

"I sell shoes." It's been a while since he last said it out loud. "In Fort Worth, there's a shitty indoor mall. 'The Sad Mall,' people call it. Half the stores are gated. Even the pretzel place shut down. There's not much left. A Sears, a Sbarro, an optical boutique. And Foot Locker. That's me."

Gwen smiles. "So, you're a business owner. What's wrong with that?"

"Not owner," Michael says.

"Manager?"

"Not manager. And I'll save you some time. I'm not the shift manager or the floor manager or a sales associate or a junior sales associate or an assistant sales associate."

"What's lower than assistant sales associate?"

He sips his wine. "Junior assistant sales associate. Low as you can go. And you know what's funny? I've been there the *longest*. Every person I work beneath, I *trained*."

Gwen's stool squeaks, and she turns back to the bar. The cheese plate's still full, slices gone sweaty under the bar lights, and she eats another piece.

"Can you imagine?" Michael says. "To be thirty-three, taking orders from eighteen-year-olds? Spending the day on your knees, lacing sneakers you can't even afford, slipping them onto other people's feet. Do you know how bad other people's feet smell, Gwen?"

Gwen looks in the mirror and fluffs her hair with both hands.

"I'm Al Bundy! My life's a joke, and I'm the punch line!"

No more flirting. She's finished with him now. Once more, his life is his own.

"And the customers! My God. You wouldn't believe how they treat employees."

Lou's back, smelling like smoke.

"He gets it!" Michael says. "Don't you, Lou? Lou, tell Gwen just how awful people are."

"People aren't awful," Gwen says.

"They *are*. People are the worst. That thing the girl said. The Jewish girl. What was her name? The girl who hid from Nazis, kept a diary?"

"Anne Frank?"

"Anne Frank! That thing she wrote: 'In spite of everything . . .' What's the quote?"

"I know the line you mean," Gwen says.

Michael knows he's drunk. He knows he should shut up.

Gwen looks at Lou. Maybe they're lovers, maybe just old friends. Whatever their connection, it's just like at the gallery. Michael is the story they'll tell all their friends.

Michael pulls his phone from his pocket and googles the quote. " '*In spite of everything, I still believe that people are truly good at heart.*' "

Things are going sideways now, the barstool beneath him loosening.

" 'In spite of everything, I still believe that people are truly good at heart.' That's the line. And you know what, Gwen? It's *bullshit*. It sounds nice, but it's bullshit."

"Please shut up," Gwen says.

"I'll tell you this much. Anne Frank never worked a day at Foot Locker."

Michael doesn't see the fist coming. He's on his barstool, then he's on the floor.

Briefly, on the floor, the boy floats by. He drifts, eyes shut, just out of reach. His limbs are spread. His face is calm. Then the boy is gone, and Lou is standing over him.

Michael's been punched before, though Lou never seemed the type to throw a punch. Maybe Lou's Jewish. Maybe he felt he was protecting Gwen. Maybe he's just had enough of Michael. Regardless, there's a reason Michael knows every watering hole in the Dallas–Fort Worth area. It's because he rarely drinks without getting kicked out. Most places, he's lucky to make it a week before pissing someone off.

"I'm sorry," Lou says. He offers a hand, and Michael takes it, lets Lou lift him to his feet. The room spins. Gwen watches from her stool.

The floor is a jumble of triangles and squares, and it takes Michael a minute to comprehend that he knocked the cheese plate over when he fell.

He pulls his wallet from his pocket. He doesn't know the price of the wine. Even if he did, he's drunk too much to do the math. He drops what cash he has onto the bar. He knows it's not enough. He's leaving, but Lou's voice stops him at the door.

"What really happened to your head?"

Michael checks the bandage, still in place. His jaw hurts from Lou's fist.

"I tried to save a life," he says. "I failed."

30.

Thad finds Nico's empty. Not closed, but unattended. He calls for Teddy, but Teddy doesn't emerge from the back.

The Blue Cross Teddy sold him has Thad anxious, that or a weekend surrounded by family, plagued by death, has Thad anxious and the Blue Cross can't keep up. He needs a strain with less sativa, maybe. But Teddy's the expert. Teddy will know what he needs. What he needs, really, is his medications adjusted. That happens every five years, give or take: '05, '08, '13. It's 2018. It's time. But that will have to wait for next week. For now, Teddy's weed will have to do.

Later, the ice cream parlor will be packed with locals and vacationers alike, the deck chairs full. But this has always been Thad's favorite time, the midday lull, too late for lunch, the evening crowd still hours away. He stands a minute more in the parlor, then checks the deck. He follows the stairs down to the porch, then follows the path through the trees to the river rock he found himself on Friday night. Smooth and wide, the rock overhangs the river like a tongue hesitant to taste, and Teddy sits on the rock, smoking a joint.

Teddy waves Thad over. His hair is greasy. His shirt, stomach-stretched and threadbare, reads: *LOVE IN AN ELEVATOR*. Thad doesn't have to look to know that the back reads: *LIVIN' IT UP WHEN I'M GOIN' DOWN*.

Teddy offers him the joint, which he takes. He hesitates, then returns the joint to Teddy without taking a hit. He wants to be right-thinking when Jake comes home. *If* Jake comes home. He hadn't planned to give his boyfriend an ultimatum yesterday, hadn't expected Jake to take off early this morning without saying where he was going. Asheville, Thad's assuming, though whether that's to tell

Marco off or to jump in bed with him, Thad couldn't say. Either way, he doesn't need to be stoned in the middle of the day. He needs to wait, sober, for Jake's call.

Teddy takes another hit. "Where's the fam?"

"I don't know," Thad says, joining Teddy on the rock. He sits. "Everyone spread out for the day. Mom's at church. Dad's fishing."

"What's he fishing for?"

"The usual. Bass, brim, crappie."

"Crappie," Teddy says, pronouncing it agriculturally—*crop*-ie—not the way Thad's dad says it, like something to do with shit. "Crappie are too easy in that lake. You get on top of them, in a few hours you'll have a freezer full."

It's true. Thad and his father have caught so many in one night that, by the third or fourth dozen, the fishing lost its appeal and began to feel like work, at least to Thad. Less so to his father, who could probably fish day and night without tiring.

"Fucking crappie," Teddy says. "I don't trust any animal that comes to you. My dinner, I want to outsmart it. Crappie are dumb as mullet. Probably you could whistle their wet asses into the boat."

Teddy is a stoner, sure. But he may also be a genius. There is much that stands in the way of this hypothesis, but *whistle their wet asses*? No weed is that good, and Thad feels the pang he feels when found poetry arrives better than any line his pen has ever put to paper.

"Give me liberty," Teddy says, "and give me trout. Give me a rainbow, a brook, a brown. *That* should be the challenge. Not how many fish a person can catch in a day. Not weight or length. One's goals should be nobler. Composition, a variety of kind. That should be the fisher's goal."

He takes a hit, and Thad can't stand it, the smoke, the smell, the river, the clear, warm day. He takes the joint. He takes a hit.

"A nobleness of goals," Teddy says. "I haven't pulled a brown trout from this river in years. Yet, should the universe see fit, should I catch three different trout from this stream in one day—a rainbow, a brook, a brown—that day I'll put down my pole for good and die a happy man."

Thad takes another hit. Already he's too far gone. On the far shore, the leaves of trees are dancing, and the trees' long arms reach over the river, as though to shake his hand. Thad pulls his shirtfront over his face.

"I should have warned you," Teddy says. "This weed's strong."

Thad tugs his shirt away. Across the river, the trees are just trees, the branches just branches.

Twice today he's tried Jake's cell. Twice, Jake's failed to answer. Thad wants this day to be over. He wants to know whether they'll stay together, relationship open or closed.

"There's a brookie who lives under here," Teddy says.

Teddy takes a last pull on the joint and flicks the spent roach downstream. The river rushes past them, but the world beyond the water lags in stoned slow motion.

Then Teddy's on his belly on the rock. He reminds Thad of a sea lion, a sea lion with hands and feet and a sweaty Aerosmith shirt. He beckons, and Thad joins him on his stomach at his side.

"Here, look," Teddy says. He has an arm in the water, face pressed to stone. "Little brookie and I have been practicing."

Thad presses his face to the rock, too. Teddy grimaces, the lip of the rock tucked into his armpit, his arm in the water, elbow-deep.

"I like you, Thad," Teddy says.

"I like you too," Thad says, a wave of gratefulness cascading down his back. When was the last time he was told he's *liked*? Not loved, not appreciated, but genuinely liked, told without explanation or expectation of commendation in return.

"You aren't like other customers," Teddy says. "You talk to me."

"You're easy to talk to."

Teddy strains, arm stirring the water. "What is it you believe in, Thad?" His face mashed to the rock looks slightly crazed.

"Like, religion? My mom's the religious one. I don't practice a faith." Which isn't entirely true. But what's the shorthand for occasional churchgoer turned atheist turned whatever Thad is now? Surviving his second attempt, he longs to believe in something bigger

than himself, but finding that something hasn't been easy. He hoped
he'd found it with Jake, but he can't even get Jake on the phone.

"You don't believe in anything?"

"I believe in something," Thad says. "I don't know what I'd call
it. Maybe love."

"I wouldn't call it love."

"What would you call it?"

"Me?" Teddy says. "The something I believe in I call the universe. The universe knows what you want. The universe knows what
you're thinking. You're responsible to just one thing, and do you
know what that one thing is?"

"The universe?" Thad says.

"The universe," Teddy says. "People will tell you the universe
doesn't matter, but don't listen to them. The secret to a good life is to
forget what people say. You and me, we don't answer to people. We
answer to the universe. And when we do, the universe answers back.
Aligns itself. Some people call this chaos, or God. You call it love.
Others say *whatever* and go about their day. But life isn't *whatever*.
We're talking about the fucking *universe*. It knows your needs. And
you're accountable to it, which means it's got to be accountable to
you."

Thad leans back so that his cheek no longer rests on the surface
of the stone.

"Teddy," he says, "I have no idea what you're telling me."

"I'm telling you the truth," Teddy says.

Thad wants to tell Teddy that his truth is cruel. That if the universe is in charge, the universe watched a boy drown and did nothing.
How is that a universe worth listening to? What manner of account-
ability is that?

A splash, and Teddy pulls a fish, flapping, from the stream.

"*The universe*," Teddy says.

"Holy shit," Thad says.

The fish is small, a brook trout, judging by the green head and
red tail. Its pupil is black ringed by gold. The mouth opens. The tail

searches for current in empty air. The trout's middle is caught in the fat of Teddy's fist. He loosens his grip, and between the fingers Thad sees polka dots, gold and red. The circles fuse into a pattern along the animal's back and melt into the red of its belly. Thad's used to seeing rainbow trout, the pink stripe, the black-speckled back, but he's never before seen a brook trout up close. The fish is beautiful, but how? How could something so beautiful spring from such an ugly universe?

Teddy kisses the fish, a brief peck on its head. He offers the fish for Thad to kiss.

"I'm good," Thad says, and Teddy lowers the trout into the water, then it's gone.

They lie awhile on the rock. The boughs of pines bend overhead.

"The universe," Teddy says. "Think about it."

"I will," Thad says.

He won't. But Teddy *has* inspired him. If the universe is merciless, Thad can't wait around for mercy. He must act. He must adjust his meds, smoke less, get serious about his poetry, or let it go. He must accept that, once Jake makes his choice, he may need to move on. And that will have to be okay. He has to learn to face his sadness and survive.

Teddy stands. "I should probably get back to the store."

Thad won't see Teddy next summer. He needs to tell him this. He needs to thank him for his friendship and for years and years of weed.

But he doesn't get the chance. There's a chirp, the sound his phone makes when it's been out of range and a signal has been found, the chirp followed by the dings of two missed calls, two messages awaiting his reply, and Thad opens the voice mail, hoping to hear from Jake.

The first message is Michael. It's garbled, though. Thad can barely make out what his brother says, and he skips ahead.

The second voice mail is clear. It's Michael again, only this time, he's calling Thad from jail.

31.

Richard is the one who found June.

She'd suffocated in her sleep, face pressed to a stuffed duck. Or she hadn't. They hadn't swaddled the child, hadn't put her to sleep on her back. Paramedics and doctors couldn't pinpoint the cause. Too many variables. SIDS is unpredictable that way. There was a brief but excruciating investigation, Richard and Lisa questioned in separate rooms. Could they be sure the other hadn't smothered the girl? Richard comprehended the legal obligation, but that hadn't kept him from threatening to punch the cop.

People at the funeral made things worse, the way well-meaning people tend to do.

"God won't give you more than you can bear," one man said, and Lisa drove her fingernails into Richard's arm. They both wanted to slap the man, to gouge his eyes and rip his tongue out by the root.

"This *is* more than I can bear," Lisa said the rest of that week, sobbing.

The year that followed was a gauntlet of a hundred little hurts: How the bassinet had to be disassembled and moved to the attic. How a thermometer or pacifier might surface in an unexpected place to obliterate Richard's day. How Lisa lactated for weeks after, shirts stained with milk.

Richard hadn't told the story in over thirty years. He can't say why he shared it with Clyde, but he did, the men in lawn chairs on the marina dock. He talked, and Clyde listened. When a boat pulled up for gas, Richard grew quiet, Clyde serviced the boat, and when the boat pulled away and Clyde took his seat, Richard resumed his story. He must have talked for an hour, every detail, all he could remember, everything. When he was through, Clyde said, "I'm sorry for your loss," shook Richard's hand, untied the boat, and helped Richard push off, so much tenderness in the other man's eyes, Richard thought he might cry.

"Crying's okay," Lisa would say. "It's healthy." But Richard isn't sure. Better to move steadily forward, eyes dry. Better to fish a few hours more and enjoy one of his last days on the lake.

He's a mile from his bay when he sees the police boats, no sirens, no lights. The big boat is not here, the dredge boat with its pulleys and hook.

It's getting late, near dinnertime.

He downshifts, idles. The police boats drift, a space opens between them, and a body floats into the open space.

Richard looks away. He doesn't have to see to know it's Glenn and Wendy's son.

Order, design. A comfort in numbers:

20: the number of seconds it takes a drowning person's lungs to fill with water.

4: the number of minutes before a dead body begins to decompose. Carbon dioxide builds. Cells rupture. The body eats itself from the inside out.

10 trillion: the number of microbes in the colon of a boy Robbie's size. Bacteria blooms. Skin discolors. Methane and hydrogen sulfide inflate the abdominal cavity and chest.

2–22: the number of days it takes bacteria to produce gas to the point of inflation. Variables include body mass index and water temperature. The colder the water, the slower the growth.

0.61: the number of degrees Fahrenheit that lake water temperatures have risen worldwide every decade for the past forty years.

54: the number of hours since the boy slipped beneath the boat.

48: the number of hours it takes a body to rise when the
water is warm.

Richard does not know these numbers yet. He will tonight, when sleeplessness has driven him online to look them up. For now, there are no numbers, only a white body in blue water.

Maybe the body is not the boy, he tells himself. Maybe the body is not a body.

He looks, sees silver swim trunks. He looks away.

No way to make this right, but there's one thing he can do. Suppose he reached the boy's family before the police? Wouldn't it be better to hear the news from a sympathetic voice, from a man who knows the grief they're going through?

He remembers their street. The cop on the boat, the young one, made Glenn repeat it twice. The street is just two bays away, their house somewhere on that street. He can find it. If he hurries, he can beat the police there.

He ratchets the boat out of idle and pilots fast toward the nearby bay. He's been there before. Fourteen miles of shoreline, and Richard's fished every channel and tributary, every inlet, every cove.

He enters the bay. No trailers here. Here, the houses are huge, their docks not rotted wood but plastic and aluminum, attendant boats suspended above the water in hydraulic lifts.

Figuring out which house is theirs will be a challenge. He circles the bay once, twice, looking for their pontoon boat.

That poor family. This will be the worst day of their lives.

And what is Richard's plan, exactly? Tie off at their dock. Knock on their door. What then? Assuming he can find the place, assuming the family is home, assuming they come to the door, what will Richard say? What words could possibly contain the horror that their boy's dead body has been found?

No matter. He's too late.

He spots the boat, the house above. A police cruiser pulls into a driveway, and the boy's mother hurries to meet it there. An officer steps out of the car. The mother falls. The officer lifts her, and she falls again.

Then Glenn is at her side. Then Trish. They are a tangle in the driveway, and Richard cannot watch. There is nothing left for him to do, and this is not his grief to share.

The sun is setting. He should be with his family. He leaves the bay and points his boat toward home.

32.

Michael shouldn't be surprised to find himself here. No small miracle he's never been arrested before. Drunk, how many punches has he thrown? How many times driven home the definition of *in no condition to drive*?

He isn't drunk. Or, he is, but he isn't *drunk*-drunk. He could have made it home. He wouldn't submit to the Breathalyzer because, *technically*, he's probably over the limit, but that hardly means he couldn't get home safe. They want to see *in no condition*, he'll show them *in no condition*. Give them a glimpse of the highlight reel of his life. Two bottles of wine is nothing. *In no condition* is still a bottle or two away. *In no condition* is throwing up to make room for more, waking with no memory of driving home, then rising and checking the grill of your car for gore.

Blow into this, or you're under arrest.

Fuck that. He hadn't crashed. He hadn't crossed a double yellow line. No way the cop could know unless he'd been waiting, casing the bar for drunks. *Entrapment.* Is that a thing, or just something from TV? Unless Lou called the cops. Or Gwen. Or the gallery owner. Or the woman he bumped into trying to navigate the sidewalk to his car. The way she'd pulled her toddler to her and crossed the street. The look on her face looking back at him. Fuck her.

He remembers calling Thad, remembers it seeming very important at that moment that his brother know they had a sister, remembers saying so into his phone, Thad's voice mail a land mine now, no way to take it back.

Then he was at his car door trying to work the key into the lock.

Then he was behind the wheel trying to work the key into the ignition.

He'd gone a block before he heard the siren—staccato, uncompromising—come on.

He got one phone call, which turns out not to be just something from TV. He tried his brother, left a second voice mail, and before long, Thad called the station to say that he was on his way. But that was hours ago.

Maybe Michael is where he belongs. On a bench. In a holding cell. In a tiny county police station with one cell, two desks, and a clock that ticks too loudly on the wall.

He's not alone. The arresting officer sits at his desk, and a drunk is with Michael in the cell. The man's passed out, or maybe he's asleep. He commands the length of the cell's only other bench, which is impressive, seeing as the bench isn't much wider than a gymnast's balance beam. The man sleeps on his back. He's bald, bushy eyebrows, pale skin. Both eyes are blackened, and blood runs from the man's mouth and down his cheek.

Michael shouldn't be here. He got into Cornell, goddammit.

"I got into Cornell, goddammit!" he yells.

Never mind that he wouldn't have gotten in had his parents not worked there, not with his grades. Never mind that he didn't actually *go*, passing up his free ride to follow Diane to Savannah instead.

The officer doesn't look up.

The cell is small, the bars close together. A low-slung, vulgar-looking toilet occupies one corner of the cell, no wall or privacy door.

What's taking Thad so long?

The man on the bench stirs. His hand finds his face, and blood streaks his chin.

This: This is when Michael's meant to change his life. This is rock bottom, right? Except, he isn't even *drunk*. He's buzzed. He's under arrest because his bail and fines and fees will pay for this year's police station Christmas party. *That* is why Michael was pulled over, cuffed, and pushed unnecessarily hard into the cruiser's backseat. Because he's not from around here. Because they want to take what little money he has left.

He didn't even swerve.

"I didn't swerve!" he yells.

"Should have submitted to the Breathalyzer, then," the officer says.

"I don't care what the numbers say. I know when I'm safe to drive."

The cop nods. Probably he's heard this before. A framed photo of his wife and kids sits on the desk. In the picture, the family stands behind a pumpkin, freshly carved, the officer younger, thinner, out of uniform.

"I'm not a drunk," Michael says.

"Sleep it off," the officer says, sounding weary more than angry. No doubt he'd rather be home with his family too. Probably lives in town, nice house, solid pension building up. Probably he has state-funded health insurance, benefits, and . . . *Is he doing a crossword puzzle?* On the clock? He's getting paid for this shit? Michael should have been a cop.

The man on the cell bench lets go a blood-flecked exhalation. His shirtfront's torn. His pants have pissed themselves. Exhibit A: Michael's no drunk. There are bottoms way rockier than his.

"What'd this guy do?" Michael asks.

"Ed?" the cop says. "Frequent flyer. Finally picked a fight he couldn't win. Word to the wise? No matter how drunk you get, never shoot your neighbor's dog."

"Jesus," Michael says. "So where's the other guy, the guy who beat him up?"

The officer looks perplexed. "Ed shot his *dog*. I'd have kicked his ass too."

Carolina justice. The officer returns to his crossword. The puzzle fills the page of one of those jumbo books for sale alongside sudoku tomes and paperback Bibles at Dollar Tree.

The station phone rings, and the cop is on the phone for a minute. "All right," he says, hanging up. "Your brother's on the way."

"For real this time?"

"I'm only saying what he said."

Still, the officer stands, opens the cell door, and lets Michael pull up a chair. From beneath the desk he produces a yellow bin, and Michael reclaims his watch, his keys, his wallet full of maxed-out credit cards. His phone is missing, then he remembers he left it in the car. He stands and puts on his belt.

"Sit down," the officer says, and he does. "Two pieces of advice: First, on your way home, buy some lice shampoo. RID is best, but any brand will do. You might be fine, but there's been a bit of that going around in here. Better safe than sorry."

Michael's scalp itches at the thought, and he fights the urge to run his fingers through his hair.

"Second, I know it's not my business, but I see people like you every day. I used to *be* you. Drunk before sundown. Hungover every morning. All I'm saying is, there's a better way to live."

"You're right."

Anticipation fills the officer's face, the start of a smile.

"It's not your fucking business," Michael says.

He says it too loud, and crossword cop is on his feet. "You want to go back in the cell?"

Fuck him. Michael's not the drunk he thinks he is. Physically, he may be alcohol-dependent, may need a drink every few hours to keep his hands from shaking, another few to make it through the day. But he's not some drunk. He's not Ed.

"What?" Michael says, angrier than he's prepared himself to feel. "What are you going to do, *double*-arrest me? For talking back? Did I make bail or not?"

"Michael!" Thad stands in the doorway, then he's through the door.

"One more word," the officer says.

"Oh, go finish your crossword," Michael says.

The cop pulls handcuffs from a pouch on his belt, taps them to his palm, and the cuffs spring open, ready for wrists.

But Thad is moving fast, apologizing, pushing Michael back into the chair. Thad sweet-talks the officer a while, trying everything. Finally, he lands on Michael as small-town hero, recounting the story of the drowning and his attempt to save the kid. Thad points to Michael's bandage.

"Shit," the officer says. "That was you?"

"Ever since the head injury, he's not himself," Thad says.

Michael laughs. He's never been more himself. He's never more himself than when he's mad and has a couple of drinks in him.

"I can let him off with a warning," the officer tells Thad, "but there will be paperwork."

Their conversation is cut off, though, by a crunch and a cage-rattling thud. Michael turns to find a bloodied Ed facedown on the cell floor. The floor is concrete, and Ed's face, when he lifts it, has the look of a face that's just hit concrete. He spits teeth, his mouth a harmonica of curiously well-spaced holes. A moan escapes the holes, and it isn't long before the moan turns to roar.

"Oh my God," the officer says. "I'd better get a dentist on the phone."

Of all the people he's been messing with all day, Michael suddenly feels sorriest for the police officer. Probably he took this job to help people, to stem the tide of hurt that floods the world. Only, no matter how hard he tries, no matter how many lives he saves or drivers he lets off with a warning, the tide, relentless, will return. Every night another Michael, another Ed, another puddle of blood and teeth to be mopped up.

The moaning grows in decibel and depth.

"Forget the paperwork," the officer says. "Just go."

Michael wants to say he's sorry for his attitude, his unkind words, but apologies don't come easy, and he lets Thad pull him across the station and out the door, Ed's screams amplifying into the evening air.

The sun is going down. It's twilight, or else it's dusk. Michael's never known the difference. They get into the car, but Thad lets the key hang in the ignition. He rests his forehead on the steering wheel. In time, his head lifts, and Michael sees the dilated pupils, the blood-shot eyes.

"Holy shit," he says. "You're stoned."

Thad turns the key. "I can't believe you made me drive to a police station, argue with a cop on your behalf, and now I have to drive you home. Next time you drink too much, I leave your ass in jail."

"I didn't drink too much."

Michael pulls the visor down and assesses his face in the mirror. His lip is swollen, jaw purpled from the bartender's punch. He wiggles a back tooth, newly loose, with his tongue. Michael flips the visor up. He can't look at himself.

"You left me there for hours," he says.

"I was afraid to drive. I've never driven high."

"I'll drive."

Thad laughs, the laugh delicate with contempt. He backs out of the parking space. But he takes too long getting the car out of reverse, too long turning onto the main road.

"Seriously," Michael says. "I can drive."

"You're drunk."

"I'm not."

Thad smacks the steering wheel. The car veers left, and he wrestles them back into their lane. "If you're not drunk, why were you in jail?"

"It wasn't jail. It was a holding cell."

"Why were you in a holding cell?"

"Because I wouldn't blow into the Breathalyzer."

"And, if you're not drunk, why wouldn't you blow into the Breathalyzer?"

"Because the Breathalyzer would say I'm drunk."

Thad's head turns, and Michael watches the road for both of them.

"Do you know how dumb you sound?" Thad says.

"Don't call me dumb," Michael says. "And watch the road."

They're quiet, then. It's ten miles to Highlands, another ten to the lake, but these are winding mountain roads, treacherous under the best conditions. At Thad's speed, it could be an hour before they're home.

Out the window, trees creep by. They crest a hill, then they're on a straightaway, past walls of rock dynamited to make room for road.

"You've got to stop drinking so much, Michael."

The flash of being found out turns Michael cold. Thad he threw up on. Thad was his one phone call. Kind of hard, now, hiding it from Thad. But the longer Michael dwells, the more he wonders just how well he's hidden it. What if he *is* a drunk? What if he's a drunk, and his whole family knows?

"If you have to drink," Thad says, "just don't drink and drive. How would you feel if your drinking ended someone's life?"

He wants to say he knows exactly how he'd feel. Two days ago, had he not been hungover, had he swum a little faster . . . Except there are too many trees, too many branches whizzing by. If he opens his mouth to speak, he might be sick.

"Pull over," he says. Pine trees pirouette down the road. His head itches at the thought of vermin swarming his scalp. "Pull over, please."

"Pull over *where*?"

"Please," Michael says, and his door's open before the car's slowed to a stop.

Then everything is out of him, the morning's moonshine, the wine, the cheese. It isn't pretty, and he hangs from the open door until he's sure the awful's out of him.

He wipes his mouth, sits back, and shuts the door.

"Tell me again," Thad says. "Tell me about how you're not a drunk."

33.

Beyond the window, the sun is up but sinking fast. Soon, the sun will hit the water and smolder, a chemical spill, orange and pink and blue across the bay. Diane's seen it a hundred times, and every seeing steals her breath. That tuck of silver water into sun, the water rainbowed like the wake a gas leak leaves behind a boat—this never stops being beautiful. She gets Monet. He has her heart. Haystacks and castles and water lilies, again and again, each one transformed by time of day. Even puddles, from the right angle, display a certain magnificence. Given enough light, Diane's convinced anything can be beautiful.

She watches the lake. She's trespassing, standing beside Thad and Jake's bed. The bed is unmade, pillows dented where their heads have been. She's alone, Richard fishing, the others gone for the day. This morning, she changed Michael's bandage, cleaned his wound, and he left, saying only that he'd be in Highlands if she needed him.

She's in this room because she's lonely, bored. The bag at the center of the bed, she didn't even have to open it. The bag was half-unzipped when she came in. She touches the bag. Jake wouldn't mind.

Of course he'd mind. But she's too curious to care. In two years' time, Jake has never once shown her his tools, what brushes he uses, which paints. She's never asked. She wants to be respectful, wants to avoid the questions he must get constantly from amateurs and the aspiring alike. But she has so many questions! And what good is it, knowing a master of the medium you share, if you can't ask him for help?

But she's Diane. And he's Jake. He's famous. Unlikely he'll ever show her the respect that she shows him. She knows this. She also knows you can't lose the respect you'll never have, so she pulls the zipper and opens the bag.

The brushes inside are good ones, not the cheapies she buys at Michaels or Jo-Ann when they're on sale. Even the ferrules on Jake's brushes are spotless, which means they're new or he's fastidious in his cleaning. She turns the bag over, and paint tubes tumble onto the bed. Something catches in the bag, and she dislodges it. After a minute's unfolding, she sees it's an easel, the travel kind composed of hollow poles like tent pegs threaded with bungee cords.

Jake's canvases, shipped in advance, lean against one wall. They're each the same size, 20 by 24, small for Jake, but fine for what she does—perfect, actually. There *are* two of them, still blank, and it's been three days. How long are Jake and Thad staying? Another day? A few more at most? No way, at this rate, Jake will use both canvases. At least, this is what she tells herself as she assembles the things she'll need.

There's a palette, but that feels personal, too much Jake's. She'll use a plate. She likes the way paint mixes on china, anyway. How it swirls, gloss-greasy. How the china seems to sway with the paint, whereas wood feels like it's pushing back.

There must be twenty paint tubes. She picks a dozen, then puts back four. Probably she can get by with eight. There's a smock, which she shakes out. It puffs and swells, new and white, geometric with the lines of its folding. She spreads the smock over the bed, but it won't lay flat, the way a road map won't flatten no matter how many times you run your hands over it. This, too, feels like too much. She has old shirts. She'll wear one of those.

She feels a kick.

Not really. Too soon for that. *Phantom kicks*, they're called. She's felt them before, worried, googled it, relaxed.

She puts on an old T-shirt, finds a plate, then carries everything down to the dock. This takes two trips, which takes too long. The sun hasn't set, but a crop of clouds is moving in, and now the light is wrong. The water's lost its shimmer, yielding to a gauzy haze.

A pair of blue Adirondack chairs are stationed on the dock, and Diane arranges Jake's paints in the lap of one of these, then marks her plate with all eight colors. She faces the easel toward the sun, away from the site of Friday's tragedy. She still can't bring herself to look in that direction.

Diane takes in the canvas and the plate, scared to begin. Back home, the one or two days a week she gets to paint, she uses acrylics or watercolors, inexpensive and quick to dry. But these are oils, which means they're pricey, slow to dry and quick to smudge. She hasn't used oils since she was a student.

She starts in on the plate and, right away, screws up. The oils are different pigments than she's used to, different hues. She tries to pull a violet from the cadmium and cobalt, but there's too much yellow embered in the red, leaving her with paint the color of a bruise. She pulls in some carmine, and, in time, she gets the violet she was looking for.

When she looks up, the surface of the water's changed again. Already the lake is less purple, the clouds less pink, the sun lower in the sky. She's never done a sunset. How does this work? How do you paint a subject that won't stay one color or sit still?

She balances the paint-streaked plate on one arm of the chair. She watches the horizon, selects a different brush. She brushes the dry canvas with the clean brush, just to feel the bristles' riffle and flick. It's only been a week since she's painted, but she feels as though she's never held a brush before, and she sets the paintbrush down.

Who is she kidding? There's a reason she teaches elementary school. *Those who can't*, and all that. Sure, she went to SCAD, but she's no great, undiscovered talent. Each time she gessoes a canvas, each time she sinks her fingers into clay, she accepts who she is, how far she's come, how far she has to go. Some days she makes art. Other days she makes a mess and wonders, *What's the point?*

If she dies tomorrow, not one person will miss her work. Her obituary will call her *teacher, daughter, wife*. And she is those things. And she's proud of them. Teaching isn't easy. Inspiring children, introducing them to the craft, is important work. Still, she wouldn't mind if her loss were remembered, secondarily, as a loss for *art*.

When she dies, what will become of the paintings and pottery filling the spare room and cluttering the garage? Say she goes first. Will Michael keep her work? Give it to Goodwill? Asking these questions feels like asking whether her husband loves her or not.

She picks up the paintbrush.

"Don't do that."

Diane drops the brush, which rolls across the dock into the lake. She turns, and Jake stands on the dock, frowning.

She hasn't prepared what she will say. In her fantasy, the painting she produced was so good, Jake was too awestruck to scold her for raiding his supplies. At least the first brushstroke has not been made. All she's done is waste a little paint.

"I'm sorry," she says. "I should have asked."

"It's fine. Someone should get some use out of them."

He approaches, pulls a fresh brush from the chair, hands it to her, and she feels like a child caught stealing twenties from her father's sock drawer, only, this time, her father isn't yelling but handing her the roll of rubber-banded cash.

"Just don't do the sun," Jake says. "I mean, a sunset can be done, but it's been *done*, you know? The sun is like birds. Everybody's painting *birds*, all of a sudden. Which isn't to say someone won't find a way to make birds or the sun interesting, but—"

"It won't be me."

"It won't be either of us."

She doesn't know what comes next. She still wants to do the sunset, but never before has Jake seen her work. Unsure as she is if she can bring herself to paint in front of him, she's doubly unsure she wants the first thing he sees to be a subject he finds tedious.

Jake steps away and seats himself in the other Adirondack chair, which seems to swallow him. He's such a small man.

She turns back to the canvas, dips the brush in paint, and rips a violet streak across the canvas. The color is too much, a mouth that wants to wail.

"Diane," Jake says, "are we friends?"

She wants to say no. She wants to point out that this might be the longest conversation they've ever had. Instead, she says, "Of course."

Then he's up from the chair and at her side. She's brought five brushes down, and he picks the largest with an angled tuft.

"May I?" he asks.

She offers him the plate, and Jake runs the brush through the carmine, then makes a comet's tail across the dish into the gold. He touches the brush to the canvas and curls a glowing yolk over her violet stripe, then tangles the gold and red into the brushstroke below. It takes all of ten seconds, and when he steps back, Diane sees the horizon before them reflected on the canvas.

"Presto," Jake says. "Sunset."

She wants to ask how he did it, except that she just watched him do it. If the seeing didn't make it simpler, she can't imagine how the saying would.

"You make it look so easy," she says.

She isn't looking for pity—she's genuinely impressed—and she shakes her head when Jake says, "I wasn't trying to show off."

"I didn't mean it that way," she says, but already Jake is setting down the plate.

"It's okay. I know I'm a show-off. I'm not even that great of a painter."

She's not sure where these words are coming from. Jake seems sad. Usually he's cocksure, pleased with himself, or at least pretending to be.

"You shouldn't say that," she says. "You're a gifted painter. It isn't fair to those of us who aren't for you to pretend otherwise."

Jake blinks, taken aback, and she wonders how many people in this man's life tell him the truth and how many tell him what he wants to hear. He could say, *No, Diane, you're talented too,* but he doesn't, and she's glad. If she's going to be honest with him, she respects him for being honest with her, too.

"Why did you ask me if we're friends?" she says.

Jake moves to the edge of the dock and watches the water, the sun. She'd like to have his eyes, just for a day. To perceive color and line and light the way he does.

"I don't know," he says. "It just struck me that we have something in common. Thad and Michael have to be here. Their parents call, and they come running. It's always been that way. But us?" He turns, and the sun is setting at his back. "You and me, we aren't Starlings. We choose to be here. We can leave anytime we want."

"You don't like them?"

"I like Thad," Jake says. "I *love* Thad. Family's tricky, though. I haven't seen mine in eight years."

She's heard the story. Not in full, but enough to know Jake's father once pulled a shotgun on him, that his mother watched and never said a word. In his family, you can't be who Jake is.

"The Starlings can be your family if you let them."

Jake laughs. "You mean I should marry Thad."

"If you want," she says, "but that's not what I mean. I only mean that Lisa and Richard would love you like a son if you loved them back."

Jake selects a clean brush from the chair. There's paint on his hands, a streak on the sleeve of his white linen shirt. She wants to ask why he's dressed up and where he spent the day, but she must choose her words sparingly. She can't be sure which questions might scare him off.

"They already love you," Diane says.

"I don't always get that from Thad's mom."

Jake stands before the canvas. He paints quickly, filling in the sky, then moving to the lake below. What he's after, it isn't quite the horizon before him, but something bigger, richer, aglow in a wider range of colors than the colors on display.

"Let me ask you something," Diane says. "Have you ever asked Lisa about herself?"

Jake says nothing. He turns his head, but she can't read his face.

Is he ashamed that he's never taken an interest in Lisa's life, or is he bewildered, wondering why he should?

"That," she says. "That right there is why she's occasionally frosty with you. You just dismissed her whole life with a look."

Jake returns his concentration to the canvas. "I did not."

"You did. You didn't mean to, but you did. And that's okay. You're young. But at some point you're going to be expected to take an interest in the lives of others. Besides, Lisa's worth getting to know. She's lived a full life."

Jake paints. He pulls color to the canvas's edge, and he's not careful about it, the way Diane tends to be. Paint splatters, and he lets it.

"Would you believe this is the first thing I've painted in months?" he asks.

"I'm sure that's not true."

Another kick that's not a kick. She should have had a bigger lunch.

"It's true," he says. "I'm all fucked-up right now. I'm too much in my head."

Say more, she wants to say, but she doesn't trust her motives. Is she hoping to help or looking for companionship in her self-doubt?

"I can't believe I just told you that," he says. "I haven't even told Thad."

The sun is setting fast, and Jake hurries to capture it, jostling the easel, bumping the canvas with his hand. He's so careless compared to her, yet somehow his work comes out so much better.

"Sometimes I think it's God," he says. "I know that's silly."

"I don't think it's silly."

Jake steps back from the canvas, squints. He's gotten more paint on his shirt, paint in his hair.

"Back home," he says, "I pick up the brush to paint, and the canvas is a magnet pushing back. The brush just hovers, like my arm's possessed, like God's stopping me. My parents wanted me to be a preacher. Dad said God told him I'd have my own flock. I know it's bullshit. I know that's just my dad. Still, some part of me can't help feeling punished. For painting. For loving Thad. It's like I missed my calling, disobeyed God's will for my life."

The lake shimmers, a drawn bath. The sun has set.

"Do you believe in God?" Jake asks.

She doesn't know, and she admits as much.

"Where I grew up, God was everywhere," Jake says. "In the air you breathed. In the songs you sang. We thanked God for the good things that happened to us, and we thanked God for the bad. We thanked God for our food, no matter what that food was. Can you imagine thanking God for waffles? I don't mean homemade. I mean *Eggos*. I can't see God wanting thanks for those."

He works the brush back over a few places, but the painting's done. Any more fussing with it, and she worries he'll mess it up.

"Yesterday I let a man I used to love suck my dick," Jake says. "Today I find out he paints Audubon knockoffs and hates my guts. Life's so fucking weird."

Diane takes a step back. She tries to keep the surprise from showing on her face, but she fails.

"I'm sorry," Jake says. "I'm not trying to shock you. It's just nice having someone to talk to."

It *is* nice. Some days, home from school, she and Michael hardly speak.

Kick, kick.

Jake puts down the plate and brush. He steps back from the painting, tilting his head left, then right. "You like Rothko? Big canvases, big color blocks?"

"I know who Rothko is." She loves Rothko's work. She wants Jake to know this, and, wanting this, understands she wants his approval way too much.

"Rothko killed himself," Jake says. "Slashed his arms to ribbons. Plus pills. Such a waste."

In the distance, a boat enters the bay, and Diane sees it's *The Sea Cow*. Richard's home.

"In L.A.," Jake says, "at MOCA, there's a Rothko room. Last

time I was there, whoever curated the exhibit placed a *mannequin* at the center of the room, some 'found object' bullshit. They have eight Rothkos, good ones, and they hide them behind a plastic man. I would have paid ten grand for ten minutes without that thing in the way. Just to fall into those paintings. To take them in all at once."

He takes two steps back.

"All that beauty, and no one could see it for the man in the middle of the room."

He spreads his arms.

"There you go. Motherfucking sunset."

The painting is gorgeous. It's more than a sunset, more than a lake, and Diane sees that her mistake was trying to paint the thing she saw. Jake understands light and design too well to fall for what's before his eyes. What he's done is stylized, impressionistic. It's the very thing Jake said a sunset couldn't be. It's *interesting*. It's all of the colors from *The Scream* blended and reassembled and made new. That Jake painted this in fifteen minutes fills Diane with too much admiration to worry about her envy anymore.

Jake turns, and his face is sweaty. There's sorrow in his eyes. Joy, too. Joy most of all.

He *loves* this.

She knows, then, that she'll never be Jake. Not just because she's not as good. Not just because she'd never pay ten grand to see some Rothkos on a wall. Because art's not her life. *Life* is her life—people. Michael, her mother, new students every year. The life that grows inside her even now. Given the choice between people and paint, she'll choose people every time. She's not convinced Jake would.

Jake wipes his face, and his sleeve leaves his forehead marked with paint.

"Come on," he says. "Let's sign."

He dabs the black, and, in the bottom right-hand corner, signs his name. He holds the brush out to Diane.

"Team effort," he says. "I couldn't have done it without your head start."

Absolutely not, she wants to say. But why is her instinct to feel condescended to? There's nothing condescending in Jake's wild eyes, his paint-smeared face, the way he holds the black-tipped brush.

"Please," he says, "I mean it." And she signs.

Up the hill, a car pulls in. Lisa gets out and waves. She pulls a long white box from the trunk and disappears into the house.

Kick, kick.

Something isn't right. Some kind of cramping or constricting, something, pregnant, you aren't supposed to feel. She holds her abdomen.

The Sea Cow nears. Above them, Lisa's coming down the hill.

The tightening worsens, and Diane drops to one knee.

Then Lisa's on the dock and at her side, asking Diane where it hurts, but Diane is having trouble speaking. The pain is too intense. She holds her stomach tight.

"Shit," Jake says. "What is it? What's wrong?"

"I'm pregnant," Diane says.

Jake looks sucker-punched, then elated. "Congratulations. Oh my God!"

"No time," Lisa says. "Help me help her up."

Things happen quickly after that. Lisa and Jake help her up the hill. "What's happening?" Richard calls from the water, tying off the boat. "Good Lord, what's going on?" But no one answers. No one is concerned with him. Lisa helps her into the backseat of her car, then joins her. Jake gets behind the wheel and waits for Richard, who's trudging up the hill. "Hurry," Jake shouts, and, frowning, Richard walks a little faster until he's reached the car and climbed in. "What is this?" Richard asks. "Where are we going?" Jake doesn't answer. He doesn't wait for Richard to put his seat belt on. He reverses the length of the driveway, then tears down the road. At which point, after taking several deep breaths, Diane pulls her phone from her pocket and dials Michael's number many, many times.

34.

In the passenger seat, Thad's brother fiddles with the air-conditioning with one hand. The other hand kneads his face. "One of my back teeth is loose." He rests his head on the window. "I need my car."

"Tomorrow," Thad says. "You're drunk. I'm high. We're going home."

"My phone's in the car. At least let me get my phone. It's on the way." He flips the visor, looks in the mirror, pokes at his teeth. "Also, if you see a drugstore, I need lice shampoo."

Not for the first time, Thad plays the mental game of whose life sucks more, which brother has it worse.

It's not a contest. Thad's father's voice is in his ear. *You're both disappointments to me.* Not that his father would say that, ever, but it's there, the judgment in the man's eyes when he asks his son what he's been up to the past year, and Thad answers, "Writing poetry."

"Have you tried therapy?" Thad asks.

Michael flips the visor up. "Fuck therapy."

"But you're depressed."

Michael cracks his window and pokes a finger out. How easy it would be for Thad to push a button, to guillotine the finger in two.

"I'm not depressed," Michael says.

"We're all depressed," Thad says. "We're a family of depressives. I'm just the only one who's getting help."

Michael pulls the finger in and rolls the window up. "Dad's not depressed."

"Of course he is. His generation's different. Men his age show it less. They just live unhappily."

"What about Mom?"

"I don't know. Mom might be okay. She's definitely the healthiest of the four of us."

Michael looks out his window. The road dips and turns, and Thad wants to ask him to face forward. He's cleaned up enough of Michael's puke for one week.

"What's so great about therapy?" Michael asks.

"For starters?" Thad says. "*Drugs.*"

"Your therapist does drugs?"

Thad can't tell if Michael's kidding or playing dumb. He's not stupid. As a teenager, Thad once went through his mother's filing cabinets. He found report cards confirming that Michael's grades were lower than his own. Then he came across two envelopes he hadn't known were there. He had no memory of taking the IQ test. Apparently, he'd done so in fourth grade under the guise of a grad student's research project. His mother was forever volunteering them for studies at Cornell. Thad opened both envelopes. Both IQs were high, two standard deviations above the mean. Michael's, though, was higher by four points. Thad's favorite part of the story, though, is that the envelopes were *sealed.* How like his mother. Getting the scores, she hadn't wanted to know. Or, wanting to know, she'd refused to let curiosity get the upper hand. What self-restraint. What bright, unbending love.

To this day, Thad's never given Michael the news or the satisfaction of those four points.

"*Prescription* drugs," Thad says. "Actually, those come from a psychiatrist. My psychotherapist can't prescribe."

"What kinds of drugs?" Michael asks.

"Me? I worship the trinity: Xanax, Paxil, Seroquel."

They approach a switchback, and Thad slows the car. On the lake, you forget you're in the mountains. In the car, negotiating a turn, it's impossible to forget.

"Why three pills?" Michael asks.

"One for anxiety, one for depression, one for psychosis."

"Wait, you're psychotic?"

"I'm bipolar. I'm at risk of psychotic episodes, yes."

A drizzle works its way out of the clouds, and Thad flips the wipers on.

"You really think I'm depressed?" Michael asks.

"I'm not a doctor. I only know what I see, and what I see is a depressive who uses alcohol—which is a depressant, by the way—to cope."

"Alcohol is a *depressant*?"

Again, Michael's fucking with him, or he's not. When he's been drinking, it can be hard to tell. Rain covers the windshield, and Thad speeds the wipers up.

"How long have you been on these pills?" Michael asks.

"This particular cocktail reaches back a ways. I tend to switch it up every five years."

"Why?"

"Because the pills stop working and I want to kill myself."

The road is wet. The wipers wipe. The weed's worn off.

"Fuck," Michael says. "I didn't know that. I knew it was bad, but I didn't know it was like that. I guess some part of me hoped that maybe you just wanted—"

"Attention?"

Thad's strangling the steering wheel. He wants to reacquaint Michael with his arm, his missing toe. But they've never had this talk before, not at any length. He relaxes his grip. Outside, the rain slows.

"It's okay," he says at last. "I've come to accept how hard it is to understand for anyone who doesn't want to die."

A sign reads: *Highlands 2 Miles*. Ahead, another bend in the road, rock face to the right, a double guardrail to the left. Thad slows the car to thirty, twenty-five.

In therapy, Steve says the best way to encourage vulnerability is to share your own, but Thad can't imagine what he might say to get Michael to admit he drinks too much.

"Steve says—"

"Who's Steve?" Michael asks.

"My therapist."

"Your therapist's name is *Steve?*"

Twenty miles per hour, fifteen. They head into the turn, and Michael's laughing.

Thad doesn't get what's so funny. Then, the more he thinks about it, the funnier it gets. His therapist's name is *Steve*. Those hairy arms on days he wears shirts with short sleeves. What kind of doctor wears short sleeves?

Then Thad's laughing too, and they are young again. They're brothers filling the car with their delight, laughing right up to the second Thad makes the turn and runs into the deer.

Thad isn't the first to hit the deer. The deer is dead, and he doesn't run into it so much as over it. He brakes, backs up, and crushes the animal again. Its entrails, peeking out before, are fully splayed now, in the road.

Michael opens his door and throws up. Thad wants to join him. He opens his door but holds his bile back.

The deer is a doe, a large one, tan and red splatter. The neck is bent. The body bisects the road's broken white line. Thad's seen roadkill across North Carolina, upstate New York, too. But deer tend to take out cars more than cars take out deer. Whatever hit this one was big and didn't stop.

But it's not the dead deer that's caught Thad's attention. It's the fawn. White-spotted rump and reedy legs, the deer stands at the guardrail, muzzle bloodied, ears up, eyes on its mother.

"Holy fucking shit," Michael says.

They wait. They sit in their seats and watch through open doors. And as they watch, the fawn moves to the doe's side. It nuzzles the neck, the face. It noses the entrails like it's trying to push them back inside.

"Fuck," Michael says.

Thad leaves the car, and the fawn doesn't flinch. Does it believe its mother will rise? Can animals fathom death?

"No, no, no," Michael says. His face is in his hands.

"It's okay," Thad says, speaking to his brother, speaking to the deer.

"I want to go home," Michael says.

Thad crouches beside the open car door, but he doesn't want to get too close. The smell is strong. Already, flies have arrived. The fawn licks its mother's face.

"Take me home," Michael says. "Please."

They were boys in a bathtub, once, singing, washing each other's backs. Boys fighting over pajamas—too small for Michael, too big for Thad—the red footies with the purple locomotives, black track circling the waist. They were boys under covers, their mother reading them the story of the spider and the pig.

Where is Thad's father in these memories? In his study. At the lab. Working. Reading. But that was Dad. They needed him, but they'd been trained not to begrudge his absence. Absence was the province of fathers, and they let their father go about his work.

But bedded down, belly warm and hair still wet, brother beside him and mother floating above as he slipped, serene and dreamy, into sleep, Thad was never happier. And never expects to be that happy again. The world was different then, or else the world's the same and Thad's too changed. Either way, there's no going home.

Then Michael's out of the car. The fawn looks up. Michael swings his door shut, and the fawn bounds across the road, over the guardrail and out of sight. Thad runs to the rail, but what looks like a cliff face, from the car, turns out to be a pine-pocked incline, one the little deer has no trouble navigating at top speed. The fawn traverses, leaps, a miracle skier slaloming downhill.

Thad turns, and his brother is a sight, battered, bandaged, lip swollen as a slug ready for the mallet's flattening. He joins Michael, and together they roll the deer onto the shoulder of the road.

In the car, Thad wipes his hands on his pants, but the smell has followed them, iron and forest and animal musk. The smell rides with them the last mile to Highlands, and when Thad pulls up behind Michael's car, the smell is with them still.

He'll never eat venison again.

Neither will he tell the story. Not to Jake. Not to his parents. Not in a poem or at a dinner among friends. A miracle loosens its grip on the miraculous each time it's told, mutating from fact to myth, from how it was to how it is remembered, until, in time, one wonders if the miracle arrived at all. The thought of being at a Christmas party, of Jake saying, "Thad, tell them about the deer," is more than Thad can bear.

The car in park, he turns to Michael. "Are you going to get your phone?"

"Diane's pregnant," Michael says.

Thad's sure he's heard wrong, then sure he hasn't. *We're never having kids*, Michael's always said. So much for that. Thad's going to be an uncle.

"That's wonderful," Thad says. "Who else knows?"

"Just Mom."

"How far along is Diane?"

"Ten weeks. Eleven, maybe."

"The doctors can't tell?"

"We haven't gone."

Thad doesn't know much about pregnancy, but enough friends have had kids that he knows you don't go that long without getting checked. There's too much to account for—nutrition, birthing classes, prenatal vitamins—not to start in right away. You find out you're knocked up, you call your doctor. You go. You change your life.

"It's not *planned*, if that's what you're wondering," Michael says.

Beyond the windshield, the sun is down, treetops lit like match heads. Soon, the Blue Ridge Mountains will shimmer like an inland sea.

"But you're excited?" Thad asks. "You've warmed up to the idea?"

"We're keeping it," Michael says, then exits the car to find his phone.

Thad checks his voice mail. Same two messages. He tries the first again and, this time, not quite so high, no Teddy talking or river rushing in his ear, he can just make out what his brother is saying. And what he hears turns his skin inside out. Michael's voice is drunken, slurred, but the words are unmistakable: They had a sister. Her name was *June*. She's dead.

Then Michael is beside him in the car. "Found it!" he says, holding up his phone.

"Is it true?" Thad says, holding up *his* phone.

Michael's face drops. "Shit. I didn't—I meant to—"

"Just tell me. Is it true?" But Michael's silence is all the confirmation he needs.

He has so many questions. Who was this sister? How long did she live? How long has Michael known, and why was he told when Thad was not?

No time for questions, though, because Michael's cursing, staring at his phone.

"Something's wrong," Michael says.

"What is it?" Then Thad's phone is ringing. Not the call he's been waiting for, not Jake, but their mother.

"Missed calls," Michael says.

"How many?"

Michael holds up the phone, and there, in black script on a white screen, Thad sees it.

Sunday: Missed Calls: 22.

35.

In the waiting room, Richard paces, and Jake watches.

Lisa bows her head. Maybe she's praying. Thad's told Jake that as kids, she dragged him and Michael to church some weeks, though these days she's less devout.

The waiting room is modest, the floor a laminate checkerboard, the ceiling low. A dozen orange chairs line the walls, and Jake and Lisa sit in two of them. In one corner, a mop handle rises from a yellow bucket of gray water. A plastic sign—*Caution: Wet Floor*—spreads its legs beside a hot-drink machine, the kind that trades quarters for bad coffee in flimsy paper cups.

No one else is in the waiting room. Small town, small hospital. The receptionist recognized Diane coming through the door. "How's your husband's head?" she asked before Lisa explained that they were here for Diane. The woman at the front desk picked up a phone. Who knows if there's a doctor back there with her even now? Could be they're waiting for one on call to arrive.

"What is it?" Richard asks at last. "Why is no one talking? What's wrong with Diane?"

"She's cramping," Jake says.

"Cramping?" Richard says. "We're here for cramps?"

Jake looks to Lisa. Lisa looks to Jake.

Richard catches all this looking. "What don't I know?"

"Diane's pregnant," Lisa says. "She wasn't telling people yet."

Richard sits heavily, and Lisa rises from her chair to take a seat beside him.

"She wasn't telling people yet," Richard says, "but she told you."

Lisa nods. "And you."

"Just now," Jake says. "On the dock."

"Am I the only one who didn't know?" Richard lets the words unfurl with too much volume, and Lisa places a hand on the back of his neck.

"Honey," she says, "the only thing that should concern you, right now, is whether Diane's going to be okay."

"Cramping," Richard says. "That's bad."

"It's not good," Lisa says.

Jake steps outside. He hates hospitals, hates illness. This talk of Diane cramping, thoughts of miscarriage, it's too much. He needs air.

Outside, night's fallen, and the parking lot blacktop glitters under lamplight like licorice laced with glass.

Fuck. Michael should be here for Diane. Thad should be here for him. Lisa spoke to them. She says they're on the way, but Jake wishes they would hurry. He can't reenter that waiting room alone, can't face the sorrow of Richard and Lisa being told they won't be grandparents.

And what to say to Thad when he arrives? Assuming he asks where Jake's been, what will Jake tell him? Assuming the ultimatum still stands, what will he say?

Is it so wrong Jake wants to have his cake, to eat it too: to have the love of one man and the excitement of many more? Must Thad really make him choose?

Jake's fault. Thad never wanted this, and Jake's known that all along.

Thad's fault. He's a grown man making grown-men decisions, and he signed up for this.

Or else they're both to blame. But no. This is America. In America, somebody takes the blame.

At least today he painted. That's something.

He checks his watch. He calls Frank.

"Jacob?" Frank's voice is raspy, honeyed with sleep, though it's not yet ten o'clock.

When Jake met the man, Frank intimidated him. He's charismatic, a toucher, hand always on your arm. But his reputation's sterling. He's never fucked a customer, never made a pass at an artist he sells. In the gallery, he's a tough negotiator, but with his painters, he's a cheerleader, a confidant and friend.

"I'm sorry," Jake says. "I'll let you sleep."

Frank coughs a cough like paintbrushes in a blender, the rattle of decades of cigarettes. The cancer, when it comes, will be vicious and unrelenting.

"It's all right," Frank says. "How's my little rock star this evening?"

"Not great. A kid drowned, my boyfriend's brother almost drowned trying to save him, and now his wife's in the hospital. But look, that's not why I called."

"Jesus," Frank says. "Where are you?"

"The mountains. It's not important. You wouldn't know the place."

Frank's quiet so long, Jake wonders if he's fallen back to sleep.

"I have to come clean with you about something," Jake says. "I haven't painted in months. I mean, I painted a sunset, but that was a fluke. Point is, you should cancel my next show. I'm not sure I'll ever paint again."

Frank coughs a substantial, phlegm-filled cough. That or he's laughing. Jake can't tell.

"Listen, Jacob," Frank says, and this is the voice Jake knows, the voice that sells millionaires on paintings they'd never otherwise buy. This voice is bayoneted, grooved for blood. "You just had a sellout show. You got a rave in the *Times*. *Of course* you're not painting. You *shouldn't* be painting. You should be celebrating. You should be freaking out. You should be doubting everything you've ever done and wondering what could possibly come next. Angst! Tears! You're twenty-five!"

"Twenty-six."

"Twenty-six! This *had* to happen. You're too much. You're a goddamn machine. You're overdue for a breakdown. Or a scandal. But stick with the breakdown. They're easier to spin. I promise you, you'll paint again."

"What if I don't?"

"You *will*. Everyone gets blocked and bounces back."

"Everyone?"

"Well," Frank says, "not everyone. Some crash and burn. But we don't speak of them."

"But what if—"

"*Trust me*. It's nothing. Call me when you haven't painted in a year."

"But my next show."

"Postponed." Frank coughs. "Make them wait. Make them think you're up to something special, which, soon enough, you will be."

There's quiet on the line, Jake unsure what to say.

"And, Jacob?" Frank's voice is stern, chrome polished to a shine. "Just make sure the next show *is* something special."

Jake *really* doesn't know what to say to that. He's dreaded this call for weeks, and in two minutes' time, he's moved from anxious to relieved to terrified.

Frank laugh-coughs. "I'm kidding! Next time, though, don't call so late. Now go to bed. And give that boyfriend of yours a squeeze from me. He's adorable."

Frank hangs up. Jake pockets his phone, and here come Thad and Michael in Thad's car. The car pulls into the nearest parking space, and Michael jumps out and runs past Jake. Thad is slower coming up the sidewalk.

"Hey," Jake says, and Thad passes him and goes into the hospital.

He should have called. He shouldn't have left Thad in the dark all day. Nothing to do now but step inside.

In the waiting room, Lisa scolds Thad. *Where were you? Why don't you boys ever answer your phones?* Meanwhile, Michael's already been led back.

Thad takes a seat, Jake sits next to him, and Thad scoots one seat down.

"Did *you* know?" Richard asks Thad from across the room, and Jake's been wondering this too.

"Know what, Dad?" Thad asks.

"Diane," Richard says. "She's pregnant. Did you know?" His voice is too loud again, and again Lisa rubs the back of his neck.

"Michael told me half an hour ago."

Richard shakes his head, stands, and lumbers to the coffee machine. He pushes the *Caution* sign aside and searches his pockets for coins. Then Lisa's there with her purse, tucking quarters into his hand.

"I'm sure they were going to tell you next," Lisa says, but Richard isn't listening. He's studying the display, selecting his drip and size.

Once, when Jake was a boy, his father rented a stump grinder from the hardware store. In place of wheels, the grinder had tank tread, and the blade, when it bit into the wood, made the most awful shrieking noise Jake's ever heard. It's that noise Jake hears when Richard pushes a button and the coffee machine shudders and lets loose a coffee-percolating scream.

Lisa moves to the seat between Jake and Thad and puts an arm around each of them. Thad doesn't lean into his mother's embrace, which Jake finds odd. He knows Thad's mad at him. He's not sure why he'd be mad at Lisa too.

The coffee machine's rattle is extinguished with a hiss, and Richard pulls a cup from the dispenser. The cup is small, the handle composed of two loops of hole-punched paper folded like butterfly wings. Richard sips the coffee, makes a face, and tips his cup into the mop bucket.

"Just to be clear," Richard says. "You *all* knew?"

"Seriously?" Thad says. "You're going to lecture *me* for keeping secrets?"

Then Thad's up, and Jake follows him outside. They stand on the sidewalk just beyond the hospital doors.

"Nothing happened," Jake says, but he's talking to Thad's back. "I went to Asheville, but nothing happened. No more Marco. That's over. I love you."

But Thad doesn't say *I love you* back. He turns, and he's crying.

"I have a sister," he says.

"I'm sorry," Jake says, "I don't understand."

"Mom told Diane. Diane told Michael. Michael told me. A sister, *June*, before Michael was born. She only lived a month."

"Oh my God," Jake says. He steps forward, and Thad lets Jake hold him in his arms. Then Thad straightens, clears his throat, and dries his face.

"I should go inside," Thad says.

Thad's still in Jake's arms, and there's so much Jake wants to say. He wants to tell Thad about Marco, about the birds, about the sunset and the painting and his phone call with Frank. And he wants to hear about Thad's day, which is when he knows the love he says he feels for Thad is real. He *is* interested. He cares. He cares about this man more than himself. Hell, he even wants to read Thad's poetry.

But he doesn't say any of that. Instead, he says, "Be with your family," and lets Thad go.

36.

Diane holds her husband's hand.

The table beneath her is wide, and, through the paper gown, her back is cold. The lights in the little room are dimmed, the walls bathed gray, and a counter runs the length of one wall. A machine that reminds her of a grade school overhead projector squats by her head, and Michael stands at her middle.

He looks terrible. His hair hugs his skull, flattened as if from a downpour. His cheeks are stubble, jaw bruised. His forehead is swollen, the bandage unchanged all day. A pinstripe of vomit marks his shirtfront, and he smells like sour wine.

At Diane's feet, a woman fills out papers on a clipboard. She wears a white coat but no stethoscope, and Diane can't tell if she's the doctor or a nurse. She wasn't among the staff on Friday who attended to Michael's head. She asks Diane questions and writes her answers down.

How far along is she? Ten weeks.

Is she on prenatal vitamins? She's not.

Has she had an ultrasound before? She hasn't.

Who is her family doctor in Texas? She doesn't have one.

Who's monitoring the pregnancy? Diane is.

A long silence follows.

The woman in the white coat thinks she's stupid, or else she sees this all the time: unplanned pregnancies, the couple refusing to make a decision, supposing that if they wait long enough the problem will go away.

Perhaps the problem is going away, her body flushing the problem from her womb. Except, the problem's not a problem, never was, not for Diane, and she doesn't want to see it go.

The woman pulls a page from the clipboard, turns it over, and clips the page again. She crosses through something, then writes some more. All of which is excruciating to watch. There's no urgency to her movements, no haste. What if time is of the essence? How can the woman in the white coat be in no hurry at all?

"Please," Diane says at last, "could you go faster, please?"

"Oh, honey, there's no rush," the woman says. "Are you bleeding?" She's not. "Are you cramping now?" She isn't. The pain subsided sometime after she lay down.

"Pretty standard. Your uterus is expanding. It's a sensation you've never felt before. Some mothers feel it more acutely than others. We'll run the necessary tests, but chances are, you're fine."

Michael squeezes her hand.

"I'm ordering an ultrasound," the woman in the white coat says. "I'll be right back."

She leaves, and Michael asks Diane what happened. His eyes are vacant. All the electricity's gone out of them, whatever glimmer proves your soul is sound.

"Contractions," she says. "Like my period's about to start."

"Does it hurt?" he asks, and she wants to ask just how genuine, on a scale of one to ten, his concern is. After all, isn't this the *Get Out of Jail Free* card he's been waiting for?

"I want my mom," she says.

"I'll call her," Michael says, but Diane shakes her head.

If she loses the pregnancy, better her mother never knew. Her mother is fragile, well-intentioned but easily upset. *Why didn't you tell me sooner?* she would ask, and Diane would have to defend herself. That isn't comfort, even if it's love. Right now, though, Diane needs both.

Michael lets go of her hand. He kneels, and his face is at her belly.

"I need you to tell me something," she says. She doesn't mean to whisper, but whispering makes it easier, what comes next. "Tell me you love me, or tell me that you don't. But I need to know."

Michael opens his mouth to speak, and she claps a hand across his face. He startles, but he lets her leave her hand. His breath is warm.

"Don't answer," she says, and she's not whispering anymore. "Don't tell me until you're sure. Because this is it, the beginning or the end. I can't live the way we've lived the last two months. I can't live the way we've lived the last two *years*. I'll love you forever, Michael, but I won't stay with you if you treat me this way."

His mouth opens behind her hand, wet lips and squeak of teeth, but she doesn't let go. Her fingernails dig in, and Michael shuts his mouth.

"If this child is still in me, I'm having it. And you, either you're all-in or all-out, no more lukewarm. I need to know if you're in, if you love me and you'd like to come along."

Her palm is wet with hot breath, fingers sandpapered by the stubble on his cheeks. She lets go, and his face sinks into her abdomen.

"I'm in," he says, and it will have to do. It's not as good as *I love you*, not the same as *I'm not going anywhere*, but he takes her hand in both of his and kisses it. She runs her other hand over his hair and finds her favorite square inch of his body, that secret indentation where spine intersects with neck, their first real intimacy in months.

"I went to jail today," he says, speaking into her stomach.

Diane says nothing, but her hand goes still. He turns his head so she can see his face.

"I might have a drinking problem," he says. "I do. I have a drinking problem. Sometimes I get up in the middle of the night and need a shot of vodka just to get back to sleep."

"We don't drink vodka." She doesn't know what else to say. She didn't know this. She knew her husband liked to drink, but this, a dependency, she had no idea. "We don't even keep vodka in the house."

"Back closet, filing cabinet, bottom drawer: two bottles. Basement, under the stairs, with the Christmas decorations: three bottles. Garage, behind the water heater, one big bottle."

She doesn't cry. She's too surprised to cry.

"How long has this been going on?"

"Three years."

Three years? "I don't know if I'm angrier at you for not telling me or at myself for not figuring it out."

"Don't blame yourself," he says.

"Oh, don't worry. I blame you. But I blame myself too." She takes his hand. She can listen. She can try. She says, "Tell me more."

He does. He tells her how it started with drinks after work, then drinks *after* drinks after work. How this ballooned to drinks to get him through the day. He tells her about bars and how many he's been kicked out of. He tells her that he's driven drunk, though he's never been caught until today. He tells her about jail, about a man who fell and broke his face, about Thad coming to his rescue.

"You have to tell your parents," she says, but Michael isn't keen on that idea. "You do. Beating this, you might have to quit work, at least take time off. You're going to need help. We're going to need money."

"I can't ask my father for more money."

"Then I will."

"Diane, please," he says, and she can see that he's humiliated. Worse, he's ashamed.

"Okay," she says. "I'll leave it up to you. But you can't be drunk when the baby comes. If you're still drinking in six months, you'll have to leave."

Michael nods. It's not the news he wants to hear, she can tell. It's not the news she wants to give. But it's the only way. She won't raise a child around a man who has that in common with her father. She won't do it.

"You can't be a drunk and be a father to our kid," Diane says.

"Okay," he says.

"I won't have it."

"I understand."

"There's no compromising here. My mother raised me. I can raise a child. I'll do it alone before I'll let you fuck our kid up."

"Jesus," Michael says. "I love you so much."

And here are the words she needs to hear. They arrive like rain to cool a sweltering day, and she pulls him to her and kisses him, their first kiss since some time before she showed Michael the little stick, the pink plus sign that meant she'd be a mom. The kiss is quick, abbreviated. Her husband smells like sickness and wine, and if he could hide this so well from her, she can't help wondering how she'll know if he's hiding it again.

"Hey," she says, "want to hear a joke?"

"Sure."

"What's the difference between a hippo and a Zippo?"

Michael smiles. Of course he'd know the punch line. He knows all his father's jokes, but she can see he's going to humor her.

"I don't know," he says. "What *is* the difference between a hippo and a Zippo?"

"The difference," she says, before saying, "Shit." She's forgotten how it ends.

Michael laughs. He pulls himself up and stands, hands on the exam table, laughing. She can't remember the last time she heard him laugh, but the laughing loosens something in his mouth, then he's choking, then spitting out a tooth. The tooth tumbles across the table and drops to the floor.

"I failed to mention, I got punched in the face today," he says.

"Let me see," she says.

Michael retrieves the tooth for her, and she examines it. It's a molar. To judge by the smooth, almost polished enamel of the crown, it's one of the teeth he grinds at night. Somehow, the tooth has come out clean, the roots intact. She hands it back, and Michael tucks the tooth into his pocket.

"Tell me," she says. "How does the joke end?"

"One's heavy," Michael says. He strokes her hair. He kisses her head. "And the other is a little lighter."

Then the woman in the white coat is back. A box sits in a wire basket by the door, and she pulls gloves from the box and stretches them over her hands.

"I'm sorry," Michael says. "Are you the doctor?"

"Ultrasound technician," the woman in the white coat says. "The doctor's on the way."

She seats herself on a rolling stool and pulls several items from the drawers beneath the counter on the wall. When she turns, she holds a bottle. Diane knows from movies what comes next and lifts her shirt. *Please, God*, she thinks, wondering whether this is a meager prayer, or whether it's the only honest one.

"This won't be fancy," the technician says. "You want one of those 3-D imagings, you'll have to go to Asheville or Atlanta."

A screen hangs on the wall just past Diane's feet. What shows up there, or fails to show, will change her life.

The technician holds the bottle over Diane's belly, and gel uncoils, cold, translucent, from the tube. The gel is spread over her abdomen, then a device is lowered to her skin. The device looks like a computer mouse, the cord-free kind. The technician taps a few buttons on the machine by Diane's head, and the screen on the far wall glows white, then black. Michael takes her hand. The black screen shivers, and suddenly the room is lit up with the image of her womb.

The technician runs the mouse over Diane's stomach, and there is a whooshing sound, like waves breaking on a distant shore. Water surrounds them. Water wraps the room.

But what are they looking at? A flutter, movement, but nothing's discernible. Nothing's clear.

Diane can't breathe. The mouse travels her abdomen until she can't take it anymore.

"Is that it?" she asks.

The technician smiles. "That's them."

"*Them?*" Michael says.

Diane searches the screen and sees not one shape, but two. As she watches, the shapes turn to bodies nuzzling.

Her hand is released, and the table trembles with the weight of Michael catching himself, then holding himself up.

"Twins," the technician says. "Separate sacs, so fraternal, most likely. Too soon to say the sex. You're definitely at ten weeks." She pats Diane's shoulder. "You can tell by the arm buds, the legs."

Buds. Diane pictures tulips trumpeting from flower beds, petals opening to taste the sun.

"Twins?" Michael says.

Before the technician can answer, a new sound fills the room.

"What's that?" he asks. He's scared, and Diane loves him for it.

"That," the technician says, "is Baby A. Heartbeat is strong. One hundred and seventy-eight beats per minute."

"That's good?" Michael asks.

"One hundred and seventy-eight is perfect," the technician says. "One hundred and seventy-eight is what we're looking for."

She finds the second fetus. They wait. She moves the mouse in ever-widening circles, then steers it down Diane's side, almost to her back.

"What's wrong?" Michael says.

The technician says nothing. She returns the mouse to Diane's stomach, and a heartbeat registers.

"That's Baby A again," she says. "I think."

"You think?" Michael's hands leave the table. "You *think*?" And he's a father, just like that.

Diane shuts her eyes. She feels the device's slow slither over her. The room is quiet but for the hum of the machine. The sound is waves and she's the shore.

"Please," Michael says.

She wants to rise, to touch his face and tell him it's okay, but there's a chance, however small, that Baby B is well, the heartbeat strong. Until she knows, she will not move, won't cough or curl a finger or open her eyes. She'll lie forever on this table to hear her child's heart hiccup to life.

"*Please*," Michael says.

A drumstick strikes the air, prestissimo.

"There we are," the technician says. "Baby B."

Diane opens her eyes. Michael weeps.

"Twins," he says.

"Twins," she says.

"Oh my God," Michael says. "I'm going to have to sell a lot of shoes."

PART FOUR
SUNDAY NIGHT

37.

Nico's is crowded—the evening cool and cooling—bat-swoop and starlight, tree-sway and sliver-moon. Shrieks, laughs, owl song. A ricochet of children across the deck.

It's late for ice cream, but, dropping Michael and Diane off at home, Lisa suggested to Richard that the parents-to-be be given some space, which is how the grandparents-to-be wound up here.

Ice cream cones in hand, Richard and Lisa cross the deck and head down the stairs.

Under a tree, a boy strums a guitar. At a table, two girls examine each other's sunburns, a bottle, aloe green, between them. Someone has planted tiki torches along the river's mossy bank. Citronella-scented, the torches cast a flickering light onto the patio, its benches bolted to tables that remind Richard of the picnic tables at state parks.

One table is empty, and Richard sits. Overhead, between the deck slats, he spies sneaker tread, a dog's paw, a nickel that hangs wedged between two boards. If he stood and stretched, he might be able to tug the nickel free. He imagines doing so, imagines, absurdly, everything above following in the nickel's wake—deck, bodies, shoes—as though the coin held it all in place.

He licks the ice cream, and his heart beats with all he's learned today, with all he wants to say. His wife watches the river, and Richard watches her.

He'd been so angry at the hospital, had felt untrusted, unloved, to learn he was the only one who hadn't known about the pregnancy. Then Michael stepped into the waiting room. Diane was well. Not only that, Richard would be a grandfather. To twins. In that instant, whatever resentment had been barnacling his heart was scraped away.

Still, the body in the water. He can't shake the image of the boy from earlier today, how pale the skin had turned with bloat.

"Honey," Lisa says. "Are you all right?" Her eyes have left the river to search his face.

"I'm fine," he says. His grief is his business. What goes on inside him has never come with a show. They almost divorced over this, long ago, when Lisa felt he wasn't sorrowful enough from losing June. But there's no wrong way to grieve. They learned that together, started over, bought a summer home, and, in this way, stayed husband and wife.

"I'm sorry I didn't tell you sooner," Lisa says. "I wanted Michael or Diane to tell you first. Honestly, I've only known a day."

"It's fine," he says. "I'm fine." A rivulet of ice cream runs down the cone, and he licks his hand.

"Just know, it wasn't *you* specifically," she says. "They weren't planning on telling anyone until they were sure they were keeping it."

"Keeping it?"

"I mean—"

"No. That's absurd. Married people don't get abortions."

Lisa's always said that, for someone so smart, Richard can be awfully dense, and the look on her face reminds him that there's much about the world he doesn't understand.

"Married people get abortions for any number of reasons," she says.

"No one I know."

"Plenty you know. You just don't know you know."

Halfway through his scoop, he's had enough, but he keeps licking, just to keep the cream from running down his arm.

At another table, a blue-haired boy, nine or ten years old, taps on a phone. His mother and father flank him, eating ice cream from pink Nico's bowls with plastic spoons. The boy with blue hair asks for more ice cream, and his parents ignore him. He asks again, this time more loudly, and his parents tell him no.

"They found him," Richard says.

"Found who?" Lisa asks, but he doesn't have to answer, and she doesn't have to ask again. "Oh, God."

"I tried to tell the parents. I thought it might be easier coming from someone who understands, someone not in uniform. But the police beat me there."

"You were there? You saw the body?"

Richard nods. He's sick of ice cream. His tongue is numb. His hand is cold.

Two tables away, the boy with blue hair demands more ice cream, *now*. A commotion, raised voices, and soon, the boy and his father are arguing.

"Fuck you," the boy says.

"Liam!" the mother screams.

Richard doesn't mean to laugh, but this night, this weekend, it's all become a bit too much.

"Fuck you," the boy yells at his mother, then, across the patio at Richard, "Fuck you too!"

At this, the boy's father stands, wrenches the phone from his son's hand, and flings it, the phone following an arc that ends underwater. The boy with blue hair screams and runs to the riverbank.

By now, the din above deck has died down. Everyone's attention is on the river, the boy. The boy turns. His hands are fists. Tears fatten his face. "Fuck you all!"

His parents watch from behind their ice cream bowls, unmoved. But when the boy takes off, heads upstairs, and runs across the deck, the parents stand and hurry up the stairs. Then they're gone. The conversations at tables start up again. The boy under the tree again plays his guitar.

"That was exciting," Lisa says.

At the other table, the ice cream dishes sit, still mostly full. Richard wonders whether the parents will come back for them, or whether they'll be too embarrassed to return.

"Do you think they have any idea what they're getting into?" he asks.

"I'm sure that's not the first time he's acted out."

"Michael and Diane, I mean. Do you think they're ready for that?"

"Nobody's ready for *that*."

"Were we ready?" he asks, regretting the words the second they've left his lips.

"What are you asking me, Richard?"

He has a choice, backpedal or forge ahead. "We were married, what, a year? Sometimes I wonder if we had kids too quick."

Lisa's been licking her ice cream. Now she lowers her cone. "That's like saying you wish June were never born."

"I'm not saying that."

Though some days he would, would trade the nightmares, anguish beyond compare, would trade away that month of love for a sense of peace, for three decades of uninterrupted sleep.

"What *are* you saying?" Lisa says.

He doesn't know. He's tired. He's sad. He wants to go home.

"I'm sorry," he says. "I don't know what I'm saying."

At the hospital, when Diane placed the printout in his hand, why had it made him, however briefly, dreamily, enraged? For an hour he's wondered this, and now he knows. Because she gets two, and he didn't even get to keep his first. And to think she might have thrown those two away.

"Talk to me," Lisa says. "Tell me what you mean."

Richard tries to speak and can't. He's tired, body heavy with the weight of all he cannot say. He stands. His legs ache, but he moves to a garbage bin and disposes of the ice cream cone before returning to the table.

"Darling?" Lisa says.

The table is cast aluminum, its grillwork sheathed in plastic coating, and it's on this surface that Lisa rests her left hand. She's not a jewelry person, but she's always worn a wedding band and the engagement ring with which Richard proposed. The diamond was his grandmother's. It's small, but it's been in his family for five generations. The thought of telling Lisa what he's done, of watching her remove that ring, it's unimaginable to him. But the thought of living this way another day is more than he can stand.

"Why are you torturing me?" he says.

He doesn't yell. He doesn't have to. He's not some petulant, blue-haired boy. He's a man old enough to know that his role in this universe is miniscule, small enough to be incalculable. He's solved equations, proposed some theories that will collapse or rise with time. Making the woman across the table from him happy, loving her and being loved in return, that's his life's last goal. But he can't do it alone.

Their eyes meet, and he's known this woman longer than he hasn't. There won't be a showdown. No yelling or screaming. They aren't those people.

"Once we've liquidated," he says, "both houses sold, what's your plan?"

"My plan?"

"Are you planning to leave me, or not?"

"Leave you?"

Her ice cream cone tips from her hand onto the table, where it splatters and drips to the ground below. She shuts her eyes. Her fingers grip the tabletop.

"How did you know?" he says.

Her head turns. She's listening to the river. "She could never tie a tie like me."

Richard scoops up her ice cream, walks it to the trash, and takes his seat again.

"Whatever you do to me, I deserve it," he says.

"Who knows what anyone deserves. I only know what I want."

"What do you want?"

"For what happened not to have happened. Short of that, I'd like us to find a way forward. Would you like to find a way forward with me, Richard?"

"Of course. Of course I would."

Her eyes open. She's calm.

"Was she underage?"

"No."

"Was she a student?"

"No."

"Good, then I don't want to know. You feel the need to get it off your chest, tell someone else. You made your choice. You don't get to burden me with the details."

Lisa's arm crosses the table, the ice cream puddle, and she takes his hand.

"How do we move forward?" he asks.

"We keep going. That's the only way. We just go on."

"Like it never happened?" he says.

"Of course not. It will always be there, what you did. I hate you for it. But I love you too. I'm learning to love you and hate you at the same time."

For a year he's longed for absolution. But this is better. This is marriage. This is love. Love is dragging things behind you—dead children, houses fallen into disrepair, infidelities lassoed to your back—and continuing on.

He wants to tell her his theory on this, but he's been expounding on his theories to her for decades. Better to shut his mouth. Better to spend their last years listening, or learning to.

"I feel like you're letting me off too easy," he says.

Lisa smiles. "I am."

She watches the water. Somewhere in that river is a phone.

"It doesn't have to be Florida," she says.

"No," he says. "Florida's fine."

She lets go of his hand. She lifts her arm and sees the mess the ice cream's made.

"You remember what you said when we met?" he asks. "I introduced myself. I said, 'I'm Richard Starling,' and you said, 'Starlings are terrible birds.'"

Lisa nods. "They are. They're invasive, non-natives. They tear up farms and fill fields with their droppings. They kill other birds and steal their nests. But they make gorgeous formations, I'll give them that. Those patterns you see, like fish schooling in the sky? That's them. A murmuration of starlings. Still, awful birds. I thought about not taking your last name."

She smiles. She stands.

He wants to say he's sorry for what he's done, but the time for apologies has passed. He stands, and Lisa moves into his arms.

"Hey," she says, "we're going to be grandparents."

His turn to smile. He smiles holding his wife, smiles watching her climb the stairs to find napkins to clean her arm, smiles following the gravel path to the river's edge.

And that's when Richard sees it, by torchlight, the reflection. Underwater, lodged between two rocks, the boy's phone glows. A video game that will never be finished is on pause, a little man suspended, mid-jump. He hovers, ready to crush his enemy, waiting to land. He'll hang there, Richard thinks, midair, until the phone dies or the current carries him away.

38.

Thad drives, the hospital behind them, high beams on and one eye out for deer.

They're close to home, crossing the bridge, the dam that keeps Lake Christopher's water level in check, when he steers the car into the crumbly, light pole–lined parking lot that overlooks the ravine. At the lot's perimeter, a handful of shut-up shops disintegrate into brick and dust, particleboard rectangles warped by rain in window frames. Down the street, the new RaceTrac, Pizza Hut, and Walgreens that put these mom-and-pop shops out of business gleam their neon gleams.

"Why are we here?" Jake asks.

Thad parks and leaves the car. He walks to the guardrail that holds the parking lot back from the ravine overlooking the dam. To the west, the lake is glass. To the east, the craggy valley floor is rubble and rock. The dam leans between, a tower of cement hundreds of feet high. Insects whine. It's a clear night, everything starlit: the bridge, the railing, the ravine. The guardrail is the highway kind, corrugated with rivets, scars where skidding cars have been repelled. Every dent is a car kept out of the air, every scrape a heart still pumping blood behind a wall of ribs.

Jake joins him at the guardrail. Below, trees sprout between boulders, weeds between stones. The guardrail's only waist-high. How easy it would be, for anyone who wanted to scramble over it, to take one step, then a second.

At a distance, a clump of mistletoe strangles the limbs of a small tree grown sideways from the cliff. The parasite's leaves are dewed in moonlight, fruit a blossoming of pink-white pearls.

"Honey, what are we doing?" Jake's voice is tender, feathered with what's gone unspoken for too long.

Thad follows the guardrail to a cycloptic pool of light spilled from one worn and leaning light pole, and Jake follows him.

"I noticed you deleted all my porn," Jake says. "You have trouble with that too, now? Not just men, but movies?"

A truck crosses the bridge, brights on.

"I can't give you what you want," Jake says. "But you knew that going in." He bends and plucks a rock from a patch of pavement crumbling into cliff. "You act like I owe you something, but I don't. I'm not wrong for wanting what I want."

"You're not wrong."

"And I'm not a bad person."

"You're not a bad person."

"Because sometimes you make me feel like a bad person."

Thad grips the guardrail. It's sharp, and he tightens his grip. "I've never said—"

"You don't have to *say* it. It's in every look you've ever given me. You judge me for the sex I have, for how often I have it, and with whom. I can't be with someone who owns my body. Heart, fine. Soul, sure, if such a thing exists. But not my body."

Thad lets go of the rail. Pink indentions mark his palms.

"Sex with other people makes me uncomfortable, yes," Thad says. "It always has. I knew the first time we tried it that this arrangement's not for me. I should have said so. But I shouldn't have had to. You knew I was uncomfortable. You knew and didn't care. You asked me to change, and I tried. I'm trying. But I'm not an *open* kind of guy. I'm sorry if that makes me some kind of anomaly in your eyes, but I want monogamy."

"And that's the one thing I can't give you." Jake draws back his fist and launches the rock in his hand toward the mistletoe. The rock flies past the plant, and Jake bends to select another crumbling pavement chunk.

"But it's not just other people," Thad says. "You *cheated* on me.

Always. Only. If. Always together. Only if we're comfortable. Never if it's an ex. Those were the rules. Those were *your* rules, and you broke them. You humiliated yourself, and you humiliated me."

Thad bends and finds a rock of his own. He pitches, hard, and misses by a lot.

"It was just sex," Jake says.

"It wasn't. You were sizing me up. Your past and present, side by side. Respect me enough to admit at least that much."

Jake chucks his rock, and the mistletoe explodes, berries raining pearlescent onto the rocks below.

Thad's handling this badly. Or else he's being honest for the first time in two years. He wants Jake back, the way it was between them that first month, before this talk of openness began. He wants the boy in the black velvet jacket back.

A few more berries cling to the mistletoe. Thad throws more rocks, but his aim is off. He isn't even close. He picks up one last rock. If this one misses the mark, then he'll give up.

"I can't give you what you want," Jake says, "but I can give you some assurance I'm not going anywhere. Let me buy the house."

"*What?*"

"That's what this weekend's all about, right? You're sad. Michael's pissed. You want the house. The house would cost me, what, four or five paintings? Let me buy it for you and Michael. Or just for you. It won't even be in my name."

"Jake," Thad says.

"Everybody wins. Your parents get the money. You keep the house. I stick around."

"Jake, you can't just buy my love."

"Then marry me."

Thad's rock drops. Cicada chant and frog chirp coalesce into a syncopated roar.

"Do you even want to be married?" Thad asks.

"You want assurance. I want to assure you. Marry me."

"That's not fair," Thad says. "You're still making the rules. You're still making the money. I'd still have to sleep with other guys, or let you sleep with them. You aren't offering me a marriage, Jake. You're offering to make me a kept man."

He won't share Jake, not now, and certainly not in marriage. Call him old-fashioned. Call him uncompromising. Call him whatever name Jake wants. He cannot budge on this. It hurts too much.

"Are you on your meds?" Jake asks.

"This has nothing to do with my meds."

"But you're on them?"

"I'm always on my meds. But meds aren't magic. They make the bad days bearable. When they don't, pot makes them tolerable. But neither makes the pain evaporate."

Jake drops to the pavement, his back to the guardrail. "I'm trapped. You've trapped me."

"I don't know what you mean."

"If I stay," Jake says, "it's on your terms. If I leave, you kill yourself."

Then Thad is on his knees beside the man he loves. "I'm not going to kill myself."

"I walk away right now, you're telling me you won't consider it?"

"I'm always considering it," Thad says. He knows how sad that sounds, but he doesn't want to lie. No more lying between them anymore. "I'm sick. I always will be. That's what you get with me. That's the deal. I won't apologize for how I'm wired."

"I'm not asking for an apology," Jake says.

"When I get back"—when *we* get back, he wants to say—he hopes it's *we*—"I'll see Steve, then I'll see my doctor, and we'll balance out my meds or try new ones. An adjustment's overdue. But that's not a good reason to stay with me if you want out. I give you my word, this won't be the thing that ends me. I promise. I love you. I promise you're not trapped."

Jake's head is in his hands. He's so small. Without his coat or product in his hair, he has no armor on at all. His hands worry the hem of his shirt, and Thad moves from Jake's side to face him, kneeling on the ground.

"You talk about the way you're wired," Jake says, "but what about the way I'm wired?"

"I'm not asking you to change. I'm just saying I no longer will."

"But if I want to stay with you, I have to change."

"If you want to stay with me, you have to *choose*."

Whatever happens, Thad must stay calm. He doesn't want to provoke another panic attack, but they must get through this. This is the talk they should have had two years ago.

"I'm sorry about Marco," Jake says. "I fucked up. No more surprises. No more exes. From now on, we agree to everybody in advance."

"Honey," Thad says. "You have to choose."

"I can't be with someone who needs that much of me."

"And I can't be with someone for whom I'm not enough."

Jake's head drops, and they sit that way a while, Thad's hands fitted to Jake's knees. When Jake's face lifts, at last, his bangs hang but don't quite hide his eyes. He smiles, and he's the most beautiful man Thad's ever seen.

"We've done it my way for two years," Jake says. "I guess it's only fair we give your way a try."

Gratefulness isn't the word for what Thad feels. This feeling transcends that. He's been afraid to hope for even this. In their lives together, there hasn't been much sacrifice on Jake's part. That Jake's capable of putting Thad's needs, for once, before his own, well, it isn't everything, but *a try* is more than Thad had a minute ago.

Thad kisses Jake's cheek, his neck.

"It won't be perfect," Jake says. "I'm warning you, I'm going to mess up. But if you're willing to be patient, I'm willing to try."

And there's nothing more to say, nothing left but for Thad to open his arms and embrace the man he loves.

39.

Michael joins Thad and his parents at the kitchen table while, outside, Diane joins Jake on the dock. It's late, near midnight, but no one's tired, no one's ready for bed.

"I just thought the four of us should talk," Michael's mother says. "First, though," she says to Thad, "I have something for you."

She disappears into her bedroom, then returns dragging a long white box. She settles the box beside Thad's chair, and Thad lifts the lid. Michael stands to see. Hundreds of comic books in plastic sleeves fill the box like files shining in a filing cabinet drawer. Thad pulls one out. The comic is bagged, and Thad peels the tape from the bag and removes the comic book. He's careful with it, turning each page slowly, cradling the comic. Michael sits.

"I found them," his mother says. "They were in the garage."

"I checked the garage," Thad says.

"They were at the back."

"I checked the back."

Their eyes meet, and Michael senses whole conversations freighted in a glance, a sigh. These are not Thad's comic books, Thad knows that these are not his comic books, his mother is sorry for throwing out his comic books, and Thad forgives her. For her to go to this much trouble, to gather these, means more than if she'd kept them all along. All of this goes unsaid—no harm done, no need to speak the truth. Better to pretend, make peace, move on. Better to live and die by the open secrets every family keeps.

Michael leaves the table. Too much to hope he can quit drinking in a day, but, say he drinks something else, he might distract himself from alcohol tonight. In the kitchen, he opens a cupboard and pulls down a mug and the instant decaf coffee only his mother drinks. He fills the kettle, stands beside the stove, and soon the kettle's whistling.

He offers decaf to the others, his mother accepts, and he retrieves a second mug. He gives the instant jar a shake, and the glass rattles with dehydrated coffee crystals. He's not sure how much goes in each mug. He pours the water, spoons some coffee in, and rejoins his family at the table.

He sips, and the coffee is too strong.

All night he's thought about what Diane said at the hospital. He doesn't have to tell his parents, but the more he considers it, the more he wants them to know. Hard enough keeping the pregnancy to himself. He doesn't like secrets, and he doesn't have to shoulder this one alone.

"Mom, Dad," he says. "I fucked up."

He gives them the history of his drinking and sees that his mother is shocked. His father nods at everything he says, and Michael wonders whether he's suspected all along.

When he finishes, he's made his mother cry.

He goes to the kitchen and returns with the sugar bowl, a pair of spoons, and a gallon jug of milk. Together, he and his mother make their coffees drinkable.

"If you need to go to one of those drying-out facilities," his father says, "we'll pay."

"If it comes to it, I might just take you up on that," Michael says.

The milk jug sweats on the table, and their spoons rest beside it.

"Do you think you can stop drinking before the babies come?" his mother asks.

It's a fair question. Quitting will be difficult, and Michael knows himself well enough to know he's never been particularly good at difficult things. But that's no reason not to try.

Still, there's so much left to figure out. How will they pay for two babies and a house that, even before the expense of children, they can't afford?

They could scorch the earth: Declare bankruptcy. Sacrifice the house, the cars. Forfeit their phones and all their fancy tech. They could learn to be happy with less—fewer channels on TV, fewer distractions, fewer bills—could learn to live their lives within their means. It isn't the American way, but fuck the American way.

Or Michael could find better work, they could stand firm, pay down their debt. Not every problem is one that requires running from.

But there is time. This problem won't be solved tonight. And, if the actuary tables are to be believed, he hasn't even reached his halfway point. In seven years, he could be debt-free. In less than seven months, he could be sober for his children's birth.

Children.

He hates selling shoes, but he could sell shoes for them. And for Diane. He could learn to put a family's needs before his own. He likes imagining he could be that man.

"The old bedroom in Ithaca is yours if you need it," his mother says. "We'll be there while I finish my last year at the lab. Then, in Florida—"

"We can't do that," Michael says.

"Of course you can. There's no shame in it. Pat and Alan, down the street, their daughter got laid off, she moved back in. It's not your fault. It's this damn economy."

She's in denial, his mother. "Mom, this one's not on the economy. It's me."

"A lot of kids your age—"

"I'm thirty-three."

"Your generation—"

"Mom." His mother sips her coffee. She won't look at him. "It's okay. You can say it. I'm a fuckup."

"That's not true."

"It's true. Your sons are fuckups."

He looks to his brother, and what his brother does next breaks his heart in ten places. Thad pulls a lighter from his pocket, then a bag of pot. Next come rolling papers, and he spreads the contraband across the kitchen table.

"He's right, Mom," Thad says. "I'm a pothead. Michael's a drunk. But it's not just that. We make bad choices. We had free rides at Cornell—*Cornell*—and we fucked those up. You gave us every opportunity, you and Dad, and we squandered almost every one."

Michael finishes his decaf in a gulp. The coffee hasn't made him want the moonshine in the freezer any less.

"Face it, Mom," he says, "your sons suck."

"Please don't say that," his mother says. "That hurts."

"No," Thad says. "That's our point. You were a great mom. You were pretty much the *perfect* mom. You're off the hook. How we turned out, that's on us."

"I know I'm a disappointment to you," Michael says, and it's as though his mother can't reach him fast enough. She grabs his face, a cheek in each hand. She holds on to him hard, gives him no choice but to look her in the eye.

"You are not a disappointment," she says. "You have never been a disappointment to your father or to me."

He wants her to let go of his face. She's hurting him, and maybe she means to. Maybe she means to hurt him just a bit.

"You are loved," she says.

"Mom, I know."

"No," she says. "You don't know. You won't ever know. And that's okay. It's not your job to know. It's your job to be loved."

She lets go of his face, then gives the same treatment to Thad. Their father looks away. Too much tenderness here. Too much emotion for one night.

Michael tips his head back, lets it rest against the wall.

Above him, Jake's painting looms huge. He's never liked it: the girl, the breast, the pomegranate half. It strikes him as pretentious, self-serious, and all wrong for the room. The colors clash, as though applied to be intentionally at odds with every piece of furniture in the house. But the man who made this makes his brother happy, and that will have to be enough.

Through a window and past the screened porch, Michael can see down the hill to where his wife and Jake stand before another painting on the dock, one they made together this afternoon. He didn't get the full story. There were more exciting things to talk about on the ride home: twins, parenthood, and what comes next. But he knows this painting made Diane happy. He needs to remember that. That, for her, art is more than a hobby or a job. Art is something she loves. Perhaps, for her, he could learn to love it too.

He wants to be a better husband, starting now.

Still, one thing needs saying, and he says it: "I told Thad."

"Son, why?" his father says before catching himself. "Wait, told him what?"

No, Michael didn't tell Thad about their dad's affair. He wouldn't do that. He wishes his father hadn't told *him*. That's no one's business but his parents'.

"I told him about our sister," Michael says.

His parents turn, ready to comfort Thad, but Thad's composed. If he's upset that he wasn't told, he doesn't show it. He slides the marijuana and paraphernalia from the table back into his pockets and folds his arms over his chest.

"Her name was June," his mother says. "She'd have been thirty-five next week. She was a month old when she died."

"What happened?" Thad asks.

"That's the hard part. We'll never know. It could have been asphyxiation. It could have been SIDS. The coroner wrote 'death by unknown cause.' With you and your brother, we kept the bassinet beside our bed. Those first months, I swear I woke every hour to check your breath."

She pours more milk into her coffee, stirs it, sips.

"We should have told you," she says. "You should have known before Diane. It's just, that boy, and with June's birthday coming up, it slipped out."

"It's okay," Thad says.

"We wanted to tell you," his father says.

His mother finishes her coffee and carries the mugs and spoons to the sink. She puts the milk and the sugar bowl away.

"Is there a picture?" Thad says, and Michael can't believe he never thought to ask. He wants to see her, and, at the same time, he's not ready to meet this girl he'll never know.

His mother returns to the table. Her purse is on the floor, and she pulls it to her lap. From her purse, she pulls a wallet, from the wallet a sleeve of photographs. Here, behind plastic windows yellowed by time, are the Starlings: father, mother, sons. From between the pictures of her sons, his mother extracts a wallet-sized photograph of June.

In the picture, Michael's sister lies on her back in a diaper on a sheepskin rug. She faces the camera, and there's a fierceness there, a curiosity. Her eyes are blue, her hair as black as night. The year is 1983, the date stamped in the corner under *Olan Mills*.

Michael passes the photograph to Thad.

"She's beautiful," Thad says.

"I'm sorry we kept her a secret," their father says.

"I'm sorry for your loss," Thad says.

He returns the picture to their mother, who puts her daughter away and returns the wallet to her purse.

"I didn't mean to kick him," Michael says. "I didn't mean to lose my grip."

He hasn't planned to say this, to confess. But, spilling secrets, he finds he can't stop.

"The boy," he says. "I had his hand. I had him, and I kicked him. I let go."

"You had to come up for air," Thad says. "You would have drowned."

"I should have drowned before coming up alone."

"No," his mother says. "Your children are going to need their father."

"You're going to be a good father, Michael," his father says.

They keep talking, his parents, but Michael's no longer listening. He's thinking of the boy in the lake. He's thinking of his sister.

That evening, leaving the deer, Michael turned and watched the carcass through the rear windshield as the car pulled away. He half expected a vulture to land, but the body lay unaccompanied where they'd rolled it onto the shoulder of the road. It would lie intact a while longer until, by whatever transubstantiation, it turned to carrion. Michael likes that idea—the notion, however naive or childish, that there might be a period of grace that keeps buzzards at bay. That even the body of a wild animal might be afforded time to lie in state, ceremonial, untouched.

And maybe this is benediction enough, to be a deer in the middle of the road, to be a boy at the bottom of a lake, to be an infant held fast in the folds of her bassinet. To lie a minute—fragrant and warm with life just left—to linger, to lie, before the rushing paramedics move forward in their rushing; before the dark fish paddle deeper in their deepening; before the truck, fender bent, hurries away, and the shadows circle darkly, and darkly drop.

Just this. To stay awhile—missed, lost, loved—before the birds descend, and you're picked clean.

40.

Lisa in starlight, stirring. Lisa Starling fast asleep.

She wakes to the screen door's slam. Out the window, beyond the open blinds, her family, minus Richard, sits on the dock around the old telescope.

She only meant to lie on the bed a moment, but the weight of the weekend, how quickly it carried her off to quiet dreams.

She's slept an hour, maybe less. It's very late. In the bedroom doorway, her husband watches her. In his hands, he holds the canvas that sat all night on the dock.

"Jake gave it to Diane," he says. "I told her we would keep it here to dry, then mail it later in the week."

Richard moves to the closet. He props the canvas against one wall, then shuts the closet door. Lisa sits up, and he joins her on the bed.

"Thad brought the telescope down," he says. "I forgot that kid knows all the constellations. Not just Orion's Belt, but the obscure ones, and all the stories to go with them."

Richard stands and, by the hand, she pulls him back.

"Please," she says. "Just for a minute. Stay with me and watch our boys."

She wishes he knew her heart, but there are worse things than being given what is asked.

She wants to believe that, in time, his indiscretion won't haunt her, and, perhaps, if she wants this badly enough, it won't.

The night is clear, the moon a crescent. How many nights has she stood at this window and listened for owls, how many mornings has she watched the birds wake up?

She'll miss this room, this house, this lake. She'll miss it all, but not enough to stay.

Next summer, the Florida surf will touch their toes. The sand will squeak beneath their feet. Their back door will open not to flickers and cardinals and jays, but to pipers and terns and gulls. Maybe it's the wrong change, but at their age, any change is good.

God, let her not grow complacent in old age. They've had lucky lives. An insult to whatever force gives life not to appreciate those lives until the end.

"We're going to be grandparents," she says.

"Very old grandparents," Richard says.

"It's going to be ridiculous how much we'll spoil them."

Them. Already she's delirious with love.

She rises from the bed, and together, they move to the family room, slip on their shoes, and step onto the porch. Her favorite great horned owl offers her its signature four hoots.

She catches Richard's wrist, leans in, and kisses his stubbled chin. "Come on," she says. Then they're down the stairs and down the hill.

They step over water onto the dock.

The boat in the boathouse creaks. The stars smolder. Her children's faces glow.

Her children sit cross-legged on the dock, and what will become of them?

Michael. The name is Hebrew, *Who is like God*, at once an invocation and a question. Naming him, perhaps she hoped to save him, that her daughter's fate might not befall her boy.

He sits up straight, Diane's shoulders to his chest, her head tucked underneath his chin. Lisa's boy is bandaged, bruised, but he's alive. He and Diane are happy, for now. And maybe the momentum of this night will be enough to get them through the pregnancy, through the twins' first months, first steps, first words, first kisses, first cars. Perhaps Michael and Diane will be good parents, love their children, never fight.

Lisa wants *happily ever after* for them. But what comes next will test them. Children are expensive. Lisa and Richard will help, but Michael and Diane will have to change their ways. And children are exhausting. There will be long nights, surprise trips to the hospital, a million unforeseen anxieties multiplied by the exponent of sleep-lessness.

And joy. So much joy.

Who they are, who they'll become, Diane and Michael, and their children—separately, together—Lisa can't predict, won't even try.

She'll pray. There's still prayer, always prayer. Prayer to a God in whom Lisa still believes. If not an afterlife, God at least. And does it matter whether her prayers work? Whether they're heard? If they're fruitless, they're no worse than hope.

Thad rises. He points the telescope at the moon, then angles it toward the stars.

Sweet Thad. Thad who suffers. Thad who is unhappy, smart, and good. The helix of possibility for him stretches on forever like one of Richard's unsolved proofs. Thad will be a poet. Or a therapist. Or, like his brother, he may spend his life helping others try on shoes. There are worse lives, and far less honest ones.

Thad sits, and Jake moves to be near him. Their arms find each other, and this does Lisa's heart some good. She worries about Jake and how he treats her son. But most days, they make each other happy, so she'll give this man some room to prove her wrong. She owes that much to the man Thad loves.

"The folding chairs aren't packed," she offers. "I could bring them down."

But no one says a word, they simply sit. They sit on planks worn smooth by a hundred summer months, and rather than seat them-selves in their Adirondack chairs, she and Richard join their children on the dock.

Lisa settles into her husband's arms. As for the two of them, what happens next?

Perhaps the skin cancer will return.

Perhaps they'll live to see their grandchildren have children of their own.

Most likely, Lisa will outlive Richard. What then? Will she stay in Florida, taking walks alone along the beach? Or will she move to be nearer to her boys?

She studies her children, their bodies curled around the bodies they love best. Her boys love Jake and Diane more than they love her. And that hurts, but that's the way it's meant to be. A mother's love: impossible, forever unreturned, or returned, but at some dim, unpolished wattage, like a star seen through too many mirrors, too thick and aged a pane of glass. As a mother, you give your child all your love because your love—if it is real and good and right—was never yours to keep.

Stars daguerreotype the night, light pushed through pinpricked tin. Orion's Belt, the only constellation she knows without Thad's help, hangs in place. A satellite winks. A distant aircraft bisects the sky.

She stands and approaches the telescope. She bends. She looks.

What is she looking for? Stars are not maps. What maps there are have been imposed on them. They do not tell the future, where to go, or why, or, going, what comes next. No, the stars she sees let loose their light long ago, light traveling decades, centuries, to reach this telescope.

The future lies ahead, unseen, unknown. And maybe this not-knowing is a gift. To rest easy, to embrace surprises as they come. The longer she lives, the more each morning will be a surprise. A pleasure just to wake and greet the day.

She hopes for heaven.

If there's no heaven, she'll never see her girl again. Wendy will never see her boy.

The world is full of wonder, and of love. This sky, these stars, this planet pinwheeling beneath. If this is all there is, it's well and good. But it's not enough. God forgive her, but one life on earth will never be enough.

Let there be heaven. Let there be reunion, recompense for all. For each soul on this dock. For each soul underwater, underground. For the souls who've come before and those who go on in their wake.

Scripture says that heaven is a wedding, and Lisa likes imagining that. Not the ceremony so much as the party after, the lights like crazy, reception in full swing. If it's true that heaven stands outside of time, they're there already. Look close, and you can almost see them. One of them is singing, one asking to cut the cake. And on the dance floor, all of them. Dancing.

What wonder. What rapturous joy. Let it be.

Lisa looks through the telescope. The eyepiece cradles her face, snug, binocular-tight.

The moon, the stars. All that light—it's traveled so far to meet her here.

She looks closer. She is not afraid.

ACKNOWLEDGMENTS:

Lake Christopher shares much in common, geographically and characteristically, with Lake Toxaway, North Carolina. The painting remembered by Jake is Margaret Keane's *Waiting* (1962), which belongs to the collection of the Memphis Brooks Museum of Art. For an eyewitness account of the inhumane torture of conversion therapy, I turned to Ted Cox's *AlterNet* article "Undercover at a Christian Gay-to-Straight Conversion Camp." SIDS statistics were provided by the Centers for Disease Control and Prevention, while statistics on body decomposition came from information compiled by the National Underwater Rescue-Recovery Institute, as well as Daniel Engber's *Slate* article "Dead Man's Float."

Thank you to the editors of the *American Literary Review*, *Chicago Tribune*, *Draft*, *Glimmer Train*, *Hayden's Ferry Review*, and *Best New American Voices*, where some of these characters first appeared in different form.

Thank you to Adam Ross and *The Sewanee Review* for excerpting a portion of this novel.

Special thanks to the Bread Loaf, Clarksville, Longleaf, Sanibel Island, Sewanee, Taos, Tin House, and Wesleyan Writers Conferences, and to the Atlantic Center for the Arts, for their scholarships, fellowships, residencies, and support of my work during the writing of this book.

This novel owes a debt to three editors: heartfelt thanks to Millicent Bennett for believing in this book before it was a book. You are an ever-present source of encouragement and an inspiration to me. Thank you to Ira Silverberg for your patience and for seeing this novel through its gangly adolescence. And thank you to Sean Manning for landing the plane. Your magnificent eye, ear, and edits have made this a far better book.

Thank you to Carolyn Reidy, Jonathan Karp, Richard Rhorer, Marysue Rucci, Yvette Grant, Lake Bunkley, Stacey Sakal, and everyone at Simon & Schuster for your devotion and support.

Thank you to Rodrigo Corral, Alison Forner, Carly Loman, and Ashley Inguanta for my dream cover, photography, and design.

Sincere thanks to my agent, Gail Hochman, who has read this book more times than anyone on planet Earth and provided the kind of care, attention, and feedback that most writers only dream of. Thank you to Marianne Merola, Jody Kahn, and everyone at Brandt & Hochman for working so hard on behalf of the book.

Huge thanks to Francis Geffard, Eugenia Dubini, Gioia Guerzoni, and all of the editors and translators who have supported this book across Europe and South America.

Profound thanks to those who read the manuscript in its various incarnations over the past nine years: Michael Griffith, Leah Stewart, Mical Darley-Emerson, Heather Huggins Sharp, Naomi Williams, Michael Carroll, and Justin Luzader.

Thank you to my friends and colleagues in the English department and MFA program at the University of Central Florida. Thank you, Terry Thaxton and Laurie Uttich, for your wisdom and your words.

Thank you to Sandra Meek and Berry College for being my home away from home.

Many thanks to Kevin and everyone at the Oviedo on the Park Starbucks team for keeping me caffeinated and giving me a place to write.

Thank you to Alicia Ezekiel-Pipkin, whose gift of childcare allowed me to finish this book.

Big thanks to Donald Dunbar and Mike Morrell for conversations that found their way into the novel, and thank you to Matt Pitt for a pep talk that came at just the right time.

Thank you, John Holman and Frederick Barthelme, for the belt fish.

Thank you, Thelma Lynch, for listening.

Thank you to Jonathan Jones for your friendship, support, and nightly talks. Your love and generosity of spirit have made me a better person and this a better book.

Thank you to my parents for sharing your love of lakes and for teaching me what it means to be part of a family. Without your unconditional love, this book would not be.

All my love to my daughters, Izzy and Ellie. Your lives are my greatest joy.

And to Marla, who saves me daily. You have my heart.

ABOUT THE AUTHOR

DAVID JAMES POISSANT is the author of *The Heaven of Animals*, in print in five languages, winner of the GLCA New Writers Award and a Florida Book Award, a finalist for the Los Angeles Times Book Prize, and longlisted for the PEN/Robert W. Bingham Prize. His writing has appeared in the *Atlantic*, the *Chicago Tribune*, the *New York Times*, *One Story*, *Ploughshares*, *Southern Review*, and in numerous anthologies including *New Stories from the South*, *Best New American Voices*, and *Best American Experimental Writing*. A recipient of scholarships and fellowships from the Bread Loaf, Longleaf, Sewanee, Tin House, and Wesleyan writers conferences, he teaches in the MFA program at the University of Central Florida and lives in Orlando with his wife and daughters.